THE TICKING ZOOKEEPER

JOHN SCHRAUB

Publishing Coordinator – Sharon Kizziah-Holmes
Cover Design – Jaycee DeLorenzo

Paperback-Press
an imprint of A & S Publishing
A & S Holmes, Inc.

ISBN -13: 978-1-951772-41-3

DEDICATION

For the Grandchildren

All imagination and inspiration begins with our kids.
Thank you Anabelle, Zoey, Nikko, Emma, Lilly, Packer, and Ellie.

ACKNOWLEDGMENTS

Grateful appreciation goes to Jola Schraub, the most honest and giving person I know. She pushed my writing with enthusiasm and encouragement. Her knowledge allowed me to keep my dictionary on the shelf and my fingers on the keyboard.

And to Sarah Stevenson, my reading partner. After the hundreds of books we discussed together, it was most fitting she agreed to read this one and offered much needed suggestions. For a book club of only two members, we cover a lot of territory.

PART ONE – THE FOUNDATION

CHAPTER 1

He remembered a lot more from before the stroke than they thought he did and slowly more pictures were forming in his head. The pictures and memories were coming without understanding. His mind's eye could see faces, see houses, see paths that once must have been walked upon, but why any of those particular images were playing in his head, he did not know. He lost most of his ability to speak and in order to avoid frustration chose not to use the few abilities he still possessed. He was playing hide and seek with the world, hiding inside a maze of confusion waiting for the fog to lift. More than mere suspicions about his past whirled around his head; he knew he'd done wrong, he knew punishment waited, but he also knew that as long as his secrets remained locked in his mind, he was safe.

Kansas unrolled before them as his daughter drove toward the home he purchased over twenty years ago. Green fields and trees, green fields and trees, a bump in the road, and hawks perched on weathered fence posts. The road was long and monotonous, the scenery ever repeating like a bad joke. He recalled a bad joke and a small smile came over Ray Lupus's face.

"Does this look familiar to you Dad?" his daughter Karen asked from behind the wheel, "The doctor said things would come back."

Ray shrugged. "Familiar," he said to himself.

What could be unfamiliar in mile after mile of green weeds fighting for space with endless prairies of wheat. What was that joke again he wondered? His smile faded. He was part of the joke now, a cruel joke.

He looked down at his nearly useless left arm, his shaking hands. He peered through tired eyes with a blurred vision. Tears filled the eyes of a man who had gone decades before without so much as a single tear trespassing on his face. That Ray was nails; that Ray was hardened steel and action. This Ray is soft and lost and what is familiar to him now is not yesterday and endless Kansas miles, but rather something from 60 years ago. The last time tears fell.

Ray Lupus started life on the north side of Chicago. He was a quiet kid who didn't make friends easily even though there seemed to be hundreds of kids playing right out his front door. He played all day long, alone, in the dirt in the street gutters or in the filthy alley behind his house.

At age five, his parents doubted that he was anywhere near ready for school, not that they spent any time getting Ray ready. Their input was to give Ray his meals, wipe the dirt off of him at the end of every day and once, in an attempt to fill his time with anything other than themselves, they let him keep an equally dirty dog he brought home around his fifth birthday. In order to keep the dog, Ray had to accept full responsibility for him, feed him, walk him, clean-up after him.

In lieu of birthday presents and Christmas presents, which never amounted to much anyway, Ray got to keep his dog. The dog seemed to bring Ray out of his darkness and even though he still preferred to be alone, the dog was a welcome companion.

He did okay in school for the first 5 or 6 years. He sat quietly through most days, not making noise, not learning much either. This was good enough for his parents and heaven to Ray.

In his tenth year, things quickly changed. Ray lay in bed one morning listening to a summer storm. Hour after hour it poured and when the storm finally passed, Ray went out with his dog to play.

The rainwater was flowing down the street along the gutter towards the sewer at the end of the block. The water was moving quickly, and Ray put a couple of short twigs on top of the flow so they could race to the sewer. Ray ran along side of them and his dog followed. For some unknown reason the dog passed Ray and was running too far out into the street. In seconds, a blue Ford Galaxie sped by, ran over the dog and sped away. The dog rolled and tumbled and never moved again.

Ray screamed and ran to his dog, picked up the limp body, and ran still screaming and crying into the house. His parents heard him from outside and met him at the back door.

"What happened?" asked his mother as his father took the dog from Ray's trembling arms.

"Dog's dead," said Ray's old man coldly.

Ray couldn't speak, his crying was still uncontrollable.

"Go to your room boy if you need to carry on. You got the dog from the alley and it's time he goes back. That's all. That's life kid."

"Take it easy hon," Ray's mom said, "we may not understand it, but Ray loved that dirty thing. Go bury it in the yard. Go to your room Ray. It's what's best."

Ray's dad took a shovel and a beer out to the backyard and a large black trash bag to put the dog in. He took a long swig from his beer, turned over a couple inches of dirt, put the dog in the bag and threw him in a garbage can in the alley. He then returned to his beer.

Ray's mom sat in the chair with the cigarette burns on the arm rests and returned to her Enquirer magazine. She was captivated by the story about a two-headed baby being born in the desert near a radioactive former munitions dump site. She was more than a little put out that Ray and his dog disturbed her reading. A few sentences in and her anger left as she completely forgot about both of them. Both Ray and the dog that is, not both heads of the desert baby.

And Ray, well he sat in his room throwing his pocket knife over and over and over again into a cardboard box. As the minutes passed, he threw it harder and quicker, angrier and more directly at something he couldn't identify or understand. The fingers on his right hand were being rubbed raw from the hundreds of throws and blood began to show. The fingers on his left hand were cut badly from pulling the knife's blade constantly out of the box for more throws. The blood dripped.

As his tears dried, Ray vowed to never cry again, not when being screamed at by his mother and not when being humiliated and beaten by his old man. He wiped the tears away with his hands leaving a trail of dried blood in its place.

He kicked the cardboard box into the corner and went outside to go somewhere, anywhere but here. His mother told him to stay close to the house but never looked up from her newspaper. His dad was busy in the yard surrounding himself with empty beer cans. He never saw Ray leave. Ray only knew death for about 30 minutes, and he didn't know it well, but in his heart, he knew one thing and that one thing that he did know well was that somebody was going to pay for this death.

Ray walked north from home paying no mind to his mother's order to stay close. He walked further than he ever had, but knew the area from the many times his parents drove this way.

He kicked at small rocks along the way, occasionally picking one up and tossing it into the street. He passed many gates with "Beware of Dog" signs boldly displayed in large black or red letters. *Beware of dog*, he thought, *what a joke, beware of people is more fitting*.

Then his heart began to race, and he closed his eyes to jog his memory. His fists clenched. He reopened his eyes and set his stare on the blue Ford Galaxie.

That's the son of a bitch that killed my dog, Ray thought. Clenched teeth joined his clenched fist. It was early afternoon and even Ray knew this was not the time for private retribution.

He kept everything inside for the time being and walked a few blocks west. In the middle of another city block, Ray saw another personal monster. Yes, another blue Ford Galaxie. If the death of Ray's dog wasn't crossroad enough, these two cars surely were. Maybe one pushed him to some sort of edge and the other meant to push him over or pull him back.

The bright sun was giving Ray a headache and for the first time, he noticed the dried blood on his hands. Ray went home, washed the blood from his hands and returned to his room. He didn't know why it was only his blood that spilled and why only he felt the pain, but he knew he wouldn't let that continue.

The local police were baffled; there must be a link, but none of the highly skilled detectives could find one. Many people were questioned, many theories offered, but eventually the case was marked cold. Two Ford Galaxies were hit, two bricks through the front windows, two bricks through the back windows. As one detective said, "Somebody's trying awfully hard to cause problems here, and my fear is this is just the beginning." A viewpoint very similar to the one Ray carried deep inside.

CHAPTER 2

"We're home Dad," Karen said to her father as they stopped in front of the garage on the gravel drive.

Ray lifted his head and forgot about his useless arm for the time being. He wiped away the mist in his eyes and looked at the house he bought such a long time ago. Very little meant anything.

"Your grandson is away at camp, it worked out for the best. He'll be home in less than two weeks. I thought you would like some time alone anyhow. Your room is just how you left it and I brought up some boxes from downstairs for you to look through. The doctor said that will stir your memory."

Ray looked at his daughter and nodded, just a little nod, but a nod of understanding, nonetheless.

Ray walked into his old room and sat on the edge of his bed. He was almost trancelike peering out of the window. The tree branches that swayed in the breeze hypnotized Ray and he sat motionless for nearly an hour. Karen brought him a glass of water and placed it on the nightstand. She left the room without speaking a word. Ray lifted the glass and played with the circle of water that the glass left on the table, his mind drifting.

Ray was in and out of trouble for a good five years after his dog was run over. He no longer failed quietly in the back of the room, but failed noisily from whatever desk they put him in. Report cards came home full of failing or near failing grades, which his mother signed without reading. In time, Ray learned to sign them for her, easing everyone's burden. Very few weeks would pass in Ray's life without him being in some sort of physical battle.

Life was neither spiraling out of control nor heading to a dark place. Life was just what it was from one day to next.

Ray graduated from elementary school through no effort of his own. None of his teachers could get rid of him quickly enough. They were tired of seeing so many good students crying at their desks and knowing Ray was the cause. Tired of the endless interruptions and refusal of Ray to ever open a book. When money and other personal items started disappearing from the students, they thought the problems had peaked. When the teacher's belongings started to disappear, they searched for a meaningful solution. There was talk after the sixth grade to double promote Ray and get him out of the system a year early. The school decided that that would be too obvious and kept Ray for the full grade school requirement.

Ray knew everyone wanted him to leave and remove the trouble he became. That is precisely why Ray stayed in school. He began high school as he left grade school, a smart ass loudmouth. He wasn't long for this school; at his age, the school would have options.

Ray started a fight, a verbal fight, with his science teacher one afternoon. This could have been the beginning of the end for Ray Lupus. Every student in Ray's science class was expected to dissect a frog. The frogs were already dead, no more killing was necessary, you simply had to go to the container, choose your frog, and cut away, looking to identify as many internal organs as possible.

Instead of heading to the back of the room for a frog, Ray headed to the front for a confrontation with Mr. Bond, his science teacher. Ray stared a hole into Bond's head and finally asked him what gave him the right to order the butchery of animals. Ray went into some detail about the value of animals and the uselessness of people like Mr. Bond. Bond was probably one of the few that hadn't yet given up on Ray, but he never found a way into Ray's head either. On this day, Bond had heard enough.

"You know Ray," Bond said rather calmly, "you're really full of shit."

All eyes in the class opened wide, super wide, and you could hear the air both fill and leave the room.

"You stand here pretending that you care about animals and you're given an opportunity to learn about what makes them tick, but you take it as an opportunity to confront me. Get the hell out of here, I don't care where you go. You've nothing to offer the students in this class and less to offer the animals of this world. Beat it Ray."

Ray left and took an extra lunch period. He sat tightly wound, alone, at a corner table. He was ready to mix it up with anyone who said a word to him, but Bond's words played in his head, "You stand here pretending that you care about animals." Words never played in Ray's head before, perhaps he never did care. He felt he did care about animals, but he had no idea about how to show it and less of an idea on what he could actually do to help them. His attack on Bond was his best effort. But those words repeating in his head started something, touched something, and Ray wanted to know more. He stalked Bond until he found him alone in his classroom and, with tail tucked between his legs, he sheepishly entered the room.

Ray didn't know how to talk to people very well, greetings were missing from his vocabulary and apologies were non-existent. Ray simply walked up to Mr. Bond and asked, "What did you mean that I had an opportunity to learn what makes animals tick? That I only pretend to care?"

Bond talked, Ray listened, really listened.

Bond told Ray that by dissecting animals he would learn about many of their lifestyle choices and begin to put him in a position to truly help them. "We build on the foundation of understanding that begins right here in high school. From here, the doors open to more knowledge and lifelong careers doing what we really enjoy and want to do," Bond said.

Bond talked of veterinary school, zoology, pet stores, farm animals, breeding, and more. He spoke in a way that nobody ever spoke to Ray. Ray thanked Mr. Bond and meant it; he came away with a fever built of a desire to get to a place in life where he felt he belonged. For the first time in a long time, and maybe for the first time ever, Ray Lupus was happy and knew what direction he now wanted to take. Nobody was going to mess this up, not this time.

Bond was excited. He thought he made a breakthrough with

Ray and talked about it in the teacher's lounge. Through the smoke, Bond explained the look in Ray's eyes, the thoughtfulness he displayed. Bond said he thinks Ray is more comfortable in a world where he can help in his own way, whatever that way might be. It may just be a love of animals, a comfort he finds in their world, a need fulfilled through their need of a protector. But whatever touched Ray must be built upon.

Bond said, "We have a chance to put this kid on the right track."

The other teachers disagreed. They felt Ray was long past finding the right path. Ray's English teacher said Ray frightened her; she saw something evil in his eyes when he would fix his stare on her. She never saw the thoughtfulness Bond thought that he saw. "The sooner we get him out of this school, the better off we'll all be. How much longer before he's eligible for the army? That's Ray's world."

It was good that Ray never heard this. He had a rough idea about what direction he wanted to go, but his long dormant brain had difficulty accepting negative words from people. Hearing harsh words would send Ray on a mission of ending those words and with his one-dimensional approach to life, his solution to problems was far from normal. Ray was still Ray, not the baby born 15 years ago in a county hospital, but the angry boy born when he watched his dog get crushed under the wheels of a speeding car.

Ray applied himself in biology class. He failed or nearly failed everything else, but he got a B in biology. He earned a C, but Bond felt the B might keep a fire burning inside of Ray. It did. Ray thought the world where he was more comfortable was open to him and he could get there. He wasn't confident enough to say that he would get there, but inspired enough to say he could get there.

The first chance he had with his parents, Ray spoke of his future. "I want to work with animals when I get out school. I'll need to go to college and figure out what to study, but I know it will be with animals."

Big mistake. Where most people have challenges on their paths, Ray had a brick wall, his father.

"College? What a waste of my money that would be. You aren't smart enough to take care of your sorry ass and you want a job taking care of animals. You quit that school when you're sixteen and get a factory job. You want to work with animals then exterminate rats for a living, there's money in that. "

Bigger mistake. Ray seethed. *Exterminator*, he thought. Ray looked at his dad, his eyes narrowed, his heart raced, and then a tiny smile crossed his face. "Thanks Dad, that helps." Ray giggled and walked confidently from the house.

"I wasn't really listening," Ray's mom told her half-drunk husband, "but I think you finally reached that boy. It was nice that he thanked you."

Karen momentarily interrupted her father's thoughts. "Dad, you've hardly even moved. Are you feeling okay?"

Ray snapped back from where wandered and nodded a confident yes.

"Would you like to watch some TV or listen to the radio? That oldies station you like comes in better now, I can tune it in for you."

Ray held up his hands and shook them from side to side, his way of saying no thank you. Karen left the room telling her dad to come out when he's ready. Ray looked at the radio on the shelf above his bed and looked at the boxes that Karen had piled in the corner for him.

I wonder, thought Ray.

Ray went through a couple of boxes and there it was, his old Seminole transistor radio that he seemed to have had forever. No one understood why Ray kept it, after all it quit working decades ago and so many times it hovered just above a garbage can only to have Ray insist on its return.

Ray returned to his seat on the bed, turned the broken radio on and played with its dial.

Ray could hear the music from the sixties almost as well as he did back then. He didn't have the earpiece pushed into his ear as he did then, but he heard. He heard tunes and ballgames and saw his dad walk into his room.

"Have you seen my new battery, boy? I want to listen to the Cub game while I take a bath."

This was a very familiar way of relaxing for Ray's dad while Ray's mother worked the night shift at an all-night diner. He would get half loaded, take his radio and a few more beers into the tub, listen to a ballgame, get completely loaded and come out bitching about anything and everything, the noise, the temperature, the Cubs, he always left the tub angry. Ray saw it often enough. And there he stood, three cans of beer in his hands, hard pressed to stand straight without banging into the door jambs on both sides of the doorway.

"I said have you have seen my battery?"

"No," Ray finally answered, "but you should take the electric radio, Koufax is pitching tonight."

Ray's old man put the beers on the edge of the tub, grabbed his electric radio and shut the door behind him. Ray sat on the edge of his bed until he heard the sounds of the ballgame come from the bathroom.

The screams from Ray's mother as soon as she came in from work startled him and he didn't know whether to check on her or to remain in bed. He turned off his radio, his Seminole, and lifted his head from the pillow while removing the cheap earpiece. The screams turned to cries of "Oh my God, Oh my God". Ray decided to check on his mom.

"Get back in your room Ray," his mother shouted, "there's been an accident."

Ray returned to his room and lay motionless on his bed. The cars came quietly, no sirens blaring in the midnight hour, no screeching tires. Ray could see the red lights however and soon talk filled the room. There must have been four or five men in the small bathroom, coroner, police officers, detectives. The dead body in the tub didn't seem to interest them too much. Ray could hear them talking about their families, summer plans and some new sergeant in the station house that was apparently some type of joke. The dead body merely served as a giant magnet drawing together a group who needed it to help pass the time.

They finally got around to looking at the body and finally packed it up in a large black bag. They told Ray's mother that they were ready to leave.

"What now?" she asked. "Do you need to talk to the boy, he was just getting close to his dad, this is really going to affect him."

"This is done." Ray heard one of the men say. "No need in upsetting your son. It's clear what happened. Your husband had a few too many, knocked the electric radio in the tub when he tried to get out and either made contact with the pipes or faucets sending the electric current through his body. He then fell and hit his head pretty hard on the tub, there's a big bump and gash back there, but he was dead or near death by the time he fell. We'll record it as accidental death by electrocution and send his body to the funeral home, they'll call you in the morning. You know that if he had a transistor radio none of this would have happened."

"He does have one," Ray's mother said, "but I guess he never bought the battery he needed. What am I going to do now? Do I get money for this? I can't work anymore than I do already. Someone has to help me. What do I do now?"

No answer came from the police as Ray heard them leave the house and saw the red lights go off. He heard his mother's voice from the living room cursing Ray's dead father and all of life itself.

Ray covered the noise by turning on his radio. The music was sweet, ever so sweet. Ray didn't know if the music sounded so good because of the obstacle now gone from his life or because of the new battery in his radio, a battery he didn't even have to pay for.

CHAPTER 3

Ray laughed then and he laughed now. When Karen came back in his room, he gingerly placed the old broken Seminole back in the box.

"You and that old radio, Dad, I swear you treat it like a friend. I have the exercise sheet from the doctor, things you need to do to make your arm strong again and words you need to read and try to say to get your talking back. When things come back enough, you can return to work, we need to talk to them next week. You'll probably be able to move back in your old place soon. But you know I'll always consider this house yours and you can stay here as long as you want. I'll leave these here, you go ahead and read through them."

Karen set the paperwork down, touched her father's cheek and left the bedroom. Ray glanced through the papers, page after page of mental and physical exercises. Ray thought that he hadn't done that much work since shortly after his father died.

"Junior and senior year of high school," Ray mumbled to himself. He sat back on the bed and drifted again.

Ray grew a lot right after his father died, physically. Mentally he was still just as challenged, still confused by long words and angered by simple putdowns. Those who knew Ray rarely spoke to him, those who didn't know him, spoke often enough to pay a painful price. Mental growth was indeed missing.

By his third year of high school, Ray was over 6 foot 2 and weighed about 225. The football coaches saw a great opportunity in Ray, not for Ray, but for themselves. A good record in high school coaching could lead to a high paying college position. Ray wanted no part of team sports, no part of school sports and for that matter, no part of any sports. The head coach asked around about Ray and found out that he had some fondness for animals and was hoping to go to college to find a career in the animal field. This was all the coach needed and he promised Ray that football was his path to college and the career he wanted.

Ray suited up and proceeded to knock out just about everyone on the football field. His career was short lived, however. When first semester report cards came out, Ray had failed just enough classes to get kicked off the team. This pleased Ray. In spite of his simple ways, he knew he was being used and felt an anger building inside. The split was timely, for coach as much as player. So, Ray turned to his books, somewhat.

A well-oiled mind can overcome a couple of bad parents and a poor childhood. Ray, however, did not possess a well-oiled mind. He couldn't get into algebra class much less pass it, and he was running out of remedial math classes to take. His senior year schedule consisted of welding, earth science, stage decoration, lunch, study hall, gym, and current history where his textbook was the morning newspaper that he stole from various house porches on his way to school.

Despite a bit of a tussle with earth science, Ray managed to pass this array of less than stellar classes. Ray felt that with his newfound intelligence, college and one day perhaps, being a veterinarian, was in his future.

Ray applied to many colleges and one by one they all rejected him. It wasn't much of a decision for the colleges to make, Ray didn't have the grades and he didn't have any of the class requirements. What he stayed in school for didn't come to be.

Unarmed, Ray was going to be launched into the face of turmoil. His fists couldn't win any more victories and his wits never could. As they handed Ray his diploma, he felt as if they were giving him his death notice. Ray secretly hoped that a trap door would open beneath him and he could slip away to nowhere. No trap door, no vanishing act. Ray took the diploma out of the envelope, laughed at it, and tossed it away on his walk home.

His mother was asleep when he got home. She was surrounded by her gossip papers, spent cigarette packs, and empty potato chip bags. Ray stood in the doorway overlooking the landscape of his life. His childhood was over and tomorrow scared him. If there were any tears left inside of him, they would have fallen now.

Instead Ray punched a hole in the wall and went to bed thinking about all the people who had wronged him, his eyes and heart as cold and dry as death itself. Sleep came easily.

Ray's mother kept her word, she said she wouldn't work any more than she already was and she meant it. The two-bedroom apartment was more than enough for her and she was getting tired of her welfare check being gutted by Ray's needs. As soon as she realized that Ray was out of school, she didn't know that he graduated only that he wasn't going to school anymore, she held her idea of a mother son chat with him.

"You need a job."

"I'll get a job. It won't do you good to hassle me."

End of mother son chat.

End of a childhood that never really began. How do the steps of a boy become the walk of a man? Ray seldom sought life, he just fought it as it came at him. The few times a spark lit, it was quickly extinguished. Now his time to truly seek a way of life had arrived, he stood on the edge of his own cliff with all his demons beneath him. The world, time, and his own mother pushed hard, but to what end? When your peak is at the gates of hell itself, how far can any push take you? Ray didn't know and he long ago quit caring. Find a job in a world he hated? Why not? What really mattered anyhow?

CHAPTER 4

Karen entered his room carrying a 2-pound pink weight. "Don't laugh at the color Dad," she told him, "the doctors said this will help rebuild the strength in your arm. They said that when we're young our mind teaches our body. Now they say after your episode, your body needs to teach your mind. Do like this." Karen curled the weight over and over again showing her father how to bend his left arm again. She curled with both arms so Ray would work his good arm too. Karen handed her dad the weight and Ray took it in his good arm and waved it over his head and tried to hand it back.

"Very funny Dad, but that won't work." She took his hand in hers and they curled the weight together. She switched hands, putting the weight in Ray's bad arm and curled again, Karen doing all of the work. "Now you try".

Ray sat on his spot on the edge of the bed and tried to lift the weight, two pounds equaling a ton. The strength was there somewhere, hidden in a motionless arm, but the muscles were good; the message to move wasn't getting through.

The arm moved just enough to lift spirits and give hope. "That arm will teach your mind to work again. Your wires may have to be re-routed, but your mind is going to work just fine. You keep playing with that pretty pink weight and later I'll show you the pictures and words you need to learn again. We're going to get you back to that strong kid that knew no boundaries. Wouldn't you like to be that wild man again?"

Wild man, Ray thought. *I never wanted to be a wild man; in fact, I don't think I was ever a wild man. People pushed me, people are always pushing me. I pushed back harder, that showed em. That don't make me wild. People shouldn't have pushed me. Not now, shouldn't have done it back then.*

Back then, back when his mother wanted him to give her money, money for chocolate, money for beer, money for gossip papers and greasy potato chips. A person needs to weigh within their means Ray believed. If you can afford to weigh 300 pounds, then weigh 300 pounds. If you can only afford 150 then live accordingly. Ray wanted to tell his mother a thousand ugly things about her lifestyle, but the words choked him when they stuck in his throat, angered him when they churned in his stomach. He would stare at her in disgust, rage building inside until she told him to quit looking at her that way. He hated the memories of those days.

"Quit looking at me like that boy! Your eyes are bugging out of your head and your chin is jutting out of your crooked face. If I had money, I'd turn you over to the doctors. I swear Ray sometimes I think you're crazy. Quit looking at me. And speaking of having no money, did you find a job yet? We need a dishwasher at the restaurant. I want you to take it."

"I ain't no dishwasher. You take it. Touch dirty people's dirty food. Think about all that …" Ray never finished his sentence.

"You ungrateful smart ass. The government money is stopping now that you're out of school. You'll be out of here next. Your father don't know how lucky he was that day he fell in the bath tub."

"Keep pushing me and maybe you'll get lucky too." Ray smiled, almost laughed out loud, and went out. The smile left as quickly as it came, and Ray looked at every store and factory on the hot city streets wondering where he could find a job that wouldn't kill him.

Ray walked into a few buildings, filled out a couple of applications but wasn't having any luck. He walked by a gas station that seemed pretty busy and thought he would try his luck there. He said he could pump gas, clean a windshield, check oil, and change a tire. Ray had a job, a 3 dollar an hour job, not bad for the early seventies, and he was to start the very next morning. He had no money so he couldn't celebrate, and he didn't have anyone to celebrate with. Ray felt successful, almost happy.

Ray reported to work in a pair of jeans and dark blue work shirt. He was promised a uniform once he got a couple weeks under his belt. It was a good job for Ray as he kept to himself doing everything the bosses asked him to. Being the new guy everyone was his boss.

He quickly learned some tricks of this particular gas station's trade. He could slice a windshield wiper and then recommend a new one, fill a container that was left by the gas pumps with gas so that the customer paid it, and never put the dipstick all the way down when checking oil. Ray was selling a lot of oil.

At 6 foot 3 now with a slightly crooked face best described as "off", few argued with Ray. One customer did complain once and checked his own oil. Full. He told Ray that he was full too, full of shit, and drove off. The guys at the station all had a laugh and one worker told Ray he needed to carry an ice pick in his lower work pocket. That way when a driver gave you crap you walk around to the passenger side of the car and stick the pick in the tire. The tire would leak slow enough to get the car home but be flat as hell by morning. With Ray's feelings for most people running from dislike to absolute hate, this was good advice. Ray purchased an ice pick later that day.

He found something to hate in everyone and he spent much of his time between customers flipping his ice pick in the air and catching it by the handle. He would even practice his stabbing style on old tires that were traded in and piled out back. Ray looked forward to his next angry customer.

This was the first time in Ray's life that he felt like part of a group. Ray made one good friend at the gas station, Lance. Lance was the station owner's dog, a German Shepard that came into work with the boss most days. Lance would watch Ray practice with his ice pick and follow him around the station all day. Ray would take his lunch with Lance and always bring a bag of goodies for the dog. The boys at the station joked about who was really following whom around the station, but it seemed to be a good situation for both Ray and dog.

A surly customer drove in one morning and asked for a fill up, a quick fill up to use his words. Ray was crouched behind the car playing with Lance waiting for the pump to stop. As soon as it did

Ray put the nozzle in the "company" container and was about to add a little gas to the community pot and a little money to the customer's bill.

"You son-of-a-bitch," Ray heard from above him. The customer left his car and snuck up on Ray behind the car. "You robbing me?"

"No, this pump leaks for a second after a fill-up, it's safer to leak in the container than on the ground."

"You're a liar, a bad liar. I should knock your fucking head off."

The customer's yelling set Lance off. Lance was barking and growling, his hair standing on end. Ray held him back.

"Get that ugly mutt away from me before I kick his teeth in."

Ray let go of the dog and got right in the guy's face. "You lift one leg at my dog, and you won't see tomorrow. Get in your car and get the hell out of here before I stuff you in the trunk."

Ray inched closer ready to haul off on the guy. Ray held back, but his fists were ready, Lance barked angrily, but he too held back. The guy inched back into his car. The owner finally came out of the station and grabbed Lance.

"You haven't seen the last of me, none of you have," the customer shouted as he slammed the car door.

"Get inside Ray, now," the boss said as he led Lance away.

Ray crouched again and bang, bang. Two stabs of the ice pick into the rear tire. Ray shook with anger and watched the irate customer speed down the boulevard.

Ray cooled quickly and went inside to face the boss. As soon as he got inside, he knelt down in front of Lance. "Good boy Lance, good boy. That's how we take care of people like that. You just let him come back, we'll really take care of him then."

The boss was not amused. "What the hell was that all about, Ray? This could be trouble for me, Lance too, and you most of all. What happened?"

"He never paid me. He owes us 10 bucks."

"You were fighting over money? He robbed us?"

"Yeah, he robbed us, but I just remembered that. He won't be back. He said I was robbing him because I put the hose in the container. Then he yelled at Lance, he shouldn't have yelled at Lance. He said he was gonna kick him too, that's why we were arguing. I scared him off. He never paid us. He's the crook."

"Damn Ray, you're a big good kid, but really dumb sometimes. No more hose in the container, understand? I'm gonna get that thing out of here. Just sit in the garage for a while, I need to think about this."

"I'll sit, but I ain't dumb. I wouldn't let anyone kick a dog, not any dog anywhere. That don't make me dumb".

"I guess not Ray. Just go sit for a while".

Ray sat, Lance sat right next to him, a rather odd sight at a business. The rest of the guys were bewildered by Ray and the distance written on his face.

A couple of the mechanics tried to talk to the boss about Ray. They thought that Ray was messed up because he didn't seem to have any friends. They assumed his home life was messed up and he needed to get out with people. They felt guilty too, they taught Ray how to steal gas on the customer's dime and supplied the container that they would then empty into their own cars.

It was decided that they would take Ray out with them to the horse track that night and loosen the kid up. He was only 18 but he looked 30. Liquoring him up would be easy.

The boss sent Ray home for the day and the four of them met that night at 7:00 back at the station. Everyone smelled of gasoline, the car reeked of gasoline, it was a byproduct of their chosen profession. In spite of the warning from the smell of gas and the warning on the cigarette package, everyone lit up. Everyone opened a beer. It was Ray's first. He was turned off by beer because of the amount his late father insisted on drinking almost every night. The first sip or two didn't agree with Ray, the third and fourth did. Ray opened another can.

The group felt good when they reached the track; a couple of the guys bought programs. Ray had never been to the track and had no idea what was going on.

They bought a round of beers and stood along the rail watching the horses trot by. Ray's boss explained how the betting works as quickly as he could and then went off to place his bets. Ray wandered down to the paddock and watched the horses get saddled up. He stopped to pet one of the escort horses and even managed to say hello to the girl riding him. Ray continued down to the stable area where horses were coming in and going out with regularity.

Ray loved the action, the horses, even the smell of the stables. He liked guessing which horse would win the next race based on his personal analysis. Ray felt good, almost euphoric. For a man who rarely felt okay, this was a big day.

There was a cat roaming the stables and when the horses got too close to it Ray scooped him up in his arms and went inside the stable area, where he wasn't allowed, with the cat. He was quickly stopped.

"Hey buddy, where you going?" a tall man in cowboy boots yelled to him.

A security guard came over right away. "Yeah, where you going man?"

"This cat almost got stepped on by the horse. I grabbed him."

"It's okay, I got this Jim," the cowboy told the officer. The security guard walked away, the cowboy looked at Ray, Ray pet the cat. "He's our stable cat, there's a couple more around here someplace. They kill the mice and keep the horses calm. They rarely get stepped on, but I can't say never, they're a weird animal. Put him back on the hay bales, but I doubt he'll stay. You could be chasing him all night."

Ray set the cat down and as quickly as he did the cat jumped off the hay and disappeared under the back wall. Ray was admiring all the tack equipment hanging up, the reins and the bits, the training irons, the halters and the blinkers. He paused to touch the leather saddle and was surprised by the softness of the seat and the hardness of the leather surrounding it.

"You new to the track, buddy?"

"Yes," replied Ray still pressing the leather of the saddle. "You polish all of this silver."

"I clean a lot of it, but don't worry, it's not real silver. None of these horses make enough to afford a real silver bridle. They are real leather though, I polish those too. You best move back buddy, the horses for the next race are coming in, they have to be saddled up."

Ray moved out of the stable and was hypnotized by the parade of horses. He was brought back to earth by his boss' voice.

"Hey Ray, where've you been? We've been looking all over for you. You learn enough to pick a winner? We're all losing tonight."

Ray studied the horses in each stall and matched them with the number painted overhead. He didn't need any names. He could tell by their looks. "Number 6."

"Alright Ray, now that you're helping us, you're part of the team." They joined the others and pooled their money. One big win would save the evening, all the guys were up, excitement had returned.

Some myths die hard. The world is flat theory lasted thousands of years. "Red sky at night, sailor's delight" has outlasted the hundreds of hurricanes that followed red skies. Leave the eyes of a corpse open and it will find someone to take with it.

Other myths die quickly like 'some people can communicate with horses and make you thousands of dollars at the racetrack.' Ray's number 6 finished sixth. Turned out Ray liked his size and when Ray saw the horse burying his face in a bucket of oats, he saw happiness. He should have seen gluttony and a horse too stuffed to run. Ray never could see any bad in an animal and was the last man on earth to ask about a racehorse.

The gas station boys had a good laugh, Ray laughed with them. Despite the losses, Ray was part of the group now. When they parted that evening. Ray looked forward to the next day. Work became Ray's safe haven. The station was more home now than his mother's apartment. Tomorrow it would be an even better place to be.

CHAPTER 5

Tomorrows were never meant for Ray, there had yet to be a tomorrow that brought Ray what yesterday promised. When he arrived the following morning, his boss called him into the office.

Before Ray sat down he asked where Lance was, the station seemed deserted without him.

"I had to take Lance home," the boss told Ray. "That guy you got in an argument with was waiting for me this morning. He said you ice-picked his tire and gave him a flat, he had a receipt for a tire repair, I had to pay him. Lance started growling at him, his hair was standing up, it took all I had to hold him back. He wanted to kill that guy. I've never seen Lance act like that. I drove him back home."

"You should have let Lance loose on the guy. Lance didn't do anything wrong, the growling is his way of yelling, his way of telling the guy to shut the hell up. That bastard said he was gonna kick him in the teeth, Lance had the right to defend himself. If I were here, I would have had Lance jump his sorry ass and I would have cold-cocked the bastard too."

"I know you would have Ray. You have some strange ideas about what you have to do to protect people. No, not even people Ray, dogs, maybe all animals. You've appointed yourself as some sort of animal protector and you're too quick and willing to hurt people in your mission. I can't have you here Ray, you're going to hurt somebody someday and I can't afford that. If you let Lance loose on somebody, I'll lose him too. Can't you see that?

"Lance didn't do anything, that guy was the one in the wrong. Now Lance is locked up at home and I'm out of work. How is that fair? How can I deal with that?" The boss stared at the ground and the silence seemed to last forever. An uneasy Ray finally spoke. "Don't worry, I won't cause you guys any trouble. I'll stay away. But I'll see that guy again, I'll see that shitty car with the bad tire, and then somebody is going to learn real clearly what it means to have your teeth kicked down your throat, real clear boss, real fucking clear."

Ray was getting more and more agitated as he spoke, and the boss tried to cool him down.

"Calm down Ray, here's a week's pay, cash. Now you need…"

Ray stopped him short, took the money, turned and walked away. After a couple steps he turned back and said, "Nobody should ever tell me to calm down and tell me what I need. Nobody."

Ray got home, it was less than an hour from when he left, and sat mindlessly in his room. The time of Ray's return was not lost on his mother and she wanted to rip him apart as he sat deaf to her words.

"What the hell you doing back here now, you got fired didn't you? I ain't paying for this apartment and feeding you and all the damn animals you bring home. Are you listening to me? Do you hear me?"

CHAPTER 6

"Pa, can you hear me? Are you listening dad?"

Karen was back in the room and momentarily brought her father back to today, back to a time that Ray was not ready, or seemingly interested in being a part of.

"It's getting late, Pa. You haven't eaten much today and it's already getting dark. Why don't you just get some sleep and we'll start over again tomorrow. You can walk the horses if you want, it will do you good to be outside. Goodnight."

Karen called it a night and Ray lay in bed thinking about the horses and how horses changed his life a long time ago.

The morning after Ray lost his job his mother started on him again. She yelled at Ray for sleeping too much, eating too much, and watching too much television. Before an hour had passed that morning, Ray had enough and left the house. He walked the neighborhood seldom taking his eyes off the ground and finding excuse after excuse for not applying for work in any of the places he passed.

That cowboy at the racetrack had it made, Ray thought to himself. He worked with animals all day and never had to listen to people moaning at him, calling him stupid or lazy, or any other hurtful names they thought of. "I should be working there. Yeah, I could work there", Ray said out loud and felt a rush of adrenaline speed through his body.

Ray walked quickly, almost running, to the bus stop and took the next bus to the track. Ray wasn't going to bet, or drink; he was going to find work. When he got off the bus outside of the track, he became part of the commotion. People were rushing to get into the park, pushing and shoving prevailed, beer stained the cement floor. But it was the smell of horses that woke his emotions. In a place where Ray had only been for a couple of hours, he felt at home. He walked with a new purpose in the track and looked for the office. Ray wanted to work now like so few others ever wanted to work.

Ray walked slowly around the clubhouse hoping to see a sign for the office. He was amazed by the huge windows offering a view of the track and stood staring, almost lost in this new world. He found the chatter from the long lines of betters exhilarating. They all seemed happy to Ray, he knew it was the horses that made people happy and his thoughts turned to the cat he made friends with back in the stables. He started heading for the stables when his eyes caught sight of a large green sign. He found the office.

Ray walked in and his eyes met those of a young lady he thought was beautiful. He stood frozen and had no answer when she asked if she could help him. Ray didn't hear her the first time she asked, and he never heard her ask the second time. She probably didn't. She just got out of her seat and began filing some papers in an old green metal cabinet that seemed out of place standing beside a new water cooler.

"When you're ready to talk you go ahead and just start up. I've got work to do in the meantime."

"I'm sorry," Ray said, "but your looks actually startled me."

That one sentence was a thousand times more than Ray had ever uttered to a woman in his entire life. Ray was a boy nearing 19 years old and, at the same time, becoming a man that was never really a boy at all. Hardness outlined Ray's life. Ray's comment was spoken in earnest, but Ray got his usual reply.

"Save your crap for somebody else buddy, I've worked this track for years and I've heard all the stupid lines that there are. I have no interest in you or anyone like you. If it weren't for the horses, I wouldn't be here. Now what exactly do you want?"

"I ain't stupid. I didn't say anything that was stupid."

"What do you want mister? Should I be calling security?"

"I want to work. I don't like people much either, they're always calling me stupid. I ain't stupid. Animals know that and I can work with them. I guess I was thinking about horses and thinking about the cat that lives here in the hay bales with them. I was in another world thinking about them. Then I walked in and saw you, you scared me. I wasn't ready to see someone like you. I'm sorry."

"Well I guess I'm sorry too. I shouldn't have been so direct to you. But did you really think that you would see a horse in the office? I'm Diane by the way. And what do they call you?"

That is when Ray met Diane Kent. Two sheltered souls, two people who didn't feel comfortable around other people, meeting like ice dropped into an already cold soft drink. No explosion, no lightning from the clouds, just two objects too close to one another and cautiously letting a little of their inner self seep out. Diane, surprising even herself, felt comfortable, and Ray felt something. He didn't know what he felt, but he felt it all right and he liked it. It wasn't comfort he felt, for he was more nervous than he'd ever been, but he wanted to hold on to the moment.

"I'm Ray," he finally said, slowly, timidly. "Call me Ray." He looked Diane over and over again.

Diane was reserved to the point of being withdrawn. She was a simple beauty. Little to no makeup changed her face. Her skin smooth, her cheeks puffy. She wore faded jeans and black cowboy boots. Her tight white top revealed what little there was to reveal about her body, her upper body, her jeans outlined a far different look that Ray feasted on from behind her. She was a woman alright, a working woman who loved animals.

"Well Ray, I know we need help around the track, and you look like the type of man who could handle the work. We need someone to help unload tracks and do a lot of park maintenance. Problem is, working for the track is different than working with the horses". As with just about everything in Ray's life he was a bit confused in Diane's words. Did he have the job, was she pushing him away?

"I'm not afraid of work," he finally said, "a little uncomfortable with some people maybe, but I would be a good worker, I promise. What kind of work would I do?"

Diane smiled and began to feel a kinship with Ray. "I think that you would see far too many people working out of this office, not that I couldn't keep you very busy". She giggled and smiled at Ray again. "But from what I'm hearing from you, I think working in the stables may be more suited to you. They're in their own world down there. You certainly look physically capable of doing whatever they ask you to do."

"I could do it. I can do anything once someone shows me how. What would I do?"

"Well slow down for a second, there's a process here we follow before hiring, but I love your enthusiasm." Diane gave Ray that look again and they both laughed just a bit.

"You know, I actually started my time here working in the stables. I was riding horses on my own for years when I applied for a job here. I got a hired through the stable as track rider. My main job was escorting the racehorses on and off the track between races. I liked it, loved it actually, but it didn't pay much money. I transferred up here doing everything they throw at me. It's okay, but not as much fun as riding every day. Why don't I walk you down to the barn and you can talk to Stuart about working there? If they have a spot for you, you'll make fair money. You'll work like hell, but you'll get paid for it. If they don't have a spot, I'll get you an application for the track. Sound fair?" She stared up at Ray for the longest time waiting for an answer that she already knew.

Ray was a bit lost. Maybe it was her words, maybe her giggle, and maybe it was just the way she looked at him but from the little Ray knew about these things he guessed she was flirting with him. "Yes", he finally answered completely forgetting the question.

Diane walked Ray over to the barns to talk to Stu. As they walked, Diane seemed to get closer to Ray with each step, occasionally they would touch arms and nervously part, putting up imaginary borders. Ray liked brushing into Diane, but he disliked it too. He felt he was trespassing when they bumped and rejecting her when he moved away. He grew more nervous with each step and felt his face grow red and warm. His raw emotions told him to hold her, his fears told him to stay away. He tried to simply walk in a straight line, jumping away whenever Diane bumped into him. His jumps however were becoming smaller and smaller and taking more and more time to happen. This ritual was running its course and there was no telling where it would end. However (there is always a however waiting for Ray), they soon reached the barn where Stuart Horky was slowly going about his work.

Stuart looked up when he noticed the pair, "How you doing Diane, you looking to ride today?"

"Not today Stu, maybe over the weekend. This is Ray, he was

looking for work with the track. He tells me that he has a real concern for animals, and I thought he may be more helpful with your workers instead. What do you think?" Diane let her words hang hopefully in the air.

Stu rubbed his jaw and looked Ray over carefully. "I know you son, don't I? You were here a few nights ago all worried about the cat getting run over by a horse."

"It's not a safe place for the cat," Ray said.

"She eats well, I'll tell you that."

"I can take her home if you'd like, I'll feed her well too. She's gonna get hurt around here."

Stu turned to Diane, "I think Ray may fit here real nice. Why don't you let me show Ray around and see what he thinks? I'll send him back your way when we're done talking."

Diane walked on back to the office and Stu started telling Ray about the work in the barns and around the track. Ray wasn't listening, his eyes, his entire self really, was glued on Diane as she walked back to work. Diane's image was burning into Ray's soul. Stu quit talking and looked at Ray staring off into the distance.

When Diane walked out of sight Ray finally spoke. "How do you ask a girl out, Stu?"

"Ray, Ray, Ray," Stu uttered, "one thing at a time. First you get a job and learn how to do that real well, then we'll talk girls. Now do want to work here or not?"

"I do Stu, I'll work hard, and it's not girls Stu, it's Diane."

"What's Diane?"

"It's Diane I want to learn about, just Diane."

"I better put you to work before you run off and elope."

Ray had his job working with animals, and a dream in his mind if not yet in his heart. Ray remembered that day well as he put his head down on his pillow. He remembered it as a completely happy time and wasn't sure where the feelings of despair and fear were coming from that loomed inside. He was glad the happy memories came back first and, as he drifted off to sleep that night, he wished that the power that he now had, the power to forget, would last forever. In his heart he knew better, he knew bad memories would return.

CHAPTER 7

Ray was up early and struggled to get out of bed. Karen was up early too, and she darted about the kitchen making breakfast for the two of them. Karen looked exhausted, the look of a girl who hadn't slept for a long time. Ray saw the look on her face, the withdrawn eyes and the beautiful hair that's been ignored for many months. Ray thought it odd that his illness would attack so many other things that were seemingly so far away.

He sat in silence eating the food placed before him. Everything was planned carefully so he could eat with one hand. When Karen asked if he wanted to go out to the barn and see the horses, he nodded. In a world this orderly, he wondered if he would ever need to speak again.

The horses were good therapy for Ray, and he brushed them just as his old friend Stuart taught him to do decades ago. The lessons lingered deep, but as with other buried memories, they were uncovered by the winds of familiar work.

Ray worked the track circuit all around Chicago for a long time and the years passed quickly. Depending on which track the horses were running on, he would either stay in a one room flop at the track or in his mother's apartment where he was mostly squirreled up in his room.

At the track, Ray was all work. He had grown to be a good size man and his love for animals grew also. It made no difference to Ray if he was grooming a valuable racehorse or feeding gourmet cans of cat food to the local alley cats. They brought him peace and purpose.

Stuart took Ray out often for dinner or a drink or two, neither ever drank very much, the work around the track was endless and a clear head was needed. One night Stuart finally asked the question that more than one person wanted an answer to, "How come you haven't asked Diane out yet Ray? You do know she likes you".

"I'm okay with the work and the horses Stu, I know Diane is way too good for me. She is happy."

"She's not all that happy Ray, I swear she's as lost as you are. You're a good man Ray. You can make her happy, hell, you two make each other happy."

"Can't do it Stu, sorry."

"Think about it, son, just think about it. Life passes us by quickly; don't leave your calling behind you."

Ray looked at Stu for a long time, rubbed his chin, scratched his head and finally answered, "I don't know what the hell you just said Stu."

Ray worked and stayed isolated from most people. After two plus years of working together, Diane asked Ray to go riding at the track on what they call a 'dark day'. Ray sheepishly said yes.

They rode together, letting the horses stroll slowly around the racetrack. They rode the escort horses that had no desire to run. Occasionally, Diane would let her horse gallop a bit and Ray followed. They talked as they rode. Years of conversation burst forth like water through a crumbling dam. They knew they liked one another and on this beautiful afternoon they learned they like being together.

Their ride was followed by dinner at a restaurant away from the track and dinner was followed by a short evening talking and listening to music at Diane's home. By the time Ray headed back to his mother's house, his quiet love for Diane turned into a blistering calling deep within him, a place seldom touched before.

Ray got to work early the next day and put some flowers on Diane's desk. They were flowers Ray picked from a stranger's front yard, but flowers nonetheless. Ray went up to Diane's office at lunch time to ask her out, but after spending a good half hour pacing back and forth outside of her door left without ever going in. He returned after work and his pacing returned also. He was about to leave when Diane opened the door.

"Hi Ray, thank you for the flowers this morning. Did you need something or are you here to see me?"

"I forget what I was going to say."

"Then it is me you wanted to see. Right?"

"I guess, I mean I think so. Can we go out this weekend? Will you go to the zoo with me?"

"Of course!

Ray and Diane began their affair. Alone, these two childlike adults may never have grown, not in the way most people do. Together they grew.

They started spending days off together, usually going to the zoo or a park, any place where they could feel alone, away from people, closer to animals. In time they started going out to dinner and every once and a while they would be joined by friends from work. It was always at Diane's insistence that they would let others join them.

Diane grew quicker than Ray and initiated the things they would do together, including the nights that they spent in Diane's bed. Ray was ecstatic and when Diane proposed marriage, Ray gave his version of 'yes'. His exact words were, "If you think it's the right thing to do".

After years of working together and dating, a nervous Ray and an excited Diane were married in a small Chicago church. It was a church because someone sent a dollar to an address they saw on a book of matches and got a non-profit business number and a twelve-inch wooden cross in return. The cross was nailed to a one story old wood frame house and 'The United Church of Souls' was born. It was legal, Ray and Diane were legal, and they never visited the 'church' again.

Diane continued to grow. She hung around more with the girls at work, went out more often without Ray and slowly turned their quiet apartment into a more vibrant home with brighter paints, wild wallpaper, louder phonographs and tape players, larger and larger TVs. Most nights, Diane would read teen and young adult books sitting alone in front of the TV.

Ray would turn in early listening to his bedside radio. If he had taken his old Seminole radio out of his drawer and played it, instead of the electric radio, things would have been identical to 20 years earlier.

He had an electric radio now not a small transistor, he had a queen-sized bed and not a single, he lived with a wife instead of a mother. Call it change, but Ray hadn't changed at all, and when Diane became pregnant and started pushing Ray to get better work, the cycle began again. He felt he was being pushed, his anxiety grew, blood rushed, fists clenched. His back to the wall, Ray cracked.

CHAPTER 8

Karen walked in the barn and saw her father holding the brush in his bad arm standing beside the horse. He didn't look lost, he appeared to be at peace.

"Brush the horse Dad, it will be good for both of you."

Ray looked at his daughter and forced his arm to move to the horse. The brush touched the horse just beneath his mane and Ray continued in a downward motion.

"You're doing it!"

Karen had a tear in her eye and Ray had a small smile on his face.

"Just like when I was little and you would brush my hair. You were as slow as you could be so you wouldn't hurt me, a small smile on your face."

The memories of Karen's early years were growing clearer to Ray, all the way back to the day his wife said she was pregnant and began pushing Ray. Ray cracked that day, but not inside. It was his hard shell that cracked from being pushed by his love for his yet unborn daughter.

Ray agreed to go to school and become something more for her. His wife told him that law enforcement or security of some sort was right up his alley. Ray enrolled in a police program at the junior college, taking classes five nights a week after work.

He pushed himself hard and when Stuart asked him why he was taking on such a heavy load, Ray told him that it was for the new baby.

Stuart said, "All about the carin'."

Ray knew from the second he heard that phrase that if he and Diane had a girl, she would be named Karen. Life would be all about Karen. With so much hope and joy inside of Ray there was never a doubt that the baby would be anything other than a girl named Karen.

Karen arrived in the spring of 1975. Ray paced in the waiting room until the nurse called him into the delivery room. All scrubbed down and wearing a hospital gown, Ray touched his daughter's cheek while the nurse held the baby. Ray was too scared to do more than touch.

As the nurses wheeled Diane and Karen to their rooms, Ray drove home. He heard a song on the radio with the lyrics, "Loving you is easy cause you're beautiful," Ray stopped at a dime store and bought the Minnie Ripperton record for Karen. They needed diapers, clothes, a car seat for Karen, and a hundred other things, but all Ray bought was the record. Life was easy he thought, and he was happy. Other purchases would have to wait.

Karen and Diane came home from the hospital after the usual 3 day stay. Eventually, Ray purchased all the things Karen needed and his life as a father began. He fixed up Karen's room, wallpapering the room with an animal pattern that failed to match up in most places. There were lion's heads on giraffe's bodies everywhere, but the room was beautiful and a custom Ray job as Diane called it.

Diane took a few months leave from work and Ray continued working and going to night school. By the time Karen was 6 months old, this idyllic way of life was over. Diane returned to work, Ray continued at work and school, and Karen spent all day with a neighbor who was home with a child of her own. It wasn't a bad life by any means and if Diane's plans came through with Ray's schooling, things would get even better.

Ray completed his law enforcement program shortly after Karen's second birthday. How he made it through was anybody's guess. He never studied and he rushed home from school every night to spend what little time he had left at the end of the day playing with his daughter. But he was a degreed man now; Ray was further along in life than anyone had ever dreamed possible.

Diane now pushed him to find work on a police force in town. She needed to do more than push, more than love, more than hope for Ray. He could never pass the entrance exams and never got accepted into the academy. Rejections long ceased to bother Ray, they gnawed at Diane, however. Shadows crept in. Life was becoming darker, but too slowly for anyone to notice or do anything about it.

Diane was getting hard for Ray to understand. She no longer seemed happy coming home from work and although she loved their daughter, she seemed to be distant in her motherly role. Ray was the closer of the two to Karen, playing games with her and riding her around the apartment on his shoulders. Most of the zoo or beach outings were now just Ray and Karen as Diane often chose to stay home. It wasn't Karen however that Diane was growing uneasy with, it was Ray.

She viewed him now as a minor failure that would never get her and Karen out of their small city apartment. At first, she minimized her time with Ray by working late, then she graduated to the bar with the girls from work. Diane would slowly sip a glass of wine killing an hour before going home, then it was two … two hours and two glasses of wine.

She never missed Karen when she was out drinking, the missing came when she got home and felt guilty about being out. As for Ray, she never missed him and never felt guilty about being away from him.

Endlessly combing through the want ads, Diane finally found what she considered the perfect job for Ray to have and give her relief, a night shift security guard. This would get Ray out of the stables and away from her at work and get Ray out of the house and away from her at home. She sold Ray on the idea by telling him the hours would allow Karen to be at home so much more and with him all day. Ray jumped at the chance and began his life as a security guard.

Ray worked various locations at his new job. Many nights were spent alone in factory buildings or construction sites nearing completion. He worked at 6:00 pm until 2:00 am and this being a little out of step from the world put Ray right in step with his family. He was up every morning by 9:00 to play with Karen and napped in the afternoon when she did.

Diane didn't get home before 7:00 anymore, so they rarely saw one another during the week. Ray would take Karen over to

Diane's parents at 5:00 and head to work. Ray was completely happy with both his home life and his work world.

Many of Ray's assignments at work included concerts and ballgames and he was working with a lot of regular Chicago police officers. He knew many of the cops on good terms and talked about one day being a cop alongside them. The cops liked Ray, but he lacked quite a few things to be a regular police officer. Ray dreamed and hoped, but was quite content if these dreams never came to be. Ray learned to accept the reality of where he was in the world.

Diane was a different story. After years of shyness and solitude, Diane was discovering and loving the world around her. With Ray off at work every night and Karen with Diane's folks, Diane saw no reason to hurry home. Her one drink with the girls had long ago grown to 2, then 3, 4 or often more, and her nights with the girls had grown to nights with the girls and boys.

Diane put her toe in the water first, spending hours in her car outside of the bar talking and listening to the radio in the company of her new male friends. Some nights would end with a kiss, some nights many kisses until Diane jumped in neck deep into the wild waters and started having occasional sex before picking up Karen. This continued for a few years with Ray totally oblivious. Each in their own ways, they found happiness. This happiness may have gone on forever, but in the world of Ray, happiness never lasted long.

Diane had grown to dislike being around Ray. She felt he had no zest for life. She was a different woman from the one he married. The inevitable happened, Diane's sexual escapades led to love. She met a man in the bar, and he became her regular sex partner out in the parking lot. Things progressed to cheap motels and finally to his place. By the time Karen was ready to start school, Diane was ready to leave Ray. She often started the talk with Ray, but it never went far. Ray's understanding of things limited the depth of their talks.

Feeling pressure to be with her lover and pressure from her lover, Diane decided to put her feelings on paper. She would tell Ray goodbye in a short note.

Leaving Karen at her parent's house, she went home with a bottle of wine and began thinking about the words to leave Ray.

Nothing was coming as Diane drank more and more of the wine. The hours ticked by and Ray would be home soon. Wringing the last drop of wine from the bottle Diane sat in front of her near empty glass and began her note.

She wrote, *"Ray, I never wanted it to end like this, but I see no other way."*

She continued to struggle for the words from there and could only see a crushed husband from this point. She swallowed the last drop of wine and put her glass down on the paper leaving half a ring on the note. Her pen grew heavy and fell. The day finally put Diane to sleep in her kitchen chair, head falling from side to side and back and forth. The door opened, slowly and quietly as it did every night at this time and Ray entered the apartment.

"You're up late," Ray said. Hearing no reply, Ray looked closer and saw that his wife was out cold. He looked even closer and saw the note, the wine stain, the empty glass and the pen on the floor. Nothing made sense to Ray now, but he was nervous, scared in fact. He shook life into Diane and when she was awake enough, he asked what the note meant.

The talk that never went far enough before was about to go too far now. The dam, weakened by alcohol, was about to burst.

"I can't be with you anymore, Ray. It just isn't working."

Words went back and forth, no yelling, no screaming, just a lot of 'you can' and 'I can't'. What Diane hoped would be the final words came at long last.

"I've met someone else Ray. We're in love. I'm going to live with him. No more zoo, no more cages. I have to go."

Ray went to their bedroom and hunted through the dresser drawers. He returned to the kitchen still dressed in his work uniform but with arms loaded with picture albums. He kneeled on the floor next to Diane and turned the pages of their life together.

"Look at these Diane. Here's Karen at the zoo when the bear pounded on the glass window scaring the heck out of her. Look how she's squeezing my neck. And here she is riding with me for the first time. Remember her birthday party Diane? Just the three of us, here's a picture of the cake me and Karen baked. We had such fun. How can you even think of leaving us Diane?"

"Us?" said Diane confused. "I'm not leaving Karen, just you Ray, Karen is going with me. You scare me. Sometimes you get mad for no reason and you disappear a million miles away. I can't do it anymore. Karen and I are leaving you."

Wherever that million miles away was, Ray was there again. The anger built, he felt it building. Nobody was going to take his baby from him. He stared into Diane's face and didn't know her any longer. He didn't recognize the eyes or know the lines on her face. He didn't like the sight of her lips and was getting sick at the thought that he once kissed them and now another man was. This woman that he loved so deeply just a year ago, a month and even just a few minutes ago, he now hated, hated more deeply than he ever loved her.

Beaten, Ray's arm hung down at his side and touched the gun he wore to work every day. Without thought Ray looked down at his gun and once more into the face he now hated. The world sped up now, grew quickly out of focus. Ray's hand shook and he bit his lip hard enough to draw blood. Just as quickly as the world sped up, it stopped. Ray relaxed. He released his lip from the viselike grip of his teeth and looked once more at Diane and smiled. She looked down at Ray and began to smile also. Then the gun rose from Ray's hip and touched the side of Diane's head.

Diane's smile left as she grabbed for the gun with both hands. Fear was all around and within Diane, her efforts to push the gun away were useless. A shot sounded, it screamed and whistled a high pitch ear piercing tone. The bullet flew through Diane's brain erasing every thought, dream and memory she ever had.

When the bullet left her head, it blew a four-inch gap in her skull and left blood and brain on the floor. The bullet came to rest high up on the wall behind her. Diane's lifeless body stayed in the kitchen chair, her hands still clinging to Ray's hands and the gun. What was left of Diane's head hung backwards over the chair. Ray slid his hands off the gun leaving it with Diane and without the slightest bit of remorse pushed her off of the chair and left her in a crumpled mess on the bloody kitchen floor.

"I guess you won't be taking my baby after all," Ray said as he left the room.

Ray walked into the bedroom, took off his empty holster, placed it on the dresser, and went into the bathroom. He ran the water until it was warm enough to wash the blood from his hands. He knew he went too far this time. Ray held his hands under the running water and looked at his image in the mirror. The cold, hollow eyes of a murderer looked back at him. Ray was frozen by his own stare.

CHAPTER 9

R ay was staring into the small barn mirror that hung above the ancient wooden tack trunk when Karen walked in.

"Recognize yourself, Dad?" she asked.

He didn't want to, but he did. The memories were returning too quickly and he recognized the murderer standing before the mirror.

"That little mirror doesn't show much but you still look like you."

How wrong Karen was. This tiny mirror showed too much. The harder he looked, the more accurate the reflection. Ray moved the hair on his head all around to get a different look, all to no avail. The eyes looked back right through him, calling him things that Ray feared others would hear.

"I brought you some coffee. You want to come to the house?"

Ray shook his head to say no and took the cup from Karen. He sat down on the trunk and watched Karen walk out of the barn. *She could have never forgiven me for what I did*, Ray thought to himself, *never love me like this for so long*.

Ray stood up and placed his coffee on the trunk. He looked again at the monster in the mirror. "What the hell did you do you bastard?"

Ray lowered his eyes from his stare in the mirror and saw Diane's blood circle the drain and leave the sink. "What the hell did you do?" Ray said to the stranger in the mirror. He began scrubbing his hands harder and harder, faster and faster almost replacing Diane's blood with his own. "How am I going to be with my daughter now? At least she won't be with Diane and her boyfriend. Anything is better than that. I can't let her see me like this. I have to end this tonight."

Ray stepped over Diane's cold body and picked up the kitchen phone. He asked the operator to put him through to the police, which she did instantly. Ray told them that there had been a terrible accident and that his wife was dead. A few meaningless questions followed and then they told Ray that some officers were on the way. Ray opened the front and back door, sat on the living room sofa and hurt inside for the pain that was about to come to him and Karen. Ray was lost in a fog a million miles away when the first police entered the apartment. They were two local uniformed beat cops who weren't used to the carnage that lay before them.

Diane's body was on the floor in a mess that was more guts and brain than blood. The police officer held his hand over his nose and mouth and felt the body for a pulse.

"She's dead," he said to the other officer.

"Yeah I figured that by the gap in her skull and the crap on the floor. Blood on the wall over here and looks like the bullet ended up way up there", he said pointing to the bullet hole about two feet below the ceiling in the kitchen wall. He picked up the note that had fallen to the floor and handed it to his partner. "Looks like suicide, only my opinion, but it looks like that anyhow. Go find the guy that phoned it in."

The officer went in the living room and saw Ray sitting on the sofa.

"Excuse me sir," he said.

Ray slowly lifted his head and looked at the cop.

"Ray? Holy shit Ray I didn't know this was your place, I didn't know you called us."

The officer knew Ray well from a lot of security jobs he worked after hours that Ray worked on with him. The officer liked Ray, thought he was a little slow, but a good guy.

"We can see that this was probably a suicide Ray. Did you find her like this? This is your wife isn't it?"

"Yes, she's my wife. Suicide? Why do you think she'd commit suicide?" Ray asked wanting to know why they thought it was a suicide.

"We never know why in these things Ray, nobody does,"

answering an entirely different question.

"Suicide," Ray repeated it as if saying it would make it so. "We can't let my daughter see this or think that about her mother."

"Stay here Ray, I have to check something with my partner. We'll take your wife's body somewhere else as soon as we can. There will be more people here soon. Where's your daughter now?"

The officer didn't wait for an answer as he left room.

These two uniformed cops were not long-term police, but not short either. The cop who knew Ray, Joe Stevens was a five-year vet. His partner, Eddie Jones had been on the force over 3 years, two with Joe. Joe laid out his issues for Eddie. He explained how he knew Ray and tried to give Eddie an idea of just how simple Ray was. He said that Ray was always the first guy in a melee protecting cops and security guards whenever fights broke out at sporting events or concerts. He was right, but it wasn't because of Ray's desire to protect, Ray just enjoyed a melee and pushing people around.

Joe went on to say that Ray's childlike mentality probably drove his wife to suicide. Eddie pushed Joe to make his point.

"It's like this Eddie, if the coroner calls this suicide then their little girl will have to live with that for her entire life, always wondering why, maybe always blaming herself. Seventy-five or eighty plus years of pain and wondering. All for what? Nothing, absolutely nothing. What are the chances the girl grows up normal or that grown man-child in the other room for that matter? Their girl goes bad because of this and that man will be the next guy on this floor we're scraping off of it."

"Spit it out."

"Simple. We lose the suicide note and put Ray's gun cleaning stuff on the table, and this becomes a tragic accident. The girl grows up missing and loving her mother and Ray raises her best he can. Hell, in two or three more years the baby will be raising the father."

"A cover-up? You want to cover-up a suicide."

"Christ sake, we'll be saving a child, and nobody gets hurt. There's no crime here, let's not create one."

"You're creating the crime, it's called a cover-up". Eddie took a deep breath and shook his head. "But maybe you're right. I've seen innocent lives ruined too often. See what this guy uses to clean his gun. Hurry before the detectives or coroner's office gets here."

Joe went back to talk to Ray and asked him if he cleaned his own gun and if he had the cleaner laying around somewhere. Ray went into the bedroom closet and returned with a box of chemicals. Ray said that he mixed his own bore cleaner and had a container of the mix in the box. He also had a spray lubricant and he said that he learned this cleaning method in school a few years ago.

Joe told Ray he was going to put the box on the table and let the detectives know that Ray's wife was cleaning the gun for him so Ray could pick up their daughter from the in-laws.

"If the detectives ask you Ray, simply say that your wife offered to clean your gun for you, that you normally clean it every Friday, if you would go pick-up your daughter. Tell them you were standing just outside the front door wondering if it was too late to go get your daughter when you heard the gun go off. You came back in the house, saw this, and from there your story stays the same."

"I don't understand," Ray told his buddy. "What good does that do? It makes my wife look like an idiot. She's cleaned my gun before. She knows what she's doing. I don't like this."

"It protects your daughter Ray. You can still live a normal life from this point on. No guilt, no pain for either of you. Got it?"

"Why would Karen feel guilty? She's not even here."

"That's what kids do Ray. They blame themselves for parent's suicides, they end up just like this a lot of times."

"Karen might kill herself if she thought her mother killed herself? We can't have that Joe. Don't let that happen. I can tell your story. I have it. Put the box on the table. I'll wait here and talk to the detectives."

The detectives never talked to Ray. It was late and they were lazy. Not a good combination in a police investigation. They listened to Joe and Eddie, saw the box of cleaning materials, took a few pictures of the body and the blood splatter, noted where the bullet went into the wall and we're ready to move on. They pulled the bullet from the wall, drop it in an evidence bag, did the same with the gun and moved everything out, sent it to the coroner's office. Bags of evidence and a large black bag containing the body of the late Diane Lupus.

"Tell that guy to clean this place up before he brings his daughter back in here," the detective coldly told Joe. "He'll get his stuff back from the coroner in a few days and they'll call him when they're ready to send the body to an undertaker. Tell him to figure out where he wants the body sent. It's getting late, time to start my weekend."

A stranger's life meant little more than this. A cover-up that only served to cover-up the cover-up. How could Ray comprehend that? He decided to wait until morning to clean up and then he would tell Karen and Diane's folks about the terrible accident. Ray laid on the couch watching the 3:00 am showing of the Marx Brothers in 'A Day at the Circus'. Ray laughed himself to sleep.

CHAPTER 10

R ay closed the barn door behind him and with head hung low walked to the house. The bad memories filled his head. He felt more now than he did then. He entered the house through the kitchen and sat for a minute at the table staring at Karen. She put a plate of noodles covered in a store-bought sauce in front of Ray and sat across from him.

"Hope that's alright, I tried to keep it warm, but you were out in the barn a long time. Everything okay?"

Ray nodded. Everything was alright for now, but Ray couldn't figure how Karen ever forgave him. Maybe she never found out. Ray wondered if he was ever that secretive.

He picked at the pasta, moving noodles back and forth across the plate. He sought answers in his head, but he was tired, and no more memories were coming tonight. He pushed himself away from the table and placed his hand on Karen's shoulder, pausing to let the feel of his daughter sink in. With a still heavy head and eyes toward the floor, Ray walked to his room. He laid in bed staring towards a dark ceiling he couldn't see. There was no laughter tonight, only fear of what tomorrow's memories may bring.

Ray woke up and walked into the kitchen. Karen was sitting in front of her coffee and jumped up to get her father a cup. The smell of fresh brewed coffee filled the house. Karen put the large white cup with the giant 'R' on it on the table.

"Aren't you glad I turned you on to coffee? I remember when you didn't touch the stuff."

Ray smiled and nodded, warmed his hands on the cup and took

a sip. Yes, he remembered when he didn't drink coffee. His wife had taken him off caffeine because she feared it wired him too much. Ray could go from zero to a hundred when someone raised his blood pressure and back in the day, his wife thought coffee and booze was a spark that Ray didn't need. Diane gradually took a lot away from Ray.

The blood had dried when Ray got up the morning after his wife's death. Ray hardly noticed. He was still amused by the amount of coffee that Groucho drank in the movie last night. Ray walked around the apartment that morning quoting Groucho endlessly, "I'll have another cup of coffee". Ray decided to have a coffee that morning.

He felt free, nobody would ever try to take anything away from him again, not coffee, not his daughter, nothing. He made his coffee that morning in an old electric percolator that he'd taken from his mother's house. He sat staring at the coffee but wasn't quite ready to drink it yet. It would be some time before he tried it again, months before his daughter talked him into the merits of the roasted beans.

He poured it out and got to work on cleaning the apartment. The floor cleaned up nicely, the walls didn't. Ray figured he would have to paint when he found the time. He poured himself a shot of whiskey, drank it and went to get his daughter.

"Yep, nobody can ever tell me again what I can have."

Ray banged on the door at the in-laws and a jubilant Karen opened the door with her grandmother. Ray said that he needed a minute of the grandmother's time, buckled Karen in her car seat, and returned with the news of Diane's death. Diane's mother gasped and called for her husband. She grew weaker by the second and eventually fell to her knees on the living room floor. While she sobbed uncontrollably, her husband took over the questions, the how, the why, the non-stop this can't be.

Ray told the story of the gun cleaning and this brought more wonderment and whys. The doubts were thrown into Ray's face and his angered boiled. Before Ray flattened his father-in-law, and that's surely where this argument was going because the lie around Diane's death had already become truth in Ray's head, he departed telling them he had a daughter that needed him now.

Ray left Diane's parents in ruin and returned to his daughter waiting in the car. Karen mentioned her mother on the ride home and Ray waited until they were inside to explain her absence.

Ray decided to use religion to explain Diane's death to his daughter. Karen was too young to make heads or tails out of her father's words. She did understand however what it meant to never see her mother again and as young as Karen was, she cried uncontrollably at this thought.

Ray said the angels needed someone special and that Karen's mom was the most special person in the world. It was an honor to be called, Ray explained. There is no telling where Ray came up with this explanation, but it was all he had. People have used worse words in their explanations of death and God takes quite a beating and blame for loss. Ray wasn't about to take any blame, so once again, God filled in for man.

Karen went to her room to cry, Ray made lunch, a sandwich and a glass of milk for Karen, shot of whiskey and a Snickers for himself. He tried in vain one last time to get the blood off the wall. He gave up and threw the moist rag into the sink.

What was left of the Lupus family ate lunch in silence and then went out for a walk. Karen's tiny hand was lost in the mitt Ray called a hand. They walked past a funeral parlor a few blocks from home and Ray thought to himself that this would be adequate for Diane's funeral. A dagger still hung over Ray's head. All evidence was at the coroner and until he ruled on cause of death that dagger hung precariously.

Karen let out a soft "Ouch". Ray had squeezed her hand a bit too tightly.

"I'm sorry dear. Maybe we best go home and wait."

"Wait for what Daddy?"

"I really don't know, but if we wait patiently, we'll find out."

Investigations don't run deep on the poor side of town, not when a cop wants to protect someone, not when a detective wants to start a booze filled weekend, and not when a coroner wants to start a summer vacation in Hawaii. Diane Lupus's case closed on Monday. Cause of death, 'Accidental death by accidental discharge of firearm'. Done.

Ray Lupus was called and told that he could come to the morgue and pick up his belongings. They also had copies of the death certificate and wanted to know what funeral home would be picking up the body. Ray mentioned that he saw a place near his home that would work, but he needed to talk with them first. The stranger on the line gave Ray a phone number to give to the funeral director. Ray said that it could be a while before he could get to the morgue because he had nowhere for his daughter. Ray was told that they could give the funeral director everything when they get the body and Ray could get his items from them if that would help. Ray agreed this was best and got Karen ready for another walk.

Ray and Karen walked to the James Brothers funeral home. It was the closest. A young lady named Erica greeted them at the door and asked how she could help them. Erica had never had a youngster come in for a funeral discussion before and was a little shocked when Ray said, "We need a place where we can say goodbye to Karen's mother."

Ray said it as a matter of fact, Karen let it breeze over her head, Erica turned pale and froze, but did manage to get out an, "I'm sorry. Yes, I can help you."

Ray looked around, clean dark wood trim everywhere, thick carpeting that absorbed all noise and soft music playing through hidden speakers. This place would do. Ray asked what they did now, the body is with the police and they need to be called.

Erica remained shocked and confused at Ray's frankness, but Ray didn't know any other way to talk. Erica asked Ray if it would be alright for one of her assistants to take Karen down the street for ice cream while she and Ray talked. Ray agreed and moved into a business office with Erica while Karen was taken out for treat and a break from the funeral plans.

Erica explained some options and costs to Ray and said she would get the body, as Diane was now being referred to, to the funeral home. All costs sounded beyond reach. Ray admitted he didn't know how much money he had. He guessed he could find a bank book somewhere in the house and be able to answer money questions by the end of the day.

Erica asked Ray about a cemetery plot, a headstone, coffin, and a vault. Ray always asked the same question, "Do I need that?" Erica, sensing Ray's reluctance to spend any money on this funeral reversed course and decided to start with the cheapest thing they could do and try to figure Ray out from there.

"Ray, we can cremate your late wife and place her remains in an inexpensive urn that you can pick-up in a couple of days. You keep that with you if you'd like or some people scatter the remains someplace special that the couple shared. No coffin, no plot, no services needed. How does that sound?"

"When could Karen say goodbye to her mother? The body lays in here for a couple of days first doesn't it? Karen would say goodbye then, and then we cremate her?"

"We can do that, but if your wife is visible for a wake you will need a coffin, I can show you our least expensive, and you will need to have a service here, one day only Ray, and then we cremate after that. I'm sure we can keep that under 4 or 5 thousand dollars for you if you'd like to check your finances. That's less than a third of the average funeral cost. We can get near one thousand if we simply cremate tomorrow."

"No, Karen needs the goodbye. Body, service, goodbyes, and cremate. I'll find my bank account today and call you."

Ray gave Erica the card he had from the police morgue and waited at the front door for Karen. She skipped down the street not understanding anything about this thing called death yet and ran into Ray's waiting arms. They walked home without a word exchanged between them.

The phone was ringing when they walked through the front door and continued to ring throughout the day. Word was out on the death of Diane Lupus and everybody had something to say. Some words nice, some words mean, some words left hanging in the air. Ray had no answers for anyone right now and wrote down everyone's name and number who called promising to get to them when funeral arrangements were finalized.

Once the phone calls lightened Ray and Karen played with Karen's farm set, making all sorts of animal noises. They shared a large can of SpaghettiOs, watched a couple TV shows and Karen went to bed. Ray remembered that he still had to see if he had any money for a funeral and finally got around to searching the house for a bank book.

Ray began his search in the kitchen drawers not believing he would find anything there. Like every other junk drawer in America, Ray found plenty of string, a tape measure, pens with business names on them, one of which had leaked in the back of the drawer, a lot of loose candy and cough drops, scotch tape and a screwdriver. No bank book. Ray held more hope in a search of Diane's dresser drawers and didn't understand his reluctance to go through her things. A shot of whiskey helped, and Ray sat on the edge of the bed and opened the top right-side drawer of Diane's dresser.

The top items, hankies, bras and underwear Ray had seen before. He pulled all these out with one grab of his huge hand and threw the items on the floor. The layer contained items that Ray hadn't seen before, all underwear, all sexy panties folded up rather small and pushed to back of the drawer. They definitely weren't gathering dust, there was plenty of age visible on Diane's private supply of panties.

Ray wasn't moved by his discovery, and he merely tossed the collection of sleepwear onto the pile of under garments that were used for his eyes. Left in the drawer was some jewelry, all cheap jewelry, lipstick, a few coins, and a dark blue bank book with Ray's and Diane's name printed inside. Ray held the book hoping that when he turned the page, he would find enough money to burn his late wife. Page after page was filled with tiny numbers and Ray kept turning looking for the last entry, and finally there it was.

Diane stashed away over 20,000 dollars. It was late, but Ray reached Erica at the funeral home and gave the go-ahead for a cheap funeral.

"We'll get your wife's body here tomorrow and take care of everything, Ray," Erica told him, "just bring by the clothes you'd like her to wear some time tomorrow and we can hold her wake on Thursday. I'll put an obituary in the paper for you. You can come any time after 7:00 on Thursday morning and we'll give you whatever time you'd like alone before we open to public. I'll put 9:00 am visitation in the paper."

Ray went through Diane's clothes and chose a black skirt and white blouse that was hanging nearest to him. He found a pair of nice work shoes that he was happy to see gone and picked through the pile of underwear. He chose a white pair that he was sure he'd seen many times and put all the clothes in a brown bag for tomorrow's delivery.

Karen nudged her father for about the hundredth time as he still sat staring into a long emptied cup. "You seemed far away Dad, everything alright?"

Ray had a good idea now about Karen's vague understanding about her mother's death. Ray was king of quiet back then and he was certain that he left Karen as much in the dark as he was able to. She seemed fully accepting of him now, so Ray saw no reason to start talking. Ray nodded once again at his daughter to say everything is okay. Karen smiled and the two went out for a walk over the miles of grassland that surrounded the house.

About noon they reached a small pond where they sat for a bit.

"Little Lake Michigan. I remember when we moved here I screamed 'Lake Michigan!' You said, 'Well, Little Lake Michigan anyway'. Time has flown."

They sat for a while in the lawn chairs, Ray listened while Karen talked about childhood games and trying to throw rocks over the pond. Karen left to do some chores and get some shopping done in one of the small towns some miles from their place. She trusted Ray to take care of himself while she was gone and told Ray that there was plenty to eat back at the house. As soon as Karen left, Ray returned to the unwrapping of his demons.

CHAPTER 11

Funeral week for Diane was a long process. Ray couldn't find any room in his heart for kindness toward a woman who planned to steal his daughter and put her into the home of another man. Ray wondered if this con man would be at the funeral, if he would have a chance to confront him in private, maybe in the back alley after everyone left.

Ray was hopeful as he grabbed the brown bag to deliver to Erica at the funeral home and had Karen get dressed for the walk over. Ray took the bank book and he and Karen stopped there first to get a check for the four thousand dollars that the funeral home required.

The teller wanted to put a name on the check in case it got lost but Ray knew no name.

"I'll put payable to 'cash' on it, sir, just sign the back. Looks like someone's going on a nice vacation."

"Vacation," Ray said to himself. Of course, she was going on vacation with this guy and using my money. Then she was going to use the rest to go live with him. Ray got very agitated in the bank and told the teller to give him the check already. "Enough talk!" Ray screamed. All eyes turned to Ray and silence fell within the bank. Ray took his check from a quivering hand and angrily left the building.

Before going to the funeral home Ray returned home and threw the underwear he had chosen for Diane in the garbage and replaced them in the bag with the flimsiest, dirtiest pair of lace panties he could find in Diane's treasure cove. He wanted to go to the funeral home and carve the word 'pig' on Diane's chest and pull her black heart through the dotted 'i' on her chest. The panties would have to do for now.

Karen and Ray dropped off the bag. "This is the real Diane, she will be herself in these clothes," Ray told Erica, "and she liked lots of dark red lipstick."

"We will be kind to your memories Mr. Lupus. I'm sure you and your daughter have been thoughtful in what you wish Mrs. Lupus to be at rest in."

"Very thoughtful," replied a grinning Ray.

"Time for lunch Karen," Ray said as they left the funeral home for a couple of days.

CHAPTER 12

"I said time for lunch Dad. It didn't look like you heard me. I swear you seem to go someplace that's a million miles from here. I wish you were able to open up about what's going through your head." Karen pushed Ray's hair back away from his eyes and rubbed his cheek. "Everything will be okay, all of your memories will come back, you'll get your strength back and when you start talking again, nobody will be able to shut you up."

Ray tried to say, "Lunch Karen" in a whisper, and perhaps he did. He grabbed a sandwich and put it on a plate for his daughter. He motioned at it, telling her to eat first. He was re-learning, Karen was moving back to her place as jewel of the family.

They enjoyed sandwiches and lemonade while listening to the songs of the birds and the sound of the long grass swaying in the wind. They sat smiling looking at Little Lake Michigan, Karen gaining more and more hope at each memory that seemed to come back to her father, while Ray was losing all hope with each image that replayed in his mind.

Diane's wake was replaying in Ray's mind. Karen watched Ray drift away and left him alone. Ray stared at the grasses dancing in the breeze and as he stared, the grasses seemed to part as the two large doors of the funeral home did once before, years ago for some, today all over again for Ray.

"We need to go in here again Karen, you need to say goodbye to your mother. She is going to the next world now," Ray was doing his best to reach his daughter, then under his breath he added, "which ever direction that next world lies."

Ray opened the two large doors for him and Karen to go through. It was not yet 9:00 and Erica was there to greet them. They stood in the small lobby where visitors stayed until they figured out where they were going. Erica pointed to another larger lobby that led directly into Diane's visitation room. Chopin was playing over the funeral home's speakers, soft, yet loud enough to be clearly heard and the beat of the music almost compelled you to walk to its rhythm.

Ray and Erica gingerly walked through the longer lobby, Karen holding the bottom of Ray's suit coat walked behind him. In the center of the lobby were two more large doors that opened the way into the visitation room and Diane's body lying in her coffin came into immediate view. Karen saw her mother and was filed with joy, death was not a part of Karen's life.

As soon as Karen saw her mother she sprinted to the body, "It's Mommy, Daddy, it's Mommy! She's not going to the other place she's coming back home with us. Mommy! Mommy!"

Ray walked with purpose behind her but not with any great rush. He felt she needed this time. Erica closed the doors behind Ray and waited in the lobby for a word from Ray telling her to open them for the day.

Karen reached the coffin and climbed up on the prayer kneeler to try to get closer to her mother. "I'm here Mama. Pick me up, pick me up. Daddy tell Mommy to wake up, I don't like this game." Karen was crying. Ray picked Karen up and they looked down at Diane.

"Tell Mommy to wake up Daddy, just one time, I'll be good Mommy, I'll be good Daddy, I promise. Can't we all just go home, I don't like it here Mommy," Karen had a hard time breathing, she couldn't see through her tears, louder and louder the child screamed. "We have to go home now, please, please."

"Mr. Lupus why don't you and Karen come into my office? I think you both could use a break. I'll have someone get you a cup of coffee."

"No coffee," replied Ray. "Karen will be okay, I'm going to get her a dog. Call me Ray please, that Mr. Lupus thing makes me think of my father. I don't like thinking about him."

"Whatever you say Ray. The dog may be a good idea, there are people that know those things better than me. I can help you find someone to talk to if you'd like."

"We don't need any help. Karen just wants to say goodbye to her mother and then we'll move on. Her friends can come visit, we'll have a dog or two, put school off for a few years. I think I have enough money to stay home for a year or two. Maybe one anyhow, I don't know. I won't let anybody hurt us. We'll be just fine."

"It's a confusing time. I hope you can find the time to make the right decisions for your family. I always suggest people slow down. Does Karen have grandparents or aunts and uncles that can help you?"

"We'll be fine."

Erica was rearranging all the papers on her desk, looking for something else to say or talk about with Ray. She found a Kit-Kat bar and asked Ray if it was too early for Karen to have some candy. Erica was thankful for the change of subject but worried about what Ray's response might be.

"Candy will be fine. Karen and I can have whatever we want whenever we want it."

Ray noticed the questionable look on Erica's face and his rising temperature was only quelled by a knock on her office door. It was Father Ken who stopped by to get some information about the lady that he was giving a service for later that evening, Diane Lupus. A relieved Erica introduced Father Ken to Ray Lupus and suggested she step outside with Karen while the two of them used her office.

Ray's eyes followed Erica out of the office hardly noticing that his daughter was leaving also. He felt that everyone was telling him what he had to do with Karen now and every innocent question was now an incredible pain in his heart. He was on the edge when Father Ken took his hand and led him to a small table and chair where they could talk.

"I know how these things work", Ray told Father Ken. "You talk about how great people who died are whether it's true or not. I'm not saying she wasn't good, but they'll be no talk like that here. I want you to just read something from your books. Understood? The cold distant stare left no doubt in Father Ken's mind. The minister would be back at 8:00 to give a generic service with readings from Psalms and Corinthians. Ray finally let a small smile lighten his face as he left the office.

Ray sat contemplating in the inner lobby looking at Diane's body, 50 or so feet away. *She had plans*, Ray thought, *maybe those plans, and evil planners will show themselves today. I can wait. Tonight, someone may just reveal a bit too much.* "Perhaps this is the day of reckoning I've heard so much about," Ray said out loud.

Ray's anxiety made it impossible for him to sit and wait for Karen's return. His head hung low and running his hand through his hair he decided to wait outside. Slowly rising he shot a mean look at Diane's body. "More troubles coming Diane, it's coming tonight."

Ray stood at the funeral parlor door biting hard on his lower lip in an attempt to calm his nerves. Seeing Karen returning with Erica, Ray began to ease his tightening muscles. Before calm prevailed, however, Diane's parents arrived bringing hate and anger with them. Ray never believed that they cared for him, but he took all their coldness for the sake of his wife and daughter. He was not in a mood for taking anything now and drew a deep breath for strength.

Diane's father, Tom Herman, nodded a hello towards Ray, his wife Ellie offered no such greeting and attacked Ray immediately. "Why in the world have you brought Karen here Ray? Do you believe for one second that this is any place for such a young and beautiful child? You're absolutely out of your mind."

Ray looked at her bloodshot eyes and swollen face and knew she was suffering, but instead of feeling compassion he was glad that she suffered as he had. He looked at Tom and shook his head in a way meant to minimize Ellie's very presence. "And who is this girl with my granddaughter? What are you up to?"

"Whoa, just a second" Erica interrupted, "I'm merely the funeral home representative. This is getting way ugly folks. Ray would it be alright if I took Karen inside so you adults can settle this on you own?"

"Of course, and thank you, but nothing's going to be settled here. I'm not gonna take much more from her. Tom you better do something." As Karen walked away with Erica and Tom scratched his head, Ellie continued. "What do you think you're going to do now Ray? You think that you can take care of Karen? You think I'll let you take care of Karen?" Her voice had grown loud and

Ray's fists clenched. "Over my dead body Ray!"

Ray took a quick step at Ellie with his fist in the air but the words 'dead body' had thrown just enough cold water on the situation to stop Ray short. He muttered some words or sounds and abruptly sought shelter back on the bench inside of the funeral parlor. Ray sat not so much as a man but as a stick of dynamite, a stick ready to explode. Ray looked at Diane's body and believed her head had turned toward him from where it was just a few moments ago. Diane laid as a fuse stalking the dynamite. The flame entered, the Hermans stomped their way passed Ray and from the rear of the visitation room saw their daughter's lifeless body for the first time.

Ellie Herman let out a heart stopping scream, "Oh my God, no, no," she wailed forgetting about Ray for a minute. She nearly collapsed as her husband Tom broke her fall. Ray sat idly by cold as ice.

Collecting themselves, the Hermans staggered to the coffin where Ellie once more collapsed falling over her daughter. The parents were left alone with their only child. Dead. Ray observed Ellie's devastation and anger and knew it could never equal his. He was waiting as he said he would for someone he didn't yet know to invade his wife's funeral.

Ellie and Tom cried themselves out at Diane's coffin and marched back to Ray in the lobby. Ray stood immediately, he learned long ago that he garnered much more respect when standing tall over people than when he remained seated. But there was no respect coming from Ellie. "Things like this just don't happen. I'm not about to let this go and you can bank on that. But for right now please just tell me why on God's green earth did you bring Karen here? Could you possibly believe that this is a place for a 5-year-old girl? Do you think looking at her mother's body in a coffin is a memory she needs? What the hell is wrong with you?"

"She needed to say goodbye."

"That's a bunch of bull."

"And just why are you here Ellie, or you too Tom."

"We're here to say goodbye to our daughter."

"Maybe that's the bull. I think you're here to make trouble. You better think long and hard about what you're doing. I'll cut you some slack for this morning, but don't push my kindness too far. It has a limit."

Another funeral representative came to the lobby and tried to quiet the family down. He spoke very quietly and his quietness only raised the volume on Ray's words. The bitter exchange continued until Ray's old friend and boss from the racetrack, Stuart, entered the funeral parlor and things began to quiet down. Noticing the tension Stuart took Ray by the arm and asked him to walk with him to see Diane. They walked together and stood before Diane.

"What's going on with them Ray? They pushing you?"

"Those are Diane's parents, and yeah they're pushing me a lot Stu. I don't think I can take much more from them, I don't think I will. I think they are blaming me for hurting Diane, but the police said it was an accident that she caused herself. They shouldn't talk to me that way. And they say I shouldn't have brought Karen here and that's none of their business either. I'm gonna blow, I'm gonna blow and explode like nobody else ever has."

"Okay, give it a minute. People say things without thinking when there's an accident. Let me talk to them. You're going to need their help a lot now, Karen needs some stability in her life. They can give you that. They can help Karen with school stuff too when you're at work. Think about all that now, chill for a bit, they'll come around."

"I don't need them. I may just quit work for a while and keep Karen home with me. No school yet."

"This isn't Alaska, we just don't keep kids home from school because we don't like our in-laws."

"They do that in Alaska?"

"They do whatever they want in Alaska but be serious for a minute. I'll straighten out your in-laws. Tell me exactly what happened."

"I got a bigger problem I want to tell you about. Let's sit down. Ellie can come up and wail again if she wants."

Stu and Ray sat off to the side away from the coffin and Ray tried to organize his words. Stu was growing inpatient and he wanted to know what happened. He nudged Ray once more.

"I want to hear your problem but just tell me what happened to Diane first. Don't let people, like Diane's folks, make up their own stories to put out there. You tell me and I'll tell them. You'll be done reliving it then, everyone will understand that."

"I hope this is the last time. I can't keep retelling it. The police and a whole lot of their people looked into it. I talked to them for hour after hour. Some things I know, some things they could see, and they told me what happened."

"Tell me from where you knew anything."

"I got home from work last Friday night and Diane was still up, which is rare, sitting in front of a bottle of wine, I think it was empty. We didn't talk. I went to see Karen, but she wasn't home, and I came back in the kitchen and asked Diane where she was. All she said was, 'At my folks.' I figured she was spending the night there and that Diane was in no mood to talk to me."

Ray went on and told Stu the story that he rehearsed so many times, everything from the gunshot to the police saying it looked like a bad accident.

I think it was a couple days later the coroner's office called and said that it was definitely an accident. That should be more than enough for anybody, especially Diane's parents. Enough is enough unless they are trying to take Karen from me. I'll tell you Stu if they try that it won't end well for them."

"Nobody is trying to take Karen from you. They just never heard what happened and are looking for someone to blame. They just lost their daughter, think how you would feel. You'd probably want to kill someone wouldn't you?"

"I don't think I'd feel that way, but I sure wouldn't push me to find out."

"Exactly. I'll tell them what happened and when they find out that you weren't even in the house when it happened, they'll let it go. They'll want to help you Ray, trust me. Now tell me your bigger problem."

"I think Diane was going to leave me and was seeing another guy. I was going through her things after she died, trying to find our bank book so I could pay for this. I found our bank book and it had over 20,000 dollars in it. She was going somewhere with someone with my money. She's been planning a long time."

"Don't be like that. I've known you a good ten years and Diane longer than that. I was with you while you were falling in love. She wouldn't run around on you, not in a million years. Look you guys don't spend money on anything. You live in a cheap apartment, you drive an old car, you never take vacation and you both make damn good money. Of course, you have a lot of money in the bank. It's for yours and Karen's future, not some strange guy."

"There's more. In her drawer I also found some dirty sexy underwear that she never wore around me. Some guy was getting her love it wasn't me."

"There had to be a reason for that. She probably wore those things for you and you never noticed. It doesn't matter anymore. Let her go in peace. Know that she loved only you, let Karen always know that."

"I know her boyfriend is coming here tonight. I don't know who he is, but I'll know him when I see him. There just might be two people sharing one coffin by the end of the day. I won't even have to pay extra that way."

"You're crazy Ray."

"I'll sit here all day and wait. He'll be here."

"Yeah, just sit here. I'm going to talk to Diane's folks. It's time to mend fences, not kick them down. Please don't move or do anything while I'm gone. Just wait here."

And Ray sat waiting - waiting for an encounter he was sure was coming. His mind drifted as he pictured himself shoving another person in the coffin with his cheating wife. Above his anger, he laughed at the scene playing in his head of lovers united in death's black box.

Time passed slowly and as the day wore on people arrived sporadically at the funeral home. Ray's friend from the police force, Joe, showed up early with a few other officers that knew Ray from his security job. Joe walked past Stu and the Hermans as they were having the beginning of a somewhat civil talk in the lobby. Joe went and sat with Ray.

"How you doing?" Joe asked his friend.

"Not so good. Diane's mom is making problems. She's going to make a big one for herself is she doesn't leave me alone."

"What's she doing to you?"

"She said that this was no accident. She said she wasn't going to let this go."

Joe went pale.

"Me and Eddie need to talk to her Ray. We'll tell her how we found everything and how the detectives investigated the entire house. Which one is she?"

Ray stood up and looked around the place.

"She's back there with my friend Stu. He's trying to get through to the bitch too."

"Calm down, that kind of talk won't help."

"You said it was an accident. I got papers that say it was an accident. She needs to go away. I can't handle this."

"Just sit here, we'll talk to her."

"Everybody wants me to sit here. I can't sit here now, I have to check on Karen, the girl with the funeral home is watching her."

"Okay, go do that. I'll find Eddie and we'll talk to the mom."

Ray stomped down the corridor looking for Karen. Too many people were telling Ray what to do, what to think, where to sit. He wasn't going to take much more. Joe better back him on this, Stu better lighten up and let him confront the man that invaded his life, and that son of a bitch better be ready for hell itself to fall on him, a hell that may soon include one Ellie Herman if that mouth won't shut up and disappear.

By now Ray was a volcano, a twister looking for his daughter. Nobody better be putting bad thoughts in her head. Thoughts that Ray was imaging with every step he took. Sent from room to room, office to office Ray finally neared the room where Erica was hugging Karen. Ray's face turned its familiar red again. Ray's heart pounding. Ray's fists uncontrollably clinched. Temperatures rising.

CHAPTER 13

R ay found Karen and Erica in a back office away from the tension of the visitation.

"She's had a long day," Erica said. "She colored some nice pictures for you. Karen is very talented."

"Yes, she is," Ray replied. "Maybe it's time that me and Karen go home. I was waiting for someone, but I guess that can wait."

"Maybe her grandparents can take her home."

"Never," Ray answered while starting to stiffen and turn red again.

Erica was a bit frightened but spoke anyway. "Karen just may need them now, at least consider it."

Ray left Karen with Erica again and returned to the wake. He noticed a friend of Diane's sitting with a couple of ladies he didn't know. The one girl he knew was from Diane's work, he thought she was working at the track even back while he worked there. He sat with them and they exchanged condolences.

The girl Ray knew was Pat Tamulus and she introduced the two other girls, one was another girl from work, the other a friend of theirs and Diane's from the bar. The names escaped Ray immediately. The bar intrigued Ray. If friends from the bar are coming, then surely his foe will be here tonight. Ray knew where his attention would be focused now. He thanked the girls for coming and moved to the sofa in the front row facing Diane.

"I got you now," Ray mumbled under his breath.

Ray was trying to keep his ears tuned to the conversation of the three girls now sitting behind him when Ellie came and sat beside him. She spoke in a calm tone now.

"Look Ray I'm sorry for what I said. The police set me straight. I'm a total mess right now and I don't know what I'm going to do without my girl. Forgive me. I'll be better. Let me help you with Karen. Please don't take her away from me"

Ray was only half listening now as his ears were laboring to hear what Pat and her friends were saying. He looked deeply at Ellie and shrugged his shoulders. "We'll see what we can do."

"I can't stay here anymore Ray. Please let me take Karen home for the night she's been through too much all ready. I can take her home now. You come over in the morning, we'll all have breakfast together. I'll make pancakes, she loves pancakes." Ellie drifted and then said from a long way away, "Diane loved pancakes."

Ray agreed to let Karen leave with Ellie and Tom. He was on another mission now and thought it would be easier to learn who's who by waiting around the funeral parlor, alone. He sought his prey, but he didn't see it yet. He knew he would.

He walked Ellie back to Erica's office and explained things to Karen. She was more than happy to be leaving and held Ellie's hand tightly. Ray watched them walk away not quite being in touch with his feelings about Ellie staying in his and Karen's lives, but that was a problem for another day.

He returned to Diane's room which was growing more crowded. Diane's 3 girlfriends had been joined by another friend, a rather disheveled guy about Ray's age. Ray's stomach turned and his muscles tightened. He returned to his place on the sofa and tried again to listen in.

Ray heard the girls call him Jake or Jase or something like that. Ray thought that an odd name and suspected this Jake might be his ex's lover. There was no such talk of anything like that now and Ray bided his time. As the evening wore on Diane's former boss from the racetrack, Ben Tanana, arrived to pay his respects. After a long prayer spoken to Diane's body, Ben joined Ray on the sofa.

"I need to talk to you in private. Can we go somewhere? Is there a coffee lounge or office we can use?"

Ray and Ben went downstairs where Ben nervously poured himself a cup of coffee.

"You don't drink coffee do you?"

"I do now, yes, but none right now. What's on your mind?"

"I'll get right to the point. If you remember from when you worked for me I give all my staff health and life insurance. I add a little to the life policy every year for my workers, you know I have to keep my good people with me. Anyway, the policy I had for your wife is worth over $500,000 now."

Ray widened his eyes as his mouth fell open, he stared speechless at Ben.

"And depending what it says on the death certificate it pays double for an accident, anything that is not health related. Do you have the death certificate yet Ray?"

"They have it for me, I didn't get it yet. It says accident, I know that."

"Then you got a million dollars coming to you Ray, on that policy anyhow."

"What do mean that policy?"

"Well about 6 months ago Diane told me that you folks were putting plenty of money away, but she was worried that it wouldn't be enough to take care of Karen if something happened to one or both of you. She had me put her in touch with our insurance agent and she took out another million-dollar policy on both of you."

Ray jumped up and got in Ben's face. Ray towered over Ben and his chin was almost resting on the top of Ben's head. "What do you mean she took a policy out on me? And why did *you* handle it and not me? Were you seeing my wife? I know she was up to something. Was she going to kill me?"

"God dammit Ray, sit down. You and Diane are family to me. Kill you? What kind of crazy talk is that?"

"Something was going on Ben," Ray said as he sat back down and hung his head. "Something in addition to what happened to Diane with the gun."

"Get a grip. You got over 2 million dollars coming your way. I called the insurance company for you, things are moving already. Get me a copy of the death certificate tomorrow. Interest rates on long term investments are nearing 20 percent. You lock up that rate with a million and a half and you'll be making over a quarter a million a year and that still leaves you a half million to use as you go. You'll never have to work again. You just take care of Karen."

"Diane had some more money in the bank too. I'll have some of that left after I pay for this. Can I go to Alaska? I hear I can teach

Karen at home there, no school."

"You can Ray, sure you can, but slow down on that. Your friends and family are here. And besides, school will be good for Karen."

"I've got nothing here. Stu told me that I can do anything in Alaska. People won't think that I'm an idiot there. "

"Come to my office in a few days and we'll talk more. I'll let you know how the insurance money is coming. They just need the death certificate now. The money won't make up for losing Diane, but it will help you with Karen. In time you'll move forward."

"I'll move forward."

They moved back to the visitation room. Ray had a small concept of the amount of money he would soon have but not enough of a concept to forget about everything else. He stared again at Diane's friends and the stranger here to pay respects to his dead wife. He sat patiently as the priest provided a stock service reading from his collection of books. The readings ended the long day for Ray and friends, at least the part of the day at the funeral home.

As everyone filed out Ray followed the shadowy figure that he felt was far too close to his wife. He stayed out of view, crouching behind cars and hiding in doorways, standing at the end of an alley, kneeling low with his head sticking out from behind a garage, oblivious to everything else around him. His eyes trained on his target Ray couldn't hear the soft sounds of footsteps creeping towards him.

Ray saw the man open the door of his car and he stared hard to make out the car that he would seek again later. The hair on Ray's neck stood up and a cool wind made him shiver. His gaze dropped from the car to the ground below where he caught a glimpse of a slowly moving shadow not caused by the trees. Ray started to turn slowly to see what was moving behind him.

Before he could turn completely around and see yet another intruder into his life, *CRACK*! Ray's skull was split by the downward swing of a heavy pipe, the heaviness alone prevented the swing from being swift enough to kill Ray. Ray's head lit up and the blinding light that he saw was emitting from his attacked brain. Ray fell to the concrete, blood oozing from his head, his face ripped by the stones and glass on the alley pavement.

Seconds later Ray took a kick to his ribs and then another. Ray offered a single groan and then passed out in silence, alone in a dark alley. The predator became prey, then prey became a bloodied mass of nothing.

CHAPTER 14

The memories of that day, of that night, of that attack, returned Ray to his current fog. He walked the line between sleep and stupor, dreams and reality. He spun in his lawn chair grabbing his head, searching for blood from a wound nearly 30 years old. The man with no voice was trying to say something. As Karen approached, she heard the garbled sounds.

"Wake up Dad, you're having a nightmare."

Ray woke up and looked around him. He soon recognized the small lake a short walk from his house and stood up to hug his grown daughter.

"That must have been some nightmare. It scared you enough to almost make you talk. That means you can do it, you will talk again, we both know that. Life can be good again, you'll see. I thought you were back in your room. I had no idea you were sitting here all day. Let me help you back to the house and get you a late dinner. It sure was a long day wasn't it?"

Ray nodded the slightest of yeses.

After dinner Ray finally made it to bed. He lay in the dark still feeling the spot where he was hit years ago. Time wasn't making sense to Ray and in the dark he felt as though he was back in the hospital where he woke up 30 years ago just as confused as he was now.

"We'll you're back with us Mr. Lupus," said a nurse in clean white uniform with a stethoscope hanging around her neck. "That's quite a hit you took your head."

Ray tried to sit up, but the nurse stopped him. "What

happened?" he asked her.

"Just relax sir. The police brought you here in a squad car. They found you bleeding from that head wound and you were lying in an alley. Nobody knows what happened. You have some meds in you, you'll be out of it for a while yet. Things will be clearer tomorrow. We got a lot of information from your wallet, but nobody answered the phone on the number we found. Is there someone we should call for you?"

"No."

"I'll let the doctor know you woke up for a while, but you should just try to sleep more, it is the best cure for you. The police will be here tomorrow to piece this together. They found a bit of money in your pocket and as I said we had your wallet, so you weren't robbed. Hope that's a good thing. "

Not robbed, he thought to himself. *Then someone wanted to hurt me. If I find them, they'll wish they did better.*

When Ray woke up, things were clearer. He knew that his mother-in-law would have been more than willing to take a club to his head, but she was too weak to hurt Ray and besides, she was home with Karen. That left only one person, the mystery man, Diane's boyfriend, the man nobody seemed to know. Ray didn't want the police to know that there was another man in his wife's life. That could cause them to relook at the shooting.

Things looked good now, if the money that Ben told him about was true then nothing but a good life lay ahead. He would never mention or think about this guy again. He could have killed Ray in that alley but didn't. It was over.

The police came with their questions and Ray had no answers. Released from the hospital Ray picked up Karen and returned home. Diane's death gave Ray a little time off work, with pay, the hit on the head gave him even more. The money he found in Diane's bankbook gave him the opportunity to take yet even more time off. But what Ray wanted now was to never return to work, but rather head for Alaska, the place where he could raise his daughter without interference of wives, in-laws, school officials, or anyone else for that matter.

He waited for Ben's call, spending his days playing with his daughter. Finally, Ben called, the insurance agent was ready to meet with Ray and an appointment was set at Ben's office. Ben offered to sit-in and help and Ray agreed. Tomorrow was getting closer.

The insurance agent, Ralph Salerno, arrived for the meeting with briefcase in hand wearing a crumpled suit. The suit seemed to need as much rest as Ralph did. Ben was loudly dressed in one of his 'racetrack' suits that he loved to walk around in. Ray wore an old shirt with an old pair of pants, didn't spend two seconds thinking about what he would wear. Ben's secretary brought in coffee for everyone and the meeting got underway.

"Just a couple questions Ray and we can wrap this up," Ralph said while rummaging through his briefcase.

"What kind of questions?" Ben asked. "I thought you were bringing Ray's checks with you. This man's been through enough."

"I have the checks, but let's not get ahead of ourselves. I just need to get Ray's answers to some questions and if all goes well, I'll sign the checks today. I'm not saying anything wrong happened here, it's just that we're talking a lot of money and we don't want any loose ends. Do we Ray?"

Ray shrugged, indifferent. Ben seemed to be getting angry.

Ralph continued. "I've read the coroner's report and see that somehow a gun accidently went off. Did Mrs. Lupus handle guns very often?"

"Not often," Ray said.

"I didn't think so, but she did that night for some reason, didn't she Ray?"

"She did."

"Handled it wrong, didn't she Ray?"

"I don't know I wasn't in the house."

Ralph again rummaged through his papers. "Oh, I see, you were standing outside the door, waiting for something. What were you waiting for Ray?"

"I wasn't waiting for anything."

"Just getting some fresh air. Interesting Ray."

"I didn't say that."

"He didn't say that," Ben added, very agitated now. "Where you going with this?"

"Just drawing the picture, gentlemen. I'm not saying anything wrong happened here, I'm just trying to wrap this up. So, let me see. Mrs. Lupus is inside with a loaded gun that she rarely, if ever, handled. Ray, you are outside, not waiting for anything and not getting some fresh air, just there so to speak. Correct Ray?"

"Not correct. Diane asked me to go pick up our daughter, so I was going. When I got outside it seemed late, so I was standing there thinking about not going. Maybe a little while, maybe a long time, I don't remember. I heard the gun fire and went back in. Diane was on the floor. Lots of blood. I think I picked her up a little, a lot of her head was missing. I called the police."

"Grace under pressure. Good for you Ray. I see from the pictures and sketches here that the coroner ruled it an accident. But I don't see how they ruled out other possibilities. I'm not saying anything wrong happened here, but there does seem to be room for questions. Doesn't there?"

"No".

Look Ralph we've had enough of this," Ben said.

"Calm down," Ray told him. "Ralph said he's not saying anything wrong happened."

"Oh, he's quite fond of those words, but that's exactly what he's saying. He's doubting you, accusing you even."

Ray got agitated. He jumped up and flew towards Ralph. "You got something to say old man, then you better say it. I'll tell you now that my head still has me mixed up since this happened and I watch my daughter suffer every day. I got nothing left to lose and if you want to see how a crazy man with nothing left to lose acts, then just say one bad word about me."

Ray lifted Ralph from his chair tearing his suit in the process. "Say it, damn you, say it."

Ralph was silent. Ben begged Ray to put Ralph down. Eventually Ray threw Ralph to the ground.

"Lying fucking coward," Ray said to the crumpled agent.

Ben got Ray to leave the room and spoke in his defense to the embarrassed Ralph Salerno.

"You asked for that Ralph, you had it coming. You cornered an injured, simple man. I should have you arrested."

"Me arrested? I should have that nut arrested."

"You'd look foolish and probably lose your job in the process. I know damn well that you talked to the detectives already and the coroner's office too or you wouldn't be here. This is your final stop and you're just trying to cover your ass. You've done that. Now sign the checks and get the hell out of here before I let Ray have another go at you."

Ralph thought for second and finally took two checks from his briefcase. "Something's not right here, but I got nothing hard to go on. If it wasn't for our respect for you, we could tie this up for months." Ralph signed the checks and handed them over to Ben. "If and when I get something, we may just be digging up a body. I'll be keeping my eye on that Lupus fellow."

"Cremated Ralph, the body's been cremated and long scattered."

"Interesting, isn't it? And it just keeps getting more interesting. This ain't over."

Ralph left the grounds. Ray sat down again with Ben and stared at the checks. Ben had some ideas for Ray about investing the money and returning to work. He cautioned Ray about doing anything major right away.

Ray had no intention of returning to work and asked Ben if it was possible to stay at home from now on and take care of Karen, by himself. Ben told him that with today's interest rates on CDs, that he could invest in a long term, insured CD and make almost a quarter million a year, doing nothing. That would still leave over half a million in spending money with over $20,000 a month coming in.

Ben thought it a good idea for Ray to keep working, get Karen started in school and reestablish a normal life before staying home. Ray was unmoved.

"But I could do it, I could stay home from this day on."

"Yes, you could for sure. Why don't you come back to the track, part-time? Work with the horses again, you could bring Karen here as much as you like."

"No Ben, that ain't gonna happen. Me and Karen are moving to Alaska. I will be her teacher, I will be her school. Stu told me I could do it."

"In time, but not now. When are you thinking about leaving?"

"Tomorrow I guess."

"Wait, wait, wait," Ben pleaded. "Let me help you set up your funds, get money available to you without you having to take it all with you. And that old beater you're driving won't make it to the suburbs much less Alaska. If you are dead set on leaving, then I'll help you."

"Dead set", Ray replied.

With Karen at the in-laws, Ben took Ray to the bank and set up a long term CD account and a checking account for Ray. Karen was sole beneficiary, so nobody could ever touch their money. Half of Ray's interest from the CD went into checking for his monthly living, the rest reinvested in the CD. Ray couldn't spend what he now had in three lifetimes, he and Karen were set.

Next Ben took Ray car shopping. The cars all looked great, but he fell in love with a large pick-up truck. Ray not only purchased that, but he bought a pop-up fifth wheel to pull behind the truck. He figured he and Karen could sleep in there while they searched for their Alaskan home. Ray filled the truck bed and pop-up with what little they were taking with them and a fair amount of food. The truck was ready for the open road.

Ray went alone to tell his mother goodbye. She had long ago gone simple, but Ray figured he owed her nothing more than this goodbye. He watched his mother rock herself to sleep in the chair she kept by the front room window. With her head hung low and a 3-month-old Enquirer on her lap, Ray said goodbye with all the bitterness his voice could muster. This long harsh part of Ray's life was nearly over.

He then returned to his in-laws' place to pick up Karen and give them the goodbye they had no idea was coming. The scene was somewhat reminiscent of the day of Diane's funeral. Yelling, accusations, tears, anger, they were all there.

Ellie told Ray he no right to take their granddaughter from them. Ray knew he had every right. The fighting was only growing uglier the longer it went on. Ray finally offered to send their whereabouts as soon as he and Karen found a place to settle. He said that the Hermans would be welcome to visit as much and anytime they wished. Ray didn't mean a single word of it and walked hand in hand with Karen to the truck. The Hermans never left the house for a final goodbye.

This long harsh part of their lives was not only over, but replaced by a longer, lonelier one. Ray didn't give a damn.

It was the spring of 1981 and a 30-year-old Ray Lupus was ready to give his 5-year-old daughter all the things he was never allowed to have and do all the things he was never allowed to do. Ray crawled along in traffic anxious to get out of the city. Down the Kennedy, over the I-294 tollway, and onto the Stevenson. Traffic finally lightened near I-80, the road Ray planned on taking all the way to the coast and then he would turn north to Alaska. The billboards on the highway passed rapidly and one for Great America St. Louis caught his eye. Karen would love that he thought as he flew past the I-80 exit.

"Let's go to the amusement park, Karen," Ray told his daughter. "Life is all about fun from now on. I've been thinking we should get a couple dogs once we're settled too. We won't hear another no ever again."

They spent two days in Six-Flags and Ray had the time of his life. He felt he was making Karen happy and wished he gotten certain people out of his life earlier. Guilt never haunted Ray Lupus.

Ray consulted his map and decided to take I-70 west right out of St. Louis. Missouri was bland and both Ray and Karen were happy when they crossed the Platte River and entered Kansas. They stopped a couple times for sandwiches and ate them at rest stops along the highway. As the sun began to go down, Ray noticed a billboard for a Cubo Zoo.

"A zoo out here in the middle of nowhere," he said to Karen, "this has 'us' written all over it".

"Can we go Dad?"

"No more no's Karen, at least not too many of them. Let's see if we can find this place. Probably 2 animals there," Ray joked.

"One for each of us," Karen replied, not joking.

"The sign said that they have horse riding too, kind of an interesting zoo."

After almost an hour of driving on narrow back roads, Ray pulled into a good size parking lot in front of a very large zoo. The lot was empty except for about 6 cars parked over to one side. Ray parked the truck and pop-up out of the way and he and Karen got out of the truck to stretch and have a look around. They were both somewhat amazed at the grandeur of the place. There was a beautiful arched entrance way which was closed and locked at the time. Karen put her face between the bars and peered in.

"Can we go in?"

"Looks closed."

"You said no more no's."

"Then I guess we'll have to find somewhere to stay tonight and come back tomorrow."

Before they turned to leave, a middle-aged man of slight frame, wearing an old train engineer's cap, came walking towards the front gate.

"You're just a little late, but thanks for coming. Can you come back tomorrow?" the man asked the weary travelers.

"That's our plan," replied Ray. "My daughter says the zoo is beautiful and we'd love to ride the horses. Is it a real ride or one for kids that goes in an endless circle?"

"It's real, sir. This is an animal kingdom. We would never allow horses to walk in an endless circle. The trail goes for miles from the zoo into Kansas wilderness. It is as calming a place as you'll find. It is a walk meant for the horses as much as, and probably more than, for people. They love it."

"Then we will be here to ride tomorrow. Don't be concerned about my daughter's age, she has been riding for years."

The man in the engineer's hat looked a little down. "I'm sure your daughter can ride, but we lost our stable hand months ago and we haven't been able to find a replacement. I'm afraid nobody here can figure out the gear, so we haven't done any horse riding in a long time. You will like the zoo part however. The animals are gorgeous."

"You know sir," Ray said, "I worked with horses at a racetrack in Chicago for a long time. I can saddle 'em up just fine. And if your boss has some people that he'd like to do this, I'd be happy to teach them. Have them up to speed in a few minutes' time."

"Well that certainly is a great offer. I'm sorry, I should have introduced myself. I'm Fred Grant and I sort of take care of a few things around here." With that he took out a large ring of keys and found one for the front gate. "Why don't you and your daughter come in and take a walk with me over to the horses. It will be great if our gear is familiar to you. I'd love to ride myself again, but I haven't saddled a horse since I was a kid."

"I wouldn't want to get you in trouble for letting us in after hours. We can come back tomorrow."

Karen looked at her father wishing he would just be quiet and go in.

"Nonsense," said Fred, "you two come right on in. I don't think that I'll get in any trouble. And what is your name young lady?"

"I'm Karen."

"Well hello, Karen. I'm Fred. Do you think we should see the horses today or wait until tomorrow?"

"I think today Mr. Fred," said a smiling Karen.

"Well then, let's go."

Karen took her father by one hand and Fred Grant by the other and off they went to the back stables.

Ray introduced himself, at Fred's prodding, as they walked to the stables. They made a little small talk and Ray explained their trip to Alaska to get away from all the people trying to tell him what to do, more like what not to do Ray added, and how he and Karen didn't need the aggravation anymore.

Fred admired Ray's resolve and said that he too had to get away from it all and that's how he ended up in Kansas. There was much more to Fred Grant's story, but they reached the stables and Ray immediately went through all the equipment.

"You've got all top of the line stuff here, Fred. Great saddles, silver bits, even real good blankets for the horse's comfort. This really is an animal kingdom. I can show you how to do all this. How early tomorrow you want to start? Don't forget we want to spend time in the zoo too."

"Let's ride for a few hours in the morning," Fred said, "it's been so long, I can't wait. I'll be here early."

"We need someplace to stay tonight. Which way should I head?"

"Looks like you have your house with you. Just open her up and stay here. Pull under the trees right where you're at, you'll have a cool morning."

"There's nobody else here, you sure it's okay?"

"Yes, I am. You want to stay here don't you Karen, and ride in the morning?"

"Yes, Mr. Fred."

"Well okay then," Ray said, "I'll pull the truck in and can you help me with the pop-up? We've not used it yet. We have a small sink inside, a few beds, a stove on the outside. I have a cooler of food too, you should stay for dinner, unless you have to be home to your family."

"No family. Dinner sounds good."

The three of them returned to the parking lot and made camp. The pop-up had everything they needed, and Ray set up a table and chairs that he bought for just this type of meal with Karen. The sun touched the top of the trees and the coolness of night arrived. Ray was a perfect host; he filled the table with chips, bread, cheese, veggie burgers, and soda pop. They all nibbled as the sun went down and Fred and Karen did most of the talking. Squirrels and chipmunks joined the party and Karen kept them happy with nice sized pieces of bread. It was the most normal evening these three had spent in a long, long time.

Ray was putting things away, keeping his home on wheels in order and Fred and Karen were relaxing in the Kansas evening. Fred wanted the evening to go on much longer as he wanted to share a bit of his world with the Lupus'.

"Well Karen thank you for a wonderful dinner. You too, Ray. Now if you two have a little energy left, I'd love to take you on a walk that is my favorite in the whole world. A walk through the zoo."

With this invitation Karen sprung out of her chair and whatever exhaustion she previously felt was instantly gone. "Can we really go in the zoo, Mr. Fred?"

"No, no. We can't let you do that Fred. I'm guessing you could get in big trouble for that, maybe even lose your job."

"Nonsense," said Fred. " I own the zoo, so I guess they're stuck with me. Now we need to be a little quiet as we walk, this is the animals' relax time. Let's go, Karen. You ready, Ray?"

Ray stood in amazement. *Fred's zoo? This must be the luckiest guy in the world*, thought Ray as he was finally able to move again and hurried to catch-up to the pair.

As they entered the zoo, Fred's talk became a whisper. "We'll save the entire zoo until tomorrow and I'll take you on my nighttime walk. In the wild, most of these types of animals sleep all night and are awake hunting or guarding their families very early. With most threats removed, they sleep a lot during the day and find this time as their chosen relax time. The bears on the other side of the zoo usually sleep all night, same with the lions and tigers. I seem to agitate them when I walk there at night. This route will let you see some playful animals like the monkeys, and the buffalo like to graze at night. But I really want to show you is back in the far corner of the zoo."

Ray and Karen listened intently, not saying anything as they wished to respect the animals' space. They walked past a building under construction and reached the far corner.

"With a name like Lupus, I figured you would like this area. These are my babies - an entire wolf family. I have a bench behind these bushes from where we can watch them. They know we're here, but the bush lets them study us and still feel safe."

"Is the new building going to be for them?" asked Ray, also in a whisper.

"No, no. That building is for me. I've been living about 20 miles from here since we built the place and I've grown tired of the drive. I love sitting here and I love every part of being here, so I thought I probably should be living here. I will be one with the animals, home with my wolf family."

"How did you get all this? This is just amazing."

"We can talk about that tomorrow. I'd like to hear more about you and Karen, but it's getting late. See the black wolf on top of the big rock? He's the alpha male. He's not paying us much attention, just enough to keep his pack safe. This pack was killing lots of cattle up in Montana. They probably left Yellowstone and staked out new ground up north. They were all marked for death, but I got a call from an animal rights group and they asked me about helping with costs to relocate them. The fear, however, was that if we moved them back to Yellowstone, they would simply migrate again and surely be slaughtered next time they reached Montana. So, I brought them here. It took a lot of money and effort, but we got the entire clan here. There were nine wolves then, Blackie was already head wolf. They've added four and lost one since they've been here."

Ray stood up and walked around to the corner of the bush to get a better look at the black wolf. He was almost impossible to see in the dark. But as Ray walked, Blackie got up for a better look at Ray. They stared in each other's direction, but in a calm sort of respectful way.

"I don't know what he thinks he sees Ray, but he's aware of you. Maybe you've made another friend today."

"Or enemy."

"Rival maybe, but my wolves have no enemies. We'd better get going. It's getting very late now."

They walked back to Ray's camper and made plans to get together tomorrow morning.

"I'm usually here by 10," Fred said, "but tomorrow I'll be here by 8. I'm looking forward to saddling up the horses and riding."

"Karen and I will have breakfast ready at 8. Will you join us?"

"I'll be here!"

Fred proceeded home and Karen and Ray called it a day, a long, great day. Karen had a hard time sleeping as the excitement of the ride tomorrow kept her awake. Ray had a hard time sleeping as he kept thinking about the stare he received from Blackie. Ray wanted to get beyond those zoo bars and visit Blackie; he was jealous of Fred and the home he was building beside the wolves. Ray dreamed while awake most of the night, dreamed of a life he now wished to enter.

CHAPTER 15

Confusion was the order of the day for Ray. The more he recalled of his past the more it melded with his present. Seeing a 35-year-old Karen in front of him and a 5-year-old Karen in his mind's eye threw Ray for quite a loop. He was going to sleep in the 21st century and waking up in the 20th, some days, the other way around. The unchanged lands of Kansas didn't help. There wasn't a human being on earth that could tell 2010 Kansas from 1980 Kansas, not around the Cubo Zoo anyhow.

Ray left his bedroom expecting to see his 5-year-old daughter but was instead greeted by the young woman she had become. Ray's head hurt and his eyes refused to focus. He looked around the kitchen. Frustration and anger were beginning to plant their seeds in him. He wanted clear memories and he wanted them now. He looked down at his weak arm and tried hard to bring his hand to his face. It was moving, inch by inch it moved towards his face as he concentrated every thought he could muster in that arm.

Karen watched as he mentally left the room and she watched the arm reach Ray's chest. Something was happening, something good Karen thought, but she was too scared to say a word. Her dad was in another place right now and she knew his answers were there too.

"It's almost time," Karen said. "Mr. Fred will be here soon."

Fred arrived before 8:00 and apologized for his early arrival confessing that he couldn't sleep well in anticipation of their ride. Ray and Karen offered similar confessions. Ray cooked a quick breakfast, some eggs, toast, and coffee. *Just like a Chicago greasy spoon*, Ray thought. They enjoyed the warm morning and ate quickly to get a start on the day. Fred's shiny boots were noticed by Ray as they cleaned up the campsite.

"Great boots Fred, you belong on a horse. We gotta get you riding as soon as we can saddle one up."

"Newly polished. Not too much is it?"

"It's perfect Mr. Fred," said Karen, "I wish I had my cowgirl boots."

"Did you leave them behind?" asked Fred.

"No, they were just too small. Dad is going to buy me a new pair before we get to Alaska."

"Well that's a good plan. Let's head to the stables, folks. Giddy-up! I've been waiting a long time to say that."

Fred opened the zoo gates for them to go through and locked the gates behind them. The three went over to the stables and walked amongst the horses. Fred had about 10 horses relaxing in the barn and said a hello, by name, to each of them.

"This boy is my favorite," Fred told Ray. "His name is Townes and I drove him up from Texas, wish I could have rode him up. Can we saddle him for me?"

"Sure thing, Fred. That's a long way to drive a horse. You know people in Texas?"

"A lot of people. I was born and raised in Texas. We can talk about all that later. Let's get on with my saddling lesson. Giddy-up buddy."

"Do I get one of the baby horses?" asked Karen, "you have a lot of little horses in here."

"Let me show Fred how to saddle his horse and then we'll choose one for you. Probably the white pony, don't you agree Fred?"

"That will be perfect. Now I know how to put the saddle on my horse, and I know to use a blanket under the saddle. It is the reins and bit that throw me."

Ray showed Fred how to work the reins on Townes and Fred helped to put the reins on the horse Ray would ride, Copper. Fred re-learned saddling quickly. He soloed on Karen's pony named Cotton, a name Karen loved, and off they rode. They took the zoo trail away from the zoo and were soon riding in Kansas forest. The trail went for miles and miles as the zoo was surrounded by public lands. It was a beautiful ride with Fred pointing out some side trails, identifying trees and plants along the way and every few minutes letting out a, "Giddy-up Townes," in a boyish way.

They reached a clearing by a small pond where Fred announced lunch. He provided cheese sandwiches from an old brown bag he brought along this morning. They tied their horses near the water and each found a comfortable rock to sit on and relax. Karen ate quickly and ran down to the horses. Ray couldn't contain his curiosity any longer and getting himself comfortable turned to Fred. "Come on Fred, tell me your story. How does a man become a zoo owner kind of in the middle of nowhere?"

"You know I've never really shared this story with anybody Ray and maybe it will do me some good telling you all about yours truly, one Frederick Grant, III. I was born on the plains of Texas to very well-off parents. By the time I was born, my family was one of the most successful cattle ranchers in the world owning thousands of acres in Texas. They also owned the railroad and miles of right of way along the tracks from mid-Texas through Oklahoma, Kansas and Arkansas. This was due to the vision of Fred Grant number one, my dear old grandpa, who wanted to ship cattle east without using a cattle drive. He felt that the cattle drive cost him too much money in lost cattle and wages to drovers. For the late 1800s, he was ahead of his time. He also felt, and rightly so, that landowners would gladly part with some of their land if it meant a railroad passing over it. The Grant lands ran for hundreds of miles through Texas providing endless options for the Grant family. The family fortunes were shaped by Fred the first and eventually run at the wishes of Frederick Grant II, my dad. The turnover from I to II was slow.

"Grandpa, Fred number one, took that number one seriously and didn't surrender it easily. He grew up pretty tough in Tennessee and fought for the south in the Civil War while still no more than a young boy. Gramps had just turned 17 when the war ended, but he managed to fight for three years. His years of fighting took him up north as far as Gettysburg and then returned him quickly through Atlanta and back to Tennessee for a series of failed attempts to protect his home. He watched his friends die and watched his birthplace burn.

"With his homelands laying in ruin, he headed west to Texas, taking with him a fair amount of gold he acquired, all ill-gotten, at the end, and after the end, of the Civil War. Fred came to Texas as one of many thieves to grow his fortune and he did just that. In addition to stolen goods which Fred brought with him, the world kept giving. Fred returned from a war that claimed hundreds of thousands of lives and left many young widows. He found a willing widow, a woman who possessed the original thousand acres of the Grant Ranch. In 1870, my Grandpa Fred married Etta Winston and took to building his Texas empire which included a cattle ranch, railroads with surrounding lands, and a lumber business. It was a steady march and by 1885, the year my dad was born, the Grants were one of the richest families west of the Mississippi. Barely 35 years old, my grandfather had seen and done things in this world that few could ever do.

"Etta didn't say or do much and it was hard to know if she was content or lost. Grandpa didn't care. He was absorbed in his world and empire and immediately tried to build my dad in his image. By the time Dad turned 4, he was always out on the range with Gramps and Etta's input was done. He learned to rope and ride, brand cattle, drive the herd, and tinker around the locomotives that rode the Texas and Grant railroads. Both Freds were hard as nails and as the 1900s approached, horns were soon to lock."

Ray was mesmerized at this point and was leaning closer to Fred with every word. Fred was really getting into his own story as he continued.

"In 1900, my Dad was a hardworking, 15-year-old cattle boy, following obediently in his old man's footsteps. In 1901, he was a 16-year-old disgruntled cattle man growing more and more tired every day that he had to throw a saddle on his horse. By 1902 he was a 17-year-old rebel that thought he had the answers to everything in the world and felt ready to play a major role in the family businesses. The tug-of-war began.

"Oil came to Texas in a big way in 1901 with the Beaumont oil strike. Overnight, wells popped up everywhere. It was harder to hit water than oil all around Texas. Fred Sr. resisted the temptation and the urging of his son to drill oil wells. He was a cattle man and damn proud of it as he liked to say. A couple years went by and by the time Fred the second reached his twentieth birthday, the battles were almost non-stop. For my Dad's 21st birthday the old man finally gave in, a little.

"He set aside the bulk of the 1000 acre plus ranch to never be drilled in his lifetime, but he gave his son 200 acres of prime ranch property for drilling and the okay to drill along all of the railroad right of ways that they owned. By 1904, Dad was bathing not only in oil, but in money as well. By 1905, he was buying every piece of Texas and Oklahoma land he could get his hands on. The guy had what they called a nose for oil and he hit another gusher near Tulsa, still in 1905.

"Back in Texas, he worked out some sort of strange deal with the government and Grant Railroad Company got control in price setting around the state for oil, shipping, and things like that. It was probably tainted if not out and out crooked, but at that time nobody was looking too hard. There was another round of oil strikes right before the twenties all around the state. Grandpa was losing his mind by this time as well as his health. My Dad was finally in control of everything with a Grant sticker on it and a lot more than that.

"He married a girl from a neighboring ranch, Marie Cesar, which just added to the size of his cattle ranch, which along with all the land he purchased was heading towards his goal of 100,000 acres. Dad never stopped for a honeymoon, and when his father, my Grandfather, passed away in 1923, he barely stopped for the funeral. The same could be said about his interest in the birth of son, that's right, me ... Fred number three. Dad didn't miss a beat of work, whether it was in the oil fields, in the refineries, on the railroad, or at senate hearings. He worked hard and he worked the system. I was raised by my mother and ever hovering grandmother. Making up for the closeness she never had with her own son, Etta smothered me with love, toys, and trips until her death in 1931.

"Thanks to all of the doting from Grandma and Mom, I grew up a lot less manly than either my Grandfather or Father. Dad didn't really care; he thought that he would live forever and had no worries about leaving everything to me. The one part of the family business that he really hated was the cattle side of things. It was a stark reminder of how his father kept the reins tight on him until after his twentieth birthday. Dad always believed those years of waiting kept him from owning the entire state. So before I was ten years old, my father gave me the entire cattle business which was to be run by my uncles, until I turned 18, then I would take 100% control. The set-up worked well and carried everyone into the forties, right up to World War 2."

"I must be boring you to death," Fred said after rattling on for over an hour.

"Hardly," answered a marveling Ray. "Sounds like you are, or at least at one time you were about as rich as a person can be."

"Yeah, I guess I was, and I still am, but I won't ever live like my father. He loved money, making it not spending it. It was his game. I was lucky that my grandmother and mother raised me right."

"So, if it's not the money Fred, what makes you tick? What brought you to the middle of nowhere with all of your animals? I'm dying to hear that part of your story."

"And I want to hear what brought you and Karen here, same place in time as me. I want to know what makes you tick Ray. But we can talk about that later. Let's get Karen back and trade these horses for a train ride if I can figure why my engine is acting up. I want you to see the zoo in daylight too."

The three of them jumped back in the saddle and rode back to the stables. Ray and Fred unsaddled the horses and they all rubbed the horses down and gave them a good brushing before rewarding the horses with a small bucket of oats. Karen took Fred by the hand and they ran over to the train.

Fred put on his engineer's cap that he kept in the train shack and started up the locomotive. It started, but ran with an uneven jerking motion. The engine sounded terrible.

Ray pulled off covers and engine parts, cleaning things very foreign to Fred. There were a lot of parts in the shack that Fred had purchased on the recommendations of past repairmen. Ray made himself at home.

In about an hour, a clean engine with new fuel line was running better than it had in years. Ray blew the train whistle and some of the few visitors to the zoo came running for the afternoon ride. Ray and Karen rode near the front and as happy as Karen was her happiness paled in comparison to Fred's. He loved his role as train engineer and seeing the happy kids behind him. The ride went all around the zoo and into the forest for a stretch. Fred wanted a thirty-minute route when he had the tracks laid and he got precisely that.

"We'll go out again at four," Fred announced and posted the time on a chalkboard Coca-Cola sign that hung on the station wall.

They then took a leisurely walk around the zoo. Fred picked up his story where he left off, somewhere near 1941, but first Fred told a tale from his youth that he felt had done more to shape him than anything else in life. With Karen skipping far ahead Fred was free to talk.

"I told you that my father made me the cattle baron before I was eleven. I didn't know anything or what my role would ever be. My mother's brothers, my uncles Bob and Curtis, ran everything and were only expected to keep me as involved as little as possible. I think that my father thought that I was being raised far too feminine for a Grant man and this was his solution.

"We had thousands of head of cattle, but my uncles thought it would be a good idea for me to run my own small herd, so they gave me my own steer to start with. That steer was born for other reasons, I know that now, but being twelve or so at the time I saw him as my pet. I loved him, I know that sounds crazy, but I did. I named him Cubo after my uncles and that's where the name of this zoo came from. It all started with Cubo. My father felt that I loved that cow too much and gave my uncles hell. He wanted a man for a son and knew just how to get through to me.

"He had my mother take me on the train to Houston for a weeklong tour of our railroads and oil offices. He wanted to hear everything I saw when I got back and over dinner he asked about any and all of my ideas for running the oil company. I was a child, I didn't have any ideas. So, after dinner he says to me, 'I hope this pet nonsense with our cattle is over and you appreciate what you need to do out in the world.' I told him plain enough, having one pet cow won't hurt anybody, animals have a right to life too. 'Not around here they don't and we won't have it around here again. The pet program is done.' I asked about Cubo, Ray and what my dad wanted to do with him. He told me that he'd done it already, we just had our first dinner of Cubo and many more would follow.

"I bit hard, I pointed my jaw forward and bit hard. I didn't let him see that he hurt me, I couldn't do that, but I walked to my room and cried my eyes out. As the tears poured out of me Ray I was starting to be shaped on the inside. I would change how we treated animals one day, I would quit eating them, I would take care of the ones I could, and I would keep my eyes open for a chance to get off that ranch.

"Pearl Harbor gave me that chance and within a month of the bombing I joined the army. I was only 17 but it was easy to join and in 1943 I found myself in Sicily and on D-Day I hit the beaches in Normandy. We worked our way through France then raced the Russians to Berlin. It was bad, but everyone knows that. The worst thing for me was the few zoos we passed, or what was left of the zoos we passed. Dead animals everywhere, starved or shot, some taken to be eaten, some burned alive in the buildings they lived in when our bombs fell. Never did I see such a thing and I never can again. I must be crazy, but I'm probably the only man you'll ever meet that had no problem firing a bullet through a person's skull but would weep like a baby for a dead animal."

"Oh, I don't know Fred," Ray replied, "we may not be as different as you think. "

"Well a couple of good things came from it. I got to meet Ike in England. He was from Texas and moved to Kansas too, he was my idol. And I vowed in a fox-hole in France that I would make it home and not only get my family out of the cattle and meat business, but I would build a zoo for needy animals and I've been able to do that.

"I got home in 1945 and put a lot of thought in the plan I would try to talk my dad into. During the war, my dad reached his goal of owning over 100,000 acres. He also owned refineries all around Texas and Oklahoma. I knew the cattle was just a pain, in fact if he hadn't turned it all over to me when I was a kid, I'm sure he would have gotten out of the business while I was away. So, one day I said to him, 'Dad, these cattle only get in our way around here with what we need to do in the oil business, and they take up too much of our time. It's time we moved on.'

"He was impressed and asked what my plan was. I told him we need to sell off the meat packing plants, kick the fences down and never buy another cow. The ones we had could simply roam the range and stay out of our way. He thought it was crazy, he wanted to slaughter all the cows first and then sell the packing company, but he finally just laughed at me and said, 'Do it'.

"I let the cows roam free, I bought some horses and let them run free. And made my dad happy working with him on the oil side. We were players in politics too and I got to really know Ike and became friends with him during his White House years. Money opens lots of doors, I have to admit that.

"By the end of the fifties, my mom and dad were gone, Ike was preparing to leave the White House and I was tired running my dad's empire. I was a very lonely and unhappy man. I came up to Kansas, I think it was 1959, to attend a ceremony for groundbreaking of the Eisenhower Library in Abilene. I gave lots of money, it meant a lot to me, and I had a good visit with Ike. We played some golf, in fact that was the last time I played, and I told him I was tired of doing my dad's business. All he said was, 'Then stop and do your own business.'

"That night I realized it was time to do my own business and the promise that I had made to myself in that foxhole had been ignored for too long. It was about two in the morning and I wanted to jump out of bed and get started, I wanted to scream to the world that I was going to create a zoo, right here in Kansas. I got up and paced the floor until the sun came up. Before leaving Abilene, I told Ike my plan and even though he never said so I'm sure he greased some government wheels for me and got lots of benefactors to join my efforts.

"I drove this way from Abilene looking for land and fell in love with this area. I bought as much land as was available, pretty inexpensive, and a year to the day that Ike broke ground on his library, I broke ground on the zoo. I spent that year stepping away from running my dad's business and I put it all in hands much more capable than mine. I built a home about 20 miles from here and moved there the day we broke ground. The oil business and government subsidies fund this place, quite nicely, and I get to be me. It's been a good ride for over 20 years now. All the animals here are the result of some sort of rescue. A lot of them have come from defunct circuses, some from other zoos that closed, and I have a cow in the kid's farm section that was tied to the gate when I got here one morning. It's been something."

They continued to walk around the zoo. There wasn't an over-abundance of animals by any means, but there was an abundance of space. Fred made good on his self-promise to take care of needy animals. Animals that had spent their years being trained by whips and prods were now allowed to just be themselves.

"You freed these animals Fred," Ray told him.

"Not really, they freed me. I could be drilling the dirt somewhere covered in oil. They brought me here. They are the freedom givers, always have been. Man just never wants to admit that."

They reached the back corner of the zoo where Fred's new building sat, and Fred took Ray and Karen in for the tour.

"It's ready for me to move into. Come upstairs. I want you to see the view of the wolves' den from my wolf room."

It was a narrow room with pictures of wolves on the back wall and a few leather chairs to rest in. The wall facing the wolves' area had a couple of viewing windows, but tree trunks blocked a fair amount of the view.

"I had those trees put in so the wolves maintain their privacy. It's important to them."

Ray and Karen looked out one of the windows and Fred the other. Blackie rose from the ground and jumped onto his private rock high above the rest of the clan. He peered at the windows and pawed at the ground.

"I don't know how he saw us through the trees, but he did. He feels something for or from you Ray."

After touring the house they continued their walk and stopped by the admin offices to visit with Fred's staff. Karen took to the ladies working there instantly and they took to her. One of Fred's assistants was going out on break and offered to take Karen with her and visit the monkeys. The other ladies asked Ray if he was from the area or just passing through. When Ray explained his desire to raise Karen in Alaska, free of overbearing authority figures, they told Ray that perhaps he was in such a place already. They had children who were in the school system in their county and doing quite well. The education included lots of outdoor and survival training as well as math and science. Much like the zoo, the school had an involved and active board of administrators and volunteers. There weren't many places in the world where you could find an education system as good as theirs.

If Ray wasn't intrigued, Fred was, you could see it in his eyes. Before leaving, Fred was asked if he wanted to get his farm listed for sale now that his new home was ready for him to move into.

"Give me a day or two," he answered, "I've got a new idea I need some time with. I want to get the train out now, promised the kids we'd be going out at four. I'll let you know about the farm as soon as I decide."

The final train ride of the day was as exhilarating as the first. The kids at the zoo exited happy and as closing time neared, families strolled slowly to their cars. The heat of day was gone, and the promise of food brought most animals to a livelier state than they'd been in for most of the day. The zoo crew tended to their final day's chores as Fred, Ray, and Karen set-up for dinner at the Lupus home on wheels.

It was Fred's turn to be curious now and he asked Ray what brought him to Kansas.

Ray was as honest as he could be. "I got tired of people always telling me what to do and telling me I wasn't smart. Everyone thought that they were better suited to raise Karen than me. I'm not stupid."

"No, you are not stupid. You took care of my horses, you fixed my locomotive, you manage a house on wheels while taking care of a beautiful little girl, looking to give her the best she can get from this world. You are in no way stupid Ray, you're one of the smartest people I know. Blackie sees that in you. Feels it."

"Animals have always liked me better than people. Yet when my first dog got run over by a reckless driver my father didn't give a damn, I wasn't even allowed to cry."

"You may not believe this Ray, but people like your dad, and mine, they pay for their behavior. Sooner or later they pay. Is your dad still alive?"

"No, he's gone. I believe you Fred. I think my dad paid a price for how he treated me and my dog. Yes," Ray added with a devious smile on his face, "he paid."

"Then best let that go Ray, he paid, and you moved on."

"I moved on all right, worked at a horse track for a long time and met and married Karen's mother. We were happy, I guess. Her name was Diane. At some point she wanted more from me, maybe more than I had to give. But there were times she wanted me to be less than I was too, less angry, less lonely. It was a confusing time. She used to love horses, even more than me, but in time it stopped. She didn't like riding with me and Karen anymore, preferred her own things and new friends. A short time ago she had an accident with one of my guns and shot and killed herself. I guess if she had given up on me and Karen then she paid the price too."

"Your freedom brought you here. Alaska may just have been a line on a map, a line you were intended to follow, but only until you found your true home. A line goes on forever, the search for home ends when you arrive there. I have a proposition for you and Karen, something I want you to try and think about for a while before making a final decision. It involves work for you, a home for the two of you, good schools and a good way of life for Karen."

"Work for me? What could I do Fred?"

While they were talking and readying their table for dinner three motorcyclists pulled into the parking lot and stopped on the other side near the east gate. Fred and Ray watched as they dismounted and began setting up a campground for the evening.

"I guess people pull in here every now and then after hours," Fred told Ray, "it's fine but I just need to tell them no fires and no trash. I'll be right back."

"I better go with you, they may not be friendly."

"People around here are all good people Ray, nothing here to worry about."

Ray stared at Fred with admiration as he strode off slowly. He let his mind wander a bit too, imagining having a father like Fred and not the likes of what he had to deal with. From Fred's war story Ray knew how much the fires and burned animals of German zoos affected him, still he was understanding enough to let people rest here providing they honor the rules. Signs were posted everywhere around the parking lot about no fires. Ray watched with his protective instincts taking over as his friend approached the bikers.

Ray glanced their way off and on as he started getting dinner ready, a little concerned for Fred's safety. Ray relaxed a bit when Fred started back. "All good people around here," he said to himself.

"All good?" Ray asked when Fred got back.

"Yeah, all good. They didn't say much, in fact one guy didn't say anything at all or even look at me. I didn't like that, but seems they understood about campfires being just too doggone dangerous Ray. I am however uneasy when a man won't look you in the eye though. I'm sure they're fine."

Ray took a few slices of bread out and put them in the middle of the table. He was anxious to talk to Fred about the work he mentioned when something else stole his attention.

"I could be wrong Fred, but that looks a heck of a lot like a fire to me."

"Guess I need to be a little more forceful."

"You stay here and watch Karen. I'll talk to them."

"Be nice Daddy."

"This is my problem, you should stay with your daughter. That one guy sitting on the rock never turned around, he may have a weapon on him, maybe even a gun. Let me talk to them."

"Don't worry Fred, I worked Chicago security for a long time, I know how to deal with punks like these. I'll be back before you know it. After all, we must protect our animals, they are our babies." Ray's confident smile reassured Fred that the situation was well in hand.

Ray went into his truck and loaded his gun, tucked it into the back of his belt, put a pen and paper in his pocket and headed over to the bikers. His walk started slow, but the old Ray anger was heating as he walked. His heart gathered speed as did his steps, his muscles tightened, his jaw jutted out as if pointing the direction to walk. The two guys put their beers down and stared at Ray, they became uncomfortable and said something Ray couldn't hear to the man sitting down, he still refused to turn around. Ray stopped beside their bikes and looked the situation over.

"My friend told you no fires," Ray said in nobody's direction.

The man sitting down spoke without turning around, "Yeah, no fires, it's dangerous. We heard him and we heard you. You can leave now."

Ray bit lightly on his lower lip and without another word he planted his size 16 boot into the gas tank of the cycle closest to him. The force sent one bike after another into each other knocking each bike to the ground. The man sitting down, the one Ray never took his eyes off of, flew up and charged at Ray. As soon as he got a good look at the size of Ray, his eyes widened and he tried to put on the brakes to no avail, he was too close to Ray. Ray reached out with both hands and grabbed him by his shirt, pulling the guy towards him and in one powerful motion, using the strangers' momentum, flung him 15 feet across the parking lot. The man slid on his face another 5 or more feet before stopping motionless on the rock pavement. Ray turned his attention to the other two travelers and his clenched fist sent one reeling into the zoo gate. The last standing man was pleading innocence and begging for mercy.

"You got two minutes to get that fire out. In exactly two minutes I'm gonna try to put it out myself with your motorcycle. I'm not sure if putting your bike on that fire will work but we're about to find out."

"I'll get it out, just let check on my buddy, he hasn't moved since you threw him."

"That's up to you. In a minute and a half this bike goes on the fire." Ray stood up the top bike from the heap and wheeled it toward the fire. "A minute fifteen."

The man abandoned concern for his friend and rushed over to put out the fire.

"You can check your friend by the gate, the other guy stays."

While the two guys were trying to make sense of things Ray took out his pen and copied down the license numbers from the bikes. He went to the unconscious man on the pavement, took his wallet and copied down his home address, throwing the wallet casually back on the ground. He returned to the less injured men.

"You'll be leaving here in couple minutes but before you go, you're gonna go over to my daughter and my friend and apologize for your rude behavior. It better be the sincerest apology you've ever made because coupled with your total lack of respect to my friend, I just couldn't handle a bad apology. I can't guarantee that I'll remain this calm much longer. Now go do it."

"What about him?"

"I'll take care of him while you're gone. He better be ready to ride when you get back however, my patience is wearing thin."

The two walked over to Fred and Karen, Ray walked over to the man now showing some small signs of life. Ray grabbed him by the throat and looked into his lost eyes.

"I should kill you now," Ray said, "and you better believe that if my daughter wasn't standing right there I surely would." Ray took his pistol from his belt and shoved it a good way into the guy's mouth. The guy was crying now, he lost control of his bodily functions and kept repeating, 'Sorry, sorry, sorry.'

Ray pulled him up and shoved him towards the bikes. "Sit down and wait for your friends."

The other two finally returned and Ray allowed them to put their gear back on their bikes. As soon as they were done, Ray had one more bit of info for them.

"We've had a great visit and we'll probably never see each other again. But you never know. I have your license plate numbers so finding you would be no problem. And I got your address already," Ray said to his main adversary. "So, say there should be some graffiti on the walls one day, or a fire within 20 miles of here, we will just have to get together, for the last time, one more time. In fact, if I hear so much as a sneeze from any one of you as you're leaving here, I will be close behind you. So, without another word, not one single word, get the hell out of here."

As quiet as three Harleys could be, the travelers continued on their way. There is no way of knowing for sure, but Ray believed it was a few hours before any of them spoke, or sneezed, again. Ray was proud as he returned to his party.

"They were very nice Dad, how come they had to leave?" Karen asked.

"They just couldn't get comfortable honey. They paid a price for stopping here and had to be on their way. There's a place in this world for all of us Karen, this just isn't theirs. Now Fred tell me about this work you think I could do."

"Well, judging by the way you protected the zoo just now, I'm thinking you could be The Zookeeper. But before we go into that I want you to see my place in the woods. Let's have dinner and then you can follow me down the road. Before I put my home on the market I want to see what you think its worth might be. You two can spend the night, nothing but room and quiet there now."

Following dinner, Ray closed up his camper and put everything back in the truck. It was another busy day, a great day, and Ray felt he was living as well as he ever had in his life. Thoughts of settling down here went through Ray's head as he followed Fred down a long winding road. It was too dark to see much of anything, but it was a peaceful drive.

Eventually they pulled down a long gravel road, headlights

bouncing lights back to Ray's eyes off of white wooden fencing, a red barn, and lastly a log ranch house. *Just a postcard*, Ray thought.

They entered the house and instantly got the full tour from Fred. There were separate guest quarters for Ray and Karen, and they got Karen's room ready immediately. She fought sleep as long as she could on the ride home but lost the battle about halfway there. Ray tucked her in, and he and Fred sat at the kitchen table where Fred laid out his plan for the future.

"Think about this," Fred offered. "You stay here for a bit and see how you like being the zookeeper, you know, patrol the grounds like security, saddle up the horses once or twice a day, help with mechanical stuff if you can. Karen can go to school here, we can have the bus stop here at the farm or by the zoo, it's right on the way. I'll pay you a salary, give you a little spending money, everyone can use that, and you two stay on the ranch, free. You'll get to see how you like it here without any pressure. In time, if you decide to stay, I'll have my Texas accountants draw something up more permanent. I know we've just met Ray, but I like you and Karen, and I think you were meant to be here. I don't need any more money, and if this works out, I could eventually give you guys this place. If I live long enough, I'll turn it right over to Karen. What do you say?"

"I need to ask Karen first, but I'm sure she'll be all for it, and if that's so, then we'll do it."

"Good! There's a furniture store in a small town about 50 miles from here, you'll learn all these towns. Let's take a ride there this week and you can buy a new bedroom set for Karen, maybe yourself also. I'll clear out the two bedrooms and leave everything else. It will be your home before you know it. Tomorrow I'll take you and Karen for a walk around the ranch, there's a small lake not far from here that I'm sure Karen will love, you too Ray. Exciting times aren't they, friend."

"Yes, they are," and Ray added sincerely, "friend."

Fred went off to bed and Ray sat alone at the kitchen table staring off into space. *Home. Yes, this could be home*, Ray thought. He liked the feel and he loved the thought of working at the zoo. Riding horses again, helping with the other animals, watching Blackie and the wolf pack grow. He was excited and hoped Karen would be just as excited as he was.

CHAPTER 16

Ray sat and his head was spinning. The kitchen seemed out of sorts somehow. Things were the same, but different. Confusion was coming again. Where was Karen? Was she alright?

He rushed to the guest bedroom where he tucked Karen in bed some time ago and burst through the door. Empty! Ray tried to scream Karen's name, but words would not come. He tried to lift the covers from the bed with his left arm, but the covers seemed too heavy. He eventually got them off the bed, but Karen was not hiding under them. A final try to yell and something, some form of Karen's name, came loudly from his heart.

Karen came flying through the door.

"Dad, what are you doing in here? Did you have a nightmare? Something made you talk."

Ray looked at Karen and around the room, still a bit confused, but he was coming home. He had a bit of hope that had been missing. Karen led him back to his bed.

"Sleep now dad, the rest will bring more memories back." Karen's hope and optimism sprung from her as she kissed her father goodnight. Ray lied down in bed and watched the shadows on the walls. *Kansas*, he thought, *home in Kansas*. Time was the question Ray couldn't answer as he fell asleep in darkness.

Ray remembered asking Karen if she'd like to try living on Fred's ranch for a while. Today he thought it odd that a grown man would ask a five-year-old a question about major life decisions. But on that particular morning, it seemed the most natural thing in the world, at least in the world of the Lupus' and Grants. That morning replayed itself again for Ray.

Fred and Ray were already sitting at the kitchen table when Karen joined them for breakfast. Both men wore sly smiles as their happiness could not be contained. Fred prepared breakfast for Karen and placed a plate of toast and a single scrambled egg in front of her.

"Did you sleep well sweetheart?" Ray asked his daughter.

"All night with no dreams. Wait, maybe I did have a dream, I remember something. Maybe not. Yes, I slept good. Did you?"

"Very, very good. I was tired. I was up early too thinking about some things Mr. Fred said last night."

"What did he say?"

"Well," Ray began slowly, "Mr. Fred is moving to his new house at the zoo and he said that if you'd like, we could move in here. This would be our home. Isn't that right Fred?"

"One hundred percent right. What do you think Karen?"

"You mean we could stay here, and I could go to school here and have new friends? We could come by the zoo too, all the time."

"Your dad would be working at the zoo."

"Let's do it. I want to, so much I want to."

"I guess it is agreed then, Fred, we will stay, I will be your Zookeeper and Karen will start school in the fall."

"And I will show you two everything around here, starting with a trip to the furniture store this weekend. But for now, let's go out for a walk around the ranch. There's a pretty little pond, almost a lake, about a half mile from here through the trees. Let's make lunch and have a celebration picnic. Time for a new start."

The new start did wonders for Karen and Ray. Karen obtained a fair amount of book learning along with her learning to take care of a ranch and home. By the time Karen was 10 years old, she was quite the home maker while maintaining her childish innocence. As one police officer foretold on the day Ray's wife died, soon the child will raise the man.

Ray was brought a long way in life by his daughter but not for one second did he ever relinquish his role as protector. As Karen inched Ray through life mentally with stories and tales from school, Ray moved Karen through life with all the confidence imaginable that a giant of a father could instill. And Ray's distant wish whispered to himself so long ago about having a father like Fred was nearly a reality. Ray loved this family a lot more than he understood it, but he understood his main role, iron fisted protector. Nobody ever messed with Karen or Fred and everyone in the county understood this just as well as Ray did.

When Ray was around Karen, he was as peaceful as a man could be, but when working or being around people he didn't care for, the body seemed to dominate the mind. Muscles would tighten, fists would clench and hot blood would chase away any cool thinking he may have had hidden in small recesses of his mind.

Once on one of his guided horseback rides, a middle-aged man slapped Ray's horse alongside the head. Ray jumped off of his mount and proceeded to pull the man off his horse and toss him to the ground like a ragdoll. The man started screaming about a lawsuit and getting even with Ray when Ray towered over him in the dirt, lifting him slightly off of the ground. Rather quickly, the man stopped screaming about lawsuits and started screaming for forgiveness. Ray gave him a solid kick in the ass and sent the man running back to the stables. The man was sitting by the barn when the riders returned and sheepishly left the zoo with his family. No lawsuit was ever filed.

These types of incidents happened often enough to worry a lot of the other zoo workers, but not often enough to concern Fred. After all, the animals were well protected and that is all Fred ever wanted out of this world.

Fred loved Ray for all he did and after 7 years of working together Fred signed the ranch over to Ray and Karen. The house, the barn, the land including 'Little Lake Michigan' as named by Karen on the first day of the new morning 7 years earlier.

Ray took his duties at the zoo seriously and many of his duties were self-assigned. He was the sole keeper of the horses to the point that when he felt the horses too old to carry riders, he relocated them to his ranch. Ray also kept the train running, although Fred was the engineer that drove the zoo express. Ray also helped with unloading trucks and getting food to the animals. Ray loved feeding time at the zoo, always done right after the zoo closed for the day and it filled the day nicely as Ray waited for

Karen's school bus to drop her off each day.

The ladies of the office took Karen under their wing and would keep her on the many nights that Ray and Fred went to pick up animals from closed circuses, wildlife refuges, or the occasional animal hospital that would call with a special needs animal. Ray's favorite part of the day was the walk-through that he performed each and every morning. He would study the animals looking for any illness or pain the animals might be dealing with. His findings were reported to the on-staff vet that worked the entire county. Every animal was treated with the highest of care and aid.

The animal that completely stole Ray's heart was Blackie. Ray loved watching Blackie as the wolf looked over his pack throughout the day. Ray would try to hide behind a tree or bushes, but Blackie would always sense Ray's presence and let out a howl to let Ray know he noticed him. Ray had found a butcher in the small town of Medford about 40 miles from the zoo that carried bison meat. Ray took to buying Blackie this special treat and tossing some to him after hours a couple times a week. Blackie would always give a little to his mate, the female that came down from Wyoming with him, and alternate some of the other pack mates in getting the treat. Blackie was getting on in years and Ray was worried that a younger male would soon challenge Blackie as leader. Ray couldn't stomach the thought.

Long before Blackie showed any signs of aging Ray would take him out for walks along the horse trails. He tried to get Blackie to walk with the horses, but the horses became too agitated when Blackie was around. So, Ray would put a muzzle on the wolf and a heavy leash, and they would walk the trails together. In time, Ray would remove the muzzle when they got a little distance from the zoo, Blackie never once exhibited any behavior that could be viewed as a threat. Fred joined Ray and Blackie many mornings on their walks and was the first to notice when Blackie slowed a step.

"I'm worried about your wolf, Ray."

"My wolf?"

"Everyone knows he's your wolf. Look how he's walking. That slight limp in his right leg is getting worse and he doesn't seem to be eating as much as usual. I watch from my wolf room most nights and some of the younger pups seem to be getting brave with stealing his food. I don't like it."

"Well, maybe it's time we moved Blackie out of there."

"Before we move Blackie somewhere else, let's have the vet take a good look at him. He'll be here next week, your boy will be plenty good until then."

"Yeah, my boy will be good, he sure will be. "

The vet, Dr. Pisarik, came to the zoo as scheduled the following week. Ray brought a muzzled Blackie into the zoo hospital and the doctor began the check-up. Blackie was a model patient.

Dr. Pisarik looked over the papers they had accumulated on Blackie over the years.

"Not much here," the Dr. told Ray, "I guess we never had a reason to look too closely at this big boy."

"No, he's been king since I've been here. Strong and healthy."

"How long have you been with the zoo?"

"Karen started school here so she must have been five and she's twelve now, so we've been here seven years."

"My, my," the doctor said, "how the time leaves us. I guess I've been coming here over 20 years now, and I feel every bit of it. Now let's look at our fellow old timer here. Blackie came here in 1983. Chart says that he weighed 125 pounds, my goodness he was a big boy. Teeth looked good, muscle tone good, estimated age was 5 to 7 at that time. Let's see if we can get him to stand on the scale."

Ray led Blackie over to the scale and where he stood without a single growl.

"109. Not what we like to see. He was eating better in the wild. Let's see him walk around the room."

Ray again led Blackie around the room and the doctor noticed a bit of a limp in his right leg. The doctor felt around and felt no obvious structural damage and believed Blackie had arthritis in his leg.

"The wolf is in a bit of pain and he isn't eating like he should. I'm going to put him under and check his teeth, if there's a problem I'll clean it while we're in there. But he's limping, he's probably over 12 years old, and he's losing weight. None of this is good. The other wolves may try to boss him around now, that's what you saw isn't it?"

"Just a little. They're testing him, but they're still scared. He's boss."

"I have to be honest with you, I don't think he'll be boss much longer, but we really don't know how these wolves will act in captivity. He's not in danger of dying right now, not from natural causes as far as I can tell. But he could mix it up with the younger pups and that could be bad news."

"I can take him out of there. He can live on the ranch. Plenty of room and I'll keep him locked safely."

"I don't know Ray, he's still a wolf after all and as much as we think we know him, he may have a streak of predator inside that we don't see. It could be dangerous to Karen, or even you for that matter, but I doubt you would mind your own danger."

"There's no risk. I'll muzzle him when I have him out at home and lock him in his own room when I'm away."

"You're going to give him his own room?" the doctor asked somewhat surprised.

"Yes, we have a room not used at all. We'll make it his."

"I guess it's up to you and Fred. He's the gentlest big wolf I've ever seen, and he obviously loves you, I just hope you know what you're doing."

The doctor went on to check and clean Blackie's teeth and prescribe some pills for the arthritis. Ray emptied out a spare bedroom and made it Blackie's room. Blackie had his own bed, that he only used when Ray wasn't at home, nights he slept by Ray. The room had toys, Blackie didn't play much but when he did he pulled the toys apart in seconds. There were three locks on the door, all with different keys, all keys kept locked in different areas.

Karen knew to keep away from the door when she was home alone with Blackie. When they were all home Blackie would wear his muzzle, it was a small muzzle that Blackie didn't mind, and the wolf would have run of the house. Blackie spent as much time lying with Karen as he did with Ray. Fred dropped by often in those days and marveled at the behavior of the wolf.

"Best thing I ever did was to agree to bring Blackie and his pack here. He would have been dead years ago without us."

"He's helped me too", Ray told Fred, "I see him control his natural tendencies and I know I can too. I've been at peace a long time now thanks to him."

"Let's just say that Blackie has been at peace with himself, you have a good way to go yet but you'll get there. At least you know which people to rough up, I'll give you that."

"I don't want too much self-control, I have just enough."

Ray lay in bed and thought about the things he'd done. A lifetime of being hurt, getting even, and somehow being lucky enough to get away with his temper driven actions against people that bothered him. The years he spent watching and hanging around Blackie were some of the calmest of Ray's life. He was surprised to learn that the wildest of creatures seldom had to bite, the showing of teeth had a much bigger impact on foes. It was the little guy that had to sink teeth and stinger to make a point. The bee would make honey, but was the quickest to attack and sting, even if it meant its own death, if someone got in its territory. And there wasn't a dog on earth that barked louder and longer when trying to make a point than the Chihuahua. Contrast that to melodic sounds of the wolves' howl and you begin to understand what being at peace with yourself truly meant.

Ray would sometimes give himself a few seconds to think about how he would react today if given yesterday's situations to live through again. He let those thoughts go quickly. It was enough to possess those painful memories that he could not share with anyone, but he couldn't let those thoughts creep into his mind and take root. He couldn't allow himself to judge himself with so much darkness in his past. He kept things locked and always found a great deal of peace when he followed Blackie's lead.

Ray recalled one of the first and most satisfying times he approached a problem through the eyes of the wolf. At great expense, Fred built a huge polar bear habitat so the zoo could rescue polar bears fighting for survival on a melting ice sheet in Antarctica. As soon as the enclosure was ready, an animal protection group rescued 6 bears from an ice floe and transported them to Cubo Zoo.

One afternoon, Ray spotted a tourist tossing marshmallows at the bears. Ray approached the man and informed him that the marshmallows were dangerous to the bears, they affected their normal eating habits and had adverse long-term effects. The man told Ray that when he was a kid, he fed the bears marshmallows and peanuts all day long at the city zoos. It was only the tree huggers that changed all that and there is no adverse effect on the bears.

Ray swallowed hard, lowered his voice and said, "You've been informed, No more feeding." A proud Ray walked away, happy with his calm demeanor. He turned just in time to see the tourist throw yet another handful of marshmallows at the bears. *I didn't show my teeth*, Ray thought.

Ray returned quickly to the bear habitat and got in the face of the offender. Ray pulled his shirt sleeves up over his shoulders revealing his Popeye forearms and massive biceps. This was Ray's idea of showing his teeth. The redness in his face and the thick vein jutting out of his neck was his subconscious way of showing his teeth.

"I warned you mister, I'm the zookeeper here and it's my job to protect these animals."

There were no more smart answers coming from the tourist. "Okay, I got rid of all my food. You don't have to worry about me anymore."

"No, I don't. You were warned and you didn't listen." Ray pointed a finger at him all of two inches from the guy's face. "I can pull you out of here by the top of your head if I decide to, and I just might. But for now, you got two minutes to get to your car and high tail it out of here. Start running."

"My families just up ahead. I can't leave without them."

"I'll give you four minutes then. Get your family and go and you better be running. I'm heading for the gate and after four minutes you won't get out of here without some animal food being shoved up your ass, in front of your family."

He made it out, running, in about two minutes and his family took about four. Fred joined Ray at the front gate, and they talked about Ray's actions.

"I learned to be so calm from Blackie and I merely growled a bit and he got the idea. It feels good to be in control."

"Ray, Ray, Ray," Fred said. "That was a long way from a little growl and a long way from calmness. You were a minute away from tossing the guy. Thank God you didn't have to. You are a great zookeeper, but we need to keep working on your attitude. Thank Blackie for how much he's helping you."

As Ray tried to sleep he kept thinking about being at peace and wondering if he would ever find what Blackie already had. He tossed and turned, in and out of sleep, watching the never-ending shadows on the wall.

The shadows were dancing now and Ray tried to raise his arm to block the vision but to no avail. He didn't know if he was asleep or awake, but he saw Blackie being chased by the rest of the pack. Ray tore out after them picking up a fallen branch along his run. They had Blackie cornered against an unclimbable sheer cliff. The pack was about to charge when Ray rushed into the pack, branch swinging and wolves flying. A large grey leapt at and grabbed hold of Ray's throat. Ray shot up in bed, sweat running down his face. He moved as quickly as he could out of bed and ran to Blackie's room. He turned the handle and the door opened. This made no sense to Ray. Why wasn't it locked? He pushed the door fully opened and turned on the light.

"What the hell?" Ray tried to say. Where am I?

He turned and looked around. This isn't Blackie's room. Ray began to shake, his eyes misted over. He tried calling out, but no sounds came.

"Dad, what are you doing? Are you looking for your grandson? I told you Freddie won't be home for a few days, you need to get used to being home first. You alright Dad?"

A shaken Ray stared at his daughter and he tried and tried to speak. Finally, a word came out. "Wolf."

"Wolf?" asked Karen. "Do you mean Blackie?"

Ray nodded.

"Yes Dad, this was Blackie's room once, but that was a long time ago. It's Freddie's room now, you know that, or at least you used to know that. I'm sorry, I shouldn't have said that." Karen was crying now, apologizing over and over. "You have no idea what year this is do you? And I thought you were doing so well. What am trying to do, I'm hurting you aren't I? Do I need to stop? Is this place wrong for you?"

Karen collapsed into her father's arms, crying uncontrollably Ray held her tight with his good arm and managed enough strength to hold her almost as tight with his bad one. He wanted to tell Karen to not give up on him, it was only moments of confusion. He would make it, they would make it.

He tried to say don't give up on him but only a garbled mess came out. Karen walked her father back to bed and spent the rest of the dark night questioning her decisions, a true Lupus trait.

Ray was up early the following morning and anxious to get outside. Karen joined him at the kitchen table, and they waited quietly for their morning coffee to be ready. As soon as it was, Karen poured herself and her dad a large mug. Karen stared into her cup and Ray drank about half of his while it was almost still too hot to drink. He then took the cup and motioned that he was going out for a walk. Karen nodded to show that she understood, but she needed to say something before her dad left.

"Dad, I need to call your doctor today. You've been very confused lately and it's not just the nights anymore, I see you getting lost in the middle of the day now. And I swear, sometimes when you look at me I could bet that you have no idea who I am. Let's get back on your rehab, maybe we checked out of the hospital too soon. I thought it would help you being here, and I don't know anymore. You were looking for an animal last night that's been dead for over 15 years."

Ray shook his head, tried to say that everything was okay but stumbled over his words again. Ray walked out the front door and headed for the lake, Karen walked to the telephone. She was still on hold when Ray reached the small lake on the west end of their ranch. He sat down and took his turn staring into his coffee mug. "And just where did you come from?" Ray tried to ask it. But answers weren't coming to Ray so easily.

Karen hoped for better results to her questions when Ray's doctor finally picked up. She laid her biggest concern out for the doctor right from the get-go.

"Was it a mistake to bring him back here so soon? Is this the wrong place for him? He seems lost in space and time so often now. He was further along when he was still in the hospital."

"Whoa Karen, you need to slow down," the doctor told her.

Ray's doctor worked out of Kansas City Memorial. The hospital was always in Fred Grant's heart and became a huge recipient of much of Fred's wealth. Fred played a part in hiring Dr. Bush, Ray's doctor, by luring him out of a top Dallas hospital and setting him up in Kansas where today he is the head of the entire Neurology Department with stroke centers in Kansas City Memorial and at a satellite hospital near Abilene, also funded by the Grant Foundation. Ray's case was being closely monitored by Dr. Bush since Ray was both patient and donor. Being a close friend of Fred Grant had opened many doors for Ray and never once did Ray need to ask for those doors to swing open. Ray spent the first couple of days following his stroke in the Abilene facility and then was flown to Kansas City as soon as he was stabilized. Dr. Bush took the lead from that moment and explained as much as he could to Karen.

"You're drawing conclusions far too quickly Karen. You're hoping to paint a bright picture of the world, but you're not waiting for the sun to rise. I have your father's file here, let me refresh my thoughts. It was less than three months since he had his stroke and you brought him home about a week ago. He was speaking a bit when he left, and we measured some strength in his left arm. All good signs and all good reasons to return home. Now this is interesting, his scans showed us that he suffered intrusion in both sides of the brain, and that is very rare. There was a small amount of damage showing on his right side and I'm sure that that is why his left arm shows weakness and is coming back, right on schedule. Now without getting technical, let me say that his scans show far more damage on his left side of the brain and that has centered on his speech and memory. That, we would expect to recover slower, but why would he regress is your question. I can't answer that with any certainty but you have to set-up an appointment in Abilene with my assistant Dr. Walden, that facility has everything you'll need and frankly I thought you would have made the appointment by now. We discussed this."

"I know doctor, but I wanted to see Dad improve before I threw more at him."

"Karen, what you're waiting to see as improvement isn't the same as a doctor would classify as improvement. Let us treat, and you be the loving daughter. Now one thing that I am concerned about and I can't say this is happening with any certainty, but your father may be having what we call TIA strokes. These are what we also call mini-strokes and they produce many of the same traits of a major stroke, weakness in the arms, loss of speech, loss of recognition of the people and places around us. These mini strokes usually only last for five minutes or so. Now we normally see TIAs before a major stroke, like a warning sign, but from what you're describing Ray may be having TIAs following his stroke. That would explain the ups and downs he's going through and the appearance of being lost every now and then. Coupling TIAs with his condition following his quite major stroke does give me cause for concern. We'll need to look into that in Abilene. Make the call Karen."

"I will, I promise."

Helpful and hopeful, they moved on. Meanwhile Ray was fast asleep on his Adirondack chair by the lake. A howl from the lake awakened Ray's senses.

CHAPTER 17

"Blackie. Blackie," Ray called out for Blackie hoping he hadn't run off hunting on his neighbor's ranch. Since Blackie had slowed a bit and weakened, he wanted more than ever to show off his hunting skills to Ray, but by hunting much smaller prey than from his youth in Wyoming and Montana. In addition to the prairie dogs and occasional raccoon that Blackie would bring home, he loved to sneak onto the neighbor's land and steal chickens. Blackie still enjoyed a fresh killed chicken, but it was more about the hunt these days than the meal.

Ray's neighbor had come over in the past and accused Ray's dog, he never got a good look at the wolf, of being the thief. Ray claimed that his 'dog' only ate breaded and fried chicken. Things remained tense between Ray and his neighbor, so Ray thought it best to keep Blackie on his own property.

For the past two years, Blackie stayed quietly around the lake, even the need for his muzzle had vanished. Blackie was spending his last years sunning himself around the lake, every once and a while he would give chase to a critter that he no longer wished to catch. The bison meat that Ray got from a butcher in a nearby town was Blackie's meal of choice now.

By the third summer of Blackie's time living with Ray and Karen, the changes had become visible, even to Ray. Blackie could no longer jump onto Ray's bed at night, so he began sleeping on the floor. He ate less and less, and his skeletal frame, long hidden by powerful muscles, was now showing through his dark coat. The walks to the lake took longer and the walks home took forever.

Ray was sitting in his chair, sunning himself as Blackie had taught him to do, feeling a bit old himself. Blackie let out a howl and then another, he sounded young and vibrant and it made Ray feel good again. Blackie came up to Ray's chair and licked his face, Blackie's version of a loving kiss. Blackie then headed back to the lake, a little extra jump in his step, and Ray swore there was a smile on his face. Blackie took about five steps and turned his face looking square into Ray's eyes. Blackie let out a howl for the ages, low, almost endless as the sound became part of the spirit of the wind.

"You old show-off Blackie, you're feeling your power today aren't you boy?"

And with that Blackie ran as quickly as he could back to the lake. Ray closed his eyes and let the sun massage his mind. Ray felt the breeze on his face and heard the softness of Blackie's howl as it was carried by the wind from tree to tree. Ray felt uneasy and opened his eyes looking for the sound, if were visible, and it frightened Ray.

He ran to lake with every bit of bit of speed that he possessed and found Blackie lying on the ground, lifeless, a smile on his face. His spirit had left his body with Blackie's last breath. When Ray lifted up his boy, the howling rose to the heavens and stopped. He was gone. Ray held the body that could no longer hold the spirit. Ray knew that Blackie had discovered something this morning and tried his best to tell Ray what that was.

Ray looked up to the sky to try and see Blackie's soul, but the clouds and the sun blinded him in his search. Ray curled up next to Blackie's body like a baby to his mother and felt the final hint of his wolf's soul enter his body. They shared one last sunset then Ray made a small cross out of tree branches and planted it into the earth where Blackie's spirit left his body. Lifting the wolf in his arms, Ray and Blackie made the long trek home.

Karen comforted her father and phoned Fred who hurried over. They sat and talked, and Fred shared how it was Blackie who finally convinced him that everything he was doing with animals was correct. With all doubts removed, Fred was able to move ahead following his heart. Protect all animals, for they are creations of the same source as man. They need love as much, and often more than humans do.

"Best thing I ever did. Blackie helped to save every animal we take in at the zoo."

"Probably brought me and Karen here in some strange way too. For sure he played a role in our staying here. Best thing I ever did too."

"Odd isn't it how much an animal can touch us. They leave a big hole too when they're gone. This is probably the worst you've felt since your wife passed away."

"By the time my wife died we had drifted pretty far apart, or maybe I should say she had drifted. She was going out on her own, drinking a lot, hiding my money. She became a stranger. I didn't feel bad when she died. In fact, I wondered if there was something wrong with me, if I was missing some emotions or feelings that everyone else had. But sadly, I learned today, I'm not missing any feelings, I'm ripped apart inside and feel plenty. I guess I just never lost someone I loved before today."

"We'll give our boy a good funeral."

"I want to bury him right on the spot he passed. I put a makeshift cross there already. He chose that spot with his last breath."

"Done. I'll get a coffin for him and have the grave prepared tomorrow. We'll have the funeral in a couple of days."

Ray knew how he would take care of things. "I'll dig the grave tomorrow, if you could take care of everything else that will be enough. Blackie will be fine in my room tonight, but you probably should have his coffin here early tomorrow. I'll bring him with me to his grave, have them bring the coffin there, I'll make him as comfortable as I can. The end doesn't leave us with much, does it?"

"Oh, very wrong. The end leaves us with everything he lived and stood for. When we take that from every death we have to witness in life it leaves so, so much. Count your blessings Ray, for they are many."

"You know you were always smarter than me."

"Yeah right," said Fred through his first smile of the day.

Ray was up early the next morning. Night's sleep came seldom and short the night before. Ray left Blackie in his room as he drove some supplies to the gravesite. The little wooden cross still stood where Ray would put shovel to earth. Before digging Ray carefully put the cross on his chair away from the lake and returned to the house in his truck. Ray picked up the lifeless Blackie and walked with him slowly back to the lake where he laid him down near what would become his final resting place.

"You picked the prettiest spot, buddy," Ray said while looking off into the horizon.

Ray spent hours digging a deep long hole for Blackie and then lined the bottom of the grave with pine tree branches. He laid two long wooden boards from the bottom corner of one side to the top of the grave on the other side. He covered the wolf with his favorite blanket that he brought from the house and sat down beside Blackie and waited.

Around sundown a truck carrying Fred with Blackie's coffin drove down the walking path to the lake. Ray got up and nodded at Fred; not a word was spoken. Fred dropped the rear gate and jumped onto the bed of the truck. Ray stood at the back of the truck. Fred carefully pushed the heavy coffin toward Ray who took hold of the outside handles. Fred jumped down and Ray pulled the coffin towards himself until Fred was able to grab the handles on the other side.

They carried the box to the front end of the grave and opened it. Ray smoothed out the blankets inside and lifted Blackie up enough so he could get a hold of Blackie's blanket. This one he laid on top of the others. He then brought Blackie over and laid him on his belly, back legs under him, front legs slightly crossed as Blackie used to love to sit. Ray positioned Blackie's head on his front legs and kissed him goodbye. Ray held his hands out to Fred, palms up, as if to ask if there was anything Fred wanted to add.

Fred said, "Goodbye buddy." He too kissed Blackie goodbye.

Ray then took the ends of the blanket and fully covered Blackie, tucking the blanket neatly all around him. The lid was closed, and Ray and Fred slid the coffin down the two lengths of board inside the grave. Once settled the boards were removed and Blackie settled squarely on the pine branches. Fred hugged Ray and still without a single word exchanged between them, walked with his head bowed low back to the truck and he left Ray alone.

Ray placed the homemade wooden cross on Blackie's coffin and returned the dirt to the earth. The sun was gone for the day when Ray tossed his shovel aside. It was a long lonely walk home that night, but Ray was comforted by the song of the wolf coming from the night stars. Ray howled along ever so quietly and apologized to Blackie for his poor howling skills. The rest of the walk was in absolute silence.

The next day Fred had a small grave marker laid on Blackie's gravesite. It simply read, 'BLACKIE, Provider, Protector, Teacher. The Lone Wolf is Never Alone.'

The ladies from the zoo office joined Fred, Karen and Ray at the gravesite where final goodbyes were spoken.

Afterward Fred walked Ray backed to the house and spoke of tomorrow.

Ray listened as Fred spoke. "We need to go to Oklahoma tomorrow. I got a call from a veterinarian friend of mine and she's got a gorilla she wants us to give a home to. She said a travelling circus dropped him off for medical treatment and she knew right away that he was being abused and she had to rescue him. When the circus folk called back to check on his progress, my friend, Dr. Stapleton, told them that their gorilla was dead, poisoned to death, probably some youngsters' idea of a joke. They understood as that sort of thing happens with theses circuses all the time. She then called me and said we need to take care of this fellow, that he's very sad and way underweight and malnourished."

"So, we are kidnapping the gorilla?"

'That's one way to put it Ray. Does it sound wrong to you?"

"No, it sounds like the only right thing to do, what time will we leave?"

"Get the truck and large cage ready by 5, we'll leave after the last train ride in the zoo tomorrow. We'll stay over in Oklahoma Friday and go home with Kingston on Saturday."

"With Kingston? Who's Kingston?"

"Our new gorilla."

"Oh yes Kingston. Need to make Kingston happy."

"And fatten him up. See you tomorrow."

Ray was waiting with the loaded truck when Fred finished his last train run of the day. Fred shook hands with all the kids and some adults who were on the ride, went to his place for their travelling cooler, and returned to the waiting Ray at the front gate. Well before 6:00 they were on their way to Tulsa, Oklahoma to greet and bring home their newest family member, a sad gorilla named Kingston.

Ray asked Fred what it was that made people be so mean to so many animals. Fred believed that it was because people didn't understand animals and when people don't understand other living things, they are often mean to them, whether it be animals or other people.

Fred became very philosophical as he continued explaining things to Ray. "These mean people, they've never heard a calf crying for its mother or seen a mother bear surrender her life in order to save her cubs, or seen the wolf family as it bonds for life and works and plays together. Put these sheltered people for one minute in the wilderness with these beautiful animals and we could eliminate a lot of hate. But so many of these people get out in the wilderness, have a few too many beers and kill said bears that only want to feed their children, or shoot a massive elk whose only crime was that his antlers would look good over somebody's fireplace. It's a crime, and these people treat you and me the same disgusting way."

"What do you mean?"

"I mean we look different than a lot of other people, we're not part of the mold. I couldn't fill the mold Ray and you broke it. I'm all skin and bone and you're a good 6 foot 6, 280 pounds of muscle Ray, aren't you buddy?"

"I don't know. Never been measured."

"Well anyhow we look different, so people think they're better than us, they want to hurt us."

"We make quite an unbeatable pair though, don't we?"

"Cause we're friends. Friends sticking together always make it rough on the outsiders. I know I can always count on you and I hope you know that you and Karen can always count on me, even after I'm gone."

"I know I can count on you, you're all the family I have, you and Karen. Do you think the dead care about us?"

"Of course they do, they no longer have to worry about themselves so all they care and worry about is us. You feel it when someone that loves you dies. You feel it around you, you feel their fingers running through your hair, it's mystical. I felt it when my mother and grandmother passed. They showed me how to live a kind and giving life. My father couldn't do that. I didn't feel his hand after he died."

"No, I didn't get any message from my dad when he died either. Maybe he's waiting for me to die and then he'll have something to say."

"I could see that."

"Do wolves care about us when they die Fred, or do they just care about other wolves?"

"They care about everyone that they loved in life. Why did you feel those fingers?"

"No fingers, but please don't laugh. I think I felt Blackie breathing on my neck last night."

"How could I laugh at that? That's exactly what you should have felt. You're a lucky man. Put on some music, we got a long ride to Oklahoma."

They drove on through the night, a bit too tired for talking and listened to the music on the radio. The stations soon quit coming in well and after a half an hour of static Fred put in a tape and played some Vivaldi.

"Your music is making me sleepy. Let's stop for a quick beer and a little rest at the next exit, the sign says there's food and drink available. I'm getting hungry anyhow."

"You're always hungry. Good idea to stop anyhow, we can log some quick miles after we eat."

Ray pulled off the road at the next exit and parked at a somewhat rundown roadhouse. There were a couple other cars parked there so the boys figured the place must be alright.

"Order me a beer and a cheese sandwich. This rear tire is a bit low. I'll put the compressor on it, it will just take a few minutes."

"Grilled?"

"Grilled what?"

"Grilled cheese?"

"It's up to them. Whatever they have."

"Okay. Check all the tires while you have the compressor out, we have a lot of miles ahead of us."

Ray began checking the truck, Fred went into the roadhouse to order dinner, still wearing his engineer's hat from his last train ride at the zoo. Ray thought that this could cause an issue based on his talk about people being mean to those that look different. Fred looked very different in his striped hat.

He'll be fine, Ray thought as he checked the truck completely. Pausing over the cage meant for the gorilla's safe travel Ray was glad Blackie never ended up a caged animal. Ray was still learning from the ways of the wolf but through his mourning a little anger stirred inside from thoughts of the cage. He knew this mission would help him move on and was ready to eat and get back on the road as he strode to the bar.

Ray dusted himself off and went just inside the door. He looked around the bar for Fred allowing his eyes to adjust to the darkness. Fred's hat stood out first and Ray took a couple steps in that direction before realizing it wasn't Fred wearing the hat. Ray stopped, took as deep a breath as humanly possible to try to slow his instantly racing heart. He clenched his teeth and began rubbing and squeezing his forehead to contain his rage. He looked over the bar again and saw Fred on the opposite side, hatless.

"Sorry I didn't notice you come in," Fred said when Ray reached him. "Just checking this map again."

"Ok, put the map away. Now I'm really working on this, but I'm not seeing straight and I'm shaking like all hell with anger. Tell me what's going on."

"Sit down, take a sip of beer, I ordered some sandwiches, they'll be here in a minute."

Ray sat and folded his hands together. "Tell me about your hat Fred."

"Okay, but you need to stay calm. You can't handle everything out of rage. I'm going to take care of this, I want you to trust me here."

Ray let out a short breath and shook his head to let Fred know he was listening.

"That guy stole my hat, for the time being, and in all honesty he said some pretty mean things to me about how I could get it back or about me leaving here now. I didn't let him or his friends get a rise out of me and you shouldn't either. I told him I drove the kid's train at the Cubo Zoo but it didn't seem to matter to him. The point is I tried Ray and now I will take it up a notch."

The bartender came over and slid a couple plates of sandwiches and chips in front of Fred and Ray.

"Excuse me," Fred said to the bartender, "do me a favor and

call your sheriff. Fellow at the end of the bar stole my hat and I'd like it back without any trouble. See how easy Ray, no fuss, no muss."

Ray stared at the bartender.

"I'm not calling the sheriff because of your stupid hat. It'd probably be an hour before anyone got here anyway. He'll get tired of your hat and you'll have it back when you leave, if not just go buy yourself a new one."

"You know mister," Fred spoke, still as calmly as before, "I fought in the war and I saw firsthand how people's refusal to get involved and do the right thing in the beginning leads to nothing but big trouble in the end. Hitler marched through all the little guys in Europe, no problem there, but his drunken lust for power was not satisfied. He caused more problems, thought he was the biggest man in the world. But eventually, and this always happens, a bigger tougher man walks through the door. Russia walked through Germany's front door and America walked through the back. What was left was ruins, pain, hunger, and death. You stand here not wanting to do the right thing all the while not realizing what just walked through your front door. I fear for you."

The bartender walked over to the man with the hat, Ray's eyes fixed on him, and spent a few minutes in speech, probably retelling Fred's tale. Nothing but loud laughter followed reaching Ray's ears.

Ray slammed his fist hard on the bar. "Dammit Fred, why does everyone have to push me?" Before Fred could say a single word Ray pushed their food and drinks off the bar and knocked his barstool to the floor. He was halfway to the group in the corner before Fred comprehended what was happening. Ray's mechanism for dealing with confrontation had kicked in.

Ray always had a built-in mechanism for dealing with trouble and aggravation. The larger the aggravation, the larger the Lupus response. Ray could be known to throw a man down a flight of stairs for shooing a dog away but looking the other way if someone was stealing booze from a liquor store. It wasn't perfect, but Ray always reacted in some way to anything around him that he didn't understand. And there was a process involved with Ray's reactions and it was happening now.

Ray's heart began to race as the blood rushed through his veins and filled his head with an anger that replaced all reason. The veins in Ray's neck jutted out for all the world to see and his fists clenched automatically without a single thought given to them.

Fred watched as Ray lumbered toward the drunk at the end of the bar. In a last-ditch effort to avoid the unavoidable the drunk threw the hat towards Fred. The hat headed north, Ray headed south at an even quicker pace. He reached the thief just as his protective mechanism was going haywire.

Ray's cold stare and anger met the drunk head-on. "You stole my friend's hat."

"It's right there," the drunk replied nervously, "take it."

Ray's heart raced even quicker now, the blood demanding more of the body as it raced quicker and filled Ray's head.

"That ain't good enough now. You mocked my friend, you stole from him, you wanted to cause hurt. Nobody hurts Fred."

"Take the damn hat, don't be stupid."

Not the word to be hurled Ray's way. He didn't react kindly to the word stupid. There may be some doubt about how much that word led to what followed or how much the death of his wolf played into it, but there is no doubt that Ray now lost all control.

He lifted the drunk up by the lapels of his ragged shirt grabbing a good deal of loose flesh in the process. Ray turned him around in mid-air and flung him into the wall a good eight feet from the bar. The crash and cry of pain were simultaneous, and everyone heard the air leave the guy's chest. He hit the wall three feet from the ground and stayed there for a couple of seconds. Then he slowly slid down the wall and ended up a human pile of crap on the floor. He sat there dizzy, watching the barroom spin around him, gasping and wheezing for air.

"You wanted hurt," Ray screamed at him, "does it hurt enough for you?"

"I can't breathe."

Ray stared at him and instead of the anger leaving Ray it continued to grow. He clinched his fists again and was prepared to finish things.

"That's enough fella!" It was the previously uninvolved bartender now trying to give Ray orders.

Ray turned around to face him and saw that the bartender had picked up a 3-foot-long oak club and was waiving it towards Ray.

"No, no, no," screamed Fred jumping from his barstool. "Bad idea. Put the club down. NOW."

Ray probably could have handled the bartender without much effort, with or without him carrying a club, but Ray had enough. He reached behind himself and pulled a gun out of his back holster. He leveled it off pointing it squarely at the bartender's nose. Now it was the bartender's heart that raced to dangerous speeds as he froze in his tracks.

"Just put the club down," Fred told him. "This man's my security guard and he's licensed to carry and use that gun. Your friend robbed me and he's lucky to be breathing at all right now. Don't be an idiot."

The bartender laid the club down without ever taking his eyes off of Ray's gun. He held out his hands, palms up as if to say enough.

"Isn't that better?" Fred asked. "Now if you'll get us new sandwiches, we'll be on our way. Four cheese sandwiches with lettuce and mustard."

Ray stood there, hovering over a room where nobody dared move, his pulse beginning to slow. He closed his eyes, took a breath and shook his head, a head filled with confusion. "That's better," Ray said more to himself than to Fred.

The sandwiches came and Fred paid the bill with a good size tip included, not that it was earned, but Fred always tipped well and he refused to allow anyone to change his nature.

Before exiting the door, Fred asked, "You okay now Ray? All the tires good?"

"I guess I'm alright. I feel good again if that's what you mean, useful. And yeah, truck's ready, tires good. I guess everything's good now."

"We better make tracks now, put this behind us."

As the men drove off to Oklahoma in quiet tiredness, Ray replayed the night in his mind. Something was troubling him. He mulled things over and over again and finally spoke to Fred.

"I did good there didn't I Fred? Those guys thought we were stupid. They're the stupid ones."

"You took care of it, you protected me, you always protect me. Let it go."

"I never have to think about what to do. I'm smart. Things just happen and I see myself doing the right thing. It's good. You never questioned me. Everyone else always has. If I got mad around my father, he'd eventually beat me. My mother would ignore me and kick me out of the house. And my lovely wife was the worst. She told me I couldn't drink beer or coffee because they set me off. Wrong actions by stupid people set me off Fred. Anger may show up, but those bad people bring it on, I have to right the wrongs. Do you see that?"

"Of course, I do. You didn't hit that guy in the bar because he made you mad, you hit him because he robbed me and tried to make a fool out of me. You know, if I were your size Ray, when that guy did that to me, I might have killed him. I probably would have killed lots of people by now. Just between you and me, there were times growing up I thought that I wanted to kill my own father. You wouldn't act like that so the Lord made you big, you control yourself Ray."

"Maybe Fred, or maybe we're just more alike than you'll ever know," Ray answered gladly.

"Looks like we got a bigger problem now," Fred said as he noticed the police car lights in his mirror. "Pull over and let me do most of the talking."

Ray pulled off the road, a two-lane black top highway, killed the engine and the boys sat patiently waiting for the cop to approach their truck.

The officer sat in his vehicle a long while he appeared to be on his radio. Finally, he exited and took a few steps out onto the highway before walking towards the truck. He unfastened the flap over his gun and withdrew the pistol from its holster. "Put your hands on the dashboard in front of you," he yelled as loud as he seemed capable of, "let me see 'em."

"I don't like this, Fred," a nervous but not angry Ray said to his partner. "He's pulled his gun on us."

"Let's be cool. Put your hands up here," Fred said while putting his hands on the dash.

The officer approached Ray's window and continued in his loud tone. "I got a call on a couple of truckers that tore up a diner, pulled a gun on the owner. Looks like I got me trouble-makers here." The officer had swung his gun up and had it pointed directly at Ray. He motioned with it and ordered Ray out of the truck.

"Do as he says," Fred told him calmly.

Ray stepped out and took the little shove the cop gave him towards the side of the truck. "Hands up here, feet back." Ray obliged.

The officer turned his attention to Fred. "So, you're the boss telling your friend what to do. Keep your hands where I can see them and slide out on this side." Fred did as instructed and was ordered to join Ray at the side of the truck where they were patted down and made to wait for questioning.

"I got an injured man back at the diner and a bag of food from that diner on your seat here boys. If I find a gun in this truck, you're both going away for a long time. Seems like two guys matching your looks busted up the place with intent to rob with a deadly weapon, that's a felony around here."

"We have a gun in there, officer. An unloaded security pistol that my security guard here is licensed to carry, as well as myself. It's in the glove box. It hasn't been loaded in years. We never seem to be in any trouble that requires a loaded gun. You got your story from a couple of drunks."

"Shut-up mister. What's in the truck? You guys pull a job or planning on one? Guess you didn't plan on me coming along, did you?"

"Just a large cage."

"For what?" The officer's tone was beginning to settle down and he seemed less on edge than he had been up to now.

"We're on our way to Oklahoma to pick up an abused gorilla. We're taking him back to the Cubo Zoo so he can have a home. It's what we do. We don't rob. We don't shoot. We support all the law enforcement people in Kansas and elsewhere for that matter."

"So, you're with the Cubo Zoo, are you? Both of you walk back and open the truck."

"He's not with the zoo," Ray said as they threw the back door open revealing the cage, "he is the zoo. His name's Frederick Grant, that name used to mean something around here."

The officer was quiet now, even appeared to be dizzy. He looked at the cage and back at the boys. He wore the look of a man who had just stepped into something mighty nasty and was trying to figure a way out. His tone was almost a whisper a now. "You two have a seat on the back of the truck here. Just relax for a minute if you don't mind. I need to call this in, someone may be trying to pull a fast one on us, but I have to check. You understand fellas, don't you?"

"Can we have our sandwiches while we wait?" Ray asked more hungry than worried. "We have a lot of road ahead of us and it's been a long night."

"You got an ID Mr. Grant?" the officer asked somewhat politely now to Fred. Fred produced his license which after the officer studied it caused him to mutter a single word. "Shit," was all he said. He got the sandwiches for Ray and Fred from the cab and went to his car to call it in.

The officer returned to Ray and Fred after their sandwiches had been eaten. He seemed different now. He reached his captain who not only knew Fred Grant but was well aware of the judges that Fred knew, the work he'd done in Kansas, and the large amounts of money that Fred donated around the counties of southwest Kansas.

"Well Mr. Grant my captain, Bill McCormick, says hello, and I apologize for any inconvenience, but I had to check you guys out. Hope you understand."

"You shouldn't have pulled your gun on us sir," Ray said a bit angry.

"No Ray, he's only doing his job, he couldn't know who we were."

"Thanks Mr. Grant, I called ahead to other districts, you guys are all clear to Tulsa. Clear sailing, you can even push the speed limit a bit to make up time. I'll straighten out those drunks back at the diner. We all love what you do for our kids and community Mr. Grant. I apologize again."

The boys returned to the truck and to the road. "They're getting closer," Fred said to a confused Ray.

"You know these guns and clubs don't scare me Fred, I only worry about Karen and what will happen to her when I'm gone. She's just a kid you know."

"Relax Ray. She's 14 years old, not so much a kid anymore. I'm sure she's doing fine and she'll be fine forever, you and I will see to that."

"How so?"

"Just relax. We're staying at the Fairmont in Tulsa, follow the signs and wake me when we get there. We'll see the vet and the gorilla in the morning."

Ray drove on thinking about Karen and trying to understand what Fred meant. They checked into the hotel after midnight. Exhausted, Fred went to his room and immediately fell asleep. Ray went to bed where he tossed and turned all night worrying about Karen and her life. He managed a few hours of broken sleep during the night and phoned Karen in the morning, waking her around eight.

"Really Dad"? was all she had to say for a while then adding, "I love you too, but can I go back to bed?"

Ray laughed a bit and felt really good when Fred knocked on his door.

"Time to meet our new friend. Kingston awaits."

Fred and Ray drove out to the veterinarian's home office in the suburbs of Tulsa, her city office not nearly equipped enough to handle a young gorilla the size of Kingston. Dr. Helen Stapleton was a good friend of Fred's and had called on him before to rescue some animals, none the size of Kingston. She greeted the boys as they pulled up, was introduced to Ray Lupus, and suggested they go inside for coffee first where she could fill them in on what she knows about Kingston.

Helen led Fred and Ray to her kitchen, a cozy mix of modern and early American décor. They sat at a long wooden table that had a tray of pastries sitting perfectly in the center. The coffee was ready, and Helen filled three cups to an inch below the rim and placed them on the table. She began making small talk with Fred as she added a small creamer and sugar bowl to the offerings before her guests. The sugar bowl contained a spoon just about as tiny as a spoon could be. Ray lifted it to add his three teaspoons of sugar to his coffee and the spoon was lost in his enormous hand. Almost unconsciously, Helen took a couple of normal size spoons from a drawer and handed them to Fred and Ray.

"Have some pastries gentlemen, they're from the best bakery in town. I picked them up last night so they will just have to be eaten today. Good things in life simply don't last too long do they?" With that Helen took some small plates from her cupboard, gave one each to Fred and Ray and sat down at the head of the table.

"So, Mr. Lupus, just how did you get hooked-up with Fred? Are you a hopeless animal rights activist like the two of us?" Helen got up again and walked into her living room returning seconds later with a vase of beautiful flowers. She moved the pastries in front of Ray and gave the flowers the center position on the table. "Eat," she said motioning toward the pastries, "you will thank me later. Now, where were we?" she added. "Oh yes, you were about to tell me a bit about yourself Ray, please do."

"Well doctor, I work…"

"Call me Helen."

"Okay doctor, I mean Helen, I work for Fred at the zoo, mainly with his horses. I lead trail rides there also."

"Ray is a little shy," Fred added. "He does take care of the zoo horses, even takes them to live at his place when they no longer care to take on riders. He also takes care of our train, all the mechanical stuff, helps with feedings and looking after all our animals. And yes, he is a hopeless animal rights person just as we are. He is the man I told you about that took Blackie home with him for the last couple of years. We just lost Blackie."

"Yes, I remember, and how it was such a sad day around the zoo, and obviously Ray's home. Do you have family with you in Kansas, Ray?"

"Just a daughter. Karen is 14 now, she's all I have. And Fred of course. He is family you know, he looks after us."

"Well thank you Ray," Fred said, "but you do a lot more looking after me than I do for you. Ray lost his wife about 10 years ago and he and Karen have been helping me ever since."

"That sounds like a good result from a bad circumstance." Helen started cleaning all the dishes from the table and tidying up the kitchen. When all was returned to its perfect nature she spoke again. "Well it's time for you gentlemen to meet Kingston. I have him in what best could be called a pen in the back of the house." Helen led the men along the walkway. "Luckily I have a full enclosure. I see a lot of cattle here, many cows and bulls, a good deal of horses and of course dogs, cats, and other domestic animals, but I never thought I would need to house a gorilla. When I had this space built for the animals, I thought I would probably have an eagle or falcon one day, so it seemed prudent to make the cage fully enclosed. I wanted enough room also so I could monitor the animals walking and trotting progress before they were released. As it turned out this area worked well for the short time Kingston's been here."

"Good foresight ," Fred offered.

Kingston soon came in to view and Ray let out a gasp. "He's far too skinny to be healthy. His head doesn't look like it belongs on that small body."

The three caregivers were quiet looking at the emaciated gorilla. Kingston sat in a corner of the large retainer with what seemed to be tears in his eyes. He appeared too tired or broken to move. Ray moved over to the gorilla and placed his hand flat against the cage.

"How you doing today big fellow? You're about to go home buddy, a real home with friends where nobody will ever hurt you again." The two stared at each other, but Kingston's grin never changed. Moist eyed, no smile, no energy or excitement from his heart. Ray walked back to the others.

"We're going to get him healthy, don't you gentlemen worry about that. I've talked to a zoologist in Chicago and put him in touch with your staff at the zoo. They all know what to do. You guys just get him safely home and his life begins anew from that day."

"Ray will handle that. I have to go to Houston today for some legal matters. Must take care of this world before I get to the next. I've got a car coming here soon to take me to the airport. I can help transfer him into our cage and then he's all yours Ray."

"I can't handle the drive today, I was up half the night, I was hoping you'd drive. I'm not the safe bet today."

"It's better you go tomorrow," Helen added, "you can stay in the guest room if you're comfortable with that. I'll have help here in the morning with the transfer, I'll sedate him just before you leave, and the two of you will have a peaceful trip. Are you comfortable with that Ray?"

"Yes, that should work. I have to call Karen of course, but I don't see any problem."

"Then it's settled," Fred said, and they moved unto Helen's veranda to relax until Fred's ride arrived.

Fred and Ray stayed outside while Helen went in for some drinks. She returned quickly with a tray carrying a pitcher of lemonade and four glasses. She placed the tray on the patio table and joined the men.

"You expecting someone to join us?" Fred asked.

"What do you mean?"

"You brought out four glasses."

"Don't you think that your driver would like some refreshment before your journey?"

"We're going to the airport, he's not driving me to Houston. And by the way, you do know that they make lemonade in cans and bottles today don't you?"

"Do your cans come with lemon slices on top or is it just the added flavor of aluminum that I would be paying for?"

Ray looked at Fred and gave a little laugh directed towards him. He then returned his attention to Helen.

"Helen how do you think Kingston came to be here? He seems so lost and out of place."

"I tried to find out that very thing and I can only tell what I've been told. It seems that these traveling circuses have got quite a pipeline to the poachers all around the world, as much as they'd like to deny it. There's a lot of dollars to be plied from unsuspecting and unwitting people with animals such as Kingston as sideshow attractions. They bring in hundreds of dollars a day and the circus folk are only too happy to deal with whatever wrongdoers are out there. They pay top dollar for illegally captured animals. I've been told that with gorillas the poachers often kill their entire family, parents and siblings, in order to easily lead away a young male. The gorilla watches in stunned horror as his family lies bleeding to death from the poacher's bullets. This happens much more often then we can fathom. I had no choice but to kidnap this youngster when I saw the mistreatment he was suffering through. I'll do it every time I can."

"You can always count on my help, mine and Fred's."

"I knew that I could."

A long black limousine pulled up looking for one Frederick Grant. Goodbyes were said, loose plans discussed, and Fred Grant headed for the airport. The driver passed on the lemonade. The tall glass and artsy pitcher were just a bit too much. He probably would have enjoyed a can.

"I need to tidy up a bit and then we can go for a walk if you'd like," Helen offered to Ray.

"That sounds good to me. I can help with the glasses and stuff."

"Just relax, I'll be done in a minute."

"I think I'll visit with Kingston, if that's okay."

"Fine. Let me give you his food for the day, you'll see the opening where it goes. I'll be right there as soon as I'm done."

Ray visited with Kingston, the gorilla picked at his food and eventually Helen joined them out back. She changed into her walking clothes and shoes and looked more relaxed than earlier in the day. She carried pruning scissors and a light pair of gardening gloves as she led Ray down a well-worn path away from the house. They talked a bit as they walked and every little while Helen would leave the path to cut down the aged colorful flowers growing just off the walkway.

"We'll have fresh flowers on the dinner table tonight. Does your daughter enjoy gardening?"

"I don't think so. She helps with the animals a lot though, she's a great kid."

"I'm certain she is."

Helen's question about Karen and gardening made Ray think. He hadn't seen a lady as feminine and yet as independent and strong as Helen in a long time. He wondered if Karen was getting the guidance she needed to be a strong lady some day. He was drifting again to Karen's future when Helen brought him back to the moment.

"You wandered on me. Thinking about Kingston's past?"

"I'm sorry. No, I was actually thinking about the future."

"That is better, but why don't we simply enjoy the moment, tomorrow will be here soon enough. Let's take these flowers back to the house, I have a perfect little vase for them. You get your valise from the truck and I'll show you to your room. You said that you didn't sleep well last night, perhaps you'd like to nap."

"Oh no, I'm okay to visit if that's alright with you, just not up for a few hours driving the truck." *I wonder what the heck a valise is*, Ray thought to himself.

"I appreciate the company." Helen took Ray by the arm and they walked back to the doctor's home. Helen prepared dinner while Ray prepared for the evening. Once both were at the table, exactly at six, a new lightness filled the room. Fresh flowers adorned the table surrounded by bowls of pasta, homemade sauce, salad, and fresh bread from Helen's favorite bakery where she had purchased the morning's pastries.

"I hope you like the spaghetti sauce, I make at least 8 bottles of it every other month or so, I'm always trying new recipes or just spice up an old one a bit. I thought this one fairly mild but tell me honestly what you think. And to help raise my grade a peg, please open this bottle of wine, I trust it will complement the sauce."

"I know I will."

"You will what?"

"Compliment the sauce."

"Very funny Ray. Would you prefer a different salad dressing? I see you didn't take very much."

Ray was a bit confused. Dinner seemed to be coming at him rather quickly, but he marveled at the way Helen was in complete control of everything. He passed on more dressing, loaded up on and complimented the sauce, and filled both his and Helen's wine glasses in a timely manner that allowed both wine and dinner to end simultaneously. When Ray set his napkin down on the table he asked very politely of Helen, "Do you think my daughter can grow up to be a real lady, like you? I'm afraid I may have sheltered her too much. I don't think I show a good feminine side."

The couple moved to cleaning up as they continued to talk. Helen sensed Ray's fears and tried to explain some very basic life lessons to him.

"I guess there isn't much feminine role play coming from you Ray and with your wife gone it's only natural that you feel you must provide that, but I don't believe that necessary at all. You show love, it just pours and pours right out of you and that is what feeds your daughter's growth. You just keep right on doing that. The feminine stuff, the hair, the fashion, the shoes, even the spaghetti sauce, all that will come when she is ready. Prepare her abilities to learn, she'll do the rest."

When the kitchen was returned to spotless, Helen handed Ray another bottle of red wine to open, she took two new glasses from her antique china cabinet and they moved to the living room. Helen put three coasters on her hand-carved coffee table and sat on the soft leather love seat behind it. "Please sit, you seem so tense." She put the wine glasses down which Ray instantly filled and picked up the conversation they started in the kitchen.

"Does your daughter remember much about her mother?"

"I know she remembers her, but not anything about her. She was only five. We don't ever talk about it."

"You may want to talk about her more, your daughter is at that age where kids want to know everything. How did your wife die, if I could query?"

"The police said it was an accident. They said she was cleaning my work pistol and it went off. But sometimes I think that she was unhappy and just wanted a way out of our life. Knowing that like I do, I could never say that it was an accident."

"Suicide is a very difficult thing to face. The survivors all blame themselves as I think I hear in your voice. Imagine what it would do to Karen if she found out her mother died in a manner other than what the police said. You don't ever want to face that. Police said it was an accident, you have to believe that."

"I know you're right," Ray said as his mind began to drift again. A future with the truth was something Ray Lupus didn't wish to ever face.

"Well Ray, I think we've covered the past about as much as we're comfortable with. I'd like to change into my nighttime clothes and we could watch a movie, or I could show you some pictures of a lot of the animals I've treated. Clients send me so many pictures of their pets in some very silly outfits after I've treated them. I guess I become family of sorts. Do you have something you'd be more comfortable wearing? "

"I do have my pajamas with me. Is that something I could wear in front of you? I think they were made for a child. Oh, not the size Helen, they do fit. I'm sorry. Oh god, I don't know. I guess I could put them on."

"Relax Ray, as long as they're comfortable. I'll meet you right back here in a few minutes."

Helen left and took the half empty bottle of wine and empty glasses to the kitchen on her way to her room. Ray changed into his pajamas and stared at himself in the mirror for a long while before deciding he was presentable enough to return to the living room. He was alone when he returned and sat nervously on the sofa waiting for Helen.

Comfortable, he thought, *I've never been more uncomfortable in my life.*

Ray suspected that he was now on a date, but wasn't sure, it had been so long since he was on one. He felt silly in his Chicago Cubs pajamas that Karen had given him for Christmas many years ago. He wished the bottle of wine was still in front of him to get lost in. What if it wasn't a date and he offended Helen? He moved to a far corner of the sofa and wished he could disappear beneath the cushions. He heard Helen make some noise in the kitchen and tensed up further. When she entered the living room carrying a bottle of cognac and two small sipping glasses, he felt sure he was on a date. She wouldn't bring out more drinks if it wasn't a date.

Helen was dressed in silver silk pajamas with matching cover-up and tiny slippers. Her hair was newly brushed, and she looked incredibly beautiful. It was a different beauty than she showed in the morning while in her doctor role and a different beauty than her gardening attire revealed. This was the beauty of a real lady, dark and warm, distant but inviting. Helen sat down and slid out of her slippers, small feet with toenails painted to match the color of her sleep wear. Sitting next to Ray was a heavenly vision that filled their glasses with the French brandy.

"I love to end the evening with a tasty brandy," Helen said to Ray. He was confused again. "I'm a bit tired, I thought we could watch this movie a client sent to me, Black Beauty. We could look at the photos another time. What do you think?"

I doubt that there will be another time, Ray thought. "That sounds perfect," he said to Helen.

They sat in a tired silence watching the movie, Ray half watching the movie and half staring at Helen from the colorful hair sitting wildly on her head down to the perfectly painted toes. Ray was emotionally moved while sitting afraid to physically move. His hands wanted to touch Helen, his mind told him he shouldn't. He filled his hand with the small glass of cognac, enjoyed the pleasure of the drink and had another. As he put the bottle and glass back on the table, he moved to the middle of the sofa causing Helen to lean sideways onto him. He positioned himself beside her to make her as comfortable as possible.

"How's that?" Ray asked. No reply.

"The cognac has a real kick to it doesn't it?" No reply.

Ray tilted his head down to get a look at Helen's face. He saw her small smile and closed eyes. She was in a sweet sleep already, it wasn't a date after all, at least not anymore.

"These pajamas really help end an evening don't they Dr. Stapelton?" No reply.

Ray gently lifted and carried Helen to the larger sofa where he laid her down softly. He stopped the movie and went into his room. He returned to the living room with a pillow and his blanket. He lightly slid the pillow beneath Helen's head and covered her with his blanket. He dimmed the lights, leaving just enough brightness to allow Helen's face to reflect her beauty throughout the room. Ray stood in the doorway to his room for a seemingly long time just looking at Helen. He felt that he glimpsed a world he didn't belong in, but a world where his daughter did belong. He vowed to be a better parent from that point on and whispered a soft, "Thank you doctor," as he went off to bed.

CHAPTER 18

Ray slept in a bit late and when he woke, he heard movement from the kitchen. He took his time getting ready as he was somewhat embarrassed by the previous night. He thought that he bored Helen to sleep and was a fool to think for one minute that he would ever be on a date with her.

When Ray was done getting himself ready to leave and his bag packed, with nothing left for him to do to kill time, he sheepishly met Helen in the kitchen.

"Well I guess I better get going doctor. Kingston and I have a long drive. I'll back the cage up to his and we'll get out of your hair."

"Doctor? Don't start that formal verbiage with me again." She put a fresh cup of hot coffee on the table. "Sit down I'm making you some breakfast. I have a crew from town moving Kingston into the truck now, you couldn't do that alone, and I've talked to your people at Cubo so they'll be ready when you get home. Kingston is going to love his new home there and your vet has all the info he needs on diet and exercise and habitat. We've done well here, as friends, so why the 'doctor' thing after such a wonderful evening?"

"I'm sorry," he paused and hung his head looking to the ground, careful to choose the right word, "Helen. But I thought I bored you to sleep last night and that you were disappointed with my company."

"Well I'm sorry, but after the bottle and a half of wine and our few let's say 'sips' of cognac I just fell fast asleep. I could blame my sleep on the fact that I'm up at five every morning and we were going non-stop for the entire day, but you would not believe that. When in doubt, blame the libation."

Ray smiled and said honestly, "You confuse me sometimes but you always make me smile. I'm not the libation, am I?"

"Always joking, Ray. You make me smile too."

"The truth is, I stood in the dark last night looking at you, I've never seen anyone as pretty as you, and I just felt that I didn't belong in your world, but I thought if I were able to teach my daughter better maybe she could be part of a world like yours."

"And just what is my world? A world of caring about needing people, a world caring for and protecting animals? A world of flowers and sunsets? What part of my world exactly do you feel you don't belong?"

"Sounds odd when you put it that way."

"Because it is odd. Our worlds, at least the part that we bring into them, are very similar. We share many goals and you shouldn't need those goals written down for you so that you compare them, just be you, just accept the people around you as you see them. You'll find that you're very much a part of the world you wish to be in already, and your daughter is too. You're a good man Ray and if I had known that my drowsiness was to cause you such concern, I would have sat up all night with you. Maybe next time."

"Will we have a next time?"

"I hope so, you're only about 6, maybe 7 hours from here and I should at least come up and check in on Kingston, shouldn't I?"

"Yes, you should," replied an ecstatic Ray.

The crew from town knocked on Helen's door and told her that Kingston was in the back of the truck. Helen gave Ray a bag of lunch for the road so he wouldn't have stop and walked him to his truck. She gave Kingston a shot, which he was very willing to take, and gave Ray another loaded needle in case he needed it, along with an air rifle with a very strong tranquilized dart loaded in the chamber. She handed Ray a list of numbers that he could call if he needed help, with hers on top. All in case of emergency she informed Ray, she had no reason to think he'd need any of it. Ray locked the back panel, the side windows let in more than enough light for Kingston and walked with Helen to the cab of the truck.

Ray put his hand out and thanked Helen for everything. Helen touched Ray's hand, stretched herself and kissed Ray on his lips, turned and walked quickly into the house.

"Why did she do that?" Ray asked himself as he started the truck engine. He would ask himself the same question for the next seven hours.

Ray's ride went without a hitch; no need for any shots or darts into Kingston. In fact, Ray stopped a couple of times to snack and talk with the understanding gorilla. Ray would talk and Kingston would tilt his head to listen, and Ray thought he nodded in approval at some of Ray's words.

Ray shared his food with Kingston and believed the sadness in his face was slowly lifting. When they reached the Cubo Zoo, there was more than enough help to get Kingston into his new home where he surprisingly began to run around instantly and investigate every inch. Outbursts of joy came from the zoo crew and Kingston walked back toward them where he held his hands through the bars motioning to Ray. Against better advice, Ray jumped the guard rail and took Kingston's hand. The group looked at one another in a minor state of shock before all heading back to work.

Ray stood alone, bewildered as he looked over Kingston's new world and he wondered about his own. Fred had abruptly left for Texas after mentioning the next world, Helen kissed him and said that her world was similar to his, but then walked away, and his daughter was home building her own world and he watched her change every day.

"They all think they'll be better off without me, a world without Lupus," a dejected Ray whispered to himself. "Well they're wrong. Just wait until they see just how wrong they are."

PART TWO - THE ESCALATION

CHAPTER 19

Ray sat at the breakfast table looking around the kitchen, he debated with himself the merits of making a pot of coffee versus sitting idly at the table. The memories of the weekend on the road to save Kingston and the memories of Helen played over and over again. The taste of Helen's kiss was still as fresh as the moment that their lips met.

He had an epiphany on this trip. He was going to start preparing Karen for the life of the lady she was going to be. A lady of charm and wisdom, cause and concern. A precious leader of immense beauty. Ray had high hopes and was filled with excitement and bursting to discuss his ideas with Karen. When she joined Ray in the kitchen his brain failed to understand his timeline. Karen's, "Good morning," failed to bring Ray back as he nodded and stared at his daughter in disbelief. She was a beautiful lady he thought but when did this happen? Who was playing games with him now?

Ray tried to say, "Kingston," but his sounds were garbled. Karen assumed he was asking for coffee and made a full pot. Ray tried to say, "Helen," but all Karen heard was, "Help."

"You don't need to help, I've got it. I'm happy that you're trying harder to talk, the doctor says that's all you need to do. He's very optimistic about a full recovery. In fact, I've made an appointment for tomorrow. We need to go to Abilene for a check-up. I thought it would be helpful if you brushed the horses in the barn today, with your left hand. I'll help you get started after breakfast."

Ray wondered what happened to Helen after his weekend visit

which to him ended yesterday and he tried to ask again. "Helen," he muttered.

"I said I would help you now please relax and have your coffee."

Ray looked at his daughter and even though he was fairly certain that she was indeed Karen new doubts entered his mind. He sipped at his coffee, picked at the scrambled eggs Karen had placed in front of him and entertained thoughts of fleeing the house. He needed time to think and sort out his questions. All he had were questions that he was unable to ask.

Ray walked out to the barn and sorted through the brushes. He picked a large one and went about the business of brushing the horses. He was hell bent on getting strength back into his arm and he brushed harder and quicker while a growing rage was seemingly boiling inside of him. Finally, he threw the brush at an imaginary figure standing at the west wall of the barn. The brush hit, the figure vanished, and Ray left the barn along with it. He stood in the loose gravel looking at the house he knew well, the shadows from the woman inside worried him. He turned his back on the house and headed down the driveway toward the main road. It felt right to Ray, he had no idea where he was going but he knew he had to go. His steps quickened until he heard his daughter voice.

"Dad stop. Where are you going?"

Ray stopped and looked back at his daughter. She seemed older than he remembered. He looked at the house and turned to look down the road again. As quickly as it dawned on Ray to head down the road, the seemingly good idea left him just as quickly. Karen walked as fast she could to her father, almost breaking into a trot and took him by his good arm. When she did so, Ray raised his left arm completely over his head and lowered it again, making a fist and flexing his muscle.

"That's good Dad! Keep exercising that arm today. You need to fix the muscle memory."

"Hel," was Ray's lost response.

"Of course, I'll help," was Karen's confusing reply.

They spent the day together in exercise, talk and music. Karen played tape after tape of old music she hoped would spawn a learning spurt in Ray's mind. She wanted her father to be as far along in his recovery as humanly possible. The progress of his left arm gave Karen a hope she didn't have for some time. It was a long day of personal work for the Lupus' but Karen went to bed that night with hopeful thoughts about the future. Ray went to bed with the music of the sixties playing in his head. Somewhere between their thoughts lay reality.

Karen got her father moving early the following morning. She spent the over three-hour drive talking to Ray about the past. She tried to transfer the seeds of her memories into her dad. Ray listened, didn't put much stock into what was said, and spent his time flexing his left arm, over and over again. There came a point that Ray didn't know why he kept bending the arm, but he kept doing so anyhow.

They reached the hospital long before their noon appointment, but the doctor was already waiting patiently in his office for Ray. Dr. William March was a member of the Kansas City neurology team and was one of their leading vascular neurologists. He and his team were under orders from the top to clear their schedules for Ray Lupus' exam today, the power of the Frederick Grant Organization always garnered results.

Armed with all of Ray's previous test results and CAT scans, Dr. March and his nurse led Ray away to meet with the small team assembled on Ray's behalf. Karen was not invited back, but encouraged to step outside for a few hours and get some coffee or lunch. She wasn't up for eating immediately, but after a good hour walk, she stopped at a chain restaurant for a light lunch.

Ray meanwhile was offered a good size lunch and unbeknownst to him his exam started while he ate. Hours of observation followed along with memory tests, recognition tests, strength tests and anything else the group thought helpful was thrown at Ray. Ray returned to a waiting daughter in March's office where the two were asked to wait even longer as the team compared their preliminary notes. After five o'clock, March and his nurse returned to the room. March recommended his nurse take Ray to the cafeteria for dinner while he talked to Karen, he felt his words better for Karen's ears only.

"Karen, quite frankly your father's case confuses me. Tell me exactly what you see in your father that worries you and caused you to bring him in today."

"Shouldn't you have asked me that this morning?"

"No, no. I didn't want any theories planted in my head or the other doctors. We needed to make our observations with a clean slate, no preconceived notions. They can really get in the way and derail the examination."

"I'm sorry. You people know what you are doing."

"It's fine. Please tell me what you've noticed."

"Well basically, there are times my father looks at me and I swear he doesn't recognize me, it seems like he's looking right through me, and then there's times he hugs me like I'm his last friend on earth. It confuses me. And the other night he was looking for his wolf in the middle of the night."

"I don't understand", said the confused doctor, "he was looking for his wolf?"

"I'm sorry," answered Karen, "pet wolf that he brought home from the zoo."

"Oh, and you think it odd that he would look for him?"

"His wolf died over ten years ago."

"I see."

"And he wasn't using his left arm much at all since the stroke and then suddenly yesterday he's swinging it around like a club. I just don't know what's going on."

"His arm does seem to be recovering perfectly. We were giving him a memory test with colors earlier and we got a different picture mixed in the group. My intern said, 'That's stupid,', and your father grabbed his arm so hard he nearly tore it off, with his bad arm."

"I can see that. Dad has always hated the word stupid. He probably took it personally."

"That brings up my confusion," March quickly added. "There are things like that which he seems to know very well, and with his limited use of words, more sounds really, he can get his point across. But he seems to be limiting responses to what we would call non-personal things. He seems to be fine with small talk, hunger, thirst, the weather, his car ride. He responds to that. Questions about you, or Fred, or your mother, even about his years in Chicago and he shuts down. One of my interns said it resembles a form of dissociative fugue."

"Dissociative fugue?" Karen's interest was piqued now.

"Fugue is a Latin word for flight. He thinks your father may be taking a kind of flight from reality. Who he is or where he is in time. He's offered for discussion that maybe there's some things in your father's past that he can't deal with."

"I don't see that. Sure, my father has had a few losses in his life, but nothing that he couldn't handle."

"We don't know what world he's living in, or what year for that matter. We asked him many times what year it was, and he gave no response. He knows that it's Thursday though, that we got from him. Perhaps with the damage to his brain, his mechanism for dealing with his past is temporarily gone, so he's looking for a safe haven, a better time, a better place, perhaps even a becoming a different person. Flight."

"Flight? It would be a flight from nothing bad, my dad's a good person - a very good person. I think you're wrong."

"I'm just a vascular neurologist Karen. We should go up to Kansas City for some new CAT scans and see if something physical is happening, I can look at that. But after that, you need a behavioral neurologist. It's one or the other, but I must caution you, even if we dig deeper, we may still remain in the dark. Something's affecting your dad's memory, maybe even scaring him. We need to get him to face reality, to come back to today."

"We'll stay in Abilene tonight. I'll call you in the morning if we're going to Kansas City."

"I recommend it. I will plan on going there tomorrow. Just come up to Dr. Wexworth's office at KC Memorial any time after ten, no need to call."

Karen checked her father and herself into a decent hotel just off the interstate in Abilene. She wrestled with the idea of going to Kansas City and replayed to the best of her own memory all the things Dr. March tried to explain to her. She wasn't buying any of the flight theory and she wasn't buying that there was anything bad that her father had to hide from. Karen worked on convincing herself that her dad simply needed more time to regain his memories, his good memories, and that was happening.

Going backward in time and place as Dr. March seemed to believe Ray was doing was a necessary part of rebuilding a damaged mind. Her struggles with this were two-fold. One, she didn't believe that it was happening so why push further. Two, if it was happening, she didn't know if her father was capable on his own of finding himself in the now, so she must push further. The more Karen thought, the more confused and angrier she made herself.

As she and her dad turned in for the night, Karen still had no decision about which direction she would head in the morning. She counted on the night to bring an answer, darkness could be a friend or foe for both her and Ray.

Ray was unnerved as he lay in bed that night. It was a long day of seemingly endless questions - questions that he was certain were intended to trick him. Why show him pictures of colors he wondered, lollipops, balls, cars, and bikes. They were looking for something and he was not about to lay his life open in front of them. While in bed, Ray tried to speak to himself, mostly garbled sounds came out, but Ray heard the words he spoke clearly.

"Will they ever leave me alone? I'm tired of the games, of the questions. They're changing time on me, moving me back and forth. Taking away my things, changing the very face of my daughter, turning her against me. She's trying to lock me away, cut me off from my animals. I need my daughter, my real daughter. She's the only one that can keep me free. Helen's the one who started to change her, she needs to bring my real daughter back. I must find Helen."

Karen lay in her bed next to her father's and tried to make out a word here and there to no avail. But she knew her dad was trying, on his own, to recapture his life. Ray seemed to be growing more and more agitated as he struggled for words in his half sleep state. Karen tried to calm him as best she could. She moved to her dad's bed and sat alongside of him taking his hand in hers.

"No more doctors for now, just try to sleep. We're going back home tomorrow. Don't think about yesterday. I've been shoving the past down your throat, the doctors misled me. We're getting back to our todays Dad, you'll see."

And during that talk it seemed to Karen that Ray began to relax. Her optimism would allow for no other thoughts. But as much as Karen sought the return of happy todays, Ray fell into a deep sleep searching for help from long ago yesterdays.

A couple of days after Ray brought Kingston to the Cubo Zoo, Fred returned from Texas. Ray was standing at Kingston's new home when Fred found him early that morning.

"It's not much," Ray told Fred referring to Kingston's habitat, "but it's a lot better than anything he's known since being stolen out of Africa."

"His eyes aren't watery anymore."

"He's getting there."

"Well, I've got good news and good news. I took care a lot of business in Texas and as we speak, our board is contacting people to build an entirely new home for Kingston and putting feelers out to bring additional primates here. They will, of course, only be animals in need. I've given them six months and a boatload of money to get this done. I hope to God that for as long as I get to live, I never have to see another starved and abused animal. I never want to see another animal with tears of pain and loss in his eyes. We've done a lot, but we're going to do more."

"Thanks, thanks for all you are and all you do. And if you ever think that these animals don't appreciate you, remember this." Ray leapt over the guard rail and put his hand through the cage bars. Kingston ran over and shook Ray's hand as he has been doing every day since they met in Oklahoma.

"That's love."

"And look who has the watery eyes now."

Ray and Fred walked together toward Fred's train and Ray's stables. "What is the other good news?"

"Glad you asked. Remember the talk we had about taking care of Karen after we're gone? Well I've taken care of everything, for both of you actually. Financially speaking, you two are set for life, quite a few lives I might add."

"We're good with money, you didn't have to do that. You know I've never had to touch the money Karen and I came out here with."

"Things can change, now you needn't fear change. Let's just concentrate on these animals now."

"I don't know how to say thanks, but thanks. How was that?"

"Just don't get watery on me. One last thing, you need to call Dr. Stapleton and tell her our plans. She'll be ecstatic. I think you need to invite her up here also. You have that big guest room that really needs a guest already."

"I don't know. I'm not so good on the phone."

"Just do it, that's as much of an order as I can give you. After" all she did kiss you, didn't she?"

"I never told you that."

"News travels fast out of Oklahoma."

Ray called Helen and shared the news of the new building and habitat Fred was going to build for primates. He told Helen about his trip back with Kingston and how he settled immediately into his new quarters. They talked for hours and finally Ray invited Helen to Kansas. Ray thought it would great if Helen came up when the new primate house was opened. Helen agreed to that trip, but suggested that they get together before then, perhaps as soon as the following month. Helen said that she needed the time away from her practice and would love to see Kingston as well as meet Karen. A long weekend together was agreed upon and Ray became instantly nervous about Karen seeing him with another woman. Ray's plans to start Karen on the road to adulthood vanished when faced with reality. He broached the subject as a father would to an 8 year old, not to an intelligent 14-year-old who hoped this day would have come years earlier.

Ray sat Karen down and began trying to explain why Dr. Stapelton was coming for a visit. He used Kingston as an excuse, he mentioned her work with other animals, he stated over and over that the doctor was his friend and nothing more and he valued her friendship. He spoke at great lengths about the innocence of their relationship and Karen listened in silence, quite bored. Finally, she spoke.

"Dad, I'm 14. I'm happy your friend is coming to visit. I'll get the guest room ready and just so you know, I won't be offended if she doesn't use it."

"She'll use it Karen, we've already talked about her staying here."

"Dad, dad, dad. Someday we need to talk."

Helen's visit was perfect, and she did use the guest room for her entire stay. She spent a good deal of time at the zoo being amazed at the speed of the work happening on the primate habitat. She visited with Kingston, who obviously remembered Helen and liked her very much. She was envious of the closeness Kingston had with Ray and loved to watch the two of them talk in their own way.

At home, Helen began a positive relationship with Karen that would continue to grow for a long time. Helen introduced Karen to makeup, fashion, and even took her to a beauty parlor for her first true adult hairdo. The influence that Ray feared he would never be able to provide for Karen was provided, and to Ray's way of thinking, in a much better way. Karen may have grown the most that weekend, but Ray and Helen certainly had the best time.

Helen was up early every morning brewing a large pot of coffee and preparing breakfast, finding time to straighten up around the house. She went out each morning to pick wildflowers and had them in the center of the table before the coffee.

After breakfast, she and Ray went to the zoo stables and rode for hours, stopping in a new place each day for a lunch picnic. They talked all weekend about the animals, the sunrises and sunsets over the hills, they watched clouds roll in and slowly float away. Helen pointed out the different plants and trees and they walked many miles following where the local creeks ran.

The time passed too quickly and when Ray and Helen said goodbye, this time it was Ray that gave the kiss. There was no confusion about the kiss this time, Ray cared about Helen and thus began the happiest time of his life, as short lived as that happiness might be. For in the world of Ray Lupus, all good things come to an end, and quickly.

Helen returned to the Lupus farm often during the next six months watching the habitat grow as did her relationship with Ray. The work on the primate habitat was complete a mere two weeks behind schedule. The workers would have been done on-time, in fact ahead of schedule, if not for the damaging Kansas storm that blew through during a 100-degree week in summer. But all was well now, and all hearts were light as the autumn of 1994 approached.

Karen was beginning her second year of high-school and after all the grand-opening ceremonies of the new primate house, now called the Kingston Building, Helen further took Karen under her wing. They spent a day together, just the two girls, driving and shopping at an outlet mall near Abilene. They talked of many things on their ride and most of those talks eventually led back to Ray. Karen opened up about her fear of dating and bringing a boy home one day to meet her dad. Helen said that is a fear all girls her age face, but it is almost always unwarranted.

"When the time is right, when you meet a boy that you feel is worthy of dating you, your father will be very warm to him. I'll even drop a hint to him that that day is just around the corner. You'll be surprised at what a little puppy your dad can be."

"Wolf, Helen. A wolf. I know he can be a puppy to me, but I think he'll forever be a wolf to anyone I date. Anyway, that day isn't anytime soon, much less around any corner. You have time to mellow the wolf for me."

"Consider it done."

With Karen in school for the better part of most days, Ray and Helen had ample time to be alone and their relationship grew. Helen, without trying, was taming the wild wolf in Ray. They walked and talked for hours, discussing Karen's future often, and also spending time walking without the need for words. Most days, mornings were filled with riding at the zoo stables and evenings filled around dinner and family discussions between the three soul mates.

Time passed and almost every month either Ray or Helen made the trip to visit the other. Ray and Helen become closer and closer and Karen, with Helen's help, developed into the young lady Ray always hoped that she would. Karen looked every bit a lady, but still hadn't cleared the final hurdle, dating.

Karen was seventeen when she began her senior year in high school. Helen suggested that she and Karen go to LA for a ladies only weekend in the big city. Karen asked her father and quickly and surprisingly he gave his blessing. The ladies shopped, dined around the strip, and Karen had a complete makeover in a sophisticated salon in Hollywood. Helen also took Karen to the campuses of UCLA and USC so Karen could begin to think about college enrollment. Her grades in the small high school were near the top of the class and the money Ray had in the bank could send 100 students to college.

Karen returned home to Ray very much an adult. Her excitement could not be weathered as she talked non-stop about the shops, the bustle of people, the schools she couldn't wait to attend, and as she put it, "The absolutely delicious taste of red wine."

Ray was happy, speechless, but happy. His daughter was a lady now and with college on the horizon she was destined to be the success he hoped she would be. He tried to find the words, but knew if he talked emotion would best him. He stared at his daughter in silence, drifting.

CHAPTER 20

"Time to get up Dad. My god you slept like a rock. Good dreams I hope."

Ray sat up in bed and stared once again at his daughter. Words were not available, but thoughts simmered. Yes, this was his daughter, going from the little girl that made life livable for him into this beautiful lady. He was right to suspect that Helen would put his mind right and he wondered where she was now.

"We're going home. I don't see any reason to go to Kansas City and see more doctors. You keep improving at the pace you've done this week and you'll be fine. I was wrong to bring you here."

Ray got dressed quickly, on his own using his left arm pretty well. When all dressed, he came out of the bathroom, looked at Karen, and said, "Home." It was as clear as he had said anything since his stroke.

"Home." It was as clear as Karen had heard anything in the same timeframe.

They were home by noon and Ray rushed through the house in search of Helen. Not finding her he changed clothes and went out to the barn to saddle a couple of horses. Only one of the horses he sought was there so Ray saddled him up and rode off to find the other that he was sure Helen was now riding. He rode into the sun fighting images of a melting landscape that tried to enter his mind.

He thought he heard Blackie call him and he turned to see nothing behind him. He looked back ahead, and he knew that it was Helen and the horse Wildflower that he saw gallop into the forest.

He rode quickly and disappeared between the same trees that his mind's eye saw Helen go by. He hadn't been in this part of the woods for some time and he was instantly lost. Lost in time, space, and place. He dismounted to find unsteady legs beneath him, his horse looked different and the trees seemed to close in around him. Dizziness followed and Ray's head seemed to be on fire, heating up from the inside until he collapsed trail-side, shivering with cold throughout his body while his mind burned.

Ray saw Helen come out of the woods and dismount her horse. She sat beside Ray and a brave Ray took Helen's hand in his. Ray leaned and kissed Helen on the lips, longer than he ever had before.

"Do you like Wildflower?" Ray asked Helen. He purchased the horse for her this past winter and had worked hard at riding and training him so that he could give the beautiful pinto to Helen on her spring visit. It was part of her birthday present from Ray and Karen and along with Fred and a couple of ladies from the zoo they had a wonderful party and celebration culminating in the Lupus barn with the surprise gift to Helen of Wildflower. Tears of happiness followed and more than one bottle of wine was consumed that night.

Ray and Helen rode as often as they could for the two weeks that Helen was visiting. Helen came to Kansas each spring the two previous years, but this year's spring visit had special meaning for Helen and the Lupus'. Karen's graduation loomed and before that Karen would be attending her senior dance with Ken Badderling. Ken and Ray hadn't met yet as Karen and Ken hadn't dated yet. Ken was as shy as Karen and his asking her to the dance shocked Karen. She answered yes before Ken was done asking.

Karen wanted her father to meet Ken before the dance and asked Helen if the meeting could take place during Helen's visit. Helen was honored and understanding of Karen's fears, telling her, "Yes, it should be no other way."

Helen prepped Ray on how to act to Ken emphasizing how important it was to Karen. An anxious Ray said that he understood. The first date for Karen and Ken was to be dinner with Ray, Helen, and of course Fred. Ken had every right to feel that they were ganging up on him, but that wasn't the case. Karen was the center of Ray's life, became the same to Fred over 10 years ago, and was now becoming the same to Helen. All felt a need to look over and protect Karen.

Ken got quite the once over at dinner that night and did himself proud. He spoke of a desire to join the military after high school and satisfy a longing to see the world. He mentioned his parents were not supportive of his idea to say the least and were in fact rather outspoken against the plan. Fred understood exactly what Ken was going through and told Ray and Karen that as long as Ken was good to Karen he had his blessing. Karen kissed Fred on the cheek and danced into the living room to sit with Ken. Sensing Ken's uneasiness, Karen asked her father if they could go out for a walk.

"A walk," Ray said in a tone that seemed to say that he didn't know what a walk was. He was silent after that and just looked at the young couple.

"Of course, you two can go out for a walk," Helen said to ease the tension. "Ray stop teasing the kids. Why would they want to sit here with us three old folks?"

"Because we're fun," Fred added jokingly. "We could play a game of charades."

"Now you're talking Fred!" Ray said without any joking in his voice.

"Dad."

"They're teasing you Karen," Helen said, again lightening the mood. "You kids go out and enjoy the evening. Take your walk or a drive. Right, Ray?"

"I guess it's okay. Just be home by ten."

When the kids left, Ray, Fred, and Helen talked about the couple. Fred and Helen tried to make Ray relax and explained to him that Ken seemed like a good kid and it was the natural flow of things for Karen to begin dating, a little slow in that regard Helen added.

"You don't want Karen to end up like us three sad sacks do you Ray?" Fred said.

"Speak for yourself, Freddie," Helen said, "I'm happier than I've ever been. A little old perhaps, but happy nonetheless."

"And we are too," Ray said directly at Fred, "both of us are very happy. The kids could learn a lot hanging around with us."

"There's no hope for you Ray," Helen told him, "but you must be supportive of Karen. Her senior dance is the biggest thing in her life right now and she's excited. You raised a happy, well-mannered daughter, be proud. But she's a lady now, you have to let her be herself. You've told me often that that is what you wish for her, now loosen up. She'll always love you, but there is room in her heart for others."

"Sounds right to me," a supportive Fred said.

"I just don't want anyone to hurt her."

"Hurt is part of life, it's is always lurking. Leave it lurk, enjoy today with your family. Share the happiness Karen feels today. It will make for a happier tomorrow".

Fred excused himself and headed home to his wolf overlook, Ray and Helen went to bed. Ray tossed and turned for the next hour or so, but Karen was home exactly at ten.

"You can sleep now," said a smiling Helen.

"And you too, I see," answered Ray.

Ray was sitting at the breakfast table with Helen when Karen awoke and gave her a nervous look. Helen touched his hand and turned to Karen, "How did you sleep Karen?'

"Not well. I guess my head was full of Ken." She saw her father's jaw tighten and head lower. "But that's all over now," she quickly added. "Time to take care of things around here. Can I use the car Dad?" She borrowed the car and drove to town just to relax in the city park and let her thoughts drift unimpeded.

Helen cleaned up the kitchen from breakfast, cleaned the living room from the night before and changed into her riding clothes. Ray went to the barn to saddle the horses; he long looked forward to this ride around home as opposed to the zoo trail rides he and Helen had been doing. He put a new saddle on Wildflower that he had bought for Helen and when Helen entered the barn, Wildflower looked like a million dollar show horse.

Helen kissed Ray and mounted her horse, Ray followed, and off they went to little Lake Michigan and a ride into the woods. The horses walked slowly to the lake while Ray and Helen made small talk about the kids. Helen promised to come back to Kansas for the dance which was less than a month away. Ray wanted to tell Helen that perhaps it was nearing time that she moved to Kansas, but he couldn't find the words or the strength to speak the words if he did happen to stumble onto them.

In short order they reached the lake and Helen said, "Let's let the horses run, try to keep up." She gave Wildflower reign and he took off around the lake. Ray sat watching and smiling as Helen's hair flew behind her matching the flight of Wildflower's tail. After her run around the lake she passed Ray and called again for him to follow. His smile grew as he loved seeing Helen having such a good time. Instead of going around the lake again, Helen and Wildflower darted into the woods.

The smile left Ray's face and he called Helen's name as loud as he could. He gave his horse a little kick and they galloped into the woods following the trail that Wildflower cut. Ray couldn't see either of them, there were too many trees, too many rocks and boulders, the small creek ahead was running low and Ray headed there, his horse taking slow deliberate steps.

Before he reached the creek, he heard Wildflower's cries carried by the wind. He didn't see anything until he was practically on top of both of them, Wildflower lying on his side in the low water of the creek, Helen lying face down on its west bank. Ray jumped off his horse long before it came to a stop and lifted Helen from the creek bed. Her head dangled back as if on a string, her arms and legs lifeless. Ray carried Helen up the creek bank and laid her in the short grass. He called her name over and over but there was no response.

He ran to his horse and took their picnic blanket out of the saddle bag, rolling it up and placing under Helen's head and neck. Her breathing was labored, but Helen was still with him, fighting for life. Wildflower's cries of pain and terror echoed behind Ray, as the injured horse tried unsuccessfully to get up. Wildflower held his right front leg in the air and Ray could see the bottom of the leg dangle uselessly from Wildflower's strong thigh. The sight made Ray sick as he ran further into the woods to vomit and scream with his own anger and pain.

He ran back to Helen and begged her to wake up to no avail. The storm of confusion ran through Ray's head, he struggled to figure out his next step and only realized that he would find no answer in his mind. In panic he jumped back on his horse and raced to the house. He called Karen over and over again, forgetting totally that she left the horse this morning. He grabbed his shotgun and shells and placed the 911 call before heading back to the creek. He kicked his horse harder and harder, dust flying behind the pair as they disappeared once again into the woods.

The scene that Ray returned to was the exact scene he left. Before returning to Helen, Ray put a shell in the gun and with shaking head and closed eyes ended the suffering of Wildflower. He then moved to Helen and kneeled next to her body. Breaths were still coming slowly, not going deep into her, strange sounds came from her throat.

"Help is coming Helen, please stay with me."

Helen's eyes opened and she looked through him. "No Ray." The two words exhausted her as she struggled for more air.

"Helen, you're alright," Ray said as he lifted her head and removed the blanket that was under it. He wiped the dust and dirt from the creek off of Helen's face and put the blanket back under her.

Helen lay motionless. "No", she said again. She knew what had befallen her, and she knew what awaited her. She couldn't go on like this and she summoned every ounce of strength to make her point to Ray. Breathing came hard and Helen chose each word carefully, she knew she only had a few words left before someone would come and strap her to a board and put her into a bed that she would never leave, not if she lived to a thousand. Never leave the prison of a hospital bed. Nothing ran through her body now except panic and she needed Ray one more time.

"Over," she began. A minute later, "End it".

"End what Helen? Us? I want to marry you Helen, I should have asked you sooner, I'm sorry. Marry me Helen."

Helen's head had hit the riverbank as square and hard as possible, she was certain she had broken her neck. "No. Life over. Finish me. Hurry"

Ray looked down at Helen, saw the tears in her eyes, felt her pain, finally realized that she couldn't move, he finally realized what she was asking. "Kill you Helen?"

"Yes."

"I can't Helen. Help is coming. You'll be okay. Stay with me."

"Kill. End this. Hurry." Each word took longer and longer to say. "Never ...move ... again."

"I can't."

"If love … must."

Ray could hear the sirens reach the house. They would never find him here, he had to go back and bring help here. Ray twisted inside himself, he had no idea what to do. He begged Helen to stay with him, but she never spoke again. She was all but gone.

He took the blanket one more time and unrolled it to fit softly over Helen's now peaceful face. He laid beside her, his left arm now under her head. His large hand covered and squeezed her face through the blanket stopping all air from reaching her. She never moved, never struggled, never spoke or moaned.

After a few minutes Ray removed the blanket and saw the peace in Helen's face. It was over. Ray shook the dust off of the blanket and rinsed it off in the creek to make it cool for Helen. He re-rolled it one last time and positioned Helen's head as softly as he could upon it. He kissed her goodbye and mounted his horse.

He started riding to the house very slowly and then suddenly broke into a reckless pace flying by the trees, rocks and the little lake before reaching the house. He jumped off his horse and yelled at the paramedics. "She's not moving, hurry. We need to run there, the car won't make it through the woods."

The paramedics grabbed a few things and followed Ray as they all ran to the ugly scene at the creek. A horse lay dead in the water, a lady lied dead on the banks. Ray stayed back and watched the paramedics work. They saw the blanket rolled behind her head, they saw the place in the mud where they knew Helen must have landed, they knew that Ray moved her way too often. The older paramedic thinking out loud said loud enough to be heard. "You shouldn't have done this Ray."

Ray was sick and the admonishment from the paramedic could not make him any sicker. He did what he had to do, what Helen wanted him to do. He kneeled down and got physically sick again. The paramedics whispered to one another and closed their bags, they walked back to Ray.

"Sorry Ray, she's gone. We couldn't do anything."

Ray knew Helen's fate, he now waited knowingly for his. What did the paramedic just say? "You shouldn't have done this". No mistaking that, not even to a shocked Ray Lupus.

"Now what?" Ray asked coldly.

"This was a bad accident Ray," the chief paramedic told him, "and I don't want to add to your pain, but there has to be an inquest, an autopsy, the coroner has to list an exact cause of death. We can pretty much see how this happened, but it would be helpful if you told us in your words. It's what needs to be done."

Ray felt pretty sure that he knew what they wanted to hear, but he learned a long time ago that it was usually better to say nothing. "I don't know what I could tell you. I can't talk now. Can you leave me alone, at least for a while?"

"It will just take a few minutes, then we can get you away from here before we take Helen out. Maybe you can just answer some questions to fill in the blanks. Would that be alright by you?"

"Okay. If we have to."

"You rode with her back here?"

"No, she rode ahead."

"Was she riding quickly or in a gallop?"

"Too fast, way too fast."

"How far behind were you Ray?"

Ray thought about the question and wondered if he should answer. His eyes glassed over.

"Ray?" The confused paramedic called. "You okay?"

"I'm sorry. What was the question?"

"How long after Helen rode back here did you ride back?"

"Minutes. Maybe 3. Maybe 5. Not 10, I don't think."

"Let's just say minutes later then. And her horse was down and she was in the creek over here?" he asked pointing to the depressed area on the bank. "Face down I'm guessing, is that right Ray?"

"Yes."

The young paramedic whispered to his boss, "This is taking forever, he's probably in shock, he's not very helpful."

"No, but I can get this done, it's all right in front of us."

"You lifted her out of the creek, and carried her to this spot."

"Yes. Her name's Helen you know."

"You carried *Helen* here and wiped the mud from the creek off of her face. You used the blanket and then put it under her head."

"Yes."

"Then you went to the house and called us, came back here and Helen was gone. Then you came back to the house and met us. That's about it isn't it?"

"I killed..." Ray started only to be interrupted by the paramedic.

"Yes, you killed the horse. I have that noted, you did the right thing. You know when I said that you shouldn't have done this, I didn't mean anything about the horse. I spoke out of turn. I was referring to Helen. I saw that you moved her and lifted her head to put the blanket underneath. Usually with falls like this, we wouldn't want to move the head at all, that's what I meant. You couldn't leave Helen lying in the water, I know that. You did what you had to do."

"Yes, I believe I did," answered a stunned Ray.

"We have to take Helen to the county coroner, there will be some tests they have to do. In accidents like this there are always tests. Someone will get back to you. Are you the contact for Helen when the coroner's done?"

"I'll have Fred Grant call you. This is all beyond me."

"Have Fred make the call. You should go, we have to get Helen's body out of here. We'll wait until you're gone."

Ray returned to the house and sat beside the phone for hours. He watched the paramedics put a dark bag containing Helen into the ambulance. He watched in stunned silence as the ambulance slowly pulled away. He moved to the phone to call Fred but just sat there for the next 2 hours. Before he made the call, Karen pulled up to the house and ran in excited.

"Dad, Helen, I got some great news. Are you two home? Dad?"

The news which wasn't really very much at all, just about her dress for the dance, would have to wait. Karen saw a statuesque father sitting beside the living room phone and knew instantly that something was wrong.

"What's wrong?"

The blank stare that Karen knew too well was back on Ray's face. He reached out and pushed the hair back away from Karen's face.

"Oh no," said a knowing daughter, "Who is it? Where's Fred? Where's Helen. Damn it, say something."

"Helen had an accident, she fell off her horse." Ray went on to describe the fall as best he could including the part of Helen flying head first into the bank. He stopped at the part of his hand covering her face and ended his story quickly. "She's gone."

Ray fell silent and hung his head down. Karen fell apart and ran to her room. Ray sat beside the phone unable to call Fred. As darkness crept into the home, Fred pulled up quickly, almost in a panic and rushed into the house. Ray was still where he sat hours ago.

"Ray I just got a call from the county coroner, what happened? You okay?"

"Helen's gone. I'm not supposed to love anyone, I guess. I cause these things."

"They said she had a riding accident, that's not your fault. Don't talk foolish. What exactly happened?"

"She rode Wildflower way too quickly this morning. She looked beautiful Fred with her hair flying in the breeze behind her. I think she was showing off, having fun, you know. She flew by me and yelled at me to join her. I was just amazed at her beauty and watched her ride. I thought she was going to turn around and run by the lake, but she went straight into the woods. I waited for her to return, but she never did. I got scared; she was going too fast for a forest ride. I followed her trail and saw her lying in the little creek about a quarter mile in, she wasn't moving. It was over, her life, my life, our life before we even got one. All over."

"Nothing's over. You have to pick up the pieces and move on. I know it sounds cold Ray, but I understand these things and I know you. You won't mourn well, I'm sorry. You have to move on as best you can. No anger Ray. Does Karen know?"

"Yes. She's been in her room a long time."

"I'll check on her. I'll be right back."

Fred went to talk to Karen and Ray went into his room not wanting to talk any more to anyone. He locked his door behind him and curled up within himself on the bed. When Fred found Ray gone, he returned to Karen's dark bedroom.

"Your father's gone to bed, probably best. He's confused, beaten right now. This is probably the worst thing that's happened to him since your mother died. It's going to take a while for him to recover."

"I was pretty young when my mom died, but I don't remember my father being lost. He probably put up a good front for my benefit. I think he was mad at my grandparents though, I have a faint memory of them arguing while my mom was in the damn coffin. I didn't even know what death was back then. I wish I didn't know what it is now. This hurts Fred, hurts bad."

"You call me if you need anything. Call me on my car phone line. I have to go see the coroner, he has questions."

"What kind of questions?"

"He has to list an official cause of death and when he's done with that, he'll need to send Helen for burial some place. When I know his schedule, I'll call Helen's office in Tulsa, they'll put me in touch with her family. I'll handle that, you and your father have been through enough. Have your moment alone now, I'll let myself out. You call if you need anything or if your father starts acting strange."

Fred cried his tears as he drove the 45 minutes to the coroner's office. He was cried out when he got there and by pre-arrangement, Sam Collins, the county coroner/pathologist was waiting for him. Fred wanted to see Helen, but as soon as Sam pulled her body out of the refrigerated crypt, he wished he hadn't.

After a painful, "Oh my God" Fred left the room and returned with Sam to the coroner's office. Fred took another minute or so to compose himself and then the men talked.

"I have some problems here Fred," said a concerned Dr. Sam Collins, "or what I should really say is I think Ray Lupus is going to have some problems here."

"I'm not following you doc. What type of problems?"

"Well Fred, what happened to Helen was a spinal cord injury due to her fall from her horse. There's no question about that. The paramedics saw where the horse went down, where Helen landed, and where Ray carried her. The level of injury is what I had to look at here. The cervical spine is made up of seven bones, C1 to C7 vertebrae separated by intervertebral discs."

"Hang on doc, I'm just a common man here."

"Yes Fred, a common man with a billion dollars."

"Well I can't handle 50 cent words Sam, give it to me in nickels."

"As I was saying, Helen injured her spinal cord and my x-rays showed the main damage at C5 causing difficulty breathing, and what we would call a spinal concussion at C4 and C5 causing paralysis."

"What you're saying is she died from a broken neck. Except for us losing a great person, where's the problem?"

"Well she didn't die from a broken neck. The broken blood

vessels in her eyes was what jumped out at me. That, and the onset of cyanosis; she was turning blue Fred. I still have some tests in progress,"

"Enough already," Fred interrupted, "what are you getting to?"

"Helen suffocated, no doubt about it."

"Are you saying Ray did something?"

"No, no. Not at all. He just didn't do anything right, that's about as nice as I can put it. The paramedics told me that Ray wasn't too helpful when they questioned him, that he was in a bad state of shock, that's understandable. But I'm able to put this together pretty clearly. Helen's horse went down in the creek, bad break of the leg, Helen flew over him, headfirst into the creek. Her head hit first causing the incomplete spinal injury. She unfortunately landed at the edge of the water, her mouth at or below the water line, her nose and the rest of her face covered in mud with water continually lapping at her. The concussion of the spine caused a temporary, I'm pretty sure temporary, state of paralysis, she was at that moment a quadriplegic. Helen couldn't breathe and didn't have the ability to move. She died of asphyxiation in the creek.

"When Ray found her, she was lying in the creek face down. He had to get her out, but he probably did so in a quick manner, not paying attention to the neck injuries. Not wrong by any means , but not exactly right either. He then laid her on the bank and used this blanket that one of them brought along." Sam showed Fred the picnic blanket. "The paramedics said that it was very wet when they got there. Ray must have soaked it in the creek and used the wet blanket to wipe the mud off of Helen's face. If he did that carefully it would have been the right thing to do, but I doubt that was the case. Anyway, after he cleaned away the mud, he must have soaked the blanket again to clean it or make it cool for Helen and he rolled it up and put it under her head. Again, in the case of a broken neck this was a wrong thing to do, but again, understandable, so not wrong, but not right by any means. Ray tried to save Helen but his actions were harmful in the long run."

"You said that Ray had a problem. What exactly is his problem?"

"He is in shock right now and I'm worried about him. You see, if Ray would have gone after Helen as soon as she went into the woods and been there from the fall, he could have done everything just as he did, and I believe Helen would have made a full recovery. He just needed to clear her air passages right away, the 3 or 4 minutes of lost time is the time Helen died. Ray's problem is that I don't think he will be able to handle life with that knowledge. The Ray I know lives in a simple world. Something goes wrong he acts to fix it right then and there, no questions asked. Someone does something he doesn't approve of, he stops them, without words. That's Ray's way. If he thinks he acted wrong here he may be moved to do something."

"You're on the money."

"If he finds out that Helen could have been saved, I'm not sure what he would do. I'm talking suicide, but how could any of us know that. I mean he does have his daughter, maybe she would keep him grounded. I don't know."

"He could take Karen and leave, he's done that before. They're all the family I have, I couldn't take them leaving, but I couldn't lie to Ray and Karen. The truth will have to stand on its own, wish it could be different."

"I'm not suggesting we lie, there are just some things here that need go no further. I told you everything and maybe I shouldn't have. Speculating that Helen would have lived and made a full recovery is fool's work. It was just a guess on my part, thinking out loud and too loud at that. The truth is that Helen died of asphyxiation caused by spinal cord damage suffered in a horse-riding accident. Ray may dig more if he comprehends that news and his problems may really begin then. For now, I think it's as much of the truth as he can handle. Let it be."

"If it's for Ray's and Karen's benefit, I'll let it be. I just could never lie to them. I hope this ends here, but I don't feel very well right now. I'll call Helen's family, I can get that info from her office and then I'll put them in touch with you."

Sometime after noon the next day, Fred showed up at the Lupus home, he was followed by a backhoe and the zoo truck. He left his car at the house and jumped into the truck, they disappeared down the road and headed toward the lake and the woods. About thirty minutes later Fred walked back to Ray's house letting himself in as he always did.

Ray sat at the kitchen table almost lifeless and when Karen heard Fred enter, she came out to greet him.

"Hi Fred, good to see you today. Just checking in on us?"

"Yes, that and I have our zoo crew picking up Wildflower right now. We can't leave him in the woods. The crew will take him back to the zoo. I thought we would just visit while they do their work."

"Lunch?" Karen asked the two of them. "I'll make some something, you guys relax."

Karen put some fruit salad, bread, and cheese on the table along with a pitcher of iced tea. Fred heard the backhoe and truck rambling down the road and turned on some music in the house. They ate without conversation listening to whatever Fred turned on the radio.

After lunch, Ray said he wanted to take a walk to the woods, he needed to. Karen said she would join them later and watched the men amble down the road. Fred talked slowly as they walked, choosing his words carefully, explaining to Ray where things stood now.

"I talked to Helen's office staff this morning, they took the news very hard. Do you know Helen's receptionist, Mary I think she said?"

"Marie. Yes, I know her. Very sweet."

"She gave me Helen's family info, sister and mom are all she had left."

"They're in Stillwater. I've been there a few times." After a few seconds Ray added, "never again I guess."

"I talked to them too. They're in a bad way now also, but they send you their prayers. They said Helen really loved you."

"She would have been better off if she didn't, don't you think?"

"No way, and you quit talking like that. Helen deserves to be remembered as she was, and she was happily in love with you. Don't take that away from her."

"I took her life from her. I can't do any worse than that."

"Life comes with death. Every day we live, it is out there looking for us. One day it finds us. You had nothing to do with her death. If you offered Helen a safe vault to hide in and never do the things you enjoy, she would have dropped you as fast as humanly possible. She lived and loved. Don't make her in death what she wasn't in life."

"I know what you're saying and I only meant that I may be the bad seed. People close to me don't seem to live too long."

"Now you're talking like a child. I'm close to you and I'm over sixty. Karen's close to you and she has years of happiness under her belt and a lot more to come. You go ahead and mourn, but you mourn right. Celebrate the life Helen had. I think we should take to the road, there's a wildlife sanctuary near Denver I want us to visit, some things there we may be able to learn from."

"You always want to take me on the road when things are bad. Why is that?"

"Well let me tell you a little story. One day, over ten years ago, I was leaving the zoo to go home. I lived in these parts back then."

"I guess you did," Ray added glibly.

"There was a pick-up parked in the lot. I went over to see if there was anything wrong. It turned out to be a rather large, somewhat decent man, travelling with a rather small extremely sweet daughter."

"A somewhat decent man?"

"Somewhat. Anyhow on that day I met what would become the closet friend I've ever had, so close, I dare say, we became family."

"And that is why you want to take me on the road?"

"You were running that day too if you remember. You had a bad death in Chicago and your answer was to run. You've had a bad death or two here Ray and your answer may just to be run again. At least if I'm running with you, I might be able to bring you back. And by being a pain in your butt as we travel, I give you all the more reason to get back home."

"Well I shouldn't tell you this, because I love our road trips and I should leave you with your reasons for getting us away, but I'm done running Fred, I'm home. This is where Karen and I belong."

"Then a road trip it is, just for the sake of the road."

"Not right away. There's a lot going on in Karen's life right now and I can't drop the ball. Helen and I picked out a car for her, sort of a graduation gift, I want to take her to buy that. Then she has the dance that Helen has her all ready for and of course the graduation itself. After that maybe, and before Karen goes away to college. I'm going to drive her in her new car to USC and fly back, she'll need a car in LA."

"We'll go in July then, just long enough to let things settle for you."

They reached the lake at the end of the Lupus property and Ray froze staring into the woods. Fred walked a few yards away giving Ray some space and threw small pebbles into the lake.

"I'm going to walk on further Fred; it might be a good idea if you went back to the zoo to make sure they're doing right by Wildflower. Do you think Wildflower is too feminine a name for him?

"No not at all."

"I thought of naming him Brown Bagger in keeping with your creative color scheme."

"I like that too."

"You know that there was not one spring or summer morning in all the days I spent with Helen that she didn't start each morning by picking wildflowers to brighten up the house. Never too many; just always the perfect number. And Helen knows which flowers are near the end of their time, she only picks those." Ray seemed almost to be talking to himself now as Fred stood still and quit tossing rocks, a quizzical look on his face. "Lots of flowers in full bloom now, we'll have to thin those beds, brighten the house you know. Helen will know which to pick, don't you worry yourself none."

"Ray." Fred called slowly, calmly. "Look at me Ray. Are you okay?"

Ray turned his stare away from the woods and met Fred's eyes. Both men were silent for a second. Ray tilted his head as if to say 'now what'. Ray shook his head no and turned his palms skyward.

"You better go. I need to face this, maybe only once but I need to face this. I did bad."

"We had this talk and it's over. Face your demons and let them go. I can walk the woods with you if you'd like."

"I'm good, I'll see you later."

Fred walked back to the house and his car; Ray walked into the woods, unsure of every step he took. He picked up a long, thin switch from the path in front of him and swung at imaginary insects as he walked. A few steps beyond the trees that lined the beginning of the forest he hesitated and looked for a friend among the birds in the trees. He tossed aside the switch and continued to the creek. He saw the place where Wildflower fell and eventually died at his hands. Ray could still feel the shotgun blast hurl him back from the creek. He saw the spot where Helen landed and the knoll that he had thought would keep her safe. He thought he saw the imprint of his knees where he kneeled and eventually took Helen's life also. Ray got sick and cried out as he vomited over the death scene.

Ray felt every bit animal at the moment - one who sees life being struggled for by a weaker being and ends it, swoops down like a vulture and just ends it. Helen saw struggles, illness, and pain and chased them all away. She was a giver of life. Ray was a taker of life and he damn well knew it. He started back to the house and collapsed under the weight of admitting what he was, a monster whose thought process went from A to B and never any further, with B meaning death to those with maladies that Ray couldn't understand.

Under the tree where Ray had fallen, he found temporary peace as he fell asleep in a mental fog. No dreams came to Ray, he lay there an empty shell reenergizing his body for its next calling. There was no longer any right and wrong, only beginnings and ends. Nothing ever lasted long around Ray Lupus.

CHAPTER 21

A worried Karen hurried into the woods and saw her father lying in the weeds.

"Dad, oh God dad wake-up. You've been out here forever, it's getting dark."

Karen helped Ray to sit up and looked into his glossed over eyes. Ray looked deep into Karen's eyes and began to panic. He touched her face and simply said, "You".

"Yes, me. Who were you expecting?"

Ray looked around himself studying the woods. His agitation was growing by the second. He heard the creek and stopped frozen, looking back at Karen.

"Helen," he shouted as clearly and loudly as he had anything since his stroke. "Helen."

"Helen? Helen's been dead for over ten years. Is that why you're in here?"

"Helen," Ray repeated and then repeated again over and over. He jumped up nearly knocking Karen down and ran into the creek. He paused where he shot Wildflower years ago and moved to where he found Helen lying in the creek. He turned around and around, lost, scared and then ran over to where he ended Helen's life.

"Helen was here," Ray tried to say to Karen. "Put," he added, and no more words came clearly. He started to smooth over the ground, slowly at first and then his paced quickened. Soon he was feverishly smoothing out the dirt trying to say, "Bring", but his speech was garbled.

Then for some reason, or perhaps for no reason, Ray started punching the dirt where Helen died. Again, and again he hammered his fist raw with his punches. Karen came over and shook her dad from behind.

"Stop it Dad, stop it. Helen's dead, we can't bring her back."

Ray pushed Karen away with his ever-strengthening bad arm and continued punching. Karen returned and threw both arms around Ray's neck, screaming loudly for him to stop.

In what seemed an eternity to Karen, Ray finally stopped and bent forward putting his face on the ground. Eventually, Karen got Ray to his feet and walked him home. She took him to his room and for lack of any knowledge about what better to do, gave him a short glass of bourbon. Once Ray settled down, she left him with his music and hurried to the phone to call Dr. March in Kansas City. His answering service picked-up and said they would get Karen's message to the doctor immediately. Less than ten minutes later, Dr. March called back.

Karen, fighting back tears, recounted the events of the evening. Dr. March listened patiently and when Karen was done speaking, March replied with questions and observations, some necessary, some not.

"I wish you would have brought Ray up here Karen, it's hard to diagnose, even harder to treat over the phone."

"Dad's just all over the place. One minute he's smiling at me or out walking, the next he doesn't know who I am or where he's at, at least not with regard to time. I thought this passed and that's why we didn't drive to Kansas City. Don't make me justify that again, just help me."

"Okay, it's late, I'm going to phone in a strong prescription for Ray, some pills that should knock him out pretty soundly for the evening and a prescription for meds to help keep him calm during the day. You get them tonight, I'll phone the pharmacist in your town. I have all Ray's info here. Tomorrow morning, I will meet with the doctors that have already discussed Ray's status and we'll study our notes again adding this latest episode. You keep him calm tonight and tomorrow and I'll phone you from our meeting, probably by 11 tomorrow morning. Do you think he will be okay while you're out for meds?"

"Of course," Karen replied. "He won't even know I'm gone. I'll go get the meds now. Reilly Drug; it's on First Street. Everything's on First Street. Talk to you tomorrow doc, the earlier the better, I'll be here."

"Goodbye Karen. Try to get some rest for yourself too."

The review group of doctors met early in the morning. After a quick review and coffee the call was placed to Karen Lupus. After a courtesy hello and small talk Dr. March put Karen on speaker and asked about Ray's night.

"The drugs calmed him down, I think he slept all night and I started him off this morning with the day pills you prescribed. He's sleeping still, or maybe I should say he's sleeping again. He was up for maybe an hour earlier."

"That's a lot of sleep from those pills, he must have been exhausted. One pill last night, one this morning?"

"No, he took one last night with his bourbon, I told him that was a questionable choice, and two of the little blue ones this morning."

"I would like you to cut back on that, it may be too much. We only wish to calm your father a bit. And I would hide the bourbon, but I understand your efforts to relax him."

"Relax him for a while if I can, until he's back to normal and knows where he's at. What does your group think of his condition right now?"

"We'll my intern, Dr. Lou Biscuit, wants to look at fugues some more. He believes some form of flight is taking place even if it isn't physical."

"Biscuit? You have a Dr. Biscuit on staff?"

"Yes Karen. Dr. Biscuit why don't you explain your theory again."

"Hello Karen," Dr. Biscuit began, "I did a lot of research on fugues and on dissociative disorders and I've studied various forms of schizophrenia. I want …"

Karen interrupted the doctor, "Schizophrenia? I thought you were stretching with your fugues thing, but this is really crazy."

"It's a personal theory of mine that schizophrenia should not be looked at as simply multiple personalities, I believe in multiple timelines. Split yes, two different times and two Ray Lupus's, one we see plainly, one hiding everything. I know that you said your father has nothing to hide, but he may be hiding something that is not even real to us but is torturing him."

"Biscuit syndrome?" Karen asked sarcastically.

"Let me interrupt for a second," Dr. March quickly said sensing the sarcasm, "we do need to consider all theories, some of these disorders can lead to violence, some to a patient fleeing his physical surroundings, and some, as we hope for here, are treated very successfully with today's medicine. We must identify an illness before we can treat it."

"Sorry. Continue Dr. Biscuit."

"If we had Ray here in Kansas City, we could do a new CAT scan or MRI and see if there is something more happening physically in his brain, TIAs, mini-strokes, swelling, or bleeding, that would explain a lot. If none of that is happening, then we have a mental disorder caused by the original stroke or as I want us to consider, caused by the actual healing and rewiring of Ray's brain. As he recalls his past, he just may be looking for a way back into it or he may be running away and trying to hide from it. This latest episode which included pushing you and punching away at the ground should be bothering everyone. Ray has reached a bad point in his recollections. I fear for your safety."

"That's crazy too, it was an innocent reaction."

"I think that's extreme too Lou," said Dr. March. "I don't see a real danger here. Karen you said that Helen died over ten years ago. Obviously that was a low in Ray's life and if in his mind it just happened yesterday, is he back in a particularly bad time, one that he had a hard time handling then and just may have an even harder time handling now?"

"No, that's not possible. Dad always could handle death. He handled Helen's death and became more protective of me if anything, more loving. He was fine immediately after her death, at least in the short term he was fine. He bought me a new car right after the accident, he said that Helen helped pick it out, that's how well Dad handled her death."

"And after that?" March asked.

"It was a special time, for me anyhow. I just started dating Kenny and we were going to the senior dance together. Graduation was coming right after that and then college. Dad was planning on driving me and my car to LA that September."

Karen stopped talking quickly as she saw her father listening at his bedroom door, bottle of bourbon in his hand.

"I have to go," Karen said into the phone, and before anyone could reply she hung-up on the doctors.

"Good morning Dad, you're finally up. Do you know it's nearly noon?"

"No dance Karen."

"What?" Karen was confused, happy that her dad was talking more, scared at his choice of words.

"No dance!" Ray shouted as loudly as he was able.

Karen was scared. She grabbed the bottle of tranquilizers, the day pills, and took two out for Ray handing them to him gingerly. "Take these; I'm not going to the dance."

Ray took the pills and swallowed them down with his bourbon. "No dance," he repeated as he walked out the door and headed down the path to the lake. He sat down in his chair with his bottle standing proud on his armrest. *I must be tougher*, he thought to himself and corroborated the thought with a good swallow of bourbon. The lake before Ray began to spin in his eyes and he sat uneasily in his chair. His bottle went out of focus and Ray knocked it to the ground when he tried to get another drink. He reached for the bottle that he could no longer see, hand flailing in the grass, images spinning wildly, dancing and melting in Ray's head. The foreseeable blackout took Ray back, again.

"I don't want to go to the dance, we've been over this."

"We've all wanted this for you for some time, we even had Ken over for a visit, he's expecting to go. Helen looked forward to it so much for you. 'Your little girl is growing up Ray,' she would tell me. Let's not make Helen's death worse by not doing the things she wanted us to do. If not for me Karen, if not for your mother, then at least for Helen and for yourself. Have some fun, it's been a rough month."

"Okay, I'll go." She put her hand up in front of her father's face, her way of saying 'enough', and shook her head as she left the room.

Linda Reynolds, one of the longtime staff members at the zoo, helped Karen prepare. Linda was a sweet older lady who had been with Fred at the zoo almost from its inception. She had known Ray and Karen from their arrival when Karen was just a child. She added the final touches that Helen had been preparing Karen for. A day at the beauty parlor, new hairdo, new somewhat professional make-up applied, a very sexy shade of lipstick, and a stunning young woman slipped into her gown, expensive by even Ray Lupus's standards.

Poor Kenny walked into the Lupus home, corsage in hand and faced Ray, Linda, and Fred Grant. His face lit up when Karen entered the living room, the little girl with dimples and freckles gone, replaced by a woman of significant charm. The young couple drove off in Ken's parent's station wagon, foregoing the classier Mustang that Karen now owned.

They reached the school where the dance was being held, Ken parked in the dark, far from the entrance, and the couple walked into their first real event. Two kids in awe of life for right now. They mingled around the gym, Karen catching more than her fair share of eyes. The DJ played Paula Cole's, 'Where Have All the Cowboys Gone', and the couple tried to dance. Ken was hopeless but game, he tried and finally gave up. They grabbed a Coke, sat at a table by themselves, and began to talk.

"You know this cowboy is soon to be gone too, Karen."

"What are you talking about Kenny?"

"Call me Ken please," he began, and just as he had started Doug Benson came to the table.

Doug Benson, a son of a bitch by any definition, a player, a self-centered narcissist. A boy long looked up to by Karen, and Karen, a girl long ignored by Doug Benson. But that girl wasn't here tonight, a sexy woman was here tonight.

"Hi guys," Doug began casually, "rough time with that dance Ken."

"You're talking to me now? You haven't said two words to me through four years of high school."

"Oh, come on, that's school, all cliques and show. We all stay within our circles, you too. That's all in the past now; we can finally be grown-up. It's a good thing. We're gonna see a lot of each other now that we'll be out of school."

"Not around here you won't, I have other plans."

"Right. Hey, I thought maybe I could get a dance with Karen, we're just old friends from way back."

"It's up to Karen."

"Karen?" Doug asked holding out his hand.

Karen accepted, remembering all the years that she thought Doug was the greatest guy in the world. Doug held her respectfully as they started to dance and dropped his first line on Karen. "God I've waited so long to dance with you Karen, it feels like a dream."

"Stop it Doug, you hardly know that I exist, but thank you for being so nice to me and Ken tonight."

"Karen I've been crazy about you from the first day I saw you way back in grade school. I've just always been scared to talk to you, you're so pretty and sweet, way out of my league. It took all of my courage to ask you to dance."

"I doubt you lack courage. You seem to be all over Sally tonight. Were you scared to ask her out?"

"To be honest I wasn't even going to come tonight, I'm not the partier most people think I am, and Sally wasn't planning on coming either, but our parents are good friends and they actually suggested we attend together. Kind of weird isn't it. My mother getting me a date at my age."

"So, you two are really not a couple?"

"Not at all, but I do want to be respectful of her, after all I did bring her here, so I will have to spend most of my time with her tonight, you understand."

"What's there for me to understand, you date whoever you want."

"What I'd really like to do is date you."

"I'm with Ken now, it wouldn't be right to say yes."

"That's just another reason why I'm so nuts about you, you're so sweet and concerned about everyone. Just think about it, we'll talk later."

"I'm concerned about Ken, not everyone. I'm not the sweet girl you think I am."

"To me you are. Always have been, always will be. I'd like the chance to make you happy, you know, see if we fit together."

And with that the song ended and Doug walked Karen back to her table. The game could have ended there with a simple thank you from Doug, but he had bigger hopes.

"Thanks for letting us have that dance Ken, you're one of the coolest guys in this town. And hey buddy, I'm sorry if you took my not talking personal, it's just me, I'm pretty shy outside of my circle. We got to get together when we graduate. You too Karen.

We go too far back to lose contact now. I better get back to Sally. I don't feel comfortable around her, but I guess I'll get through the evening."

"Unusual to see Doug acting nice," Ken said.

"You don't think he's sincere?"

"I guess there are worse people in the world; maybe not in our town, but somewhere in the world there may be someone worse."

"He just asked me out."

"Yeah I heard him. I think it was innocent enough."

"I don't mean that small talk at the table, while we were dancing, he actually asked me out. I said no of course, I said I was with you."

"It's okay if you see other people."

"That's not a very nice way to talk Kenny, I mean Ken. Would it kill you to be a little thoughtful?"

"I'm sorry. There's just something I should tell you. Can we get out of here? I can't dance and if I drink one more cup of that sugary punch, I'm gonna get sick."

Karen agreed to leave with Ken and after a few goodbyes they walked out to car.

"Where to Ken?"

"I don't know, why don't we park at the ravine? We can talk there at least until all the kids from here show-up."

"What's the ravine?"

"You've never been to the ravine? Everyone goes there for privacy, you know to drink or make-out in their cars. It's okay, I'll behave. I always do."

They drove out to the ravine, no other cars were there when they arrived, so they took a walk around. It was dark, and it made the landscape look somewhat scary. They walked out on a flat rock overlooking the ravine.

"Be careful Karen, it's narrow through here, but very deep."

"It must be pretty in the daytime."

"It is," Ken agreed, "there are a few places you can get some footholds and make it down to the bottom, but it's hard to get back up. You'd kill yourself trying to do it at night."

"Let's go back to the car then."

They walked slowly back enjoying the spring air and smell of the trees and flowers. In the car Ken hunted for a radio station.

Karen stopped him and asked what was so important that he needed to talk about. Ken opened up.

"You can't tell anyone any of this. If word got back to my parents, they'd find a way to stop me, this town is just way too small, and they'd stop me."

"Stop what, you're scaring me."

"Not a word."

"Not a word, I promise."

"Well my folks are all set for me to take over the farm right after graduation, no college, no nothing. I can't milk cows and bale hay for the rest of my life. So, come July I'm going to Chicago to join the Navy. I'll take the train and enlist there, all Navy recruits train at Great Lakes, it will be great. After basic I'll get assigned to a ship. I can't wait."

"How are you going to sneak away?"

"I told my parents that I wanted one long weekend as a graduation present before I start working full-time on the farm. They agreed. So, me and a couple of buddies are going to Kansas City for the Fourth of July weekend, do some partying, tear it up a bit, you know. Then on the morning of July 5th, I'm catching the train in Kansas City riding right into Chicago. I stay that night in downtown Chicago and Monday morning I bus it to Great Lakes. By noon that Monday, I'll be a Navy man. Nobody knows except you now, not even my buddies. I'll tell them that weekend."

"Your parents are going to be pretty hot. They may even try to get you discharged before you start."

"I thought about that, but if I join under another name, you know some form of my own name, they'd never find me. I'll call them sometime after basic training. If I get any leave I may even come home for a day. I'll call you if I do."

"You better."

"That's why I don't want you to pass up the chance to date other people, I'll be gone a long time, maybe forever even, and you need to live your life. Doug can't be that bad and you've always liked him. Give it a whirl. I would like to see you more before I go though, just like this. I need to talk to someone to keep me from going crazy the next nine weeks."

"Wow, nine weeks and you're gone. Your secret is safe, and I'll even keep you sane, until you leave. After that I guess you're on your own."

"And that's exactly how I want it. Thanks Karen. I better get you home."

The area around the ravine filled up with carloads of kids from the dance while the couple talked. Ken maneuvered his car around a few other cars, turned on his headlights and cast the light on a group of kids passing around a bottle of something and turned back onto the highway. Heading back toward Karen's house he casually said, "Wasn't that Doug's car at the ravine?"

Ken walked Karen to the front door and said goodnight, a small awkward kiss, missing most of Karen's lips, followed. *He needs an awful lot of basic training*, Karen thought as she walked in the door to an anxious father and calming guardian Fred Grant.

"Hi honey," Ray instantly said while giving Karen a big hug. "Did you have a good time? I want to hear all about it."

"It was good. Ken is fun to be with and all the other kids were there. I danced once or twice, had some punch and cookies, Ken drove me home and here I am."

"That's it?" Ray asked.

"That's it," said Fred, "and it sounds wonderful Karen. You must be tired sweetheart, why don't you get some sleep. I'll visit with your dad a little longer and be gone soon. Let us know if we're too loud."

"Thanks Fred, goodnight. Goodnight Dad."

She went off to bed leaving her father staring blankly at Fred. "That's it?" he asked of Fred.

"For now, Ray. Leave her have her night to herself. When she's ready she'll tell you more, and you won't even have to ask. Just be patient."

"This dad thing just gets harder and harder."

After Fred left, Ray stood outside of Karen's bedroom door, hand near the knob, wondering whether to go in or not. His daughter was growing up so rapidly that it scared him. He wanted to tell her to slow down, take life one small step at a time. "Damn it," he said somewhat aloud and turned and went to bed. He sure could have used a night of advice from Helen, but instead, four dark walls were the only things to turn to. Graduation and then college Ray thought. "Damn," he said again a little louder.

CHAPTER 22

Ray rolled around in his chair by the lake trying to get comfortable. The pills were wearing off which made him feel better, but the bourbon was wearing off too and it made him feel worse. He tried to gather his thoughts, but he felt at odds with where he was sitting. He looked around and tried to get up and walk but failed miserably at getting out of the chair. He slumped over the armrest on the chair and mumbled to himself. He spied the bottle and treated himself to a few swallows. *The dance*, he recalled, *the damn dance*. If she went to that dance, there's going to be trouble.

More booze, more anger. Ray drifted off again to a very bad place.

The months after the dance started innocently enough and Ray was proud of himself for giving Karen the space that everyone told him she needed. Ken didn't come around the house anymore. Ray knew it was because Karen was picking him up in her new car. He figured things must have been going well for the couple because Karen was going out nearly every day and Ray always shouted, "Have fun," as Karen went out for the evening.

May seemed a good month for Karen and Ray was happy while still dealing with the loss of Helen. With June came changes in Karen's mood and she started staying home more and more evenings. Ray blamed the upcoming graduation, thinking that Karen had finally fit in well with her classmates and now she would have to begin all over again far from home and the security that Ray provided. After graduation, Karen's mood worsened and she grew very quiet around the house, spending good portions of her day locked in her room. Ray couldn't take it anymore and set about quizzing his daughter.

He waited one morning near the end of June to talk to Karen. Sitting alone nervously at the breakfast table, Ray drank cup after cup of coffee. Karen finally emerged from her room and poured a cup of coffee for herself. Without a word she turned and headed back to her room with her coffee.

"Just a minute, Karen. I want to talk with you. Please sit down."

"I don't want to talk, it's too early."

"Sit down honey, please."

Karen sat and Ray rubbed his hands together and tapped at the table.

"Your car running well? Was the Mustang a good choice?"

"The car's great. You and Helen chose wisely. Can I go now?"

"I haven't seen Ken around here in a long time, are you still seeing him?"

"Not really."

"Is that what has you so depressed? Has he been mean to you? You know I pass him on the street now and then, I can straighten him out in quick order. Tell me what he pulled on you?"

"Nothing. Ken's leaving that's all."

"Leaving? Leaving for where?"

"Oh, hell, I shouldn't have said that, forget I said that. Ken and I agreed that I would keep quiet about what he's doing."

"Keep quiet about Ken? Just what the hell did he do? Don't make me hear it from Ken, I'm pretty good at making people talk when I want them to."

"Oh god", Karen said crying now, "this is just getting worse, let me lay down for a while."

"You tell me where Ken's going and why and then you can lie down." Ray was speaking about as loudly as he ever had to Karen before.

"Promise me that what I'm telling you stays between us. We can't let Ken's parents know any of this. They'll make things bad."

"You have my promise, begrudgingly, but you have it just the same."

"All right. Ken's leaving here and joining the Navy. His parents would never let him go so he's sneaking off. He's catching the train out of Kansas City after the Fourth of July weekend and on July 6th he'll be in Chicago and join the Navy there training out of someplace called Great Lakes. That's it."

"Why is he going?"

"He just can't handle the responsibilities that will be facing him here. I'm going to my room."

Karen walked away with tears falling from her once happy eyes. Ray understood the pain of losing friends, but he thought that Karen was too hurt by this and wanted to reach out and explain that this was nothing in the big picture. He wanted Karen to look forward to college and planning her own life, meeting the right man one day.

He entered her bedroom well intentioned, but it only aggravated Karen again. They shouted a bit back and forth, Karen finally yelling that she's not going to college. Ray yelled back, neither was doing much listening as they both tried to be the loudest combatant. Tears, rage, and anger filled the room, and then Karen delivered the knockout blow square between her father's eyes.

"I'm pregnant."

Words were exchanged now at break-neck pace. All the 'hows', all the 'whys', the predictable 'now whats'. It was an ugly afternoon. Ray left the house pretending that he had to be at work even though he now had ample help in the zoo stables and never really needed to be at work anymore. Karen lay on the bed and cried the few tears she had left inside of her. Anger grew inside of her also, but she had no idea where to direct her rage. Karen was in strange waters for her and she felt as though she was going under.

Ray raced to the zoo because he knew of no other place to go. He sped into a parking place in the zoo taking up two spots and walked around the grounds. He hopped the safety fence by the primates and Kingston came running over. Ray poured his heart out to Kingston and the few people at the zoo thought it was simply amazing that Ray would stand so close to the giant gorilla.

When Ray finally noticed the crowd that had gathered, he said goodbye to Kingston and walked over to wolf house. He sat on the same bench that he sat on his first night at the Cubo Zoo. Fred noticed him from his private viewing room and quickly joined Ray on the bench. Fred knew immediately that something was wrong and without much prodding got his friend to open up.

"Karen just told me that she's pregnant. Pregnant."

"God that's wonderful Ray, congratulations."

Ray was dumbstruck. "Congratulations? This isn't a good thing."

"So, you're going to be a grandpa, don't let that bother you, you'll be great."

"Come on, that's not it. Karen is just a kid herself, and Kenny, that bastard is getting out of town. Karen won't be going to college now. This is terrible and I let Karen know it."

"Oh no Ray, you didn't. Let's look at this logically for a minute, okay?"

"You can't make this better."

"Let me try. What's troubling you the most?"

"For one thing Karen's supposed to be going away to school."

"Which you've moaned about a thousand times saying you wish she wasn't going. Next."

"Next? How about no father around here?"

"What about me and you? Can any man in this world be a better father than the two of us will make?"

"What about Karen's education? Her career?"

"Karen has more money than she could use in ten lifetimes, what in the world does she need a career for? If she longs for the education and a career, she can do it quite easily down the road, or take one of those computer classes that's all the rage now. Next."

"The father leaving, Fred. That really bothers me."

"Oh, I see, your lifelong wish has always been to have a son-in-law."

"No, but I want a good husband for my daughter."

"This doesn't stop that. If the right guy comes along, Karen will know it. This isn't the right guy, you should be overjoyed that this joker is leaving, and we can give our grandchild, yes, I said ours, everything he or she will ever want. This is going to be the best time of our lives."

"Damn, you make sense. We have everything in the world, why not add a baby?"

"There you go. Now we need to tell Karen how happy we are for her. She needs that and some space alone for a little while. We never took that road trip we talked about after we lost Helen. How about in a couple weeks we scout out the wildlife refuge in

Denver? We can do some shopping for the baby's room while we're there."

"You and me shopping for baby things?"

"Maybe I should wait and take Karen, she has better taste than you."

"You do that. I think I need some time away too, maybe take a horse or two out on the prairie, probably over the fourth weekend. The weekend after that we'll hit Denver. It will give Karen plenty of time alone. Let's go tell her how wrong I was, you'll enjoy hearing that."

The two dreamers rode back to the Lupus ranch together and called Karen in their loudest happiest voices.

"Karen sweetie, we need you. Get on out here!"

Karen came out of her room and was greeted with a big hug and kiss from Fred. "Congratulations Karen, I hear you're going to be a mother."

"I'm sure my dad told you how disappointed he is in me. I've ruined his life."

"That's not what he told me."

Ray finally spoke. "Karen I was upset when you gave me the news and for that I apologize. When I had time to think about it, I realized whatever happened has happened and we have to let that go, we've lived our lives that way forever. And looking ahead, I can honestly tell you that I am the happiest man in the world. This will be great, and you are going to raise a wonderful child."

"Are you telling the truth? Fred, is he?"

"He sure is, and in a couple of weeks we're going to do some shopping for baby stuff when we're in Denver."

"You two are going to Denver? Baby shopping?"

"We have some business there at a wildlife habitat," Fred explained, "but yes your father and I are going to look for some baby things. Nothing big for right now, your father said we can do that later with you. I'll leave you two alone now, I have to take the train out at the zoo this afternoon. Ray I need to take your car back since I came with you."

"I'll take you. My girl needs to start planning remodeling for the baby. Look the house over sweets, let me know what you want to do. I'll give you all the space you need. Next weekend I'm taking a horse out and camping for a few days and then the week after that me and Fred will be in Denver. You should have your design plans ready after that and we can get to work."

Karen kissed her father on the cheek. It seemed as though the weight of the world was lifted from her. She knew who to thank. Another kiss and a smile, "Thank you Uncle Fred."

Early the next week, Ray was wondering which horse needed some work on the prairie and was getting his camp gear ready for his Fourth of July getaway. On Tuesday he bumped into a hapless Ken Badderling walking down First Avenue. Ray remembered his promise to Karen and walked on eggshells around Ken. The old familiar Lupus anger was boiling at the mere sight of the Badderling boy. As best he could, Ray held it together.

"Hi Mr. Lupus," Ken shouted somewhat happily.

"You got time to be wandering around town in the middle of the day boy."

"What sir?"

"You heard me."

"I had to come to town to pick up some things for the folks. Something wrong?"

"Isn't that a bit too much responsibility for you?" Ray stared a hole right through the center of Ken's head. Ray's fist was clinched, and the volcano was about to erupt.

"I see what this is about, Karen told me she wasn't going to say anything."

"She didn't say anything. I know when something's wrong."

Ken took a few quick steps away from Ray, the hulking figure scared the hell out of the boy. A few doors down the street he turned and yelled, "Nobody can make me do what I don't want to do. I'm not staying here for somebody else's plans." He turned again and ran to his car like the scared chicken he was.

Ray took a step to run after him and knew it was senseless. He walked down a side street and kicked the door down in an abandoned building. Inside he punched hole after hole in every wall in the house. There was an old broken chair lying in the living room, Ray picked it up and flung it through the kitchen window, the chair came to rest in the mud in the backyard. Standing alone shaking, lost in anger, Ray slowly regained his composure. The chair came into focus and Ray had a few words for the chair. "I wish you were Ken Badderling," was all he said.

CHAPTER 23

Ray and Karen spent a quiet week at home. Karen was looking forward to a weekend by herself without the uneasiness of her father watching over her. She felt the pain over the supposed happiness of Ray. The morning of the 4th, Ray headed to the stables with a truck full of camping supplies. Karen looked genuinely happy as they said their short goodbyes. Ray said that he would be back Monday, maybe Tuesday at the latest if he was finding contentment in the country.

Ray thought about Karen's angelic face and the life she deserved. Ken's devilish sneer interrupted his good nature. Without thinking about it, without hardly realizing it, Ray turned off the road to the zoo stables and headed north. He reached I-70 and headed east to Abilene. He arrived at the small old west town of Abilene without any thought that he was even heading that way. The feel of the old days appealed to him as he walked the streets once walked by Masterson and Hickock and had himself a soda in the old west bar. *They knew how to handle things back then,* he thought, *yes sir they did.*

He left a dollar and his drink on the bar and went back to his car. Driving onto I-70 he headed east again. "Well Ken," he said out loud to himself, "Karen tells me that you're leaving Kansas City tomorrow morning. Don't count your chickens, punk."

Ray squeezed the steering wheel of his car pretty damn hard as anger rested in those massive fists. He had no plan, Ray seldom ever did, as he drove toward Kansas City. A face-to-face with Ken before the boy made his final escape to Chicago and out of the

Lupus world. Ray finally asked the question he should have asked long ago, "Then what?"

Ken will probably be with his friends at the depot, they'll want to see him off. They'll keep me from getting my final two cents in. Dammit. Ray was lost and getting angrier, he wanted to pull off the highway and hit something, maybe even someone if that was easier. He banged hard on the steering wheel with both hands causing his car to swerve from lane to lane. Horns blared at Ray and he cussed at the other drivers through his rolled-up window.

Feeling in danger and dangerous himself, Ray exited the highway at the next exit, Topeka. Driving through downtown Topeka the 5 o'clock traffic, light as it was, disturbed Ray. He pulled into a public parking lot and sat there wishing he had a plan to confront Ken Badderling. Looking across the street, Ray's eyes fell on a medium size building with a large sign on its side, Topeka Amtrak Station.

"Interesting," he said. He exited his car and went inside the depot to ask some questions.

At the ticket window he began his interrogation of the agent.

"This is the train to Kansas City isn't it?"

"Yeah, but you'll make better time walking. The train's sitting in Albuquerque waiting on a part. It's already a good 5 hours behind schedule and she always loses more time just east of the Duke City. Add to that losing its pecking order on the tracks to the freight trains now and the hours are going to pile up. If you wait for the train, you won't see Kansas City until late afternoon tomorrow at the earliest. You could drive there in about two hours you know."

"I see," answered a bewildered Ray. "Tell me, is there an outdoor area on the rear of the train, you know, where people could visit, have a little alone time?"

"Are you crazy, we'd be losing people all the time, probably have a bunch sneaking on too. You've been watching too many movies."

"I don't watch many movies," he said a little agitated now. "What time would we make Chicago?"

"I'm only guessing right now buddy, but I'd have to say a good eight, nine hours late, maybe worse. You'd probably get in about two in the morning."

"Two in the morning? Union Station's nothing more than a ghost town at that hour."

"I've never been there sir, but if want your alone time so badly I guess that's the place. You planning on proposing to someone?"

"Something like that. Exactly, I need the right mood. I'm still getting my plan together, you've been helpful. I think I will drive further. Getting a train part on the fourth of July could be tricky. I don't want to disappoint my girl, I better make my own tracks."

Ray walked back to his car, the city was filled with the noise of firecrackers and darkness would be bringing fireworks that Ray had absolutely zero interest in. He had been traveling nearly ten hours now without food and very little to drink. He left his car again and walked the streets until he found a café that looked comfortable. He sat with a blank stare molded on his face looking into a thick dark cup of coffee. A tasteless tuna club followed it and Ray kept trying to think of what to do. *I can make Chicago in less than ten hours*, he thought. *Of course*. He took half of his sandwich with him and went back to the train station for a schedule. Sitting in his car he planned his new trip.

Ray thought it through to the best of his abilities. *I can't confront Ken around his friends in Kansas City and I can't have a face to face with him on the train. Too many people, not enough room. I may lose my temper with the punk and if I do, I want to make him feel my pain. I need somewhere dark, somewhere alone, like Union Station Chicago at 2 in the morning. Ken will be at the station in Kansas City tomorrow morning expecting his train at seven-thirty. That train won't get in until at least 3, maybe 4 or 5. Our little boy will be exhausted by time his train pulls out and when he gets to Chicago, he'll be little more than a walking vegetable. I'll confront him then and there. I can get a good sleep at a rest area on the interstate, maybe even a nap tomorrow and I'll be fresh. I know Chicago and Union Station as well as anybody. He can't get past me, he needs to hear from me. I'm off to Chicago.*

Ray's plan sounded good. Somewhere in Missouri, Ray asked another question, "*And what if Ken goes back home or flies to Chicago because of the delays? I'll worry about that later.*" Ray was set, his plan for now set in stone.

Ray drove until midnight and pulled into a rest stop in central

Illinois. He made dinner from his camping supplies and with his gun at his side had a very relaxing sleep. He awoke and caressed his gun. He had but one question now, a question for his gun and he asked aloud, "You want to see Ken Badderling now? I thought you would."

Ray cleaned up in the public bathroom and stopped on the road for breakfast. He was only 3 hours outside of Chicago while Ken was sitting, he hoped, at the Kansas City train depot. Ray had a lot of time to wait and didn't want to be seen in Union Station all day. Almost noon he said under his breath, "I could go see my mother, it's only been 12 or 13 years. Nah, she's got to be dead by now. Hey Mr. Gun, want to go see my ex-wife's parents? I'd love to introduce you."

Ray saw a sign near Utica, Illinois for Starved Rock park. "Starved Rock, I remember it well. A few hours of hiking here, some dinner, a nap, and then Chicago. Perfect!"

Ray left the Interstate and found a secluded parking spot in the park campgrounds. He didn't pay for a campsite, but cooked up a little lunch by his car, his camp stove and mac and cheese was sufficient. He followed his lunch with a 3-hour hike toward Ottawa and back, bought himself dinner in the lodge and returned to his car for a short nap. At 8 pm on July 5th, Ray Lupus headed to Chicago Union Station. He was on the hunt now, hunting an animal called Ken Badderling.

Ray made Union Station a little after ten and parked his car on the north side of the depot, Adams Street. He entered the depot at track level off of Clinton and checked out the big schedule board. The Southwest Chief and Ken Badderling were due in at 1:30. *Three hours to kill*, Ray thought and laughed at his choice of the word kill.

The station was already changing over from its usual daily crowd to its nighttime inhabitants. Summer offered quieter nights than winter when the warmth of the station is needed by the city's many homeless. The plan Ray had now ended when he saw Ken. Then what? He thought things over again. He sat in his car tapping on his gun.

"You can't shoot Ken, you're not that stupid Ray," he told himself. He sat imagining the feeling of shooting this person who can't be bothered with the responsibility of Karen and her child.

The thought felt good, but Ray knew he couldn't shoot Ken. He removed the bullets from his gun and put them and the gun in the glove box. He felt exposed sitting on Adams and took a drive around the building and headed up Jackson. He thought about driving to his old neighborhood and turned his vehicle onto the lower Wacker Drive.

Wacker was a mess from the fourth, garbage was everywhere, and overfilled dumpsters marred the roadway. He drove through the darkness and came to the homeless village. Small fires burned everywhere, and the wall was lined with shopping carts and large boxes and crates serving as homes.

Ray got out of the tunnel near the lake and decided against seeing the neighborhood that he now hated. He took a slow drive north on Lake Shore Drive, exited at Fullerton, and took Wells back towards the station. It was near enough time now to sit and wait which Ray decided to do on Jackson Boulevard. He played the radio, jumping from station to station, talk radio, oldies, news, back and forth, nothing held his interest. He opened the glove box. "No Ray, no!"

At one in the morning, Ray left his car and the deserted street and returned to the depot. The schedule board carried a happy message, 'The Southwest Chief was arriving on track 23.' Ray's stomach tightened and he had to breathe deeply to get enough oxygen in his system. He positioned himself where he could see all the passengers exit the train. He waited and waited, a parade of exhausted angry people marched off the train. Finally, near the back of the line, small duffle bag over his shoulder, crept Ken Badderling. Ray planned his steps and came face to face with Ken in the huge main waiting area. Ken spoke first.

"Mr. Lupus. What are you doing here?"

"Hi Ken. I'm in town to take care of my mother. When I was talking to Karen this morning, she said that you were coming in today and you may just be lost in this city. I felt bad about yelling at you the other day, that was mean on my part, and I thought I could make it up to you by making sure you're safe around here. It's a rough city. You have a place to stay tonight?"

"I need to find a street called Monroe and walk west about half a mile. There's supposed to be hotel there."

"I know it well, let me drive you there and we'll be square. I just couldn't forgive myself if I didn't."

They left the depot and walked to Ray's car. Ray unlocked the doors and glanced at his glove box. He shook his head.

"Hop in. Gimme that bag, I'll toss it in back. You got your name on your stuff in here boy? You need to mark your stuff around here."

"Just the tag on the outside."

"Sounds good." Ray tossed the bag on the back seat. "Your clothes are falling out, I better fix your bag." Ray slid in back behind Ken.

"Thank you, sir."

"You're welcome." And with those words Ray took the rope that he had hidden on the back seat and wrapped it around Ken's neck in a perfect choke noose. "You are so welcome you son of a bitch." Ray pulled tighter and tighter as all life left Ken's body. Ken was out of air in seconds, out of life in a couple minutes. Ray tightened the noose for five, ten minutes, screaming at the dead body. "Too much responsibility? My daughter's not good enough for you? A bullet's too good for you. Suffer. SUFFER!"

It was almost fifteen minutes of strangulation. Ray blacked out somewhere during the process. He came to his senses and released the rope. Ken slumped slightly forward. Ray moved quickly to the driver's seat and started the engine. Seconds later Ray was back on the lower Wacker parking beside a dumpster in a dark, black section of the street. He emptied Ken's pockets and then half emptied the dumpster, throwing black garbage bag after bag alongside the dumpster. With the dumpster half empty he threw in Ken's body and then covered it over with bags. By early next morning if luck was with Ray, Ken would be landfill never to be heard from or about again. He took the cancer from his daughter's and grandchild's life, a surgeon in his own right.

Ray ripped the name tag off of Ken's duffle bag and drove up to the homeless village. He threw the bag of clothes to the underground residents and drove off. In a matter of minutes, he was heading south down the interstate.

"Home," he said to himself gleefully, "home sweet home". He felt good about what he had done and felt physically good also with one minor exception, Ray Lupus was hungry. "I've worked up quite an appetite."

Ray made tracks down I-55 and hit St. Louis as the sun was coming up. Sunday traffic was light and as quickly as he hit the city, he put it behind him. Exhaustion was gaining on Ray, so he pulled into the first rest area he saw between St. Louis and Kansas City. He bought a coffee, a thin watery coffee, from the vending machine and munched on some of his camping food. With what seemed like the weight of the world gone from Ray's shoulders, he kicked back in his car and slept for over four hours.

Minutes after waking, Ray was back on the road. Mile after mile passed, Ray was physically awake, but his mind slept. No radio, no music, no talk. A rock behind the wheel, he drove. Sometime before the sun went down, Ray went through Kansas City, but he couldn't remember it.

Feeling home in Kansas, Ray stopped at an all-you-can-eat café. The poor café lost money that night. Ray ate mounds of mashed potatoes, beans, salad, peas, and he may not have eaten an entire school of fish, but he came close. A few desserts followed before Ray began the final leg of his trip.

The July night turned cool as the sun went down. Ray rolled down the window of his car and the breeze reawakened him. He tuned his radio to an oldies station out of Colorado and sang along with every song. At 10 pm, he entered his driveway and killed the engine near the front door. Sixty hours to change a few lifetimes. Ray was proud of himself.

Ray walked into the house, tired, stiff, hungry again, and just a tad bit lost. As time passed, Ray was wondering if he had done right, done right by Karen. He knew what he did was right for him, but maybe he jumped too quickly for Karen's needs. He became nervous as he heard her get up from the sofa and head for the kitchen where he now stood.

"I didn't expect you until tomorrow. Did you have a good trip?"

"I think I may have had one of the best weekends of my life. It was amazingly relaxing. I guess time will tell if it makes a difference in me. Did you enjoy your alone time?"

"I think I am coming around. And you're right, time will tell."

The following Thursday, Ray and Fred left for their weekend trip to the wildlife habitat near Denver. Karen drove Ray to Fred's place at the zoo and the boys left from there. They talked about the valuable time Karen was getting alone at home. Fred thought that it would put her in the proper state of mind towards becoming a mother. Both men were optimistic about the future and Fred commented to Ray about how far he seemed to have come in a week's time.

It was a good long weekend for Ray and Fred. They loved the habitat and thought it would be a good home for Kingston. Ray was far too close to Kingston now to ever move him again. Fred was in agreement and suggested that he make Kingston's primate grounds even larger at the zoo.

The boys then visited a couple small towns far from Denver, the city was not appealing to either Fred or Ray. They stopped in a couple of bars, just for a beer or two, and all stops went without incident. In Ray's newfound state of tranquility, it would have been a little hard, or at least a little harder, to upset him.

They visited a baby store near Colorado Springs, looking rather comical as they viewed the items they considered buying. They decided to let Karen do the shopping and settled in Monday night in a fancy hotel.

They talked a lot that night, about Karen and the baby, the zoo, the past, the future, and of course Helen and the void she left in both their lives.

They got back home to Westgate early Tuesday evening and had dinner at Fred's. Karen joined them as she had to pick up Ray and sat through dinner somewhat quiet. She blamed her silence on all the thinking about raising a baby that she had been doing and how much she missed Helen and all the help Helen would have been to her now. Ray understood and tried to offer assurances of good times ahead as they walked to the car.

"Trust me Karen, you'll see," Ray said as he opened the passenger door. He then commented on the rock Karen had left on his seat. It was like a small boulder, almost too heavy for her to lift. "What in the world you driving around with this rock for?"

"Well," Karen started and then hesitated, "I rather not say."

"Oh, come on, you can see my curiosity."

"Don't laugh. I was walking the other morning picking wildflowers like Helen and I used to do, and this rock was in the middle of a great bed of Indian Paintbrush. So, I took it and thought I would drive it out to where Blackie rests and build a monument for Helen. This is my first rock, all of them will come from a special place. Too silly?"

"Not silly, but what if we build a real monument, one that will last forever. Kind of like a headstone but without Helen under it. You could write some things to engrave on it, you're so good with words."

"I like that."

"Can I throw your rock away?"

"I'll put it by Blackie for now, it will be symbolic while we're planning Helen's monument."

"Okay, but no lifting for you, young lady. I'll carry it out tomorrow. I need to talk with Blackie tomorrow anyhow. I'm sure he wonders where I've been."

"You do that."

Ray felt light. He believed that he took care of any problems that could upset the Lupus household. He was taking Fred's suggestion and looking at Karen's pregnancy and the coming birth of his grandchild as a good thing. He knew he didn't deserve it but felt strongly that great days were coming. He should have known better by now, things don't work that way in Ray's universe, but he had no idea at this time just how badly the past and present could collide.

CHAPTER 24

Ray woke up once again in his chair by the lake and looked around. All he saw was his empty bottle of bourbon. He walked to the edge of the woods but didn't go any further. He walked back to the house trying to recognize the trees and flowers along the way. He felt old, it pained him to walk, his heels heavy in the dust. He tried to ask himself what was going on, but his words were a mumbled mess. He reached the house and it looked the same as it always has. He went in just as Karen was leaving. Alone again with his fractured memories was a bad place for Ray.

The bourbon at the lake made Ray feel good, but old memories coming back didn't. Ray hunted through the kitchen cabinets and found himself another bottle. He turned on his stereo but forgot to put in a disc. He sat and waited for music until he forgot what he was waiting for. He walked around the house looking for Karen but ended up back in his room. He began looking through his box of old photographs.

Karen must be out, he thought, and it troubled him. He fell asleep for a while and woke up when he thought he heard Karen in the other room. The noise stopped and he put his head back down on the pillow. He repeated this sequence about ten times and was still without an hour's worth of good sleep when he got out of bed in the morning. He had an urge to walk back to his little lake, he felt there was something he was supposed to have done there.

Karen got up as soon as she heard her father in the kitchen. Ray stared at her with an angry look in his eyes.

"Lake," he tried to say and did a good enough job so that Karen understood.

Karen looked out the window at the rain that was now pouring down and listened to the wind that blew the rain sideways. "Not now Dad, look at the rain."

"Must go."

"As soon as it stops, I promise."

Ray gave her a slight push and went to the back door. He looked through the window at the rain and nothing else out the door looked too familiar to him. Karen was worried about the shove and wondered if the violence that the doctors had warned her about was about to escalate. She cautiously pulled Ray back from the door and stopped abruptly when he yelled at her in his way, with fractured words, but loud voice, to leave him alone. She went and got a couple of Ray's pills and a glass of juice. Ray took the pills and let Karen walk him back to his room. Karen saw the second empty bottle of bourbon on the floor in Ray's room identical to the empty bottle she found on the sofa last night.

Picking it up she scolded her father, "This is why you're acting like a fool this morning. You're not a drinker, don't start this now. Lie down and let the pills help you relax, I'm sure you need rest." She expected no answer and did not get one, just another mean look from Ray as he sat in his chair by the window.

Karen left him alone as he tried to feel the rain through the window. He traced the path of the drops with his finger, top to bottom and top to bottom. He looked at his fingertip and wondered why it wasn't wet. The old bourbon with the new pills was beginning to spin Ray's head. His mission at the lake was unclear to him but calling just the same.

"I need to get out of here before they come." Ray had absolutely no idea where he was or why he should be leaving, but the last thing he said to himself before he passed out stuck with him, they were coming. The rain, the bourbon, the pills, Karen banging things in the kitchen and his first deep sleep in days put Ray back in the middle of one of his dark times.

Officer Butler had driven to the Lupus' place in the pouring rain. He parked as close as he could to the door and ran from the car to the front door. Standing dry under the porch roof he knocked and waited for someone to answer. Karen came to the door.

"Hey Jim, what brings you out here?"

"Burns wants me to bring your dad in for a little bit, says he saw something in town that your dad may know about. Wouldn't tell me what."

"Brad Burns? Always thinking outside his brain. Probably some new angle on getting votes. I tell you if that guy ever becomes sheriff, half the folks in this county will move. Him just running for office is bad enough. Does my dad really have to go out in this rain?"

"I guess that's why he sent a car, his way of being polite."

Karen got Ray and Officer Butler explained again that Burns wanted Ray's help with something. His story sounded different as did his tone when face to face with Ray.

Karen noticed his change and questioned him. "You sound odd Jim. Is there something you're not telling us?"

"I don't know anything, you know Brad, always planning something. Can we just go Mr. Lupus?"

"Yeah, let's go see Mr. Burns."

"You probably want to grab a slicker or a jacket sir, it's coming down pretty hard."

"It's a little rain Jim, let's go. I'd like to be back before the sun comes out."

"The car's right in front, let me wipe up this mess I made and I'll be right there."

Ray walked out and Karen started to go for a towel. Jim stopped her. "I just wanted to tell you to call someone for your dad, have them meet us at the station. I think Burns might be up to something and he could get your dad saying all kinds of stuff."

"About what? My dad hasn't done anything."

"I don't know, just call someone. Maybe it's about that boy. I don't know. Brad will do anything to win this election and if hurting your father will bring him votes then he'll do it."

Karen got sick and put her hand on her stomach. Her motherly instincts immediately thought to protect the child. She sat on the edge of the sofa and went pale.

"You okay?" Jim asked.

Tears filled Karen eyes as she spoke to Jim, "I'll be okay, I'll call someone. Do me a favor and tell my dad to not say a word to Burns. Tell him he must stay calm. Help will be there soon. My dad had nothing to do with that boy."

"I'll tell him that you said to keep quiet, that's all I can do. I better get going."

Off drove Ray and Jim Butler, disappearing quickly in the rain. Karen picked up the phone and made one call. There was nothing to think about, the only person to call was Fred Grant.

Jim Butler pulled the squad car into its parking space at the station. He kept his promise to Karen and had a quick talk with Ray before they went inside.

"Mr. Lupus, Karen asked me to tell you that you shouldn't say anything to Officer Burns. She says you must remain calm and quiet. She'll have someone here for you as soon as she can."

"Keep quiet about what?"

"I really don't know Mr. Lupus, just please don't say much."

Jim and Ray went inside and were directed to the lower level meeting room. It was a much larger room than the small rooms upstairs, there was a long table in the middle of the room and Burns arranged for coffee which sat in a large container on the far end of the table. At the other end of the table sat Brad Burns and police station secretary, Charlotte. Joining them was an older man that nobody seemed to know. He was tapping his pen on the table, his nervousness obvious to all. Jim tried to excuse himself from the meeting but sensing there might be trouble, Burns asked Jim to stay. Jim sat near the coffee container feeling as nervous as the old rumpled man at the other end of the table.

"We're all here so we better get started," Burns began. "Ray you know Charlotte, she's here to take notes, I'm just trying to clear up a death in town. Do you recognize this gentleman Ray?" Burns asked motioning to Ralph Salerno.

Ray looked the man over, squinting as hard as possible to bring the guy into focus. "No." Ray was so far intent on keeping his words to a minimum.

"I'm offended Ray. We met quite a few years ago in a racetrack office, we had to settle your wife's affairs."

Ray looked at Ralph again and spoke again, "I've put those days out of my head, but I remember enough of them. What the hell are you doing here?"

"I know what you..." Ralph began, but was cut-off by Burns.

"Keep quiet until I ask you something. Well Ray, Ralph here

tells quite a tale of your wife's death in Chicago."

"You son of a bitch," Ray screamed at Ralph and jumped out of his seat, "you no good son of a bitch."

Jim Butler jumped up too and grabbed Ray trying to hold him back.

"I should have beat the shit out of you then. You won't be so lucky this time. Why you bringing that stuff up here after all this time?"

"Sit down Ray," Burns ordered, "Ralph thinks it connects you with this and I think there's something to it too." Burns handed Ray the Omaha newspaper that Ralph brought down and a copy of the Westgate paper that carried the original story. Ray looked at both of them and scratched his head. He hung his head and stared at the floor.

"Let me see those," Jim Butler said. He had to take the papers from Ray, as Ray never heard the request. The room was silent now and a smug smile covered the face of Ralph Salerno. The silence may have lasted forever but was interrupted by a knock on the door. Sam Waterford, the county coroner entered the room and was startled by the number of people standing around.

"What's going on here?" Sam asked of the Officer in charge of the meeting.

"I'm guessing you have something for me Sam, but hang on. Ray was just reading the story. You have something to say now Ray?"

"Yeah, I do Brad. Who the hell is Doug Benson?"

"Don't play dumb Ray, we know he was daughter's boyfriend."

"I think you're nuts, you get that from this fool?" Ray asked pointing at Ralph.

"Oh boy," added Sam Waterford, "you are making a mistake here, you're heading down the wrong road."

"Doug Benson probably got your daughter pregnant Ray, and everyone knows you're none too happy with it," Ralph blurted out. "Spill your beans."

"My daughter's pregnancy got nothing to do with anyone in this room or in this town for that matter. I oughta kill this bastard for dragging us in here." Ray tried to get at Ralph and Jim and Brad held him back and the room was about to explode when a new voice entered the room.

"Hey, let's calm down here," Fred Grant spoke, and the room quieted instantly. "You're running a noisier zoo here than we do at the Cubo. Somebody want to fill me in?"

"Brad thinks I killed some kid named Doug Benson. I've never heard of a Doug Benson."

Jim handed Fred the newspapers and Fred read them quickly. "I read about this boy, sad story. High school kid got drunk and fell into the ravine, happened a few weeks ago. What's this got to do with you bringing Ray in here?"

Brad was not as sure of himself as when the meeting started. Fred had taken over the meeting and when Brad now looked at Ralph, he saw a bitter twisted man, nothing more. "Fred, I know Ray is your friend and I meant no disrespect, I'm looking after you here too. But I need to look into the possibility that this was no accident and Ray played a part in something very bad here."

"That's not possible," the coroner said.

"No, that's not possible at all," Fred added sternly. "Doug Benson went missing Friday night, July eleventh, they found his body Sunday July thirteenth. Me and Ray were in Denver much of that week and all of that weekend at the Wildlife Habitat. Ray wasn't even in this state when Benson had his accident. You stupid asshole, you're done in this town Brad."

"Wait everyone, I'm just going by the info this Salerno guy brought in. I had to look at it, Sam you see how this looks, explain it to them from my viewpoint."

The coroner spoke straight, "You have no viewpoint, I wish you would have talked to me first. I relooked at the scene and the photos. Doug had some small cuts on the front of his face from falling face first into the ravine. I have pictures of the area where he first hit the rocks and we got his blood from there. He landed straight under the big flat rock. That's what cut his face. He then free fell and hit the very top of his head on a boulder at the bottom of the ravine, there was large amount of blood there and brain matter if you care to look at the photos. His blood alcohol level was almost triple the legal limit. You had a blind drunk wandering around the rocks at the ravine and he staggered off the flat rock to his death. Even the boy's parents blamed his drinking and held themselves responsible for the accident."

"You saying there's no way Ray could have been involved?"

"He wasn't even in town," Fred shouted at him.

"Listen to me," Sam ordered him, "if Ray would hit him with a blow to knock Doug into the ravine, the first cut would have been to the back of his head and it would have sent the body flying further from the side of the cliff towards the middle of the ravine. And my god, if Ray did hit Doug in the face with a rock, he would have cracked his entire skull, not bruised him a little. It would take a mighty tiny man to inflict that little damage. You owe Ray an apology Brad."

"You owe this town an apology," Fred told Salerno, "I suggest you leave the area. If not, I'll do everything in my power to make your life hell. Let's go home Ray, I know Karen's worried about you. This isn't over," Fred added as they prepared to leave.

Ray walked over to Salerno and clinched his fist. He thought about hauling off and laying him out but then just waved his finger in Ralph's face, finally turning and walking away.

"They keep getting closer Ray," Fred said as they started their drive home.

"You say that to me a lot, but I never know what you mean."

"It's just a feeling I have. They're coming after us, after you. I can't explain it. But you have another issue now that we should deal with. The words obviously out about Karen's pregnancy Ray and one day that Ken kid is coming back. I assume he's the father isn't he?"

"He's guilty, but he's no father. He's dead to me Fred. I've just been trying to be positive. I can't remember who gave me that advice."

"Good advice, you are wise to follow it, but we should address the father question, protect Karen and the baby. We don't need anybody coming around trying to lay claim to the baby's estate."

"I wouldn't worry about Ken, he ran away and I doubt we'll ever see him again. I really believe that now, part of my positive outlook."

"Seriously Ray, it could be anyone who comes around especially if something happens to you or Karen after I'm gone. We need protection."

"Maybe. Are you cooking something up Fred?"

"Yes. Artificial insemination."

Fred was serious, Ray was shocked.

"A little late for that isn't it, Fred?"

"Not at all Ray. If my money's worth anything it's about buying the truth, any truth. I've got hospitals and clinics all over the place. I'll get the paperwork done and filed showing Karen had the procedure done in May. The papers will be more official than official papers, locked-up tight. She'll never have to worry about anyone from her past coming around making trouble for her and your family."

"You could do that?"

"Easily."

"If she says yes, do it. I like that our family stays our family"

Fred dropped Ray off at home and said he would talk to Karen when the time was right. He was off now to start the ball rolling on the paperwork on Karen's procedure.

Ray sat down with Karen and filled her in on the morning's events at the police station. He blamed it all on Ralph Salerno and his twisted view of her mother's death. Needing to be alone after their talk, Ray walked down to the lake. Karen sat bewildered at the kitchen table until she was disturbed by a knock at the door. Karen opened the front door to a disheveled stranger in a wrinkled suit.

"Can I help you?" Karen asked, giving him a strange look.

"You must be Karen. I'm Ralph Salerno. I need to see your father before I leave town, I owe him an apology. I guess. I blamed him for killing Doug Benson and I know now that wasn't the case. Your father didn't kill anyone. I'm sorry."

"You don't need to tell me anything. Dad's by the lake, you can drive. Follow that narrow road. You really messed with him today."

With head hung low, Ralph made his way to his car and drove out to the lake. Ray rose from his chair as soon as he saw Ralph and picked up a rock sitting at his feet. Ralph held his hands up over his head and tried to get Ray to grant him a few minutes time to apologize.

At the house Karen sat on her bed and pondered the past yet again, yes, she knew that her father did not kill Doug Benson and the days that followed the school dance were replaying for the hundredth time in Karen's head.

Doug found a way to 'accidently' bump into Karen in town and suggested that they go out for talk, just to visit, talk about the old days, not really a date. Karen agreed to that and since Ken was moving on and wished the best for Karen, he was no longer the issue.

Doug and Karen had a great visit, parked out at the ravine, just talking and laughing. Doug knew his way around a first date and how to build for a second. Karen was a little uneasy that Doug brought a bottle of whisky, but didn't want to seem like a child. Doug asked and received Karen's permission to drink, but Karen refused the whisky for herself saying she was more of wine drinker. Doug sipped at his bottle and kept up the sweet talk all night. Doug explained to Karen that somehow Sally got a little attached to him following the dance and asked Karen to keep their relationship quiet until he had the chance to break things off with Sally.

Karen was used to keeping secrets about boys. She believed from Ken that that was how the world worked. Seeing Doug, as friends, was not a very big secret to keep and Karen had no trouble doing so. Doug acted so excited about their evening together, going on and on about all the time he admired Karen and all the time he lost not asking her out sooner. They planned a second date, a real date, and Karen felt like a million dollars after their first night together.

The real date was different. The kids met on Main Street in Westgate and left Karen's car there. Doug drove them to another town almost fifty miles away for dinner, he claimed it was a great restaurant and wanted the evening to be special for Karen, more special than a night in Westgate. After dinner they drove back to town and parked at the ravine. Doug went to the trunk of his car as soon as they parked and got his bottle of whisky and a small bottle of red wine he bought for Karen. They talked and drank a bit and soon Doug was all over Karen, the couple kissed and groped for a long time, only taking time out to drink. Surprisingly, Doug merely sipped at his booze and although Karen started that way she soon was drinking very quickly and polished off her bottle in minutes.

Karen's head was spinning, and her body was screaming for affection. She knew she wasn't drunk, but couldn't resist the urges of her body.

Doug suggested they get some air and took Karen and a large

comforter from the back seat out to Flat Rock at the edge of the ravine. Before Karen knew what was happening, she was naked, and Benson was on top of her riding her like the drunk trash that he was. Karen didn't argue with this, she was excited at the time and her moans filled the night air.

After sex, Doug left her on the rock and returned to the car for his whisky. Karen dozed off for a short time and awoke scared and groggy. Her vision was blurred, but she eventually regained focus and saw Doug sitting on the hood of his car drinking his booze. She recalled a bit of the sex, but not much and began to cry.

She dressed herself and went back to Doug. Crying, she asked Doug what happened and Doug blamed Karen. He said that she was all over him and he only did what she wanted. Karen cried the entire way back to her car while Doug kept telling her to grow up.

Doug told Karen he would call when he had time and left Karen standing in the street next to her car. Karen's legs were shaky, and her head was a mess, all the result of the pill Doug Benson slipped into Karen's wine. Karen never knew of these pills and never knew she was drugged. She moved forward blaming herself for the evening wondering how long the darkness of guilt would sit on her shoulders. To most, this would have been a mere night of sex, but to Karen, it was the loss of innocence and the beginning of deception she didn't even know existed. Things would only get worse.

Within two weeks, Karen knew something was different, everything felt off. Within a month she was sick every morning and scared. She asked all the girls she knew from school about what it could be. She heard lots of talk of pregnancy, some of it joking, some of it serious. Soon enough there was no doubt in Karen's mind, she was indeed pregnant. She got a hold of Doug and met him at the ravine over the fourth of July.

Doug denied everything and threw insults at Karen blaming Ken Badderling. Doug even went so far as to say he heard from lots of the guys and they would all claim that they had sex with her. Karen's sickness continued and when Ray went away for another week's trip, she confronted Doug one more time.

Meeting at the ravine Karen told Doug that she was letting go and wanted nothing more to do with him. She promised to never mention their night together and as a peace offering brought Doug a quart of whisky. Doug hardly needed more whisky as he was pretty lit up when Karen arrived.

They talked coolly toward one another, with Doug fonder of the bottle than of Karen. With the bottle half empty, Karen said that it was time for her to go and only wanted one favor of Doug, a final kiss goodbye on the rock where they made love, their rock as Karen called it.

They walked to the rock, Karen doing all she could to hold Doug steady, and stood on the edge of the ravine in a final embrace, there was no kiss. Karen told Doug to look out over the ravine as she didn't want him to watch her walk away. Doug stood swaying in what little breeze there was, Karen walked away from Doug and jumped off the flat rock on its meadow side. She looked down at the eight-inch rock she placed there and lifted it above her head. She jumped back on the rock and ran at Doug

As soon as he turned to see Karen, the rock caught him just above the eyes bruising his head. The blow, coupled with the booze, caused Doug to lose his balance and pass out. He fell straight down into the ravine smacking his face right below the rock and falling the rest of the way, headfirst like a missile, splitting his skull in two near the bottom of the ravine.

Doug was dead and Karen knew it. With her rock still in her hand, she returned to her car and threw the rock on the seat next to her. By the time she got home her shock passed. She poured herself a glass of wine and sat in what would become the baby's room planning the new décor.

The next day her morning sickness had gone, and she felt unbelievably good. Karen was a good girl and her actions did give her pause and one major regret which Karen summed up best, "I wish I had done that sooner."

At the lake, with hands held high, Ralph tried to make his peace with Ray. "I just came by to say that I'm sorry. Sitting in the police station today, I realized that how I've handled things over the years was wrong. I made people justify the deaths of their loved ones just so I could save my company money, everything for the job, you know. I was a bastard, I know that now, I'm sorry."

Ray, still holding the rock, still holding his anger, heard enough. "You leaving for good now?"

"Yes."

"You know I had nothing to do with the Benson kid's death?"

"I do. You weren't in town and like the coroner said if someone had hit Benson it would have had to have been a very tiny man, certainly not you. It had to be an accident like everyone said, I doubt that there's any tiny man in town that had an issue with Benson."

"I guess not," Ray agreed.

"I guess I should have looked for an angry lady instead," Ralph said joking, "a young lady would be tiny enough."

Ray looked at the rock in his hand, the rock he brought over from Karen's car. Ray went pale.

"What's wrong Ray? You know a lady mad at Benson?"

"No."

"What about," Ralph stopped himself. It came instantly clear to him now just as it had to Ray. Karen killed Doug Benson. "I better run along Ray."

If Ray had stopped to think for a minute, he would have known that Ralph would be running right back to Burns, but Ray didn't stop to think, he didn't need to. He rushed Ralph with rock in hand. He gave Ralph a forearm blow with his left arm knocking him to the ground, in almost the same motion he brought the rock down with his right-hand smashing Ralph's face. He brought blow after blow down on Ralph until long after Ralph was dead.

Then he dragged Ralph back to his car and stuffed him into the truck. Ray drove the car around to the far side of the lake to its deepest point and rolled the window down. With the car in neutral, Ray put the rock on the gas pedal revving the engine for all it had. Ray got out of the car, slammed the door, reached inside and shifted the car into drive. The car took off like a fired cannonball into the lake. It floated for a bit as it moved away from the shore. It teetered, it bobbed, it swayed, it sank like a stone putting Ralph Salerno in his final resting place.

Ray felt good about what he had done, ever the protector of his family, always certain to bring things to a fitting conclusion. Before walking back to the house Ray spoke his final words to Ralph Salerno, "I wish I would have done this sooner."

CHAPTER 25

Ray woke up in the chair in his room and looked out the window. The rain had stopped and the heat from Ray's breathing and agitation had fogged the inside of his window. He used the side of his fist to wipe away the fog and looked out onto the sun drying the fields. He looked down the driveway thinking someone may be coming. He looked down the worn path to the lake, Karen's Little Lake Michigan, and wondered if he should be hurrying to get there. He recalled a car sinking in the lake, but wasn't sure now if it would stay on the bottom. He was trying to recall why he sunk the car. There was someone in there he remembered now, someone trying to hurt his family. *The guy from Chicago, he must have followed us here after Diane died. He wants to take my daughter.*

The memory was getting clear, but Ray was not placing it where it belonged, almost ten years in the past, but Ray's memory had him pushing the car just last night. He looked again down the driveway and recalled Fred's words, "They're getting close."

Ray thought he should run and started packing his suitcase. Careful at first, he soon began to throw clothes in his bag as haphazardly and as quickly as possible. He was startled by a noise from outside of his room and heard footsteps nearing the room. Ray hid next to the door and waited. The door slowly opened and Ray reached out grabbing the intruder by the throat.

Karen jumped back breaking Ray's hold on her. "Dad, what in the world are you doing?"

Ray looked at his daughter and whoever Ray thought might be

coming, she wasn't them.

"Sorry," he said.

"That's it, no more drinking, you're becoming paranoid." Karen charged into the room and grabbed the bottle of bourbon. What's with the bag? She asked noticing the bag of clothes on the bed.

"They're coming," he said somewhat clearly.

"Who's coming?"

"Ralph. Police."

"Nobody's coming, you're chasing ghosts. Why don't you see my mother instead of this Ralph person? We can go to the hospital and have them run all the tests they have on you or you can calm down and try to get your bearings. I have to keep you on your meds, and you have to stay off booze. Are you ready to do this?"

Ray didn't answer but sat in his bedroom chair and willingly took his pills. Karen doubled his dose hoping to bring the calmness the doctors said that he needed to correct his mind. At bedtime Karen gave Ray two more strong pills and left him to his demons once again.

Not doing much better than a comatose patient, Ray relived the happier days of the end of the last century and the bright beginning of the next one in his mind. As long as the pills rushed through his system, Ray floated to a good place. In sleep, Ray landed in the times beginning with the birth of his grandson.

Karen gave birth on February 20th, 1999 and she promptly named the newborn boy Freddie Ray Lupus. Both Ray and Fred doted on the child and as Freddie grew, he spent more and more time at the zoo. Just like his grandfather, Freddie had a strong tie to Kingston as well as most of the other animals, and had a hard time fitting in with the other kids from the town that visited the zoo. Freddie preferred running around the stables or playing in the Wolf House with Fred and Ray. Freddie would watch the wolves for hours from the viewing room Fred had built originally for himself.

As with the birth of Karen, the first five years of Freddie's life was a time of great joy for Ray. He was able to shut out the rest of the world and draw what little family he had tightly around him. By the fall of 2004, things were beginning to unravel yet again for Ray. Freddie began school and from day one he was an outsider, a loner. Karen was called into school on numerous occasions for Freddie's fighting or his tuning out in general. She always attended the meetings without Ray because she feared Ray would not handle the meetings well at all.

The biggest change in Ray's life was the failing health of Fred Grant. Eighty years old now, Fred was nearing the end of his days. He stopped operating the train and would only ride now if Ray drove the engine. He would sit and smile, always with Freddie, always with a tear in his heart if not his eye. Moving became so difficult for Fred that Ray and Freddie would have to help him in and out of the train. Fred's legs didn't work well anymore and one day after a long struggle to get into the train, Fred announced that this was going to have to be his last ride. Ray fought back the tears and blew the whistle many more times than he ever had before. Fred and Freddie held tightly to one another as Ray whipped the train around the tracks. Fred asked Ray to stop the train for a second and told Freddie to sit with his grandfather and help pilot the train home.

"I have a better idea, you sit up here with Freddie and you two bring her home."

After another long struggle with Ray carrying Fred to the engine, he finally got Fred in the driver's seat. As he put Fred down, Fred held onto Ray's neck an extra little while, a hug usually given from father to son. Ray gave Fred the nod of his head and the love of his smile and sat behind his family in the train car.

"Let's take her home Freddie," Fred said for one last time. And the two Freds had the ride of their lives, the train going as slowly as possible while still considered to be moving.

Back in the train station, Ray helped Fred out again. Fred took a hanky out of his pocket and wiped the engine down a bit with a soft touch. "I should have built a bigger engine forty years ago Ray, this one's a bit tough to get in and out of."

Fred walked back to his home, the Wolf House, and watched the young pups playing in the rocks. Fred smiled at the young wolves as they jumped and tumbled all over each other and felt his heart breaking with the realization that he was no longer a part of that world that he loved so much. Born into a dualism that he tried hard to overcome, Fred felt for a brief moment, that perhaps he failed. Perhaps he missed out on the special moments.

He limped to his couch and sought comfort from his pains and relief from his doubts as he lay flat on his back. He heard a pup howl trying to be strong and then another, a third wolf-pup joined the song and then they all got quiet and listened along with Fred as the alpha wolf howled the wolf's song of goodbye. Pains gone, a lasting smile on his face, Fred was assured in song of the oneness he sought in life. *Be at peace Fred Grant, you are home.*

Fred Grant had worked and planned hard for a future where he would have an actual presence without having a physical one. Immediately after his death, following the wishes of Fred as outlined in his will, his body was transported to Texas for a family and business associates' wake. At this point, Fred's executor and longtime CEO, Vince Gutterson, implemented Fred's plan.

Vince Gutterson began working for Fred in 1960. Fred hired Vince to manage his companies so he could spend his days setting up the Cubo Zoo. Vince admired everything that Fred Grant did and what Fred stood for. He fought every day of his life for the betterment of Fred and the Grant Foundation. There were some very specific things to get done which Fred had discussed in great detail with Vince and all outlined in Fred's will.

Fred took care of the Lupus' in many ways and good to his word he made sure that Karen would be comfortable if she lived to be a thousand. He left Karen millions of dollars and he did the same for Freddie. Freddie's money was put in trust and Freddie would gain control of his money at age 25. There were also stock gifts and options in the Grant Foundation for both of them and Karen was given a board position in the Frederick Grant Foundation, the managing board of all Grant industries.

In keeping with the wishes of Ray Lupus, Fred left him the Wolf House, and a lifetime job as zookeeper at a modest pay of one thousand dollars a week. Ray insisted on receiving nothing more, he had never even touched the money he received from his wife Diane's insurance policy. With the gift of the Wolf House, Ray was able to gift the Lupus Ranch to Karen and Freddie so they could have a more traditional mother-son relationship. Ray would be quite happy with his time in the zoo and his private time watching the wolves from his new home's observation room. Many provisions and safeguards accompanied this inheritance and Vince was the perfect legal mind to handle everything. The Lupus' were set for generations to come.

Fred had a couple minor requests for himself also that Vince took care of. By prearrangement with Dr. Helen Stapleton's family, and for a tidy sum, Helen's remains were moved to the Lupus Ranch along with Fred Grant's following his wake in Texas. Helen and Fred would join Blackie in what was to become the Grant/Lupus Family plot along the edge of Little Lake Michigan where Blackie was already at rest. Within a week of Fred's death, the private funeral at the family plot took place.

It was an odd funeral by funeral standards, but in the world of Ray Lupus it was perfectly normal. Normal as it could be when you start a cemetery with a wolf, bury a lady that died years ago, bury a man on the property he bought and once owned but had given away, and leave enough land in the cemetery to bury yourself and your descendants - a cemetery on the edges of a lake where a murdered man rests and backed up by a forest where a young lady and a stallion met a violent death. Yes, in the world of Ray Lupus, it was a perfectly normal funeral.

A minister from town handled the services, speaking kind words about Helen and glowing words of Fred. The minister never mentioned Blackie which didn't sit well with Ray, but the few people there listened quietly all lost in their own thoughts. The three ladies that comprised the zoo board were there, very shaken as they had all been with Fred at the zoo almost from the beginning. Karen and Freddie stood together, inwardly emotional, but appearing very stoic. Also attending was a couple of people from town who knew Fred as well as he allowed them to, and three or four workers from the zoo. A small, quick funeral and everyone was on their way.

After all the cars had gone, Ray, Karen, and Freddie walked back to the ranch house. With the sound of burial equipment in the background, Ray summed up his feelings in his comment to Karen.

"He never mentioned Blackie, don't let that talk guy say one word at my funeral."

Some deaths leave an emptiness in the world, but Fred Grant's left a black hole that continued to swallow life as it grew. Fred left money in his place, but the money could not bind together the people and things he loved. With their anchor, their glue, gone, people moved on to live their own lives. They always gave consideration for, as they say, 'what Fred would have wanted,' but the tight family bond Fred created became a loose group with individual goals.

Following the wishes of Fred, Ray moved into the Wolf house. From there Ray pretty much ran the physical demands of the zoo. He drove the train, led trail rides, helped wherever he could with the animals, and ran security. He was law and order at the zoo. Ray knew his move inside the zoo was the right move, Fred convinced him of that long ago, but he missed the togetherness of family and felt his absence from the ranch house left his family vulnerable. He did feel personally home inside the zoo and watched those around him move on with their lives.

The three ladies of the zoo board retired one by one. The last to go was Ray's best friend Linda Reynolds. Other workers that Ray knew left the zoo also. No more human faces that Ray felt comfortable enough with to talk to. He found more and more comfort in Kingston and the wolf pack. Losing the calming effects of Fred and replacing those actions with animal instincts began to change Ray once again. The cyclone was on the way and no warning was sounded.

CHAPTER 26

When the pills wore off, a less agitated Ray Lupus woke to face the day. He sat on the edge of his bed organizing in his mind and the memories that came with last night's sleep and medication. His urge to run vanished for now; his fear to speak was fleeting. He was confident his distant past was safely behind him and only the most recent of years needed to be reconciled.

He flexed his muscles, right arm, left arm; he felt strong. He clenched his fists, right fist, left fist; he felt extremely strong. He was ready to seek his enemies, first in his mind and then wherever else that should lead. Ray still felt lost in time. Today wasn't yet today for Ray. He didn't know what or who knocked him for a loop, but just knowing that something was off inside of him was a major step. Ray knew that he needed to know more, and his mind was rewiring well enough to bring answers.

"What happened to me?" Ray asked himself. "Who would want to get me?" His words were clear, and they brought Karen to his room.

"I heard you talking, more than you've talked in months."

"Freddie? Home? Work?" Ray had questions about everything, and finally with a somber look in his eyes he asked, "Karen?"

"Of course I'm Karen. Remember that for good this time. I don't know about home or work, I'll call Dr. March."

Ray interrupted Karen, "March an idiot."

"He's been good to you, I'll ask him about you being on your own when we talk today. We should go to the zoo and talk to the board, let them know you'll be back in the Wolf House soon and you'll be working again with the horses at least. Does that sound good?"

"Maybe."

"Take these now," Karen said as she handed her father the pills that March had prescribed. "Two of the strong tranquilizers and one blood thinner and I'll call March now. He'll be happy to know that the pills are working and you're finally on a positive road. Long way to go but we're finally heading in the right direction."

"Maybe," Ray repeated. "What happened to me?"

"Something in your head, we're fixing it now. That's all. Just listen to me from now on."

"Maybe."

"Is that all you're going to say?"

"Maybe, just maybe."

"Well I have another surprise for you I think you're ready for, but you must stay calm, take your pills, and keep doing your exercises and reading if you can. You need to get more of your words back. But anyhow, remember I told you that Freddie was staying with Linda Reynolds while you recovered?"

"Maybe."

"Well Linda is bringing Freddie home today. Time we got back to normal. Take those pills." Karen handed Ray his coffee and Ray swallowed his pills. Karen went to call Dr. March and Ray went to the kitchen for breakfast.

Normal, Ray thought as he stared blankly at his toast, *what in my world is normal? Something happened in my head, she says. I didn't do it to myself, I need to find answers.*

Ray began to get agitated at the table. He was certain the lost days and months were the work of an enemy, perhaps someone whom he had hurt before. As quickly as his anger rose, it quieted back down. The pills were doing their job and Ray soon forgot he was ever mad. He walked to the bar while Karen was on the phone and treated himself to an early brunch of bourbon. Three, four swigs of the smooth elixir and Ray went out to the barn to do some work.

Before he reached the barn he forgot why he was heading there. He stopped in his tracks and turned in a slow circle looking for the reason he was going anywhere. It wasn't there. He retraced his steps back to the house, stopping again at the bar and reacquainting himself with the drink. Five, six more swigs. Ray was getting warm, dizzy, confused, and finally lost once again. He stumbled over to the sofa where he collapsed in a dream state and he listened to Karen's voice as she spoke with the doctor.

Karen told March about Ray's increased abilities, seemingly overnight. Better physical movement, more words, clearer speech. She expressed sheer optimism. March said it was a good sign and what he expected all along. March also told Karen that the staff did a thorough review of all the tests Ray took on his Abilene visit and there is concern about blockage in a vital spot of Ray's brain. March said that he and the other doctors believe that this blockage caused Ray's stroke, is causing TIAs, and is preventing Ray's quick recovery. March said that the blood thinners are finally getting sufficient blood to Ray's brain and that explains the seemingly sudden improvement.

Karen thought this all good news and wondered if increasing the dosage would be even more helpful. March stopped Karen at this point and read from the other side of the coin.

"Thinners are only a temporary relief. It could be a day, it could be years, but Ray is going to sooner or later have more TIAs and eventually, in all likelihood, he'll have another major stroke. You're going to see the father you knew come and go. I'll repeat what I've told you, we need to get Ray in Kansas City and get him tested on the state-of-the-art equipment we have here. I think it's Ray's only chance for a complete recovery."

"He won't go to Kansas City, and in all honesty, you don't know if you can do anything more for him than the thinners. Surgery could kill him too and, as you said, he could live years with this issue and never have another major stroke."

"That's the optimistic view, I'd like to get a complete look at Ray's brain and make a recommendation from there."

"Not now - not as long as he's improving, we're going to stay the course. Can he be alone? Dad wants to go back to work and move back into his house at the zoo."

"I guess work is okay, but you'd better be on call, just in case. I wouldn't let him move back home yet. If he has another TIA, and he will, he could come out of it completely lost. No telling what he would do in that state. Keep him with you for a while yet, we'll talk again next week."

"We're going to meet with the zoo board soon. I'll tell them that Dad is going to be working again, whatever jobs he chooses to do, and that he'll be back at the Wolf House soon. I'll mention that he has your support for both of these moves."

"Yes, you have my support. You know that. And on another subject Karen, if you could say a thanks to the Foundation Board, I'd appreciate that. The Frederick Grant Wing is open now and we wish you'd come and tour the hospital. We're doing some great things for children now, really making a difference thanks to Fred and your father. I know this wing was meant to be one of their proudest achievements. I was so happy that you agreed to be on the Foundation Board, Fred often told me he knew you'd be amazing with that responsibility."

"Well thank you doctor, it's rewarding work, I try to follow Fred's dreams. I'll talk to you soon, goodbye."

As intent as Ray tried to listen to their talk, he slipped away from today early on. He fell quickly back to the time of Fred's death.

Ray didn't mourn the loss for long, he worried more about what Fred's death would mean to little Freddie and devoted himself to keeping Freddie strong, safe, and happy.

Freddie spent time at the Wolf House with Ray and many days at the zoo with him. By age eight or so, Freddie could drive the train quite well and was nearly strong enough to saddle a horse. Freddie and Ray spent hours together at the zoo, tending to the horses, watching the wolves, and visiting with Kingston. They would sit far too close to Kingston and have long conversations. Kingston would move his head as if understanding everything that was said and Ray was certain that Kingston did understand.

It was a functional time for Ray, more lows than highs, only to be further broken when Freddie began school. That began a slow downturn in Ray and his depression took over most of his days. But as sad as Ray was for himself, he was happy for Karen and Freddie. In fact, Ray was a better pseudo parent to Freddie than he felt he ever was to Karen.

As time passed, Ray realized that he was far too protective of Karen and perhaps stymied her growth. It was the great lesson that Fred Grant taught Ray and finally after Fred's death the message got through. Ray was never going to stop being overprotective of Karen, but he was doing what he could to help Freddie be independent and strong.

Any doubts that Freddie was following in Ray's footsteps were put to rest when Freddie completed second grade. Karen got a call from the school principal requesting a meeting which she quickly agreed to attend. Ray insisted on going along.

"Thank you both for coming in today," Principal Dean began as everyone took a seat in his inner office. Ray looked around almost in horror as his mind recalled the many days of his youth spent on the hot seat in this same environment. He almost had his fill before the real meeting even began.

"Always happy to help the school," Karen replied, "what can we do for you today?"

"Please, call me Ed, Principal Dean sounds so odd, I've never grown accustomed to it. It does beat Dean Dean, however, I think that's why I've stayed away from teaching at college."

Ray found no humor and was confused by the entire joke.

"How can we help the school this time, Ed?" Karen asked.

"Well there are some things that we'll be discussing at the next PTA meeting, but this meeting is to discuss Freddie and his behavior. It seems that Freddie got into an altercation with another student and my understanding is that if the teacher did not pull Freddie off of the other student Freddie would have injured him quite badly."

"Oh," said a surprised Karen. Ray didn't see the point yet and sat befuddled. "What riled Freddie up?" Karen continued.

"Freddie told us that the other student called him stupid or said that he looked stupid. Forgive my bluntness Mr. Lupus."

"That's okay Ed, I always try to teach Freddie to be strong and defend himself and the family. I appreciate you sharing this with us. Freddie's a good boy."

"Dad," Karen interrupted, "I don't think Ed has called us here to praise Freddie's fighting ability or righteousness."

"I don't understand," Ray replied, "why are we here then?"

"Well Mr. Lupus," the principal continued cautiously, "we don't encouraged fighting for any reason. We would hope you could explain this to Freddie."

"A kid called him stupid Ed, what did you want Freddie to do?"

"He can bring his concerns to his teacher."

"Why would he do that when he can handle things himself? Besides, what would you have done if he brought his so-called concerns to a teacher? Where is this foul-mouthed kid that called him stupid? Where are his parents?" Ray was speaking louder now and quicker, his face red with anger.

Karen asked him to slow down and then repeated Ray's question to Ed.

"Where is this other student and his parents?"

"In all honesty, we haven't gotten that far into this yet, we wanted to stop the violence in these young children first."

"You stop the damn words first," Ray yelled at Principal Dean. "I can if you won't. Who is the kid that thought it was okay to call Freddie stupid? If my grandson is being attacked, I have a right to know who's doing it. If you don't tell me then Freddie will, that won't go well for anybody."

"Please calm down Mr. Lupus, it was George Dickson's boy, Curtis. I assure you I will be talking to George, we'll stop this. These are just kids Mr. Lupus, we mustn't overreact."

"You overreacted, you should have let the kids handle it. I better see that jackass Dickson in here tomorrow getting the same crap from you that I just got. If not, I'll be at his house tomorrow night, you'll see who's stupid then Ed."

Karen heard enough and asked her father to leave. She explained to Ed that she understood the need to teach children the wrongs of fighting and promised to talk to Freddie, but she added, the school better reach out to George Dickson because if there is a next time, her father will likely insist on handling matters one on one with George and perhaps one on one with Ed also.

"My dad will come alone next time you call. Fix this, the clock's ticking." And with that Karen left too.

Ray was proud of the lessons he taught Freddie and they replayed fondly in Ray's mind. And Ray was certain his way was the right way, after his talk with the principal the Dickson boy never ever said another word about Ray or Freddie Lupus again.

CHAPTER 27

R ay sat in his fog, remembering the years with Freddie, their walks, their talks, their hours together at the zoo and at the home ranch. While very young, Freddie was given lessons in caring about the animals, caring about the land around his home, he heard tales of the lake and the woods. Most important to Ray were the lessons necessary for a protector to learn. Ray needed Freddie to grow up and be the protector of the family, mainly of Karen Lupus.

In addition to the words of Ray Lupus, well intentioned and perhaps ill directed words, Ray added some lessons of what he called righteous fisticuffs. Freddie had seen his grandfather straighten out a good many folks at the zoo and by age ten he wasn't opposed to raising his voice and correcting any wrongdoer at the zoo. Armed with knowledge of fighting learned in the Lupus barn, Freddie was walking the footsteps of Ray and Ray loved it. In Ray's mind, the family would be safe for a very long time. As talks from the past played in Ray's mind, he thought he could see Freddie standing in the corner of the room. Ray heard voices.

"Freddie?" Ray shouted.

"Grandpa?" Came the reply, but not from the past nor from within the room but rather from the kitchen and it was shouted today, it was shouted now. Freddie was home and Ray was getting close.

Ray lumbered out to the kitchen and saw that Freddie was home and standing with Karen and Linda Reynolds. A big smile came over Ray's face and he was almost moved to tears to see the boy.

"My god how big you've grown Freddie, how long have I been away?"

"Hello Ray," Linda said trying to help everyone focus on happier things than Ray's missing months.

Freddie ran over and gave Ray a big hug as he nodded to Linda.

"Dad I was just telling Linda that you think you're ready to return to work and move back to the Wolf House. You still feel that way?"

"Yes, for sure. How've you been Linda? Tell me later, me and Freddie are going to take a walk to the lake. Halloween's getting close, maybe Fred or Helen will pay us a visit. What do you think Freddie?"

"Whatever you say Gramps, but I've never seen a ghost."

"Wait until you're my age, son, I see them all the time."

"Dad, take your pills before you go, you want to keep your words coming. Take a long walk, no more ghost talk, Linda and I have a lot to talk about, no hurry."

"Tomorrow we visit the zoo?"

"Yes, tomorrow, now focus. Go for your walk."

Ray and Freddie went out the door and headed to the lake. Linda was confused and wasted no time asking about Ray.

"Was Ray kidding about the ghosts? That's a good thing if he was, isn't it?"

"I don't know anymore, Linda, I do think he sees things. I've seen him in the middle of the night looking around here for Blackie."

"That old wolf that he brought here to live? Oh, I remember how Fred made us come out here for the funeral. I thought it weird at the time but knowing those two, I guess it made sense. Do you think Ray's ready for work?"

"A little work yes, he doesn't do much at the zoo anymore, walks around and talks to people. That will be good for him. Living alone is another story, he's really only been talking well for a couple of days. The doctor thinks his meds are getting more blood to his brain, it takes them so damn long to figure things out, I guess we should have stayed in the hospital longer but he was doing okay. He just quit talking when we got home and got worse by the day. Can I tell you something Linda?"

"Of course, anything."

"I don't think Dad knows what year it is any more and there are times I'm sure he doesn't know me. He expects his little girl to be here and when he looks at me he can get confused, mad even,"

"Do you think you had me bring Freddie home too soon?"

"No, I think Freddie will help Dad's memory, ground him in today I hope, and the pills are working. We may be past the worst."

The girls continued to visit, and Ray and Freddie returned to the house. Freddie went to his room to do whatever it is ten-year olds do. Ray sat and listened to the ladies' gossip. When night fell, Linda joined the Lupus' for dinner and talked turned to the old days and old friends. It was a nice night and an exhausted Ray turned in as soon as Linda left. Before Freddie turned in, he had a few words with his mom.

"Grandpa said he's going back to the zoo and the Wolf House tomorrow. He said if anybody gives him any grief there, they'll pay like nobody's ever paid before. What'd he mean by that?"

"I don't know, I'll talk to Gramps. He shouldn't talk like that to you."

"That's the other thing, he wasn't talking to me. He said he was talking to Fred and Helen."

It was a sleepless night for Karen; Freddie's comments were disturbing. If Ray thought he was talking to Fred and Helen, then there is no way he is ready to be left alone. He needed more healing time, professional rehab perhaps, but there was no way she was going to put him through that all the way in Kansas City.

She decided it best to push her dad a little, have him go back to work a few hours a day and work his way back home to the Wolf House. She had seen the quick improvement and believed, if built upon, her father could recover almost fully. She could spend the time at the zoo with her dad and drive him back to the main house afterward. She talked herself into her plan and had great confidence that it was the right course.

When Ray woke up and came to the kitchen, Karen had his pills ready. After so many months of climbing back, this was a first step on the old road, doing it without those who have passed away would be the preferred manner. A worried Karen was nonetheless feeling excited. She saw her dad more deeply than others; she knew he was in there someplace.

"Good morning Dad," Karen said with pills in her hand, "take these and I'll get you some coffee. Big day today."

Ray swallowed the pills with the juice Karen had before him. "What's so big about it?"

"Our meeting with the zoo board, letting them know you're coming back to work and to live there again soon. They'll be happy to see you."

"We seeing those guys today? I don't think they like me. Are we safe there? Where's Freddie? Is he safe? When did this zoo thing come up?"

"We're all safe, stop being silly. Freddie's in school. What's troubling you?"

Ray sat silent, almost frozen in is chair. "I don't remember. What's wrong with me? Someone tried to hurt us though, I remember that."

"You had a stroke. It's over now and you're healing. No one tried to hurt you. This is what you wanted, work, the zoo, home, everything that's your life. You can do it. Relax and let these pills calm you. We'll go when you're ready."

They sat and didn't say much. They both had a couple cups of coffee and Ray turned his cup around and around until some things finally made a little sense in his mind. "I'll get ready," he said as he disappeared back into his bedroom.

The ride to the zoo was quiet. Karen understood that she was just being respectful in letting the zoo board know that Ray was coming back. Ray had what amounted to a lifetime contract to work at the zoo at whatever hours he saw fit, and the Wolf House was now Ray's, so he didn't need anyone's permission to be there. But as a board member of the Grant Foundation herself, Karen wished to maintain a civil working relationship with the zoo group. She felt nervous about the meeting, but didn't really know why.

Ray sat very relaxed; the extra pill Karen gave Ray was, what you might say, 'just what the doctor ordered,' even though it was exactly what the doctor didn't order. Dr. March cautioned Karen about over medicating, but Karen knew best and could see day to day what worked best for her father. She had a handle on how many blood thinner pills it took to keep Ray's mind working and how many tranquilizers it took to allow Ray to handle his renewed thoughts and memories. As Ray sat quietly, off in some other world, Karen was certain that they were on the right course.

At the zoo, Karen drove around to Ray's house and parked on his driveway. Entering the front door, Ray stopped, looked around, and smiled. "The Wolf House," he uttered and ran upstairs to look at the wolves from the room overlooking their den. Friskie, the alpha wolf ever since Blackie left, saw Ray and scratched at the ground. He did a short leap in the air and spun around. Ray laughed and tried to do the same. He stopped his actions when he heard Karen come up the stairs.

"We should go to the office and see the group, I'm sure they're waiting for us."

Ray and Karen walked back downstairs and out the back door of the Wolf House which led into the zoo. As Karen closed the gate behind them, Ray wandered off again, this time to the primate area. He was off to visit Kingston. Karen knew that there was no point in calling him back now, he would have to visit with Kingston before the meeting.

Kingston sprung over to the bars at the outside of his cage, Ray hopped over the protective fence and touched hands with the gorilla. Kingston jumped back and ran over to his fruit only to bring an apple back to Ray. Ray took a bite and handed it back to Kingston, the apple then disappeared. Ray talked for a while with Kingston and then visited the horses in the stable and toured the rest of the grounds.

Karen noticed a worker giving them the eye as they walked. She didn't wish to rile her dad up, so she said nothing.

A couple hours later, they finally entered the administration building and were ready for what should have been a short meeting. Karen and Ray sat at the table across from two of the board members. At the head of the table sat the CEO and off to the side sat the CEO's secretary, apparently ready to take notes.

Karen knew all of these ladies. They all came on board after the death of Fred Grant and the subsequent retirement of his original board. Linda Reynolds stayed on the longest after Fred passed away and helped Karen and Vince Gutterson make these hires. Vince sent out feelers to find candidates to interview and got responses from all over the country. The board positions were only a part of the job as each position also came with day to day zoo responsibilities. There was much travel involved, good pay, and a self-managed workplace. These were indeed highly sought-after positions.

All the women who were hired possessed intelligence, knowledge of wildlife, and ambition. Of the three hired, Karen only felt comfortable with Sue Vrablick. Sue was from Chicago, as was Karen, and they often talked about the things in the city that Karen missed out on by having left it so early in her life.

Sue knew the neighborhood that the Lupus' were from and Karen loved to hear about Sue's days there. Sue's background was in conservation biology where, along with her Ph.D., she also possessed over twenty years' experience with zoos from Chicago to Denver. She stayed mainly out in the zoo with the animals and limited her involvement with donors and office politics.

As friendly as Sue had been with Karen today, she kept her eyes low.

Janice Simons sat next to Sue. Janice came from Texas and was one of Vince's favorite hires. Janice majored in business management, marketing, and communications. She came recommended by Vince's contacts at the Texas Zoo and Wildlife Association where Janice was in charge of finances and fund raising. If and when Janice left the office, it was to attend posh, out of state gatherings to help raise funds. Vince believed this role would take a lot of responsibility off of his back even though most of the large donors came from his leads.

The energy companies that swam in the same waters were tapped into for large amounts of donations to the Cubo Zoo. The Cubo wasn't a very big zoo by zoo standards and it didn't have half the animals of major zoos, but through the work of Fred Grant, it was one of, if not *the* richest zoo in the country. Janice went out of her way to take credit for the zoo's financial standing even though just about anyone else would be equally successful.

Janice and Karen were cool toward one another. Karen was raised to live simply and never think much about all the money she had; Janice lived in constant chase of dollars as a personal scorecard of success. They seldom talked and this afternoon was no exception.

At the head of the table sat the CEO, Barbara Tummelvic. Barbara was a high-wired east coast transplant, coming to Kansas from the zoos of New York. She possessed fundraising skills and business management acumen and graduated college with a degree in animal behavior and biology. She was driven by a love of power and to a lesser degree money, and although she worked with and for animals, they weren't that deeply entrenched in her heart. They were a job.

The coolness she displayed towards the animals could not be viewed as a failing to them. She was involved in research and studies and funding that made life a thousand times better for these animals. She was all work and no play and always had her sights on higher rungs on taller ladders. She insisted on org charts and chain of command loyalty. She spent money on her office and personal comfort where she felt necessary. She would have been a great military commander and because of that, made an acceptable CEO.

Barbara's belief in following a set hard line structure may have been in the best interest of the zoo, but it was not in the interest of Ray Lupus. There was no love lost between these two and Karen had known that for a long time. Ray's official role was to come and go as he pleased and oversee whatever he wished, all for a very nice monthly paycheck that Ray never needed. He was the thorn under Barbara's saddle. The stone face that Barbara wore this morning underscored that feeling. Barbara spoke first.

"Good afternoon Karen. I had you scheduled for this morning I must have misunderstood you."

"Not at all Barb, Dad just got caught up in seeing all his friends around the zoo, took a while to get past them."

"My secretary will take notes. Karen you asked to meet with us here so please state what's on your mind."

"A secretary? My how we have grown, good for you. I doubt you need to take notes, but do what you wish. Before we start, who is the worker walking around in the cowboy hat? He seemed to be staring at me and my father."

"That is Clyde Endel," Barb said coldly and sternly, "he's a supervisor on the grounds, does quite a lot of everything. He's filled the void your father left, before and after his illness. I knew Mr. Endel in New York and he is a most valuable person to have around the zoo. Ray and Clyde worked together for a few weeks before Ray's stroke. I'm surprised you never shared this info Ray. But please move on, why are we here?"

The temperature in the room was dropping quickly and Karen

had no idea why. Ray sat quietly, his meds keeping him relaxed and somewhat out of the loop. His thoughts were on Fred and Linda and the other board members that used to laugh and tell stories in this room. Calmer in those memories, Ray still managed to stay in the present as his mind fought to go back in time once more. Being able to think about the past without disappearing into it was a big moment for Ray, but he had no idea of any difference.

"We're only here as a courtesy," Karen began, "Dad feels he's ready to return to the zoo and do some odd jobs and eventually he'll be back living in the Wolf House. I just wanted everyone here to be aware of that and ask that if he should ever seem a bit out of sorts, that someone calls me. Strokes can repeat themselves and we should all look after each other."

All eyes looked down at the table and the room was quiet, even Ray sat motionless not sure what he just heard. Barbara Tummelvic spoke next.

"It surprises me, that Ray has plans on coming back. The last time we spoke, before Ray's illness, we explained to Ray that the zoo was interested in re-annexing the Wolf House and using it as a new administration building. We badly need the space and it makes much more sense than erecting another office building. You folks will be paid fairly for the building, but you must understand that a building connected to zoo property has little or no value."

Karen was in shock. "You actually think you are going to take away my father's home given to him by Fred Grant? Are you insane? For money? We could buy and sell all of you."

"Please calm down Karen. Here's our lawyer's card, you can call him if you wish. He's currently handling all the paperwork to make this sale possible, if you should fight us on this, then we will have no choice but to go the courts and invoke eminent domain. Fred should never have taken land away from the zoo for personal use, our lawyer is certain of that, and we merely want to get on the right side of the law."

"And Dad just drives to work every day and becomes a stranger in the zoo he helped build over the years?"

"Number one," Barbara said to Karen, "that's life and it happens to many of us, but secondly, and I did discuss this with Ray, we feel that it is in everyone's best interest if Ray retired from the zoo. He's been known to be a little surly to visitors and he has, on occasion, threatened Clyde and some other workers. I don't like saying this again, but Karen, we simply can't have him here anymore. Time has moved on."

Karen stomach turned and tears welled up in her eyes. She stared at her father and could not believe what this board was trying to do to him. She grew lightheaded and words wouldn't come. Ray looked in her eyes and saw the tears. Anger followed.

"What the hell are you people doing to Karen? You better have a good answer," Ray shouted at the group as he rose from his seat, towering over the room.

"You see the problem clearly now, don't you? Our lawyer will have a price on the house ready by tomorrow. I'll have him call you."

"Tomorrow?" Karen said quietly, plotting inside. "Just give us the rest of the week and the weekend Barb. We can all meet again here on Monday, have your lawyer bring the offer then. I'll be here, I'm not sure about Dad yet."

"I go where I want," Ray shouted at them.

"You've made a wise decision," Barb said, "the sooner we wrap this up the better."

"We'll see you on Monday. I'm just going to take Dad home for a while, we'll be in the Wolf House."

On those sad words, the meeting adjourned. No one else spoke a word and all was recorded into the zoo record. Karen and Ray returned to the Wolf House and were upstairs watching the wolves when they heard the back door open, it was Sue Vrablick. Ray and Karen went down to talk to her.

"Karen I just want you to know that I have nothing to do with this," Sue said with a fair amount of nervousness in her voice.

"Exactly what is the 'this' you are referring to Sue?"

"Getting Ray off the grounds and taking his house. I should have called you sooner. The day Ray had his stroke was the day they sprung this on him. I think the threat may have led to his stroke, but I guess I don't really know."

"Why don't you tell us what you do know."

"Well Barb, and to a lesser degree Janice, are a couple of really ambitious people. I think they feel buried here. The cocktail parties and fundraisers they fly out to are probably okay for Janice, but they're not enough for Barb. She wants Westgate to be LA and if that can't happen, she'll try and change this place and get more action here, whatever that is in her world. I heard her talking to Clyde about getting the Wolf House and living there and hosting big moneyed events here."

"What does Clyde have to do with anything?"

"I think they're a couple. Barb brought Clyde here soon after she started. He was with her in New York, real eastern attitude. I see them arguing a lot, but they come and go together much of the time. They want this house and they want this zoo to be a player on the national scene. My understanding is that is not what Fred Grant ever wanted and Ray is a link to Fred, so in their minds, Ray must go. They'll do whatever it takes to get rid of your father and I can't help, I'm one vote and if I go against Barb, then I'm gone and I love it here, I need to be with these animals. Please don't tell anyone that I said these things. I just wanted you to know. I like you and your father, Karen. Good luck in whatever you do."

And Sue was gone, taking her nervousness with her and hoping nobody saw her walking out of the Wolf House. Ray looked to Karen, confusion on his face. "Don't worry Dad. I haven't said much today but I've got this. I just need to know all I can about those women before firing back."

Karen and Ray took a final walk around the house and the zoo before heading back to the ranch. Ray's meds were wearing off and his mind was becoming agitated. As Karen began driving, Ray began complaining.

"They're after me, they won't stop until they get rid of me and my animals. We're all in trouble. I have to act first." Ray spoke quickly, not loudly yet.

"Did they threaten to move you out of your house before?"

"I don't remember. Why are they trying to move us? Do they want our ranch too?"

"Don't worry I'll take care of this."

"I think yes."

"Yes what?"

"I think I've been through this before. Maybe not. My mind's not good anymore. I'm dizzy, I need to lie down."

Karen drove the rest of the way back to the ranch in silence. Ray mumbled, "They're after us. They'll be sorry. We need to run. We need to find them first." Back and forth, whispers and shouts.

Karen feared she was losing her dad again and wondered about his previous meeting with Barb. Did she cause or at least push his stroke? Was another spell coming? How should she proceed with Barb's threat? She pulled up her drive and parked alongside the house. Ray exited and stood looking down the road. Karen ran in and got a few more of Ray's blue pills, the ones meant to calm him down. Ray swallowed them quickly and let his anger loose.

"Those bastards, those rotten bastards! This isn't over Karen," Ray Shouted. "Fred said he would take care of us. Where's Fred now? I can't take this anymore."

Karen tried to give her dad a reassuring yell of "don't worry", but it was too late. Ray took off for the lake cursing away as he walked. Karen went inside to phone Vince Gutterson.

Karen was on the line with Vince long before Ray reached the lake and the monument area. She filled Vince in on the dealings of Barb, Janice, Sue, Clyde, and Barb's lawyer Walt Samuels, reading his info to Vince from the business card Bard provided. She talked a long time with Vince offering apologies often along the way. Things obviously got away from everyone associated with the zoo.

Vince said that he would arrive in town either Saturday or Sunday and he would be at Monday's meeting. He let Karen know that he would be staying at the ranch where he always does when visiting Westgate, about twenty miles southwest of Karen's place. If anything else came up, Karen was to notify Vince immediately. Vince left Karen with some somber words.

"You know there's no way this ends nicely."

"I understand."

"Have you ever thought about what you and your family would do without the zoo?"

"I don't think that's an option. I better go see how Dad's doing. He's been away a while now."

The wait before the battle, Karen thought, as she walked down the road. Her nerves were twisted as tightly as they've ever been. Months of dealing with the past was turning to dealing with the future. Life had its hard turns for the Lupus'. As Karen neared the monument field, she saw her father lying on the ground. Her walking steps turned to a run as she flew to her father's side.

"Dad! What's wrong? What happened?"

Ray looked up, he wasn't having a seizure or a battle with a

TIA. His battle was with his vision, his memory of where he was. His hands shook as he reached up to touch Karen's face. *My daughter*, he thought. He felt a bruise and large bump on the back of his head.

"Dad, your heads bleeding. Did you fall?"

His speech was still forced, words far from perfect but understandable. "I'm remembering now, a little bit. This happened before. It was a while back I think, not real long ago. Those zoo people did this to me. They told me to get out. Get out of the zoo, get out of my own house. I remember coming here after they spoke to me. I was mad at Fred for not taking care of us; he promised to always be here and take care of us. Oh god, Karen, I was so mad. I was cussing and yelling at Fred, I picked up this boulder and I was going to smash Fred's monument. Thank god I didn't do that. Something stopped me, I don't know what. I had this boulder over my head, and I was cussing at Fred and that's it. I woke up in that hospital in Abilene and you were there. Everything was foggy and I've been trying to piece it together from there, I was scared that I did wrong, scared that I hurt someone, but I remember now, it wasn't me, it was them. The threats from Barb and that Clyde person hurt me and they're starting all over again. I came here and knew it was happening all over again, the same thing over again. I picked up this damn rock. Now turned into then and I was blaming Fred all over again. I was ready to smash these monuments, but just like last time I blacked out. I wake up in pain looking at you. I never was the problem, Fred never abandoned us. I know who the problem is now. You understand, don't you?"

"I think I'm starting to Dad. On that day they told you that you'd have to leave your home and the zoo. Your anger raged and your heart raced. It hurt you and you came here and had a very bad stroke. It has taken quite a few months for your memory to come back and just when it has, Barb said the same words again. It's not your mind playing tricks again. And you're right, we have to stop this person. Vince will be here Monday. You spend a nice weekend with Freddie, I'll take care of everything. Do you have any interest in moving on without the zoo in our lives?"

"Not an option. I gave my word to Fred on that."

"That's good. Let's go back to the house."

Ray paused in yet another moment of confusion and felt the

growing bruise on his head. "I don't think I had a stroke Karen."

CHAPTER 28

Ray and Freddie spent the weekend together just hanging out. Karen didn't appear to be doing anything to prepare for Monday's meeting, but Ray didn't let that bother him. October was drawing to a close and Ray thought it would be a good idea to take a couple of the horses out for a final gallop. He and Freddie drove to the zoo and parked in the main lot. Ray sat frozen for a while staring at a white SUV parked in front of him.

"What's wrong Gramps?" Freddie asked him. "You look mad."

"I know who owns that white car. She wants to hurt us. Wait here." Freddie sat in the car as Ray walked over to Barb's RAV4. Ray looked in the windows without having any idea what he was looking for. He thought about smashing the windows in, but knew that would only cause problems. He let the RAV4 stoke his fire and took his anger back to the car with him.

"Feel better now?"

"Worse, so yes, in my own way that means better."

"Is it whose you thought?"

"It is the car of our enemy, I'll take care of it. I don't feel up to the zoo now, let's go buy you a Halloween costume."

"I have one already."

"Then you'll have two, and some candy too. It will be good to shop. Mindless even."

The weekend came to an end following days of tension and nervousness for Karen. Ray seemed at peace as he spent the time with Freddie. Freddie was not yet 12, but possessed the look of a wild teen. When Freddie and Ray walked down the street, you couldn't miss them.

Karen and Ray drove Freddie to school on Monday and then went straight to the meeting at the zoo. This time they parked at the main gate and walked quickly past the animals to the admin office. The same group was seated in the same room and they were now joined by Clyde, who sat alone in a corner, and Barb's lawyer, Walt Samuels. Barb once again started the meeting.

"Well I guess we're all here. Let's make this quick. Karen, are you and your father now in agreement with giving up the Wolf House and moving on?"

Before Karen could speak Walt spoke up. "I'm sorry Barb I had a call on Saturday from someone claiming to be Ray's lawyer and he said that he would be here this morning and advised us to wait."

"We're under no obligation to wait," an agitated Barb said, "I want to get past this. Who is your lawyer?"

"That would be Vince Gutterson," Karen said calmly.

And as if on cue, Vince Gutterson walked through the door larger than life. "Sorry I'm late folks, the Kansas cold hit me unexpectedly this morning, so I stopped for a cup of hot chocolate. Kept bumping into old friends of mine and Fred's. I really love this friendly community. Don't you Barb?"

Barb was startled by being singled out but replied nonetheless. "Yes, Vince. It's good to see you, but you didn't need to make this trip. We're just discussing a local matter today, nothing the foundation board needs to be concerned with."

"I would recommend that you quit stating the foundation's responsibilities, best I inform you about what they are. I have a packet of legal documents here for everyone I'll pass out and I'll go over these items with you. Ray, I brought a packet for you, but as you know it's up to you if you wish to stay or not. I can fill you in later if you prefer."

"I think I'll stay and listen, make sure nobody gets out of line."

"Good," Vince said. "Let's start with this annexation of the Wolf House. Explain this."

"The zoo needs the space and the building. We can't afford to buy new land and build from scratch."

"Well we sure as hell could if we needed to, but continue."

"To save money, I felt it was in everybody's best interest to reacquire the Wolf House for the zoo. Walt and I felt it was wrong for Fred Grant to take personal land from the zoo. We are attempting to right that wrong."

"You started this process a good six months ago. You tried to move Ray out about four months ago. What's your hold up?"

"Things slowed down when Ray took ill. We were being respectful, and now were just hitting some walls finding the transfer documents of the Wolf House to Fred and now Ray. When we have those, we'll file to get the property back."

"You're awfully quiet, Walt. That seems like a long time for a high-billing lawyer to find public documents."

"Papers may have been misfiled, Vince. I'm trying."

"Six months of searching concerns me Mr. Samuels. Makes me wonder if you're doing an honest day's work. You could make a lot of money delaying this. Or here's a wild thought, what if you found something that didn't help your mission here, you could try to move this along by conning people and getting signatures. But of course, that would be illegal and at best you'd lose your license and perhaps even end up in jail."

The room sat in absolute silence. Barb's face went stark white as she stared at Clyde. Walt Samuels looked down at the table.

Vince continued. "But there couldn't be any wrongdoing on your part Walt, could there? I'm sure that after we talked this weekend you got busy and found some of your answers, didn't you?"

"I don't know what you mean," Walt offered meekly.

"I'm just saying, that if you found the answers you have been looking for and share them here we have no crime, you will skate. But if you don't have any new info, I will provide it and you can see just where you'll fall."

The silence returned as all eyes were on the table except for Clyde and Barb who tried to communicate with odd head motions. Minutes passed and Vince gave up.

"Very well," he said, "let me explain some things."

"Excuse me Vince," Walt jumped in, "I did get some info sent to me on Saturday that may be helpful. I haven't had a chance to share this with Barb yet, but may I introduce it here?"

"Well how fortunate Walt, yes please enlighten us."

"It seems that the land that Wolf House was built on never had been transferred to Fred Grant and there are no documents in that matter."

"What do you mean?" a nervous Barb asked.

"Fred Grant bought all the land around here in the 1960s. He bought the land that the zoo currently sits on, the land that the Wolf House sits on, and miles and miles of land surrounding the zoo."

"We know that", Barb said, almost in a shout, but what he bought for the zoo, including the Wolf House land belongs to the zoo."

"No, it doesn't," Walt said. "It seems that Fred bought all of the land for himself personally, and merely leased land to the zoo for zoo use, and only the land that the zoo sits on, not an inch more. This zoo leases the land, one month at a time for one dollar, paid by the Grant Foundation to the Grant Foundation. It was Fred's way to protect himself in the beginning and his family now."

"I don't believe this," Barb moaned.

"It gets better," said Vince

"What I found in court documents, on Saturday, was that when Fred Grant died, he left all of this land to Ray Lupus and his family. There are thousands of pages filed on this, the Lupus' will control this area for years to come. It's locked up tight."

"So, Ray can kick the zoo out of here?" Barb asked.

"Not exactly, but he could close it," Vince replied.

"We would never do that," Karen said, "Dad told me that that was not an option."

"Well then accept my apologies everyone, especially you Ray. I'm sorry and everything remains the same and we move forward," said Barb.

"That's not going to happen Barb," Vince said. "Fred lived for this zoo and wanted it to live forever provided it was run correctly and his true family, the Lupus family, was safe and protected here. That's my sworn responsibility. If you open your packets and look at the documents in the appendix, I want you to focus on numbers one and two."

Everyone opened their packets as Vince continued. "Number one is a copy of the letter that Walt faxed me on Saturday requesting Ray end his employment with the zoo. Number two is a section from Fred's final will. It states that if there is ever an attempt to move Ray Lupus or any of Ray's family off the zoo in any fashion, then the foundation may close the zoo in the manner spelled out in other court documents. The decision on the future of the Cubo Zoo now belongs to Ray and Karen."

A shaken Barb hunted for a way out. "Well just tear up the letter. No need to get crazy here. I'm doing good work for this place."

"Too late." Vince was beyond forgetting anything now. "I don't know what the hell gave you the idea that you could pull such a stunt, or why you would even want to. The Foundation board makes all final decisions and you would have never gotten away with this. Ray and Karen and I are lifetime board members of the foundation. Karen has agreed to also be a member of the zoo board."

"I thought the zoo board was supposed to handle all local animal related items, that's me. Don't bring Karen into this."

"And you thought that stealing Ray's home and firing him from the zoo was a local animal related item? You got a hard sell on that one Barb."

A confident Karen now spoke with greater assurance. "I made the decision to be a zoo board member, not Vince. I am going to be more active from now on and my father is going to have an increased voice on this board also."

"I guess we'll just have to learn to work together," Bard said.

"That's not going to happen. You're fired Barb," Karen said in her first order of business.

"Gone!" Ray said loudly and slowly with as much pleasure as anger, "Gone, gone, GONE," Ray actually sang.

"Janice you're gone too. Sue, you're dangling. You may want to look for other work." Karen continued. "I'll see. You two be out of here by the end of the month."

"Two days' notice?" Barb asked. "Legally I'm due more than that."

"Two days," Vince added. "Legally that's more than you deserve. Halloween is your last day to clean out your offices."

"Clyde is out too," Ray said looking at him through narrowed eyes.

"There will be no severance, no unemployment and no references." Vince informed them, "and if I were any of you, I would not list this zoo on my resume. I don't want to see any of you after Wednesday."

"I don't want to see any of you in town either," Ray said. "Might not mind bumping into you, Clyde."

"You bastard, Lupus. Be careful what you wish for," Clyde snarled.

The meeting had broken into a near war. Roles reversed and some of them disappeared. Barb's head was spinning and she knew she had to retreat for now. "Enough. Let's go. We'll come back for our stuff some other time. Maybe Wednesday."

In parting, Clyde left them with a "You all suck." Barb grabbed him by the arm, and they left the zoo. They had much to discuss as they headed home with their anger and their fears.

A pall set over the remaining group. Ray watched as Janice gathered up her belongings and said a tearful goodbye. She apologized for not being stronger and for the first time mentioned the fear she had of both Clyde and Barb. "Be careful," she cautioned Karen as she left the office for the last time. Ray's expression went blank.

Sue also apologized again and begged to be kept on. She said too that she blindly followed orders, orders given in raised tones, and ordered many products and signed many forms without taking the time to read everything. She said that she did vote, and signed papers intended to remove Ray from the premises and couldn't explain where the fear was coming from. "It seemed so real and right at the time," Sue offered.

Karen liked Sue and asked her to leave her things in the office for a few days and that they would talk in more detail after Halloween. Sue left the office leaving Ray, Vince, and Karen to discuss the status of the zoo.

They talked about re-staffing the zoo positions that were filled by Janice, Barb, and Clyde and eventually adding once again to the zoo board. They wondered about the fears the women felt from Barb and Vince blamed himself for ever trusting Barb and letting her run wild. Vince said he couldn't imagine any reason for the hostility that Barb and Clyde felt towards Ray.

"Just to play devil's advocate," Karen put in, "my dad could be scary. He probably had a run in or two with Clyde so Clyde pushed to get him out. Barb just stupidly listened to her boyfriend, it's the human thing to do, but she should have known better."

"She would do this to Ray for her love of Clyde?"

"I don't have another answer right now."

"What about this so-called fear Janice and Sue felt. Should we be worried?" Vince asked with caution in his voice.

"I doubt it," Karen said, "they'll be gone for good once they get their stuff out of here. We'll be okay."

"I have an idea," Vince said as he opened the office door and spoke to the secretary. "Call maintenance and have them change all the office locks and all the locks to the zoo gates, have that done right this instant." He turned back to Karen and Ray, "I don't want either of them in here without us or security watching them. Better to be safe than sorry."

"Makes sense, we'll pick this up next week," Karen said. "I plan on being very busy with my son over Halloween. There's a big fair at his school Wednesday night and he's really looking forward to it. Thursday, school's closed and we'll be doing something fun. You should join us Vince."

"That sounds good, now Ray, I want to see this Komodo Dragon that we brought in from Indonesia. We paid enough for him."

"Komodo Dragon? We don't have a Komodo Dragon. They don't do well in zoos. In fact, I think they're only sold on the black market. Very dangerous people. Fred would never ever have allowed that."

Vince stared at Karen whose face went from confused to worried. The winds of Halloween blew louder through the zoo.

The threesome took a slow, quiet walk around the zoo, parting at the Wolf House. Vince returned to the ranch where he was staying; he had full use of the office there and tons of work to stay on top of. He asked Ray to stay at the zoo until all the locks were changed and have ample sets made for himself, Karen, and any of the crew that he felt needed them. He repeated his concerns about Barb and Clyde once more to Ray.

Karen offered to come back for Ray after she picked Freddie up from school, but Ray said he wished to spend the next two nights in the Wolf House. He said that some of the kids go a little crazy over Halloween and zoos and cemeteries are prime targets. He felt it important to be on site.

Karen reluctantly agreed and the three agreed to meet back at the zoo Thursday at noon. At 1:30 that afternoon, the long ugly part of the day came to an end. The zoo was nearly empty and Ray walked around feeling that he was finally back home but not back to normal. He met the locksmith at the front gate and as he watched him change the locks, an uneasiness deep inside was haunting Ray Lupus. Just outside the zoo gates the cause of Ray's dread stood arguing, a raging Clyde and a defeated Barb.

"Your stupid plan to get rid of Ray and takeover the zoo got us on death's doorstep, you useless bitch. We gotta move like hell now. You grab that damn kid, he's our only ticket out. Nobody comes after us once we have the kid."

"Ray will come," a deflated Barb muttered.

"I'll take care of Ray once and for all. You just get the kid or the black market henchmen will be the least of your problems."

As the wind blew colder, the wolves howled at the dark sky, Clyde and Barb went their own way each carrying their sordid part of the plan, a nervous Karen tucked Freddie into bed and Ray stood peering out his window at the restless pack. No one had a true grip on reality.

CHAPTER 29

Halloween morning. Anyone unfamiliar with the date merely had to look out the window and they would say, "Must be Halloween."

Summer held on for a long time and as a result the leaves stayed alive on the tree branches well into October. A week of cool days and cold nights ended the fullness and the green beauty of the trees. The leaves were falling faster than rain drops, flying sideways for a few seconds and then rolling down the streets and through the fields. The ground turned hard and morning frost iced the tops of all the houses. It was seven in the morning, but the darkness made it look like five.

The entire town of Westgate was moving slowly except for the children, they were all up early putting on their costumes and readying their trick or treat bags. Freddie was slowly getting ready for school, slipping into the green hoodie that was part of his costume and putting the Frankenstein mask, the rest of his costume, into his pocket. He walked to the kitchen where his mother stood at the back door, holding her coffee mug with both hands, using it as much for warmth as for coffee. She seemed distant and Freddie noticed the faraway look immediately.

"What's wrong?" he asked. "Are you mad at me?" Kids almost always blame themselves for their mother's unhappiness.

"No, I'm not mad at you, and if I knew what was wrong I would tell you. It's something inside crawling around, I can't say what it is. Maybe it's just autumn and seeing everything die, the trees and flowers, the birds are gone. Not a good time I guess." She paused when she saw the sad look come over Freddie and tried to change her tone. "But it will be a great day for you, I promise. Where's your mask?"

"In my pocket, I'll put it on when we get to school. It's kind of hot under it."

Karen poured out the half cup of coffee she had let go cold and poured herself a fresh hot cup. Her stomach churned and she had no idea why, she also didn't realize that she wasn't alone in her nervousness.

Ray Lupus slept well on his return to the Wolf House, however as great as he felt physically from the night's sleep, he was lost mentally. He had no pills with him and no one to tell him to take them.

He went to the wolf viewing window and Friskie looked up toward him and pawed the dirt. Ray waved back as you would to a casual friend. Ray then made himself a pot of coffee and sat listening to the wind race through the zoo. After a couple cups of coffee, Ray went out into the cold, windy weather that he loved and looked in on all the animals. Things were coming back to Ray as he walked, and the sight of Kingston brought a smile to his face.

He hopped the protective fence and touched hands with the gorilla. Kingston climbed the fence and jumped down making new sounds as he did. The wind knocked some branches off the trees and the deserted look of the zoo caused Ray to wonder why he was alone. As he looked around the zoo, he saw a person here and there and his paranoia took over. He now felt he was being watched and followed by everyone.

He told Kingston that he had to leave but would see him later. Ray crept behind some of the zoo workers who were tending to the animals and eventually made it to the safety of the stables. Watching from behind a small window in the barn, Ray didn't recognize any of the faces. He thought about saddling a horse and riding through the zoo, but didn't know why he would do so. He decided to stay hidden until he knew more, until a better plan dawned on him.

Standing by the window he watched as people scurried from one place to the next, running ahead of the fallen branches and among the dead leaves. Heavy clouds continued to block the sun and the darkness surrounded everyone he looked at. Ray tightened the collar of his jacket around his neck and waited, clueless as to what in the world he was waiting for.

Karen made a quick stop at home for Ray's pills after dropping Freddie of at school. She drove to her father's front door, but there was no answer, so she drove around to the zoo's main entrance. She passed by the employee lot and parked at the main gate which was now very empty. She entered the open zoo and stood just inside the gate debating with herself on where to head first, the admin building, Kingston's habitat, or the stables.

She pulled her coat tighter around herself to get some protection from the wind and the cold and started walking quickly towards Kingston. Before she walked too far, she heard someone call out, "Hey, I'm over here."

Karen turned and saw her disheveled father leave the barn. He reached Karen and asked if she was looking for him. He knew Karen, but not her name right now. As Ray waited for Karen's reply his eyes darted all around the zoo. "What's going on around here? Who are these people?"

"Do you know me?" she asked.

"Of course," Ray replied.

"What's my name?"

Ray thought for second and finally said, "I don't remember, but I know it's you."

"I'm your daughter Karen. Let's go back to your house, I have your pills and we'll have breakfast. It's a cold Halloween, nothing that should disturb you."

"Karen. You're Karen."

"Very good, let's go make some coffee. I'm freezing."

School let out at three and Karen was there to meet Freddie. They walked up and down the streets surrounding the school and Freddie knocked on every door shouting, 'Trick or treat,' whenever a door was opened. Other kids were running full speed to and from every door, but Freddie chose to stay with his mother. When Karen suggested that Freddie go with his friends he casually replied, "No Mom, I think I've had my fill of that Chester kid, he's a real asshole."

Karen was somewhat shocked. She got the goose bumps and didn't know if they were from the cold or the words of her son. "Is that any kind of language for an eleven-year-old to use?"

"When I told Gramps some of the things Chester says and does in class he said that Chester must be a real asshole. You don't like that word?"

"No, I don't, and just because your grandfather thinks a certain way about someone he's never even met, doesn't mean you should. Think for yourself, okay?"

"Sure."

The pair hit a few more houses and called it a day. Karen promised Freddie she would have him to the school fair on time tonight, but they needed to have dinner first. Freddie was content but noticed the discomfort in his mother's behavior. He blamed his use of language for her unhappiness and knew where to direct his anger. "Damn Chester," he told himself.

By 6:30 that night the full moon had risen just above the horizon casting eerie shadows through town and throughout the meadows and fields surrounding it. The wind died and the temperature dropped a few more degrees. The town's 6:30 curfew for trick or treating caused the town to go from bustling to appearing as a ghost town to anyone passing through. The zoo was locked, and the last few workers were finishing their daily tasks with the sounds of hungry animals echoing throughout the zoo. Ray walked among them watching with suspicion at everything they did.

In town, the shadows were shifting on the school and the banner advertising the fair snapped in the wind. The school doors were still locked as the staff prepared the final touches on decorations and activities for the kids' night. A Halloween sound effects recording blasted on the school's P.A. system. Everything was indeed falling into place. More importantly, in addition to the kids who were dressed as murderers and monsters, walked real life versions of similar, but far more sinister souls.

At 6:45, the church bell rang a tune and then blared three times. The sound carried on the wings of the wind so everyone in or near town was able to hear and feel what seemed tonight to be a warning. Something mysterious in the air was falling on Westgate.

Karen kept her promise to Freddie and a few minutes before 7:00, they were driving to the fair. Freddie carried his mask again, Karen sat quietly and appeared very unhappy.

"I could stay home if you'd like the company," a concerned son told his mother.

"I'll be just fine."

"You look worried about something."

"I'm going to a party for a little bit while you're at the fair. I don't know most of the people that are going to be there so yes, I'm a little nervous."

"What party?"

"At Linda's house. My costumes in the bag."

Freddie lifted and looked into his mother's bag, "It's just a mask of a man. That's your costume? You should be nervous."

"Leave the bag alone. That happens to be Dick Nixon. I'll be fine," And Karen added in a soft whisper, "I hope."

Right at 7:00, Karen parked behind a bunch of cars and let Freddie out. "I'll be right here at 9:00. Don't dawdle." She watched until Freddie entered the building and took her mask out of the bag. She tried it on and was pleased that after so many years it still fit nicely, and she had ease in seeing through the eye holes. She put the mask and her bag beside her and made tracks to her destination. Time was a factor now and Karen was counting the minutes.

Back at the zoo Ray was alone. He made a sandwich and went to visit with Kingston while he ate. He was oblivious to the car that just parked in the lot and wasn't sure if the noise he heard coming from the front gate was real or just in his head. He stared down the path that the dead leaves were rustling down. He thought he saw a large shadow move but refused to get lost in another time shift. The security light reflected off of something as Ray stared harder, something metal maybe, a belt buckle, he wondered. He felt for his gun, but it wasn't there. A gun reflecting, he now thought.

He stood frozen and whispered to Kingston, "You see anything boy? I don't know if this is even real."

Kingston became agitated, grabbing onto and shaking the thick bars. Ray tried to calm him when his attention was grabbed by the sound of footsteps steadily drawing near. Even in the moonlight nothing was visible.

When whoever it was got within ten feet of Ray he broke into a full run, their steps now a flurry of sound one right after the other, then the deadly crash, a metal pipe full force on the top of Ray's head. Ray collapsed in a heap like a large felled tree. He was hit again as he lay face down in the dirt. The attacker with a burning purpose walked around the body and kicked Ray over and over until he rolled over facing the night sky. He then went through Ray's pockets and found the master set of zoo keys. Ray was no longer needed.

"I just wanted you to see my face one last time before I kill you Lupus."

"Clyde Endel," Ray whispered before passing out.

Clyde lifted the pipe above his head to begin the fatal blows, but before he could strike even one more blow he was grabbed from behind and pulled back. He couldn't pull the arm away from around his throat and felt something cold on the back of his neck. Life was quickly leaving his body and his mouth had not even the strength to utter a single plea or cry for help. Soon his arms went limp and he slumped down dead next to the still breathing Ray Lupus. A strange quiet fell over the zoo as not a single animal there moved a muscle. Even the wind had died.

On the other side of town Karen made it back to the school by 9:00 and waited patiently for Freddie to leave the fair. Nine o'clock, nine o-five, ten after, no Freddie. She felt she had always done everything in her power to protect her son, but now had a knot of fear in her stomach. She moved her belongings from her bag to her purse, threw her mask in the back seat and hurried from her car to go inside the school and find Freddie. Before she took any steps, Freddie left the school and hustled over to the car. "Sorry I'm late, I had some things to say to that Chester kid before I left, he is an ass, sorry."

Karen bent down, not very far, and hugged Freddie. "It's okay, I just always worry when I'm not with you. It's been quite a night, I need a little rest."

"Your party good?" Freddie asked.

"Yes, it was, turns out I knew someone better than I thought. Put some things to rest you might say." And they drove home leaving their anger, their fears, and the bitter night behind them. Yet, as Karen parked the car and listened to the howling from the woods behind her lake, her uneasiness gnawed away at her insides. Life in Westgate still seemed out of kilter and she wondered how her father's night in the zoo went.

Near midnight Ray thought he was awakening from a bad

dream. He rolled to his side but soon returned to his back. Life was slowly coming back to Ray as he tried to open his eyes and focus on the dark sky above. He couldn't open one eye and he couldn't move his bad arm again to rub life into his eye. When his good eye came into focus, he looked around him and for the first time saw the dead body of Clyde lying against Kingston's cage, bars pressing against his neck and Kingston's powerful arm still wrapped around Clyde's throat.

Ray had a hard time getting up and a hard time speaking. His arm useless, an eye useless, his legs unstable, his head growing more painful by the second, memory of what had happened tonight there someplace, but fleeing. Ray stumbled to one knee but righted himself quickly. He took Kingston's arm away from Clyde and tossed Clyde with his one good arm like a sack of garbage. He then put his arm through the bars and hugged his friend. He tried to speak and knew the words he wanted.

"You saved my life Kingston, but you shouldn't have. They'll put you down for killing this bum and you don't deserve that. I have to hide the body."

Kingston looked at Ray, his eyes watery. The words coming from Ray were not as clear as they sounded in Ray's head, they were nothing more than slurs and gibberish and Kingston had to hold Ray up or he would surely crash to the ground again. Ray no longer knew much, but he understood that his life was saved and now he needed to save Kingston's.

He tapped the back of Kingston's head and Kingston released Ray causing Ray to immediately slide down to the ground. He sat and tried to think of a plan while some strength returned to his body. He knew he couldn't get far in this condition and felt he had to hide the body away from Kingston. The howling of his wolves gave him an idea. Bury Clyde in the wolves' lair.

Ray knew something was happening in his head. Thoughts were unclear, ideas coming and going too quickly. He looked for his keys and after a short panic found them on the ground near Clyde. He stumbled over to the shed and started the backhoe, driving it as best he could to the dead body. He managed to lift Clyde's body and dump it in the shovel of the backhoe. He drove over and into the wolves' habitat parking behind their small dirt mound between the trees and brush.

The controls for his digging were on the wrong side for Ray and he lacked strength to get started. As he sat in the operator's seat, he was growing less and less aware of what he was doing. The wolves, led by Friskie, were circling and growling low at the tractor and the two trespassers in their world. Ray passed out for a few minutes and when he came to, he didn't know where he was. He saw the wolves circling around him but had no idea how he got there.

He then saw the body lying in the shovel of the backhoe and jumped down between the wolves to see who it was. Ray didn't recognize the body and when he tried to lift it, he collapsed again with the dead body of Clyde falling down on top of him. Friskie let out a howl to his pack and three of the larger wolves grabbed Clyde's body and dragged it away from Ray. They sunk their canines into Clyde crushing his skull, ripping open his chest, and tearing away limb after limb in an angry attack on their intruder. The smaller wolves came last and tore away at what was left of Clyde.

When they were done, whatever was left of Clyde was scattered in pieces all over the den. Bone, blood and the few uneaten body parts marked their territory. The pack, with blood surrounding their mouths and saliva dripping thick, now stared at Ray. Friskie and his two lead pack wolves moved on to Ray. The moonlight lit Ray's body and the cold chill of night brought out every ounce of wilderness behavior the wolves possessed.

The pack attitude that Friskie displayed on Clyde was not the behavior he had for Ray. Ray was viewed as one of the pack, the former alpha wolf who cared for and protected the pack now needed its protection. Friskie laid down close to Ray as did the other wolves making a wolf fort and a warm surrounding for Ray. They protected Ray from the cold of night and whatever other intruder may be coming there.

It was here they lay as a pack, one against the world, only as strong as their weakest member. Night passed slowly, but when the sun came up the following morning and the workers saw the bodies lying in the den, the heart of Ray Lupus was still beating.

"I recognize that jacket, that's Ray in there. What the hell's going on?" asked one of the workers. "I hate Halloween. Call the office, hurry."

Sue was the only former staff member in the office, she was meeting with Vince about her job when the call came. In shock they rushed to the wolf den and met all the workers at the gate.

The wolves came to the gate and growled at the group, it was definitely a warning growl, the wolves did not want anyone else inside their domain.

"There's something else in there with Ray," Sue said, "look at all the rags laying around."

"I don't think those are rags, I think it's clothes. Someone else went in here with Ray." Vince said.

"Do you think they're dead?"

"Whoever belongs to those clothes is gone. I can't tell about Ray from here, we have to go inside."

"I'll get a couple dart guns from the office; we'll be able to tranquilize all of these wolves quickly. We'll get Mr. Lupus out." The workers hurried into panicked action as organized as they could be.

"Get it done. I'll call an ambulance from the hospital," Vince said.

"We don't have a hospital. Call the fire department, they'll take Mr. Lupus to the clinic. It's a good clinic, don't worry."

They both ran back to the office, Sue grabbed the dart guns and was out the door in seconds. Vince made a quick 911 call saying Ray Lupus was dying at the zoo, send an ambulance and the police. The phone then fell to the floor and Vince was out the door right behind Sue.

There were a number of workers at the wolves' cage now able to help Sue get Ray out. Three of them slowly opened the gate and moved in. Four of the larger wolves crept back slowly but kept growling. Sue ordered each worker to shoot on her count, one dart per wolf only, more is dangerous and not needed. On her count they fired, Sue shot darts into two of the wolves and the workers handled the others. Within seconds all the wolves were down, and the smaller remaining wolves ran and hid behind the trees. Sue moved toward Ray.

"He's alive, I think barely, but he's alive. Hardly breathing and it sounds like a huge effort for him. Is help close?"

"I hear the sirens. They'll be here right away."

When the emergency vehicle arrived, Vince went into the

compound with them. The two workers stood watch over the sleeping wolves, guns ready. The field medics from the fire department ran some quick tests on Ray while loading him onto a stretcher. The medics pointed out some bruising on the back of Ray's head and Sue found a pipe amongst the clothes. "This is what did it, I think," she said.

"Probably," said one of the medics. "We can't gather up the bones and body parts from whoever this is, or was, not a lot left. We got an ID here from his wallet, name Clyde Endel mean anything to you?" Sue and Vince exchanged a panicked look. "We'll have to come back for his remains. We have to get this other guy to the clinic if he's gonna have a chance. The police can figure this mess out. Tell them this guy was beaten almost to death. We need to motor."

The fire department left with Ray while Sue and Vince stayed to talk to the police.

"Clyde was the guy Karen and Ray fired yesterday, along with his boss, Barb." The words were no sooner out of Vince's mouth when the two officers high tailed it to their car and peeled off for Karen's place. On their way, they radioed in to send a car after Barb Tummelvic. Sirens blaring, they pulled up Karen's drive. Karen was standing at the window in a near trance when Freddie came over to see what the commotion was.

"Why are they here?" Freddie asked.

"They probably need something from me, don't worry. We may have to take you to Linda's house though if they need me in town," a very calm Karen said. She then opened the front door to let in the one officer who came from the squad car.

"Thank god you're okay Karen, Vince was worried about you."

Karen looked confused. "Why were you talking with Vince?" she asked. "Is something wrong?"

"I'm afraid so. It looks like some guy named Clyde tried to kill your father last night. Your dad's alive, they took him to the clinic. Clyde's dead. Sue from the zoo thinks that the wolves killed Clyde to protect your dad."

"How bad is my dad?" Karen asked finally coming out of her trance.

"I don't know, he was going to the clinic when I got to the zoo. They say he was hit hard on the back of his head."

"Can you take me there? I can't drive now. Freddie too? The back of dad's head is already injured. This is very dangerous for him. I need to get his doctor now."

Karen made the call to Dr. March and was assured he was coming immediately before she returned to the officer.

"Clyde got into the zoo?" she asked the officer, still confused by everything.

"His remains were in the wolf compound this morning."

"Odd," Karen muttered. "Why was Vince worried about me?"

"Something about a Barb. I really don't know. We're picking her up now. Vince thinks she's tied up with that Clyde guy. I better get you to the clinic now. You'll be safe with us, Freddie too."

Karen grabbed a few things she thought she would need for her dad, his pills mainly, and moved the items from her bag into her purse. She threw a clean shirt on Freddie and the four moved quickly to the squad car and with the siren back on, sped to the clinic in the humble downtown of Westgate. Along the way, a radio message was received in the car, sent by the squad that went after Barb.

"We got another dead body out here, I'm sure it's Barb. No bullet hole but she has a gun in her belt. Can't see what killed her, maybe someone strangled her, just guessing. But she's dead. I need the coroner out here."

"What the hell is going on in our little community?" The officer driving Karen and Freddie said into his radio. "Is this all because of that Clyde guy?"

They all sat quietly in the car as they continued to the clinic. Finally, Karen spoke. "Don't you have to respond to that?" she asked.

"No, that call goes out on all our radios, the station responds. They'll send out a detective and the coroner. You're safe Karen, you and Freddie are safe. They'll sort everything out. I know you feel vulnerable, helpless, but don't, we have you safe now."

"Thank you. I appreciate your help."

The car parked right at the doors of the clinic and Karen took Freddie inside where they were met by Vince and Sue. Hugs and tears began the greeting, and things were quickly summed up by Vince. "It's very bad Karen. I'll get the doctor to fill you in. Sue can take Freddie out for a walk. We'll need to talk to the officers, I asked them to arrest Barb. I think she's involved in Ray's attack."

"Barb's dead, Vince. We picked up the call in the police car on our way here."

"Dead? Why? How?"

Before Karen could say anything more the doctor arrived.

"Miss Lupus, I'm Dr. Kearn. I've been looking after your father this morning and we are doing all we can, which unfortunately isn't very much. It isn't a clinic problem, we have the best of equipment, but your father may need a lot more."

Karen quietly spoke, "I called Dad's doctor, Dr. March, he's flying in from Kansas City right now."

"That was a good call. Dr. March called me already," answered Kearn, "Per his instructions I've taken x-rays and scans of your father's head, the trauma area, March is bringing Ray's file to compare things. We'll know very soon the correct course of action."

"What's your best guess Dr. Kearn?"

Dr. Kearn looked around the room and looked back at the room that Ray was resting in. He spoke slowly. "Well Miss Lupus, your father has come in and out a couple of times and seems very agitated when he's somewhat awake. Once he asked about you, I'm sure of that, and once he was very angry about a dog of his he thought I killed. He seems to be bouncing all around in his mind. Dr. March told me he was concerned about possible blockage leading to your father's brain and the new head trauma may have further damaged that area and caused a significant stroke. That could explain the confusion."

"March always feared another stroke would happen. We'd be back to square one with Dad's recovery if that's the case. You seem hesitant on that."

"I can only tell you what I see today and without knowing Ray's history I think I see something a little different."

"Please tell me."

"I think your father has blood vessel damage from a couple of extremely hard hits on his head. The area was weak to begin with. I can see blood on the scans in areas where there shouldn't be any. I'm fairly certain Ray has a subdural hematoma, acute or chronic, and he will need emergency surgery, and that can't be done here. If that's the case, your father needs to fly back to Kansas City with

March and have emergency surgery. Every second we lose is dangerous, but what we're doing with March and the plane is the quickest we can do from this town. By some chance if this is a sub-acute hematoma, we'll have more time."

"What can I do?"

"You need to sit with him, talk to him, even though you think he can't hear you. He needs to be calm in whatever world he's living in on the inside. I fear if he works himself up, he'll bleed quicker and more dangerously into his brain. Calm him down if possible. Is his dog alright? That might help calm him."

"His childhood dog? I guess you could say he's fine considering he would have died over fifty years ago."

Karen walked into her father's room quietly closing the door behind her. She sat next to his bed and watched his labored breathing. She wondered what to talk about, what could calm him. She took his hand and held it softly, just hard enough so Ray could feel her hand. "Dad, are you ready to start rehab again or do you just want to go back to the zoo?" Karen laughed at her own silly question but thought if it reached her dad it would calm him in some way. Tears were about to begin when Karen thought she saw her father's eyes open. She jumped up and wanted to shout to her father but remembered the orders for calm. "It's Karen, Dad. I'm here. Everything's alright."

She looked into her dad's eyes and saw that it was only one eye that was opened. In that eye she saw no peace, no recognition, more hate than blank. Her father was agitated as the doctor said. Ray mumbled something that sounded like "killer" to Karen, but it could be all in her head. Before she could say another word, the doctor knocked on the door and burst in.

"His monitor is racing," Dr. Kearn told her. "Heart rate's a bit too quick. See this number," the Dr. said pointing to his heart rate monitor which read 120, "I'd like to see this a lot closer to 80. Has he been awake? Is he making any sense to you?"

"Not yet, but he just opened his eye, only one eye, why's that?"

"Part of the trauma. I have some medicine in his IV drip, it may help calm him, the rest is with you. I'll leave you now, I only came in out of hope. If we could bring Ray to understand what time he's in, I'd feel a lot better about things. I'd think his mind was working a little."

"I'll try to reach him. Some pleasant stories from way back should relax him."

"Maybe some pleasant stories more recent would help. Is there such a thing as a relaxing Halloween story?"

"Sure. I'll think of something."

Kearn left Ray and Karen alone again hoping March would arrive soon. This situation was more than Dr. Kearn ever thought about doing in this small town. He went back to his office and stared at the remote monitor, 100, 96, 91, 102. "Where the hell's March?" Kearn asked himself.

Karen studied the monitors from next to her father's bed and watched the numbers bounce back and forth. She felt that somewhere inside of her dad's deepest thoughts he was worried about her and Freddie. Karen had worries herself and needed to both unburden herself and relieve Ray's fears. Following what seemed to be a painful sleep, Ray awoke again and stared blankly at the machines he was plugged into. His heart rate increased again, and Karen leaned over to talk into his ear.

"You can relax Dad, everything's been taken care of. Your wolves, I'm sure Friskie led them, took care of Clyde. They ripped him apart like a piñata and protected you through the night."

Ray's breathing was still labored but his heart rate was below 100 and Karen felt certain she was reaching him. She looked back at the door behind her and quietly continued.

"I killed Barb." Karen checked the monitor again and continued. "I saw her car at Freddie's school one day and then saw her following us home. She thought she was out of sight, but she stood out totally clear to me. She followed us all the way home and made a u-turn when I turned up our drive. I was concerned, but not worried Dad, and then I saw her at Freddie's school again Halloween morning. I was worried then and went to the school early to pick him up, I realized right then and there that Barb was after Freddie, no other reason for her to be at his school parking where she thought she wouldn't be noticed. I knew what I had to do. I drove Freddie to the school fair and had everything I needed with me to take care of Barb. We got to the school at seven and I let Freddie out of the car telling him when and where to meet me.

"I tried on my mask that I brought to get close to Barb and it fit well. I drove over to Barb's and parked down the street. It was quiet as all the kids were now at school. I put on the mask and pulled my sweatshirt hood over my head, I walked quickly and rang her doorbell."

Karen stopped, checked her dad's monitors and let the night replay in her mind before continuing. She recalled the anger building inside of her as she waited for Barb to open the door. The memory of the night flooded back.

"I could tell right away that she was in a flustered state. She told me that I was a little big for trick and treating, and she was getting tired of having to give candy to all us damn kids. I was boiling then Dad, everything about Barb sickened me."

Squeezing her father's hand she continued and through her empty stare into his eyes she watched the night play out as if watching complete strangers.

"She turned to grab a candy bar just to get rid of me and I don't know if I lost it or found it, but I reached into my bag for the hypodermic needle I brought from the zoo. It contained a small of amount of animal tranquilizer, just enough to knock her out. As Barb was bent over I walked up behind her and stabbed the needle into her neck and released the serum. I grabbed Barb around her throat and lowered her to the floor and held her tightly until she was completely passed out. I get a little vague here Dad, but I kind of remember that I duct taped her hands, feet and mouth and sat to collect my thoughts. Within 30 minutes a glassy-eyed Barb was trying to come to and focus on me. She tried to speak until she realized her mouth was taped and then she noticed that she couldn't move her hands or feet either. I had her Dad; I felt good."

Karen stood up and wiped her dad's forehead with a cool wet towel that's was sitting on the clinic table. She saw that the heart monitor read 95 and was confident that her story was bringing her dad peace. She returned to her seat and continued talking almost in a whisper meant only for Ray to hear.

"I was the one in control and I told Barb I wanted answers and if I didn't get them I was going to kill her right then. I told her to keep her mouth shut when I take the tape off until I asked her to talk. "She nodded her agreement and I pulled the tape away from her mouth. I remember hoping that the tape hurt. I know it's weird Dad, I had just threatened to kill her and I was hoping that the tape hurt. Still do, to be honest. I started questioning her.

"I told her I noticed her following me and Freddie around town. I told her I didn't know exactly what she was up to, but that I knew she was planning something. I told her that nobody hurts anyone in my family, not anyone. I demanded she tell me what was going on. "She asked for water, I think to buy time."

"I told her I'd get her a glass but told her to not even try to get her gun from her belt. I already took it. I was getting angrier and losing my patience with Barb. She must have felt death drawing near because she was sobbing when I returned with a small paper cup half filled with water. I poured it into her mouth, but very little got down. 'Talk,' I said.

"She started with a ridiculous story. I wasn't doing anything wrong, she said, I would never hurt you or Freddie. I like the both of you. I was trying to know Freddie's habits, what he does before and after school. She said she thought if she could be there if he got in trouble, even if she had to be the one to put him in trouble, then she could help him, and I'd be grateful, and she'd get her job back at the zoo. She said all she wanted was for me to be grateful to her.

"All lies Dad and I let her know that I knew it and I was losing what little cool I had left. She thought she would put my son in harm's way and then bail him out? And I'd somehow be happy? Bull shit! I told her we were done here."

Ray's monitor showed his heart racing again, but Karen kept explaining the night as she saw it in her mind.

"I held Barb's gun in my hand and waved it in her face. 'Wait,' she screamed at me. 'I'll tell you more, the whole truth this time, please don't kill me.' She was crying and shaking by this time and I gave her one more chance to explain what was going on and she finally opened up.

It was all Clyde she said. He got her involved in the illegal selling of animals on the black market. They were using the zoo for what you'd call laundering. Money, paperwork, and moving the animals. It's a billion dollar industry in the world and Barb and Clyde stood to make millions off of animals they were pretending to save. Dad, Barb said that Kingston was next. They got themselves in a bad situation with some bad people and the money from selling Kingston was their ticket out. When we fired them, their scheme blew up and they were looking at death or prison any way they turned. None of this made any sense to me Dad and I still didn't know why Barb was following Freddie and my moves. I guess I lost it there. I shoved Barb's own gun hard against her face and demanded she tell me how Freddie fit into all of this. She cracked and blamed Clyde again. She said that Clyde believed that they could trade a kidnapped Freddie for Kingston, make their sale and disappear from here. I think that was her plan Dad, but she said that they realized it was a bad plan and dropped it. She claimed that they decided to just run and fly to South America last night. She had a bag packed in her room, I checked on that, but I didn't believe her story. I taped her big mouth shut again Dad and told her that she was a threat to our family and I wasn't about to let her run free. I took out the second hypodermic needle I brought and made sure she had a good look at it. I told her that there was enough tranquilizer in there to kill a horse.

"She really lost it then Dad, she started fighting against the tape, squirming and twisting on the floor to no avail. Sounds were emitting from her throat, but nothing discernable. I pushed Barb's face against the floor and injected her with the tranquilizer. I held her head down and still until Barb was dead. I then removed all the tape putting it back into my bag and returned the gun to Barb's pants. No guilt Dad, I did the right thing."

Karen's story almost done, she sat and studied her father's monitor and print out. The tape revealed a small heightening and lowering of his heart rate as Karen was talking. She was certain the pattern would match that of her story if she could compare them. She knew she reached him.

Karen being calm now, wanted her father to be at peace as she finished the story. "After that Dad, I went to the school and picked Freddie up. When the police came over this morning, I thought they were after me. I should have at least suspected that you were in danger too and did something, but I was out of it. I'm sorry, but understand Dad that we're all safe now, we beat them our way."

Ray didn't move a muscle or open his eye. His monitor stayed down around 90, but his breathing seemed to be even more labored. As she stroked her father's hand, a short rap on the door preceded its opening. Dr. March and Dr. Kearn entered in a hurry to examine Ray.

Dr. Kearn spoke first. "That must have been a beautiful talk you had with your father, he seems to be much more relaxed now. You can feel comfort knowing that you reached him."

Karen nodded and greeted Dr. March with a soft hello and then added, "You always knew this would happen, didn't you?"

"Not by trauma. I've looked at the scans with Dr. Kearn and compared them with the files I've brought along. Your father has suffered a lot of damage. The mass that was sitting in the back of his head has dislodged due to the hits and there is a new mass, I'm afraid building blood where we can't allow it to be. Once again, we're fighting multiple issues, some we can't even pinpoint. For a person so open and one dimensional as your father, it seems unfair that he would have such hidden health issues. I'll examine him and then we can discuss options. I think there's a police officer here that wants to talk to you."

"Talk to me?"

"Yes, I'm sorry," Dr. Kearn said. "I forgot that he was here. I told him I would let you know. He's in the lobby. We'll look at your father and see you out there."

Karen walked out apprehensively to meet the police officer. Like every other officer in town Karen knew the face, but not the name. "I'm Karen. You wanted to see me?"

"Yes, I did. It's about Barb Tumelvic. We found her dead this morning in her home."

"I heard on your car radio on our way here."

"Well I was there with our new detective and it's pretty clear what happened last night although some things just don't make sense. When you're dealing with murder, things seldom do."

"What do you guys think happened?"

"There was a message on Barb's phone from Clyde. He threatened to kill her if she didn't go along with something. We don't know what that something is, we may never know. But Barb got a gun, we think to protect herself from Clyde, but he overpowered her and ended her life. We don't even have a cause of death yet, but we know that Clyde killed her. Whatever Clyde's deal was included your father and after killing Barb he went to the zoo to kill him. He would have succeeded too if the wolves hadn't stepped in. That's pretty strange right there isn't it?"

"I don't think that the wolves protecting him is strange at all. It would be strange if they didn't. My dad and his animals shared life on a different level. You said that there were things that didn't make sense. What else is bothering you?"

"Motive for one, but I think we'll get that. We're looking hard into Clyde and Barb's past. We're sure we'll find something. The thing that bothers me, and I asked the detective this, why would Clyde kill Barb and leave her lying in the middle of her home, then go and try to kill Ray and go to such lengths to try and hide the body."

"What did the detective say?" a concerned Karen asked.

"He said I ask too many questions. A murderer's methods are always the result of a twisted mind that we usually can't understand. He said Clyde probably hated your dad and wanted him to be ripped apart by the wolves, but it backfired. He said killing Barb was probably just a necessity to him. At any rate, I don't know how much more time we're going to put into this since we have our case pretty much solved, but we will need to talk to Ray when he's able."

"When he's able? Officer have you heard how bad he is? He's in there fighting for his life and you wonder about talking to him?"

"If he's able."

"Leave me alone. This case is solved as you said. Let us, let this town, move on. I swear I'll never lift another finger to help your organization if you hurt my father or anyone else over this. You look into Clyde and Barb, you leave the Lupus' alone."

"I'm sorry. I guess it would be wrong to bother your family anymore. I'll let everyone at the station know you've suffered enough. I'm truly sorry about all of this."

Karen didn't say another word and as soon as the officer left, Vince, Sue, and Freddie came back into the clinic. They sat and talked to Freddie about school, about the Halloween parties yesterday, and anything else to keep all minds off Ray for a while. Silence eventually took over and the group sat waiting for the doctors to return to the lobby with updates on Ray. Karen recalled the loss of her mother and same sick feeling she was witnessing now, how life changed overnight, how her father just wanted to run away after that. *Alaska,* she remembered, over 25 years ago they were headed to Alaska.

"How would you like to go to Alaska, Freddie?" she asked.

"Where did that come from?" a nervous Vince asked. "We'll

need you here now more than ever, please don't do anything rash. And I'm sure Sue will stay on to help." Sue nodded her support and Karen looked at Freddie.

"Mom, after I take care of Chester, we can go anywhere. You decide." Karen only chuckled.

Dr. March and Dr. Kearn finally exited Ray's room and went into the office with Karen and Vince to discuss options. It was Dr. March's meeting and he had his mind set on one course of action.

"Karen, whatever our suspicions in the past were, they are irrelevant now. Your father is bleeding into his brain, and we have to go in and stop that and remove the build-up."

Karen asked about the previous blockage and chances of another stroke recurring.

"He's had a second major stroke. That blockage shut blood supply down to his brain and then in simple terms, released and ran through him. We won't know the extent of the damage until we get the bleeding of his vessels under control."

"You want to cut into his head? Can he even make it to Kansas City?"

"I think he can make it to Kansas City and yes we have to cut into his head. It's his only chance. We can't let him lie here in pain waiting for death."

Karen walked to the window and looked outside. With her back turned nobody saw the tears running down her face. She tried to think as if she was Ray. What would he choose for himself?

She had no answer and asked the others.

"Surgery Dr. Kearn?"

"I'm not sure about current pain versus recovery. I guess I'd say no."

"Vince?"

"Fight until your last breath. I say yes."

Karen remained speechless for so long, it forced March to talk once more.

"If we don't move soon, there will be no decision to make."

"Make the arrangements, we'll go. I need to fly with you and Dad. While you're getting everything ready, I need to have Freddie talk to his grandfather."

"No matter what happens Karen," Dr. March told her, "this is the right decision."

"One last thing doctor; no heroic measures. If Dad goes on the way, then we leave him be, that would be his choice. I believe in his way Dad will make the ultimate decision."

"Of course. Why don't you take Freddie to visit Ray and Dr. Kearn and I will call rescue and get the ambulance sent here. We'll meet them outside. You have about 5 to 10 minutes."

Karen left the office and took Freddie inside to see his grandfather. Freddie broke down immediately, his crying took over as he grabbed his grandfather. Ray's breathing was harder now and his monitor numbers were unchanging.

"This isn't Grandpa any more. He told me to never ever make him go through something like this ever again. He hated life after his last stroke and you're giving him more. Why?"

"I have to do what everyone can live with Freddie. Trust me. Tell your grandfather goodbye for now and wait for me outside. I have to get him ready for his trip."

Freddie kissed his grandfather goodbye and lightly shoved his mother as he left the treatment room. He came close to telling his mother that he hated her, but knew that would be a lie he couldn't live with. He ran over to the sofa in the lobby where Sue and Vince were sitting and buried his face into Sue.

Karen tried to fight off her tears but had no luck. Seeing through her tears was impossible and she looked in her purse for a tissue. After drying her eyes she continued to fumble in her purse for what she needed and held it lightly, being careful to not accidently prick herself.

Before leaving the room, Karen kissed her father goodbye. A calm Karen sat beside her son and waited for the rescue team to arrive.

She heard the ambulance and looked out the window as they parked and frantically unloaded the stretcher. Two paramedics and two doctors banged the door open and came running full speed across the clinic floor and into Ray's room.

They seemed to be in the room a long time and finally Dr. March emerged alone, all panic gone and motioned for Karen to come over. Dr. March spoke to Karen as quiet as he could and still be heard, "It's over, I guess your father just didn't want to go through this again. He went peacefully. He was already gone when we entered his room."

"I better tell my son."

The shock passed quickly and Karen's and Freddie's tears were soon behind them. Before Ray Lupus' body could be rolled by them, they headed to the car.

"This is best," Freddie said, "I don't know what I would have done to that doctor if he put Gramps through useless surgery."

"You can't settle everything with fists."

"I'm a Lupus, what else can I do?"

THE END

ABOUT THE AUTHOR

John Schraub was born in Chicago and lived there until his love of the outdoors called him west. Following a series of road trips, John eventually called Colorado home. He settled on a quiet piece of land in the San Juan Mountains sharing his space with bears, mountain lions, elk, and numerous other new friends. John now spends his summers kayaking and hiking and his winters skiing and snow-shoeing. A new trip or adventure is always in the works. John shares this simple message with those he meets, "If you don't feel each and every day that you are one of luckiest people in the world, make a change."

www.ingramcontent.com/pod-product-compliance
Lightning Source LLC
Chambersburg PA
CBHW031712170626

46808CB00005B/1719